Our Little Life

SILENCE AND SHADOWS BOOK 2

DODIE BISHOP

For my husband, Alan, always eager for the next instalment

And, like this insubstantial pageant faded,
Leave not a rack behind. We are such stuff
As dreams are made on, and our little life
Is rounded with a sleep.

Shakespeare, The Tempest Act 4, Scene 1.

Prologue

SUMMER, 1676

Raphael

Our sail to fetch Penny home from Hampshire was rather more comfortable than our earlier one returning from Southampton, after leaving her safely at Chewton Court with Susannah's grandmother when threats were made to her life. This time our passage was arranged by Susannah's father, though the King must have had a hand in it too or someone had on his behalf, for we were given the captain's spacious cabin on a Royal Navy Man-o'-War first rate ship of the line, taking up the whole width of the aftcastle beneath expansive windows. After a dawn sailing, and with the speed expected of this ship, the captain would reclaim his space overnight so no one would be ousted to a hammock with the crew as had been expected of me on that first voyage.

1

We boarded HMS Persephone at the Deptford victualling yard where she was being made ready for a voyage to the Americas and would land us at Southampton before heading out to the Atlantic. That this passage took only three days to arrange proved the level of influence behind it. We learnt from Sir Richard that the King would grant us a marriage ceremony in the Chapel Royal at Whitehall on our return. Not something I had ever foreseen in any notion of my future ... just like my spell in the Tower. And this time my father would be overjoyed. Though he would not learn of it from me. *Cristo.* I began to understand just how different my life would be now as Susannah's husband. Eighty guns and a six-hundred-man crew would do that.

Lady Sylvia's coach waited for us on the dockside when we were delivered there by one of the ship's tenders in mid-afternoon after making excellent time with a favourable wind, and we were soon on our way back to Chewton Court and Penny. 'She'll be overjoyed to see you. You've been apart for rather longer than we'd expected, I think.'

'And I shall be overjoyed to see her.'

She did indeed look very happy at the prospect and the contrast her appearance made now with the last time we had travelled together in this coach – on our way back to London with Sam Carter still imprisoned in the Tower – was remarkable. 'You look quite breathtaking, *cara mia.*'

She closed her eyes. 'I think we both look a little

more relaxed now.' Yet she chewed her lip, still. 'So, I must tell Penny I'm her mother? It feels rather daunting now I truly have to face it.'

I put my arm around her. 'I'm sure she'll accept it without question. Children do at this age.' I shrugged. 'So much knowledge comes from what they're told.'

She smiled. 'I don't think I can tell her Sam is her father yet. How could she understand? It's probably best to make one revelation at a time. Though–'

I moved in to kiss her. 'Don't try to plan it too much.' I kissed her again, which turned out to be a very pleasant, if frustrating, way of passing quite a considerable amount of time. After a while we were forced to stop, for consummating our desire in a moving coach in broad daylight seemed neither feasible nor entirely proper. I rested my head back against the soft squabs, whilst Susannah stared out of the window. We were driving through what appeared to be an extensive tract of woodland. We both panted a little. 'That was probably somewhat foolish of us.'

'Never start what you cannot finish.'

This made us laugh like silly children which took up further time.

Susannah fanned herself. 'Glazed windows are all very well but not without means to open them.'

'Perhaps our activities haven't been especially helpful?'

She gave me a look suggesting my words were superfluous before putting her hand inside my shirt again, still untucked from our earlier goings on. 'It's fine for you. You've shed your coat and waistcoat while I have nothing I can decently remove.'

She moved her hand down towards my breeches. 'Stop, I beg you–' She did not.

'I think I'll make you a little hotter. See how you enjoy it.' She did halt then and flew to the window. 'Jesu. We're very nearly there.'

She laughed, watching me try desperately to tuck-in my shirt, and struggle into my waistcoat and coat. My cravat had gone missing somewhere on the floor as had the tie for my hair. In truth, Susannah's hair looked somewhat dishevelled too, and her pale green gown decidedly creased. '*Merda.*' We would arrive looking like we had just been ... well, doing what we had been.

'Er, Raphael?'

I looked at her and saw she held my cravat and ribbon. 'And when I said nearly there, I didn't actually mean all that close. Forgive me.' Her lips twitched.

I frowned. 'How close is not all that close, exactly?' I began to feel decidedly suspicious.

Her eyes widened. 'Perhaps, half an hour or so.'

I grinned and moved to her, taking her face in my hands. 'Perfect. Shall I now remove all your clothing so you might arrive at your grandmother's naked?' I kept my face entirely serious, shifting to pin her so she could not move at all, one hand already reaching behind her to find the laces to her skirts.

Her eyes widened and she took a sharp breath. 'For God's sake, Raphael. I beg you, don't.'

I saw something cross her face so fleetingly I barely had time to register it. '*Cara*?' I pulled her to me and spoke softly into her ear. 'Very well. Not now but I give you my word I shall do so later.' I shifted to search her face. And became even more alarmed. 'You didn't really think I'd do it here?'

She moved away, appearing vexed and uncertain. 'How would I know what you might do. You're Italian.'

Said with the same sense of suspicious disdain her grandmother had once used to me. I laughed. Though, in truth, I was not amused at all. I was dismayed. '*Si*. I'm found out. Undressing ladies in moving coaches is indeed a common pastime for my countrymen.' Thinking of it though, I had probably spoken more truth than I meant.

She gave me a hard stare. 'Hmm.'

I smiled and watched her, holding her gaze. Hoping. Waiting for her to come back to me. When she sighed and returned into my arms, I closed my eyes. Thank God. 'Forgive me, *cara*. I frightened you, I think.' I must be more careful with her. Perhaps we did not know each other quite as well as we thought we did. But we would. I crossed myself.

'What?'

I shrugged. 'Habit.'

She kissed me for some minutes and then was quite herself again. 'Well, you can make it up to me later.'

'I intend to. Believe me.'

'Come here.' She lifted my cravat and fastened it

for me. 'Turn.' She smoothed my hair with her fingers and tied it back.

Now it was my turn to tidy hers, pinning up the loose strands. 'There. We're respectable again.'

'And just in time for now we are truly arrived.'

When the coach clattered in under the gate arch and on up the gravel drive towards the house and the sea beyond, I felt her press against me. 'Don't be afraid.'

She laughed, shakily. 'I think I am, a little. Penny is about to discover not only am I able to speak, but also I'm her mother.'

'She'll be delighted by both.'

We halted in front of the marble porticoed porch where Penny waited, beaming, and almost quivering with excitement holding Lady Sylvia's hand while she restrained her – with both her words and a firm grip – from running down the steps to climb inside the coach with us, I felt sure. When we were safely out onto the gravel, she was released to cannon down the steps straight into Susannah's arms before trying to hug us both at the same time.

'Do let them to come inside, child.'

Penny ran back up, watching us eagerly as we followed after her. 'Are you and Raphael truly married now, Sukie? Grandmama says you are?'

Susannah hugged her and glanced at me, smiling. 'Yes, little one.'

Her eyes widened when Susannah spoke, though she said nothing. I wondered why? But more, I wondered how Susannah and I could possibly be together at all? It seemed unreal.

'She held out her ring for Penny to admire. 'Raphael made it for me.'

'Oh, Sukie, it's so beautiful.' She turned to me. 'You must be very clever to make such a thing for my sister.'

'He is.' Susannah offered her hand to her grandmother.

Smiling, she ran a finger lightly over it. 'It is indeed exquisite.' She pulled her granddaughter into her arms, kissing her on both cheeks. Then she held out her hands to me and did the same. 'Welcome to our family, Raphael.' She grasped Penny's shoulders. 'Run down to the kitchens and ask Sarah to have tea sent up, there's a good girl.' She moved away. 'Come. Let's go in. It's a little late for tea but no matter.'

Susannah and I followed her to the drawing room.

'How did you know we were handfast?' Susannah said. 'The King has granted us a ceremony in the Chapel Royal when we return.'

Handfast. An English custom she had told me, joined us for life when I placed my ring upon her finger.

'Sit.' Lady Sylvia gestured to a sofa. 'Your father has written to me, so I know Sam is safe, thank the Lord. I did tell Penny some of what he said, too. She knows you have recovered from the illness that took your voice. I suggested she not question you about it.' Her nostrils flared. 'And, as you are already living as man and wife, I thought it simpler to tell her you were married and leave it at that. Handfast is not an easy concept to explain.' She cleared her throat. 'Though, I believe it is still quite common amongst the poorer sort.'

'You haven't told her–'

'Of course not. That's something only you can do. And, in due course, who her father is.'

'Papa told you?'

She sighed. 'Don't be tiresome, Susannah. Why would you imagine I needed to be told?'

She looked bewildered and then upset. 'So, everyone knew when I thought no one did.'

I took Susannah's hand. 'Yet you understood she should not marry him?'

'I did.'

Susannah looked away, her eyes bright with unshed tears.

'May I ask you why?'

She sighed, appearing resigned. 'When Susannah would not name her child's father, though Jane and I thought it must be Sam, but when she refused still, we accepted it. Then I was made aware of the company he kept at court in a letter from someone who thinks to amuse me with all the latest gossip there. Though we never understood how Susannah knew he was a sodomite–'

'No.' Susannah stood. 'How dare you. How is this anything to do with you? I won't have it.'

I rose, too, and grasped her hand again. 'It doesn't matter anymore.'

She looked at me, taking a long breath before placing her palm on my face. 'I know, my love.'

Lady Sylvia watched us. 'Forgive me, Susannah, you're right. It's not my business to speculate about such things.'

She held out her hand and Susannah went to her, kissing her forehead. 'No. You must forgive me for becoming so heated. I'm only now beginning to understand so much of it myself.' She glanced at me. 'Because Raphael is helping me.'

Penny dashed in then, followed by a footman carrying a tray of tea things. She sat between us, telling of her time at Chewton Court interrupted by bites of cake and gulps of milk. 'I've ridden nearly every day and been sailing lots with Sir Douglas on Gloria. That's his yacht he keeps at Mudeford.' She looked at her Lady Sylvia. 'He is Grandmama's special friend.'

Susannah looked at her, too, raising her eyebrows. 'Special friend? Really? But how intriguing.'

Lady Sylvia coloured. 'An old friend back from the Americas. Penny dear, tell Susannah and Raphael about Joshua.'

Penny leapt to her feet. 'You must come and see him. He's so beautiful, Sukie.'

'Who's Joshua?'

'Madrigal's foal.'

Susannah turned back to Sylvia. 'And you called him Joshua? Why? It's horrible. Surely something musical like his dam?'

I noticed Penny blushing and crestfallen. 'Did you choose his name, *piccola*?'

She nodded. 'It's Kitty's little brother's name.' She chewed her lip just as Susannah does. I touched her cheek. 'Well, I like it.'

Susannah pulled her into her arms, kissing her. 'It *is* a lovely name now I know why you chose it, my sweeting.'

'Will you take us to see him?'

She smiled again. 'Oh, yes, Raphael. He's so tiny. Leeman only let them out into the paddock for the first time this morning.'

Lady Sylvia placed her empty teacup down onto the tray. 'Fetch her an apple, then you can be sure she'll come to you. Joshua will stay with her.'

Penny scampered away to do as asked.

Sylvia studied Susannah for a few moments. 'She foaled two days ago. Penny was very interested in the birth. I believe some explanation had been given to her friend when the new infant arrived which was passed on to Penny, naturally.' She raised her eyebrows. 'So, while the foal might prove a useful way of raising the subject, you may also face some rather unexpected questions.'

Susannah looked at me. 'Well, I'm certain nothing will faze you.'

I raised my eyebrows. In truth, though, very few

things did.

When Penny returned with an apple cut into pieces on a tin plate, I stood and offered Susannah my hand. 'Come. Let's be introduced.'

We found the mare and foal, both glossy black and long-legged, in the field behind the red-brick, cupolaed stable block.

Penny climbed onto the bottom fence rail, clinging to the top one. 'Madrigal. Madrigal.' She held out the plate with her other hand. 'Apple. It's apple for you, Maddie.'

The horse raised her head and seemed to contemplate for a moment before walking slowly towards us, without a thought for the suckling foal that had to scramble away and chase after her. Penny fed her the pieces which were accepted with great delicacy from her hand.

Susannah dropped onto her knees to look at the foal who stood staring back at her. 'He's so beautiful.' She looked up at the mare. 'What a clever girl you are, Madrigal.' Then she glanced up at me. 'This is her first foal.' When Penny knelt down beside her, Susannah put her arm around her and pulled her close.

I stroked the mare's velvet nose. '*Sei una ragazza carina.*' I looked down at them. Shall I leave you for a while, *cara*?'

'Jesu, no. Sit down here with us, Raphael.' She patted the long grass beside her.

I did as she asked, and we all sat close together in the early evening sunshine. I looked down at Penny, startled to recognise her dark blue almond-shaped eyes. They were Sam's. 'Susannah?' I nodded. There seemed little point in delaying it.

Taking a deep breath, she nodded her agreement. 'Penny?'

She turned to her, smiling. 'Yes?'

Susannah swallowed. 'There's something I must tell you.' She glanced at me, then back at Penny. 'I hope it'll make you happy–'

'Are you to have a child, Sukie?' She clapped her hands. 'That would make me very happy. I could help care for him like Kitty does with her Joshua.'

Susannah hugged her. 'Yes, I hope so. I hope I shall, but that's not it.' Another long breath. Another glance at me. 'When I do, though, it will be my second.' She gazed intently at her. Because you, my dearest little one, were my first.'

Penny frowned. Then her eyes went wide. 'Are you saying you are my mama? But how can you be when you're my sister?'

Susannah closed her eyes and pulled Penny into her arms again. 'I've always been your mama. It made me sad I had to pretend to be your sister.' She glanced up at me once more. 'But I don't have to do that anymore, dear one.'

'You mean you truly are my mama? Please say you are?' She clutched at Susannah's arms.

Susannah smiled, nodding. 'I am, Sweetheart.

That's just what I'm saying. I'm your mama. I was very young. The family ... well ... it had to be a secret until now.'

Penny pulled away, frowning once more. 'So, Papa is your papa–'

'And your grandpapa. Though he will love you just as he always has. That will never change.'

They clung to each other. And I knew Susannah would weep, especially as I blinked away a tear myself. Poor little Penny. How happy she must be to have a mama again. There would be many questions as she began to understand it, though I felt sure we both knew what the next one would be.

Penny looked up at me. 'Are you my papa? Did you put me in Su ... Mama's belly?

Susannah's eyes widened. 'No, Penny. We didn't know each other then.'

'But you can be, can't you? I want you to be my papa, Raphael.'

I smiled. 'Of course, *piccola*. I'm married to your mama, which makes me your step-papa.'

'So may I call you Papa?'

I hoped my face did not betray the great wave of emotion that request brought. There was so much Susannah still did not know. Christ, I must tell her. But when? How? I bowed. 'I would be most honoured, *Signorina*.'

She scrambled to her feet and this time launched herself into my arms. *Santo Dio*. It is hard to put into words how I felt at that moment when my past and

13

future seemed to come together. I now had a wife and a daughter. I held her close and knew it would be my duty to protect them both for the rest of my life. It was a duty that both terrified me and filled me with indescribable joy. I truly felt God's blessing upon me then ... and his forgiveness, too. I set Penny down and kissed her forehead before standing and offering my hand to Susannah. I helped her to her feet and into my arms for a long kiss. Penny watched us, looking very pleased indeed.

Back in the drawing room, she ran to her grandmother, clutching her hands. 'Sukie is my mama and Raphael is my papa. I'm so happy.'

Lady Sylvia looked rather content herself. 'Well, isn't that just wonderful. Now take the plate back down to the kitchens and ask one of the girls to give your sticky hands a good wipe.'

Sylvia waited until we were alone and turned to me. 'She doesn't think you her natural father?'

I shook my head. 'Being her step-papa seemed enough. For now, at least.'

Susannah put her head onto my shoulder. 'She'll need to know about Sam. She's loved him her whole life.' She frowned. 'And when she's old enough I must try to explain why we didn't marry.'

'Well, that's some time away yet, I imagine.' Sylvia stood. 'I need to talk to cook. Your room is ready. I'll have hot water sent up. I expect you'd like to bathe?'

'Thank you, Grandmama. Where have you put us?'

'La Chambre Fenêtre.'

Susannah nodded and put her arm through mine. 'Where you were last time.'

I held her face between my hands. 'You did so well with Penny, *cara*. I was very proud of you.' I moved in to kiss her, but a knock on the door parted us. Three footmen brought in a copper bathtub, a stack of towels and two large churns of steaming water. The bath was set down beside the hearth, lined with towels and quickly filled and steaming.

When we were alone, I took off my coat and waist-coat and began undressing her. And when she stood before me naked, her flaxen hair cloaked around her, I kissed her. This time there was a bed and, well, not un-surprisingly it took very little time for either of us to slake our need. 'So have I kept my promise?' I said, kissing her, still catching my breath.

She smiled against my lips. 'For now, my love.'

Smiling too, I moved from the bed, holding out my hand to help her stand. 'Come. The water will cool.' I helped her down into the bath and kneeling, lifted a pot of lavender-scented soap and a small sponge to wash her before picking up a pewter pitcher. 'Close your eyes.' She did, and I poured water to wash her hair. I handed her a towel to dry her face before soaping it and rinsing again, then taking the towel from her, I began drying the wet strands.

'May I ask you something, Raphael?'

'Of course.'

'How is it possible to love you like this? It fills me. It overflows from me. It's difficult to even comprehend it.'

I closed my eyes, almost overcome by her words. *'Cristo, dovrei sentire queste parole.* It is the same for me, Susannah. You're a part of my soul.' I think we both wept a little in the steam and kissed a little before I helped her out and into a towel.

A short while later, I kissed her neck tying her laces, helping her to dress for dinner. 'Your hair is a touch damp, still.'

She turned to feel mine. 'Yours is very wet. It's such a thick mane. You must leave it loose to dry.'

I thought, then, of her tenderness as she washed me, every touch telling me of her love. And how had we ever found each other? Florence. London. How? I thought of Plato's *Symposium.* For we had truly found our soulmates. Our other halves. Philosophy. A Greek myth I had thought it. I crossed myself.

She touched my arm. 'What?'

I shook my head, lifting her silver clip from the toilet table to wind her hair up into a simple twist. 'You look stunningly beautiful tonight.' She wore the same indigo gown I had admired the last time we had been here together when everything had been so very different.

She placed her palm against my face. 'And you look very fine indeed, particularly without that rather unpleasant waistcoat.'

'*Merda*. I thought you hadn't noticed it.'

She smoothed my hair and kissed me. 'I didn't think you wore it to sell Grandmama sapphires, it just reminds me of, well–' She shook her head. 'No matter. Let's go down or the hour will become overly late for Penny.'

I touched her chin, moving her head so she looked at me. '*Cara*, I must still sell gems at court and the women were never part of it. You know that.' But they had been a bonus, had they not? And one so often made available to me.

'Of course I do.'

I took her hand. 'Come.'

In the dining room, we were seated as we had been the last time with Penny already beside Lady Sylvia, though she rose to kiss us. 'Mama. Papa.'

I looked at Susannah. It would take some getting used to for both of us. 'You and your mama look especially pretty this evening.'

Penny smiled and blushed just like her mother. 'Thank you, Papa.'

After a supper of scallops in a rich butter and parsley sauce, a lattice-topped capon pie, loin of lamb with plums and a summer pudding, just as before, Susannah left with Penny to take her to bed leaving me alone with Lady Sylvia. The difference this time being a kiss from them both and Penny calling me Papa.

'That must seem very odd to you, Raphael?'

I looked at her, remembering her hostility when last we sat here alone. 'No. *Meravigliosa*. Not odd at all. Wonderful.' How startling it must be to see her granddaughter happy with me.

She seemed to read my thoughts. 'I'm very glad to see Susannah so happy and to know she can have a life with you.'

I tilted my head, studying her. 'But perhaps not quite the one you had once hoped for her?'

She laughed. 'Well, perhaps not but things changed, did they not? And when circumstances change then aspirations must change with them.'

'Indeed.' I finished my wine. 'You asked me before if I were her lover. You warned me to leave her alone, and I understood it was because you thought me not good enough for her. Well, I wasn't her lover, but I did love her then.'

She placed her hand over mine. 'Raphael. You know now why I said you could harm her. I could see the way you looked at each other. You cannot blame me for being concerned for her, surely?'

I moved my hand away. She sighed. 'No. But I can blame you for assuming I could get her with child and abandon her. I can blame you for not asking if I loved her.'

She looked down. 'Yes. Forgive me. I should not have made such assumptions about either of you. You will be a wonderful husband for my granddaughter and a wonderful father to Penny and your own children, too, I'm sure.'

I forced a smile. Why was it so difficult? 'I intend to be.' What could I say now? She did not think me good enough for Susannah alone, but Susannah with Penny was a different proposition. And I thanked God for her. I thanked God for them both. I crossed myself. She saw and said nothing. But what was I thinking? Why should I expect any different? And despite all this, Susannah was my wife. What more could I ever wish for? I took a breath. 'Susannah was close to her mother. I know it was hard for her when she lost her.'

'My daughter.' She closed her eyes for a moment.

I was suitably chastened. 'Forgive me.'

She waved her hand in dismissal. 'It was hard for all of us.' She poured more wine. 'They were very close just as I was with Jane and Susannah is now with Penny. It's not always so. I hated my own mother. Thank God we seem to have bred that out of us.'

I thought of my father. Though I did not hate him, I was merely indifferent to him now. 'Perhaps you learned from her how not to be a mother?'

'Perhaps I did.' She looked at me with renewed interest. 'For if I were ever uncertain what to do as one, I would think of how she would act and generally do the opposite.'

I rather thought I would take the same approach with my father. My children's lives would belong to them, not to me.

The door opened behind me, and Susannah joined us again. 'She's asleep. There were questions.' She raised her eyebrows, looking at me. 'I'll tell you later. Now, mothers and daughters? I heard from outside.' She kissed her grandmother's cheek followed by my lips for more than a few moments. Lady Sylvia cleared her throat. Susannah laughed and sat down beside me. 'What about fathers and sons, Raphael? Tell us about that.'

'Well, I believe it is more Italian sons and their mothers, no? I'm very close to mine, as you know, *cara*. Perhaps difficulty between a father and son is more common for us? We think more of fathers with their daughters.' But for mine there was not even that.

Susannah took my hand and kissed it. 'You haven't spoken of him much.'

I smiled. Beside his penchant for mistresses. Though I was unsure whether I wished to in front of Lady Sylvia. Yet it appeared I had little choice. So, in that case, I would be as perverse as possible. If Sylvia despised artisans, she would get them. 'At fourteen, my father was apprenticed to a distinguished jeweller in Rome. His name will mean nothing to you, so I shall not trouble you with it.' I saw a faint look of distaste cross her face. I smiled again. 'At twenty-one he began our business in Florence. He chose the city for its dearth of high-quality competition at that time, and its position as the centre for all of Tuscany, but mostly for the court of Grand Duke Cosimo de' Medici. My mother is a Florentina and also from a family of jewellers. The Morettis were his main competitors there, so the alliance was an important one. She worked with my father after their marriage. In Italy, a family business means just that. All the family contribute.'

'Your sisters too?'

'Of course, *cara*. Usually only until they marry when their husband's interests take over. Claudia would still come back if needed, though. Perhaps if there were a large commission or the workshop was particularly busy.'

'What about you, Raphael?'

We faced each other now. This was a conversation between only us. 'I absorbed it, of course I did. I can't remember not knowing how to cut and polish a stone or fashion a chain. But Papà had a different plan for me. I was sent to Latin School. Then to Rome for three years with his old master. After that I returned home until he judged me ready to go to Paris and sell to the French court.' I shrugged. 'Then he changed his mind, and I was taught rather rudimentary English and sent to London instead. He thought the profligacy of the English court a better prospect. After so long under puritan rule, he decided there would be a good market for our sort of jewellery and gems and fewer established competitors.'

'Expensive jewellery perfect for a King's many mistresses. And all things Italian very much in vogue at court.' Her expression told me she included me in this. I raised my eyebrows, making her smile. Hers rose to mirror mine. 'So, there is a high demand. He was right.' Susannah stood. 'I am quite tired, Raphael, I think we should retire.'

I grinned and finished my wine. 'I agree, *cara*.' Though, I thought she looked far from tired.

Lady Sylvia had a strange expression on her face when Susannah kissed her goodnight. When I did the same, I actually felt a touch sorry for her.

In our bedchamber, we sat on armchairs before the window, looking out at the full moon hanging low over the sea, sending its gleaming track down across the water until clouds made white by its light raced across the sky. After a time, she turned to me. 'I think you misjudge her. Her father was a tailor. Perhaps your papa's life reminded her of his. She married into the landed gentry and wanted the nobility for me because of her beginnings. My mother married for love to a friend of an exiled King. Raphael, she is truly happy for us.'

I closed my eyes. Is she? I tried hard to believe it was so. '*Che sciocco sono stato.* 'Perhaps I've been the prejudiced one, when I thought it was she. I'll apologise in the morning.'

She reached across to pat my hand. 'She's very taken with you. You've cast your spell over her just as you always do, my love.'

I sighed. 'What is this spell I know nothing of?'

'But you do.' She stood and I stood with her. 'You know it perfectly well.'

'Come. Let's go to bed. I know how tired you are, *cara*.'

She took my hand and walked with me. 'Not so tired, in truth.'

I kissed her. 'No, that's not what I meant.' I slapped my forehead. 'My English, eh? What I meant was, I know how tired you will be.' Yet we made it into bed with only kissing. There would be more. But this was good, too. 'Do you remember what you said about how kissing makes you feel?'

'Yes. It makes me feel like this.'

I sighed. 'I think I need to talk to you.' She frowned and I smoothed the line between her brows with my thumb. 'About this afternoon in the coach–'

'It was just foolishness. We were play-acting. Why are you so concerned?'

I propped myself up on an elbow to look down at her. I could see her quite clearly in the moonlight. 'You were afraid of me.'

She reached up to touch my face. 'How could I ever be afraid of you? I was pretending, Raphael.'

'Play-acting?' Could it be true?

'Yes. It was childish and silly. We are responsible parents now.' Her eyes danced. 'Let's never do it again.'

I shook my head. '*Cara*, I saw something on you face for a moment. I'm sure of it. I thought it was fear.'

'Jesu. I think I know. It was when you held me so tight, I couldn't move?'

I nodded.

'That wasn't fear, Raphael. It was ... recognition. I

realised just how powerless women are against a man's strength. How easy they are to hurt. To rape–'

'*Cristo.*' I felt completely lost. 'You thought I would *rape* you?'

She pulled away to look at me. '*What*? Why would I think such a thing?' She grinned 'And you couldn't, anyway.'

I frowned. 'But you've just said I could, had I chosen to.'

She rolled over me. 'You couldn't because I would want it as much as you and that's not rape, is it?'

I laughed. Confused. Relieved. And then, I admit, I took it as something of an invitation. When I brought her climax before my own, I thought to slow and take her there again.

She smiled, cupping my face. 'No. Just you now.'

So, I went fast and hard and, what can I say? *Santo Dio.* It was ... well, extremely enjoyable. When I came to myself, I moved to look down at her, still catching my breath, my sweat dripping onto her face. 'Forgive me.' I brushed it away with my fingertips. Her eyes were wide. Was she holding her breath? '*Ti ho ferito.* Did I hurt you?

She released it, smiling. No, my Raphael. Well, only my heart which is sorely full of love for you.'

I kissed her. 'I feel it, too.'

'Why have you never done that before? Taken your own pleasure so freely? I loved watching you. Feeling you. I loved that I could give you such a thing.'

'*Cara.*' I smoothed her damp hair back from her

face. 'Well, I'm glad I gave you pleasure even when I thought only of my own.' We lay in each other's arms, kissing again for a while. 'So, what were these questions of Penny's? You haven't told me.'

She laughed. 'It is quite difficult to answer her when I don't know what Kitty has said. I fear I chose evasion.'

'Answering a question with another? Always a good tactic.'

'I'm sure you'd have handled it better.'

I kissed her. 'I've a feeling I won't be entirely immune. Though the general rule is girls with mothers, boys with fathers.'

'So, sons it is for us. Can't have you missing out now, can we? But why do fathers need to talk to boys when they have all those other boys?'

I rolled my eyes. 'I believe fathers need to see their sons squirm because they were forced to do so themselves. And to tell them all the unpleasant consequences awaiting them, both physical and spiritual, should they fall into sin.'

She grimaced. 'Well, I hope you will discontinue the tradition. It sounds most unpleasant.'

'It is. And I most definitely shall. Now, what did she ask you?'

'Just as expected. How does a child get out? So, I asked her how she thought it did, and she didn't know.'

I smiled. 'You changed the subject?' I watched her

nod, a little shamefaced. 'And I wager I know the next one. How does it get in there?'

She grinned. 'That one was easy. I told her to ask you.'

She had done it again. Taken me completely by surprise. But I kept my wits about me this time. 'No, Susannah, you didn't. You did exactly as you had earlier. You changed the subject.'

She laughed. 'You know me too well, Raphael.'

'I think I am beginning to.' I truly hoped I was.

I awakened to a room bathed in sunlight, finding Susannah had moved away from me in the night to curl up near the edge of the wide mattress. I slid across to her, startled to see her weeping. 'Amore mio, what is it? Tell me what's wrong? She rolled over into my arms, pressing against me. I held her, soothing her in my own tongue until she was able to calm herself. 'Tell me, Susannah?'

Her lips trembled and more tears fell. 'My courses ... I'm bleeding.'

I drew her tighter into my arms. 'Hush, *cara*. Hush now. We have so much time ahead of us to enjoy each other and that is all it takes, no?'

She pulled away to look at me. 'I so wanted our–'

I put my finger on her lips to quiet her, kissing away her tears. I had never really expected it anyway. I smiled. 'It will happen. I know it and you know it, too. Yes?'

She nodded. 'Yes. You're right, of course you are. Forgive me for being so foolish.'

I kissed her nose, which ran a little. 'Nothing to forgive.' In truth, I was quite certain of it for she already had a child ... as had I, once. But I had still not told her. And how would I explain why I had not? *Cristo.* For it was shame and cowardice. I had acted shamefully and was afraid to tell her. She had already found so much of my life distasteful. How could I risk losing her with this?

She blew her nose. 'I think I'll stay here for a while, but you must go down to breakfast, Raphael.'

I shook my head. 'We can breakfast together here.'

'I'm not hungry and you must speak to Grandmama.'

'*Merda.* I suppose I must.' I moved in to kiss her. 'I love you, Susannah.'

She watched me shave and dress, silent, but looking more cheerful. I went to kiss her again before leaving her. She clung to me, and I rubbed her back.

'All shall be well, I know it.'

I smiled. 'It will, I promise. Now, can I do anything for you?'

'Just never stop loving me.'

I crossed myself. *Pray God you never stop loving me.* 'No more than I can stop breathing.' Her eyes were closed when I left. I hoped she might sleep a little.

. . .

27

Lady Sylvia and Penny were already seated at the table when I arrived. Again, Penny rushed from her chair to kiss me.

'Where is Su ... Mama? Is she not coming down?'

I bent to kiss her. 'Not yet. She is a touch unwell this morning.'

Her face fell. She turned to Sylvia. 'May I go up to her?'

'Good morning, Raphael. May she?'

'*Buongiorno*, Lady Sylvia. I believe so. If you go in quietly, *il piccola mia*, in case she sleeps.'

'I won't wake her, I promise, Papa.'

I smiled shaking my head, watching her go. 'She'll soon raise Susannah's spirits.' I sat down opposite Sylvia and began helping myself to breakfast. Eggs. Smoked fish. Cheese and soft white rolls. Strawberries. And this time a good dish of coffee. Someone now knew how to prepare it.

'I'll have a tray sent up for her.' She watched me closely. 'Is she with child?'

I finished chewing and swallowed. 'No.' How had I forgotten her disconcerting candour?

'But she hoped for it?'

I frowned. It seemed such an impertinent question. Yet perhaps she had some right to ask it? But before I found a response she spoke further.

'Forgive me. Not a question for a man, I'm sure.' She sighed. 'Susannah had a rather singular experience of getting a child. I shall talk to her.'

I closed my eyes for a moment. I knew she meant

well. 'No. That won't be necessary, thank you. We have already talked of it. I understand why she hoped for it though, for how could she not?'

Her eyes widened. 'Well, I'm glad you are knowledgeable in such matters.' She raised her eyebrows in an unspoken question.

Yet if I did not answer, she would be free to speculate. So, with great reluctance I did so. *Merda*. 'Sisters.'

I finished my breakfast in silence. When she poured more coffee for us, I knew I must speak again. I cleared my throat. 'Lady Sylvia—'

'Sylvia, please.'

'Sylvia. I must ask your forgiveness—'

'Indeed, you must not, Raphael. Had Susannah not given birth to Penny I would never have wanted ... or even accepted you for her. That is the truth.'

Yet might I still excuse her, knowing the why of it. Perhaps I could? 'Well, it matters little now.'

'And, Raphael, you need to know this also. I have thanked God for Penny every day of her life. Every single day.'

I hugged her then, closing my eyes. We had made our peace ... or so I thought.

'When you're ready to return to London, my coach can take you as far as Winchester, where another will meet you for the remainder of your journey.'

We could not return by sea, of course, because of Penny's seasickness. 'Someone is sending a coach? Who?' Not the King, surely?

'A close friend of yours, I believe. The Duchess of

Richmond. Very generous of her, is it not? She'll arrange overnight stays for you in private houses along the way, so you'll be spared the privations of coaching inns.'

So, Sylvia knew of my affair with Frances. More letters full of court gossip, no doubt. 'Well, how very generous of her.' What was it about this woman that brought out the worst in me? 'I shall be sure to thank her profusely when next I'm in her company.'

She frowned a little, though I could see she hoped she had concealed it. 'You will be very careful with Susannah, won't you, Raphael? She has been a little ... hurt by her life so far, I fear.'

Christ, this woman. This damnable woman. I would not allow her to force me into defending myself. Into justifying myself to her. Yet, once again, I had to say something. 'I love Susannah.' I stood. 'Now, if you will excuse me, I must go to her.'

'Raphael.'

I looked back.

'Perhaps you can ask her when she feels she'll be well enough to travel, then I can have a letter couriered back to Her Grace.'

God help me. 'How kind, Sylvia. But I shall write to Frances myself.'

I found Susannah alone, propped up against pillows. She smiled and I went to sit beside her on the bed. 'How are you feeling?'

'Cramps.' She searched my face. 'What's wrong? Your eyes look a touch flashy.'

I placed my hand on her belly. 'Flashy?' I closed my flashy eyes and sighed. 'I find your grandmother rather difficult, *cara*. I allow her to provoke me, and I don't know why I do?'

'Oh, my dear. Do tell.'

So, I did.

She looked a little disappointed in me. 'Well, you have all but admitted you are still Frances Stuart's lover, which was hardly sensible of you.'

'I agree, especially when I'm damn well not.' I took a breath. 'Nor ever will be again. But I did try to apologise to her and was told I was only allowed anywhere near you because of Penny. I fail to understand why she felt the need to spell it out for me.'

'Raphael. Dearest. None of this is her business, nor would it ever have been her decision to make. And I would always have chosen to marry you. Always. Penny is a gift we share now just as our own children will be.'

I stroked her face, our eyes locked together. 'Christ, Susannah. You're right, of course. None of it matters now.' What in the name of God was I doing? I already had everything I could ever want. In truth, more than I had ever dreamt of.

'My papa and mama married for love. And to do it they had to run away together, back to the exiled Stuart court. I think it was in Cologne then. His family are extremely wealthy, with vast tracts of farmland in the west country, tin mines in Cornwall, and an estate in Tavistock. Many of them, and his friends as well, thought her too far beneath him. Luckily, the King was less pejorative. He was in love himself then. My papa believes in love.' She chewed her lip. 'Perhaps too carelessly, of late. I trust he'll learn from it.'

I took off my coat and moved onto the bed beside her, pulling her into my arms. 'I'm sure he will.' Though Catherine Villiers had proved a damned hard lesson. 'So now I find your grandmother even more difficult to understand.' I shook my head. *Leave it now. Fool.*

I rolled over her and we kissed for a while, most enjoyably.

Susannah moved away with a sigh. 'I should dress. And you, dear Raphael, must write a letter to your lover.'

I smiled. 'Indeed, I must. But first I shall help you.'

When I brushed out her flaxen hair on that beautiful summer's morning, I felt we had entered a state of grace together, where everything had settled into perfect alignment, finally. Where the future would be ours. But what I should have understood then, and prayed for God's protection, is such things never last. The abyss always looms around one corner or another. And it lay in wait for us.

CHAPTER 1

Raphael

LONDON, 1676

That we shall have a child seemed certain to me, though Susannah cannot quite allow herself to trust it. I watched her sleep. The knowledge of it filled me with so much joy and gut-wrenching terror, too, for I could not live without her. Valentina haunted me and I crossed myself, whispering an act of contrition asking for God's mercy on me. Susannah must know of her but not yet. Not now. When they are both safe, please God. But I think she will not understand why I have kept it from her for so long. And how can I explain? She opened her soul to me, and I withheld mine from her.

The King did not attend our wedding ceremony in the Chapel Royal though, unexpectedly my mamma, who had fortuitously decided to visit quite unaware of my forthcoming marriage, did. There was a Mass afterwards in the Queen's Chapel in St James's Palace where I was able to make my confession – something I had not done for some considerable time – and take the sacrament. Well, not unsurprisingly, my confession was long and unpleasant, resulting in a penance of many decades of the rosary. No more than I deserved.

Mamma is with us still, in our Cheapside house, occupying the chamber which had once been mine and we have taken the larger one on the same floor, which has a closet for use as a dressing room. I looked around our chamber now. Gilded cream furniture. Silk drapes and upholstery in vibrant jewel-like colours. Carved and gilded Carrera marble fireplace. A ceiling painted with frolicking cherubs and putti, reminding me disconcertingly of the one in Frances Stuart's Richmond House bedchamber. Not something I have pointed out to Susannah. She had not wished the room altered, though I know it is far too ornate for her taste, wanting me to have this reminder of my Florentine home. God bless her.

I lowered myself softly onto the bed to sit beside her, but still, she did not stir. Her eyes were moving madly under closed lids, and I had no wish to wake her from her dream. Then, after a tiny snort, they flew open.

'Raphael?' She reached for me. 'Did I snore? Oh, Jesu, was I snoring?'

'Christ, it sounded like a pigsty in here.'

She looked so mortified, I quickly pulled her into my arms. 'I'm teasing, *cara*. Forgive me.' She pulled away to look at me and I smiled, a little shamefaced.

She narrowed her eyes, running her hand down my satin coat. 'You're ready to leave? Why must she have you there at such an hour?'

Meetings with Frances Stuart always caused a little unease between us. I shrugged. 'She is the patron. I do as I am asked.' *Merda.* Not the best choice of words. I bent to kiss her before she could reply. It took a while until I felt the tension leave her. I moved away, cautiously.

'I want you, Raphael.'

'I wish I could, *cara.*' And I did, very much. 'No time, I'm afraid, especially if I am to return the coach for you.'

She sighed and fell back against the pillows. 'I could always take a hackney.' She sighed again. 'All I want is to make love or to eat. Is it normal? How can it be?'

It sounded rather perfect to me. 'I think it a further proof you are with child.'

'You do?'

'I think so. Ask Mamma. Now, I must go.'

'Find me when you get back.'

I kissed her forehead. 'Of course.'

Giuseppe waited outside with the leather bag holding the samples and drawings for the duchess. A chill in the air already suggested autumn with little warmth now in the early morning sunshine.

'Why she want you now, eh?'

I sighed. 'I have no idea.'

'Maybe she meet you in her *camera da letto*?' He grinned.

I snatched the bag from him. 'I have a wife whom I love very much. Now, where is that damn coach.' As I spoke, I heard the sound of hooves approaching from the mews behind the house, and he was able to gesture smugly towards it. I really must not rise to his goading. There would be more when I returned home. I would ignore it.

He lowered the steps and opened the door for me, but before I could climb inside, he touched my shoulder. 'Raph, you know I joke with you, no? I see how it is with you and Susannah.'

I nodded, punching his arm lightly in response. 'I know, *Amico*.' And, in truth, I did. And I also knew he would never stop his banter and in time it would wash over me as it had always done before. For now, though, the reality of my marriage was still too new to be the target of his humour and any suggestion of infidelity too offensive, for I knew without a single doubt it would never happen. I had vowed it before Susannah and before God.

The streets were quiet at this hour and there were even a few rakers' carts still trundling along, carrying their reeking load from the city's cesspits out to the laystalls beyond. I held my handkerchief to my nose as they passed.

Rory halted at the turn into King Street and climbed down to speak to me. 'A cart be over further up with nothing moving. What do ye wish of me, Master?'

Time was pressing for my appointment with Frances. 'Go down The Mall and through the park.' The route towards the Park Gate was kept free from carriage traffic on most days but if King Street was blocked, I had no compunction about using it. Driving down the deserted track, I noticed some of the trees were already taking on their vibrant autumn colours. It still surprised me how much brighter and more varied they were in England. Perhaps it was all the rain, for there had to be some purpose to it? Then, amongst them, I glimpsed bright hair gleaming in the sunshine and spotted two small girls dressed in identical pale blue gowns, sitting on the grass. One of them was Penny. I knocked on the wall signalling Rory to stop and jumping down, I cupped my hands around my mouth, 'Penny.' The air already carried a hint of autumn. Damp earth and wood smoke. I sighed. Soon coal smoke from London's countless chimneys would pall the sky once more.

She looked up, scrambling to her feet, and ran to me, grinning. 'Papa.' She flung her arms around me and turned to her friend, who approached more slowly. 'Kitty. This is my papa.'

'Surely, you are not alone here, girls?' I looked around and spotted a young woman talking with a man further in under the trees.

Kitty saw me looking. That's Abigail. She's taking care of us.'

It certainly did not appear so to me. Far from it. 'Stay here. I shall speak with her for a moment.' I had walked some way towards them before the man noticed me. He looked decidedly disreputable, with threadbare clothes and grimy skin. The woman, heavy-set and freckle-faced, was clearly enjoying the kind of male attention she would likely not receive very often. 'Abigail?'

She made a clumsy curtsy. 'Master?'

'I believe your attention should be on your charges, one of whom is my daughter.' I gave the fellow a hard look and he stared back, insolently, before finally lowering his eyes. He spat on the grass, then slunk away deeper into the shrubbery.

'Forgive me, Master. I shall get back to 'em right away. Please don't tell my mistress, I begs you. They was right there with me. I never saw 'em wander off, like.'

'I'll make sure Penny tells me if anything like this happens again. Then your employers will hear of it.' She looked suitably chastened. 'Make sure they're back in Wood Yard by midday when my wife will collect our daughter.' As I walked back to Penny with the woman scurrying after me, I wondered whether to return them safely to Whitehall in my coach and said as much when I reached them. They were making chains out of small white daisy flowers. Penny already wore one on her head like a crown, and it gave me an idea for a necklace. I could craft the flowers with enamel in Susannah's kiln. A skill she had been happy to teach me, and it had proved a popular addition to our designs. My suggestion to the girls was not well received.

'Not yet. Please, Papa.'

'We haven't finished,' Kitty added.

I sighed. I was already late. I turned to Abigail. She really was most unprepossessing, poor girl. I smiled at her. 'Remember what I said.'

'I will, Master.' Blushing did nothing for her complexion, unfortunately.

I climbed up into my coach, telling Rory to hurry as I did, and we were soon pulling up at the Park Gate. I walked briskly along beside the bowling green to arrive at Richmond House, where the door opened immediately, and a footman led me upstairs into the drawing room. 'Frances.' We kissed each other on both cheeks. 'You look well.' She was dressed in pearl grey silk with a violet mantua just the colour of her eyes.

'So do you, my dear. And how is Susannah?'

I decided to tell her. 'She's with child.'

She hugged me. 'Raphael, I'm so happy for you both.' She stepped away smiling. 'And little Penelope will have a brother or sister. She'll like that, I'm sure.'

I tilted my head, studying her. 'You knew about Penny? I mean–'

'I know what you mean, Raphael. And I did. And that she was Samuel's. Who else could it be?'

Just what her father and grandmother had said. 'The King knew?' I was fairly certain of it.

'I never spoke of it with him. Now, I have breakfast for you.' She led me to a low table placed before a sofa affording us a good view over the bowling green, where a game was now underway. 'We can eat while you show me what you've brought.'

And that is what we did, eating hot-buttered rolls and coddled eggs while I showed her the drawings of a necklace she wished for, which would feature some of my new enamel work. When the plates had been cleared away, I laid out the mock-ups of a ruby brooch I would make once she had decided on the design. 'These are the three you chose from the drawings.'

'These always make a decision so much easier.' She studied them, lifting each one, and taking it to hold against her in front of one of the many mirrors there to reflect light from the large candelabras set in front of them. 'This one.' She handed it to me.

I nodded. 'I'll begin it right away.'

She patted my arm. 'Now, my dear, I have another appointment.'

I kissed her hand. '*Buona giornata*, Frances.'

CHAPTER 2
Susannah

I rang for the maid as soon as Raphael left me. I was extremely hungry now the first part of my craving had been withheld. I smiled thinking of him, knowing there would be time later. I felt heat on my face, imagining it. *Jesu, how I love him.*

Maria helped me dress and pinned-up my hair. She was my height but heavily built with thick black hair scraped into a tight bun. As she had accompanied Raphael's mother from Florence, it seemed easier to make use of her skills as a lady's maid rather than try to find a girl myself. Though she spoke little English and I less Italian, we managed with smiles and goodwill and Raphael's help when he was there. Perhaps my previous maid Bess's betrayal, which had nearly cost the life of my dearest friend and Penny's father, Sam Carter, accounted for my reluctance to find a replacement for her. The girl had stolen his sword so it could be discovered hidden in a Whitehall courtyard, providing the only evidence Sam had committed the murder for which he had ultimately been convicted. Only her eleventh-hour confession had saved him from a traitor's death.

As I made my way down the wide staircase to the dining room, reflecting on how different I felt with this child – and, yes, I do believe there is one though I have not admitted so to Raphael – than with Penny years before. Then I had vomited so much I thought I would die from it. Now I could not stave off my hunger pangs. Did this mean I carried a boy? Please God it might be so. I wanted it for my husband.

I found his mother, Lucia, seated at the table buttering a hot roll. She looked up at me and smiled. I returned it, thinking how much of Raphael I saw in her, though she was so tiny. She stood to kiss me on both cheeks before holding me away to look at me. 'Susannah you are *una bellissima ragazza*. More so each day. I say this to my Raffaello; how lucky he is. Is *Meravigliosa* ... wonderful to see him truly happy at last.'

I sat beside her at the table and began to load my plate while she poured coffee for us. I could not help wondering why he had not been happy in the past. He had always seemed so in the time I had known him. I smiled. But perhaps not quite so visibly as he was now. 'Yes, it must be.' I admit I wanted her to tell me about it without realising I did not already know. It seemed a little unkind to try and trick her like this, but I sensed this was something perhaps I needed to hear, for he still hid secrets from me.

'After Valentina.' She shrugged. 'Though, it was to be expected after losing them, *credo*?'

Valentina? Them? Jesu. What was she talking about? I had to find out. 'Yes, of course.' What could I say to make her tell me? 'He hasn't said much,' I lied. 'Perhaps if I knew more, I could help him?' I lowered my eyes, feeling horribly guilty for misleading her so shamefully.

She tilted her head, studying me with some care. 'Maybe you're right, *cara mia*. Has he told you about Rome?'

I nodded. 'Yes, he spent three years there.'

'He met her there. She was married ... what can I say about his behaviour? If he hasn't told you, then I do not wish to shock you–'

'I shall not be shocked,' I said, quietly. I knew all about those activities. There had been many such at court since he arrived in London.

'She came to us in Florence far gone with child.' She took a sip of coffee.

His child? I felt dazed, which must have shown on my face. Luckily, she read it as deepening concern.

She took my hand and squeezed it. 'Her husband had put her out, you see. He knew the child couldn't be his.' She shook her head. 'Allessandro believed she'd come to Raffaello because he was conveniently far away from Rome. But I knew the girl was his as soon as she was born.' Lucia looked away. 'Valentina had meant her for Raffaello, so a dead child was of no matter to her. She said she'd go back to her husband.' She held my gaze. 'Then the childbed fever took her. Capitano Gentileschi fetched her. We took care of the child.'

I thought I would vomit, my hand pressing on my belly where this child was just beginning. 'Jesu.' Tears spilled.

Her eyes widened. '*Dio mio*. You're with child.' She crossed herself. 'God forgive me, I should never have spoken of this to you now.'

I seized her hand. 'You didn't know, Lucia.'

She paled. 'And you didn't know of it at all, did you? *Dio mi perdoni*. I never dreamt he would have told you nothing.'

'I wanted to know. Forgive me. I made you think I already did.' All at once, I was angry. Very angry, indeed. 'He should have told me. I had a right to know.' Especially as he knew everything there was to know about me. He would have some explaining to do. I stood, patting Lucia's shoulder. I had quite lost my appetite. 'Forgive me, I'm a little unwell. I think I must retire to my chamber for a while.' She looked so distressed, I bent to hug her, kissing her cheek. 'Please don't blame yourself. You've done nothing wrong.' Which was more than I could say for her son.

Giuseppe. His manservant. Assistant. Friend. What did he know of this? Surely, he could explain why Raphael had kept it hidden from me. I hastened down into the workshop, stark in light and deep shadow, sunlight blazing in through the skylight casting a dark grid beneath it. Giuseppe's black hair gleamed just as Raphael's did. I stood beside him while he finished mounting a large diamond between two emeralds, set into a slender gold band.

He looked up. 'What's happened?'

I cannot say it surprised me he could read it on my face. I glanced at the apprentices and journeymen at their benches. 'I need to talk with you.'

He took off his leather apron and led me out into the mews behind the house. 'Raphael?'

I laughed, if somewhat grimly, for what else could it be. 'What do you know about Valentina Gentileschi?'

He looked genuinely surprised. 'Why you ask this?' He studied my face.

'Did you know he has told me nothing? When his mother spoke of her at breakfast, it was the first time I'd ever heard her name.'

His eyes widened. '*Merda*. He hasn't shared that with me, no.'

'Why would he do such a thing? You've known him most of his life? Why?'

He touched my arm. '*Padrona*, it's him you should be asking this.'

I held my forehead. 'Oh, believe me I shall, but you must have some idea.' I chewed my lip. 'Is it so shameful then, so depraved, what he did? Is he afraid for me to know of it?'

'*Santo Dio*. Is no that at all. You think he could do

something so bad? You know him. You really think such things of him?'

I took a long shuddering breath. 'Jesu, no. I do know him, Giuseppe. While I know how he used to live, I also know how he lives now. So, why hasn't he told me about this? There was a child. I had a child.' I shook my head. 'I simply can't understand.'

He squeezed my shoulder. 'You ask him. One thing I say. He always hard on himself. Too hard. You know this, Susannah. Talk to him.' He walked away back to the workshop.

I did not return to the house but went instead to my studio over the coach house. I would wait there until Raphael returned. Hugo was already working, cutting the metal disks and ovals from sheets of silver and gold that I would need for my enamel portraits. A task he had proved particularly adept at. He was a cheerful boy with a round, guileless face and unruly copper hair always trying to escape from whatever means he used to restrain it. Today it was a leather string.

He turned and smiled, plainly surprised to see me so early. 'I've done your box for the palace, Mistress, just like you asked. Don't you worry yourself.'

I smiled. 'I knew you would.'

'Who's you painting today, Mistress?'

'Henry Hyde, Earl of Clarendon. He is close to the Duke of York.' I studied him for a moment. 'I shall take you to court with me one day soon so you can make your own watercolour.' He copied each of mine after I returned with them and had been making a fine job of it. And he had just begun learning to transfer to enamel. I should have thought to take him with me sooner, though not today, for my mind was too occupied elsewhere to make much of an instructress.

He glowed with pleasure. 'Thank you, Mistress. I shall work hard to learn, I swear it.'

I heard the coach wheels on the cobbles, then, and stood. My husband had returned.

CHAPTER 3

Raphael

As my carriage drove back through the park, I kept my eyes open for Penny, hoping I could bring her home with me to save Susannah the trip to Wood Yard. I assumed Abigail had taken them back there when there was no sign of her. The return journey to Cheapside unsurprisingly took considerably longer than my outward one and I became concerned Susannah would indeed be forced to take a hackney if she were to get to her sitter in time.

When we halted finally in the mews, I jumped down and ran upstairs to the small studio we had made for her above the coach house, with a kiln and everything needed for her portrait miniatures. She was there still, talking quietly with her young apprentice, dressed for court in indigo satin that clung to her body, with her box waiting beside her on the floor. I scooped it up and winked at Hugo. He grinned. 'Come, Susannah.' I took her hand and hurried her down the stairs. 'I saw Penny and her friend in the park on my way in. She was wearing a crown made from daisy flowers. It's given me the idea for a piece using enamel again.' Then, I walked her backwards against a wall in the dark empty coach shed, pressing close against her, kissing her. I knew immediately there was something wrong. 'What?'

'Valentina Gentileschi.'

'*Dio mio.*' My mind spun away with shock. Her name felt like a physical blow coming from Susannah's lips.

'She had your child.'

'Christ.' Bile rose in my throat. 'My mother told you?'

She moved around me. 'She did, indeed, Raphael. What I can't understand it is why you never have.'

I grasped her hand to stop her walking away. 'Susannah, please. Let me explain.' *God knows how.* When she pulled away from me, I followed her outside to the coach, reaching for her again.

She shrugged me off. 'Later. I've no time.'

She didn't look at me as I helped her up inside. 'I can explain.' Well, at least I now had time to decide what to say, or so I thought.

Rory appeared and climbed up, fisting his forehead before taking-up the reins. 'Privy.'

I watched them clatter away before going into my workshop through the mews door. First, though, I must speak to Mamma.

Giuseppe looked up. 'Which did she choose?'

'I shook my head, to clear it. 'The one I expected.' *Cristo.* My thoughts fragmented like shards of shattered glass on the floor.

'You know how to please her, *Padrone*,' he said, flatly, his grin not quite reaching his eyes.

I ignored him, turning to my mother working at her bench. *'Mamma, una parola con te per favore.'* When she looked up it was clear she knew what it would be about.

She walked upstairs with me to the drawing room, looking troubled. Strange how this ornate setting felt more hers now than mine, with its plethora of carved and gilded white marble and bright silks.

'Forgive me, Raffaello. Though, how was I to know you hadn't told her? Or that she is with child herself?' She hugged me then. 'Which pleases me more than I can say, *cara mia*. God has indeed blessed you, my son. With such a wife and now a child.'

I hugged her, kissing her on both cheeks. How could I be angry with her? 'Susannah hoped for a child as soon as we married. It seemed something not to tell her in view of that.' This was only part of the truth, of course. While I did not want to bring such a vision of the abyss into our life together, there was also the self-serving wish not to show her yet another example of my past behaviour to disappoint her when there had already been so much. In truth, there was more to it than I cared to face. Things about my father and my toxic relationship with him. I sighed. It would not be an easy conversation to have now. I hoped she could forgive me for it. 'Come.' I held out my hand. 'We should go back down.'

Giuseppe followed me to my bench and bent to speak into my ear. 'Susannah, she ask about her ... about Valentina. Why you no tell her?'

I closed my eyes. 'Christ, Giuseppe. I don't know. How can I explain when I don't truly know myself?' He squeezed my shoulder.

I tried to lose myself in work for a while. I could see Mamma did the same. She had always worked alongside Papà, though he rarely acknowledged her skills as a jeweller. Yet they had started out alone together to build what was now an extremely successful business.

It was Giuseppe who saw him first. I picked up his tension and followed his gaze. A man, resplendent in uniform, ran down the stairs. An equerry in the Richmond livery. I took a loud breath. A groan.

'Raphael Rossi?'

I stepped towards him. 'Here. What can I do for you?' My heart pounded. Christ. Sweet holy Christ. Frances would not send this man without good reason. Something terrible had happened. *Dio mio*. Not Susannah? He handed me a letter. I crossed myself and snapped it open.

Raphael. Penny has disappeared. Susannah is with me and distraught. Come now.

I dropped it onto the workbench, struggling for breath. Giuseppe read it and shook me, slightly. 'Go.'

I turned to the equerry. 'Have you a coach?'

'Horseback, Master. It's best.'

I charged outside with Giuseppe behind me. We both knew to take Vixen. I bridled her whilst he dropped her rug and saddle down, fastening the girth strap before giving me a leg up onto her back and tightening it again.

'Off,' he cried, slapping her rump.

She shot forward and we began our breakneck dash back to Whitehall, ending with a gallop through St James's Park beside the canal. I arrived again at Richmond House, silently repeating: she's safe already, followed by: but what if she is not? Again and again, like slow torture. I swung my leg up over the pommel and vaulted from my horse.

The equerry grabbed the reins. 'I'll tend to her, Master.'

I glanced up at the big drawing room window. Susannah was there looking down. I ran inside through the open door and up the stairs two at a time. She turned to look at me when I entered. Her eyes were dry now, though I could see she had wept for a long time. They were hot-looking and bloodshot, her pale skin blotched with red. '*Cara*?' And, Holy Mother of God, I watched her break.

Somehow, she was in my arms on a sofa, and I held her while she keened, pushing against me as though trying to find somewhere to hide within me. I wished I could give her that. I had no idea what to do or say, other than hold her and gentle her in my own language. When, I heard footsteps, I glanced up. *Cristo*. It was the King, dressed in grey worsted with a touch of silver lace at his throat. Sombre for him, especially against the bright greens and gold of the room. I never thought of trying to rise. It was only when he waved his hand to say it did not matter that it even entered my head.

'You saw the children in the park?'

I nodded, trying to order my thoughts. This is King Charles of England, but he is not my King. 'Is the other little girl–'

He sat down on the sofa opposite. 'Missing. And the maidservant.'

I saw his eyes were fixed on Susannah who was quiet now, her face pressed hard against my chest. I stroked her back. Still murmuring words of comfort from time to time when I felt her stir. 'What is being done?' He showed no sign of objecting to my lack of protocol in speaking to him as a man and not a King.

Before he could answer, Frances came in. 'Raphael.' She hurried to me, holding my face, and kissing my forehead. Then her hand joined mine on Susannah's back for a moment. 'We can tell you what's been done already and what will happen now.'

Susannah raised her head and turned to look at Frances and the King. 'Yes.' Her voice sounded small and hoarse. 'Please. If you can do that. I need to know.'

I moved so she could sit more comfortably facing them, though I kept her gathered tight in my arms. It occurred to me then that the King must have been with Frances when Susannah arrived here – the appointment she had spoken of – and what a huge stroke of luck that was, even if luck was a strange concept to apply to a catastrophe like this. But because he was, everything that could be done would have been. Immediately. All he had to do was order it so because, of course, Susannah is his goddaughter.

There was a sharp rap on the door. 'Enter.' The King turned his prominent, dark eyes to the newcomers, Tom Monkton and Sir Richard Gresham. They made the required subjugations, but he waved them away. 'Lieutenant, if you please. Tell us what has been accomplished so far and what you intend now.'

Susannah held out a hand to her father. He took it and bent to kiss her, brushing away her tears with his fingers before sitting beside her.

'Sukie. We'll find her, I'm sure of it.'

The King gestured at Tom to begin.

'Mistress Rossi. My men have searched St James's Park and are doing so within the palace boundaries as we speak. I've talked with Mistress Foyles concerning the maidservant, Abigail Dobbs, and she has told me all she can of her. Nothing is helpful. None of them were seen at the house again.

'Poor Anne,' Susannah murmured.

I turned to her. '*Cara*. I told you I saw the girls in the park on my way in this morning. I stopped my coach because I thought they were alone. But the maid was with a man under the trees. I went to remonstrate with her because she wasn't watching the children–'

The King leaned forward, hawkeyed. 'Describe this man.'

'He looked like every vagabond. Ragged clothing. Dirty.' I closed my eyes, trying to remember more. I shook my head. 'He was a man like so many others. A beggar.'

The King turned his attention to Tom. 'Lieutenant. What else is to be done? Manpower is not a concern. Do everything necessary. Do it immediately. And ask the other child's mother about this person.'

'Your Majesty. I must now send men to all docks within the pool of London. Anywhere a ship might sail to the West Indies or the Americas.'

'Explain.' The King held up his hand. 'No. We see it, now. But you cannot think such a thing possible in this case? Not taken from a Royal Park?'

'Unfortunately, I do. It is rife everywhere, Your Majesty.'

I felt Susannah stiffen beside me and held her closer. 'What are you talking about?' She looked from the King to Tom. When the King gave a slight nod, Tom sighed.

'Mistress–'

'Susannah, please.'

'Susannah. Sending men to the docks is a precaution.'

'But why are they needed there? What are they to do? And how is it relevant to my ... our daughter?'

'There is a very slight possibility that it might be. There is a particularly unpleasant criminal activity prevalent at the moment ... because it's so lucrative.' He paused to take a breath. 'Colloquially it's known as Spiriting. Many otherwise reputable shipping companies employ so called 'spirits' to kidnap people, taking them ... spiriting them away to the colonies.' He looked down at his hands. 'They are sold into servitude ... usually that means for the rest of their lives. Much like slaves from Africa.'

Susannah gasped. 'A child? Why would they want children? The girls are so little. They're but eight years old. What can they do as servants?'

'Children are cheaper than adults and they grow. They work now, Susannah. In London and throughout the Kingdom. Children the same age as your daughter and Kitty Foyles. Many work, or they beg.' He looked again at the King who turned to Frances.

She pursed her lips. I knew whatever he wished her to say was unpalatable to her. She sat up straighter. 'Some children are sold for different purposes. Pretty children. Pretty boys and girls. Some are even stolen to order.'

Susannah's groan tore at my heart. 'Not Penny? In the name of God, you can't be suggesting such a thing.'

Tom closed his eyes for a moment before looking from me to Susannah. 'No. I'm saying we'll search ships to make sure it doesn't happen to her. We shall find her very soon and bring her back to you.'

She turned to me again and began to weep silently,

tears washing down her face. '*Amore mio.*' I held her to me again without any idea what to do.

We waited at Richmond House for many hours, hoping for news and hearing nothing good. All searches had so far proved fruitless. Frances stayed with us, maintaining a constant supply of refreshments. I ate a little, Susannah nothing, though we both drank claret. As afternoon began to fade into evening, I stood at the big window looking out over the privy garden, a few bright-clad courtiers wandered there. On the bowling green a game was just concluding, with the last of the sun shining ruby on upper floor windows and rooftops. Life went on outside whilst ours had frozen. I turned to Susannah, white-faced on her sofa, Frances sitting patiently beside her. 'We should go home, *cara*. Word will be got to us when there is something to tell.' She turned to me, her face blank as though she had not understood.

I moved back beside her, meeting Frances's gaze for a moment. I cupped Susannah's face in my palm. 'Let me take you home. Let me care for you there.'

Frances touched her arm. 'I shall send an equerry with any news, however small.'

I stood and offered my hand to her. 'Come, Susannah.' She allowed me to help her stand and I pulled her into my arms, holding her close and feeling her tremble.

Frances moved to the bell rope. 'I'll have my coach sent round.' She left the room and returned with Susannah's cloak.

I took it and wrapped it around her shoulders. How little time had truly passed since I drove through the park this morning and saw the girls playing happily in the sunshine, yet it felt like eons. Holy Christ, why had I not taken them safely into my coach. I crossed myself and prayed for God's mercy.

Once inside the carriage, Susannah stared ahead, appearing not to see as we journeyed through streets now falling into shadow. What could I do but pray? 'The holy mother will protect her.'

She turned to me. 'You really believe that?'

I crossed myself. 'I do. I have faith it is so.'

She moved into my arms, pressing herself against me. 'Then I shall try to have faith in yours.'

I had sent messages to Cheapside, so no explanations were needed when we arrived. My mother waited quietly in the drawing room and hugged us both without asking questions. She poured us wine, and I sat beside Susannah once again, on a different sofa in a different, somewhat less grand, drawing room this time.

My mother sat beside her, too. 'Have you eaten, *carissima*?'

Susannah seemed not to hear her.

I met Mamma's eyes and shook my head.

'Tell me everything,' she said in Italian.

So that is what I did, including my failure to see the girls home myself.

She wiped away tears, shaking her head. 'Don't

blame yourself, Raffaello. Save blame for those who took her then leave them to God, my darling.' She stood. 'Get her to bed and I shall have a tray sent up. She must eat. You know why.'

I nodded, rising to my feet. I put my arm around her to help her up. 'Come, Susannah. You should rest. Let me help you.' She allowed me to lead her up to our chamber and stood meekly before me while I undressed her. She had sent her mind elsewhere. I was glad she had but also a little afraid she would not come back. I loosened her hair from its pins and moved in to kiss her, hoping I could call her with my body. After a time, feeling no response, I gently moved her to sit on the bed while I fetched her a nightgown from the press.

'Raphael.'

I turned to find her standing, holding out her hands to me, her face wet with tears once again. 'I'm here, *cara*.' And then she was in my arms kissing me and clutching me hard to her. I held her around her waist, pulling the quilts back to guide her into bed. She lay quiet, chewing her lip, her face white as chalk, watching me shed my clothes onto the floor. I wanted to make love to her gently; to offer her comfort but it was not that she needed from me. She wanted fast oblivion. And when those few precious moments of unknowing faded bringing her back to herself, she wept as though her heart had finally shattered. I held her close. I had nothing else to give her. God help me.

After a light tap on the door, Giuseppe came in

with a tray. Our eyes met and he closed his for a moment, seeing Susannah held tight in my arms with her face pressed against my chest. He placed the tray down softly onto the table and lit all the candles before closing the drapes to shut out the last of the twilight. Then he bent to retrieve my clothing from the floor sorting what should be hung-up from what must be laundered. 'Thank you,' I mouthed.

His eyebrows shot up and he mimed a stagger of amazement.

'Idiot.' I murmured as the door closed behind him.

Susannah raised her head. 'What?'

I pushed her hair back from her face. 'You must eat now, *cara*.'

She moved away to lie on her back, her forearm covering her eyes. 'I can't. It would make me vomit.'

I rose up onto my elbow to look at her. 'You must, Susannah. You're with child, so you must.'

She let her arm fall away and held my gaze for a moment. 'Jesu.'

I climbed out of bed. 'Stay there. I'll fetch a plate.' At the table, I filled a large one with enough bread, cheese, fruit, and cakes for both of us before pouring two glasses of Chianti, bringing them to the table beside the bed. She sat up higher against the pillows. Her white tear-streaked face tore at my heart.

'Wine first.'

I smiled. 'Cake first. Best I can do.' I handed her one and watched her eat it with her eyes closed. She opened them after a final swallow, and I handed her the wineglass. And so, she ate with wine as a reward, and I more or less did the same, though I ate more and drank less. Then, she slept in my arms or rather what passed for sleep for both of us with short dozes followed by agonies of remembering.

CHAPTER 4

Noah

PORT ROYAL, JAMAICA 1676

Noah sat at the battered mahogany table out on the long, covered porch of their beach-front house close to the more salubrious end of Port Royal, which unfortunately happened to be within sight of Fort Charles squatting up on the headland. This meant they were rather closer to the English authorities than was altogether comfortable. But it was never possible to have everything, he had long accepted that. He glanced up at Sam sifting through a small stack of letters, his skin browned by the sun, chestnut hair sun-streaked, looking healthy and happy ... and loved. Noah returned to his ledger only to look up again a minute or two later when Sam groaned. 'What, Lad?'

'Christ. Holy Christ.' He stared down at the letter he had dropped as though it burnt him. All colour had left his face. 'Susannah ... I don't. I–' He held it out for Noah to read.

Cheapside
  August 17, 1676

My dearest Sam.
  Raphael and I are married and happy beyond anything either of us could ever have dreamed of.
  And, dearest Sam, we will have a child as soon as possible ...

Noah scanned on through domestic detail and news of Sam's father, trying to find what could possibly have shocked him in such a way.

... So, my Sam, there is something I have to say to you. First, I must tell you that Penny lives with us here now because she is my daughter and not my sister – she calls me Mama and Raphael Papa though, of course, he is her stepfather, though very happy to be so. Well, I don't quite know how to tell you this, dearest Sam, but you are her father.
  I hope I have not shocked you too much. I only wish we could talk of it now but fate has been unkind in that regard. She will know you are her natural papa when she is old enough to understand it, and I pray one day you might meet again as father and daughter.
  Until then, I hope you can take comfort from her joy at having a mama and papa of her own now.

I love you my dearest,

Always your Sukie.

Noah handed the letter back to Sam. 'Christ, Laddie.' He shook his head. 'Does it make any sense to you?'

Sam took a long breath. 'Of course it does. I think I told you of my one experience–'

'With Susannah Gresham? Holy God, Sam.' How could he have got her with child and not known? From all he had heard of their years together, they had been more or less inseparable.

Sam seemed to read his mind. 'How could I not have not known? It is a good question with a shameful answer.' He scrubbed at his face, looking out across the water ruffled and aglitter in the afternoon sun.

Noah stood and pulled up another chair close beside him. 'Do you want to tell me?'

'No. But I think I shall have to.' He sighed. 'It was once, only. I told you that–'

'Not good enough, Laddie. Not by a long way. I know about you and Susannah. I know you loved her ... you love her still. You didn't suddenly stop being all but her brother to throw her onto your bed and rape her, now did you. So, either tell me or don't. But there is a child from it so don't try to pretend it was nothing.' What the hell was he doing sounding so judgmental before he had even given him a chance to speak? All right, it had shocked him, but he should know by now when to hold his tongue.

Sam stood. 'Then, as you've so generously given

me the choice, I believe I shall not tell you, Sir.' He scooped up the letter, tucking it inside his shirt, before running down the steps onto the beach.

Noah brought his fist down onto the table, watching him go. 'Christ's fucking wounds.' He should have left him to tell it as he wished. What in the name of God was wrong with him? Now he must give the lad some time to understand it himself before going after him. He paced for a while, too short a while he knew, and then set off to follow Sam along the beach.

He found him sitting on a low bough sweeping out over the white sand, the flame tree covered in blossom. When he sat down beside him, though the perch groaned and dipped, it held. 'Forgive me. Tell me as much or as little as you like. I've no business pressing you ... or judging you.'

Sam closed his eyes, tilting his face up to the sunshine dappled through the leaves. 'It's shame holding my tongue.' He looked at Noah. 'I have a place where I hide such things. Things that won't bear too much scrutiny if one is to keep a reasonably good opinion of oneself. Perhaps everyone has such a place?'

Noah nodded. Determined not to interrupt him this time.

'I don't know why things changed between us. Why we started kissing or even which of us began it. I liked it well enough.' He bit his lip. 'I liked her touching me.' He laughed, mirthlessly. 'Making me hard.' He picked a bright red flower and twirled it between his fingers. 'I can, of course, offer the excuse there was a certain amount of pressure from boys at school. Each new term some came back with tales of poor little scullery maids deflowered behind the gardener's shed or some such. And here I was with a wonderful opportunity to deflower my dearest friend in my own bedchamber. Christ, what a shit I was.'

Noah could not help himself. He placed his hand down onto Sam's shoulder. 'You were just a boy. You didn't know what would happen–'

Sam shrugged him off. 'I knew I shouldn't do it. God help me. I knew I didn't even damn well want to.' He took a long breath and composed himself. 'I can scarcely bear to tell you what I did.'

'I know what you did. And neither of you expected to get a child.'

Sam shook his head. 'You don't, I'm afraid. You truly have no idea at all. Yes, I took her to my chamber but ... well. I wasn't kind to her. I just lifted her skirts and–' He looked up into the branches again, heavy with flaming blossom. 'It hurt her. I felt her tremble from it, but she didn't cry out. She held me so tight. Then I was done. It was over before I'd scarce begun. When I rolled away from her, I saw her blood and my seed smeared on her thighs. Jesus Christ help me; I began to weep. She moved to me, holding me, and telling me she loved me. And what did I do, Noah? Did I hold her and tell her I loved her, too? Oh, no. Not at all. I told her not to touch me and to go home.'

Holy fuck, Laddie.'

'It certainly wasn't that.'

Noah snorted. 'No.'

They sat in silence for a while.

Noah, listening to the whisper of the sea foaming in lace frills over the sand a few feet away, still questioned how Sam had not known of his child. 'Can you tell me the rest?'

'Tell you the worst of it, you mean?'

'I love you, Sam, for the man you are. Boys are fools. Often selfish fools. I was one myself and I have two sons. I know quite a lot about the mindlessness of lads.'

'Indeed. I was a selfish prick. I still can't understand how I could have done it. I loved her. I never stopped loving her.'

Christ, Lad. What did you do?'

'I left. I left that evening. I packed my box for school and went to a friend in Richmond. I stayed with him until term started.' He closed his eyes. 'When I next came home, they'd gone. Richard told me they were with Sylvia – Susannah's grandmother – and Jane was with child. They would stay there for her confinement. I didn't see Susannah again until they came home with Penny.'

'Fuck. And it never once occurred to you that Penny might be Susannah's child and not her mother's?'

'Noah, I was utterly self-absorbed. I'd found myself. Found myself with men ... at school. At court. I was happy. God, I was so pleased to see her, though.

She looked wonderful. Softer. Rounder. Bonny. I told her country life suited her.' He tilted his head back. 'She'd just given birth to my child, and I told her that, God help me. What can I say to her? How can she ever forgive me?'

Everything Sam had told him seemed so out of character for the man he knew now. He had to keep reminding himself of how long ago all this had happened. And he already knew it was not as straight forward as Sam thought. 'Well, she has forgiven you, hasn't she? You're as close as you ever were. She fought hard beside me to save your life.' That she bore him no ill will was clear. The opposite, in truth.

'Very well, then. Why did she forgive me?'

'Because she loves you.' Noah frowned, thinking. 'And she never wanted you to marry. If she had, she would've told you about Penny.' Christ, the girl had paid a high price for what sounded such a grim encounter. Poor lass. Yet she had a much-loved child from it.

'Well, I can understand that. I ran from her. I can't have seemed like much of a prospect as a husband. No wonder she was so unhappy she had to hide herself away. Much of that must have been because of me.'

'Had you known she was to have your child what would you have done?'

'Married her, of course.'

How naïve he was. He must understand what a lucky escape it had been for them both that such a marriage had not taken place. Susannah had understood it. Sam needed to now. 'Would either of you have been happy, do you think?'

Sam walked to the water's edge, letting the foaming ripples wash over his feet. 'I might have made her happy. In time I could have learnt how.' He turned back to Noah. 'You did.'

Noah ran his hands through his thick unbound hair. 'As happy as she is now with Raphael?'

Sam chuckled a little. 'Ah, dear Raphael. Now that's probably something of a tall order.'

Noah reached him in two strides, closing his arms around him. 'Could you have been as happy as you are with me?'

Sam shook his head. 'No.'

'Then you've nothing to blame yourself for–'

'Apart from running away.'

'Boys run away. You were a boy.' He held Sam's face between his big hands. 'You have a daughter. It is a wonderful thing. Leave the rest of it behind. Susannah has.'

Sam sighed. 'I must write to her. Christ knows what I'll say.'

When they arrived back on the porch, Noah called for wine before sitting beside Sam on a hide-covered sofa close against the wall of the house, now in deep shade.

'I wish you could know her. She's the image of Susannah. It's strange how the women in that family all look so alike. Though Susannah is taller than her

69

mother and grandmother.' He turned to Noah. 'I won't see her grow up, will I? In truth, I shall probably never see her again.'

'We can't know that for–' Noah broke off at the sounds of breathless cries of female satisfaction soon followed by groans of male pleasure coming from the chamber at the other end of the porch. 'What the–'

Sam smiled shaking his head.

Noah closed his eyes and tried to ignore it for long enough to feel some virtue over it, until anger won. He stood and glared towards his son's room. 'Hal. Come here now if you please?'

Sam sighed. 'For God's sake, Noah, leave him be–'

'Leave him be? Leave him fucking be? Have you not just learnt how easy it is to get bastards?'

Sam stood, too, clenching his fists. 'If I thought I wouldn't break my hand doing it, I'd punch you in the face you crass imbecile.'

'Imbecile, is it? *Imbecile?*' Noah took a step towards him.

Hal strolled out onto the porch and walked towards them, wearing only breeches. 'Good afternoon, Sam. Papa. What can I do for you?'

Sam began to laugh and collapsed back onto the sofa. 'Go ahead, Noah. Do tell.'

Noah narrowed his eyes. 'Perhaps you'd be so good as to give me a moment to speak to my son in private?'

Sam raised his eyebrows in an eloquent *'really?'* and shaking his head, rose to go inside the house touching Hal's arm and rolling his eyes as he passed him.

Noah pointed to the sofa Sam had just vacated. 'Sit.'

Hal tilted his head. 'Am I a dog, Sir? I shall stand.'

Noah wanted to insist but doubted he could force it. 'As you wish.' Christ. Why did he now find he had no clue what to say? Shit. 'Who was that in your room?'

'A young lady, Papa.'

'Well, I didn't think it was a fucking goat.' He whipped around, sure he heard laughter from the parlour. He would deal with him later. 'Who is she?'

'Marianne.'

'Where is she now?'

'Gone.'

Noah sat on the sofa realising his mistake immediately when it left him looking up at his son. He closed his eyes for a moment. 'I would prefer it you didn't indulge yourself here–'

'Indulge myself? What can you be talking of, Papa? We had congress. I wasn't pleasuring myself.'

More laughter from inside. Just wait, Noah thought. Just you bloody wait, my lad. 'Don't try to be clever, Hal. I know exactly what you were doing, and I forbid it.' Laughter from inside and outside now.

Then, Noah watched contempt bloom on Hal's face. 'And just how, dear Papa, are you planning to stop me?'

Noah stood again, shoving Hal out of his way.

'Fine. It's your choice. Carry on if you're content to be pox-ridden and leave a string of bastards behind you everywhere you go. Fucking fine by me.' With that he blundered down the steps and disappeared into the gathering darkness.

CHAPTER 5
Hal

He shook his head, watching his father stride away. 'What the devil's wrong with him?'

Back outside on the porch, Sam sighed. 'Sit down. I'll do my best to explain but first ...' He handed him a letter.

Hal read it and looked up. Whatever he had expected it had not been this. 'Shit.'

'Now, God help me, I think you need to know what I told your father about how it happened, so you can understand his reaction.'

His eyes widened in surprise as he listened. Yet he knew how deeply Susannah cared for Sam regardless of what had happened between them in their shared past. How could he forget her waiting white-faced for news of his release, after he and his father had discovered who was really responsible for the murder he had been sentenced to death for? 'Well, I can see how he's arrived at this.'

Sam shook his head. 'Perhaps he transferred the anger he feels towards me onto you. He can't ... or doesn't think he can be angry with me now for something that happened so many years ago.'

'But he can always be angry with me.'

Sam sighed. 'Yet why can't he be so with me? Everything I did then I knew to be wrong. Still did it though, didn't I? Maybe I need him to be angry? Christ, Hal. I wasn't much younger than you are now. How would he have reacted had this been you?'

'Not well.'

They both laughed a little at that.

Hal turned to him. 'He imagines me so reckless and careless always. I never know what to do to make him think better of me. But I do think of such things, you know. There might not be much to be done but I do it. He watched Sam's eyes widen now as he told him. 'Not that you need know of this, of course.'

Sam laughed. 'Well, I shall certainly bear it in mind should such need arise.' He took a breath. 'Tell me about your young lady. I hope she wasn't too alarmed by your Papa's blustering.'

Hal grinned. 'She's extremely pretty ... and she makes me laugh. In truth, we laugh a lot together which I rather like. And I think she understands all about difficult fathers. Hers is in charge at Fort Charles.'

Sam poured them each a glass of wine. 'There's

something I've wanted to say to you for a while ... and it's something your papa and I have spoken of quite a bit.' He took a breath. 'The way you've behaved with us, well, you've been very understanding–'

'Of course. Contrary to what Papa thinks, I really do want him to be happy.' He smiled. 'And I can see he is with you.'

'And he wants the same for you, even if it doesn't always seem so. Hal, I do wish you could talk to each other more.' He grinned. 'I'm probably not the best person to be offering such advice. I only talked properly to my papa for the first time when I was in the Tower contemplating execution.' He raised his eyebrows. 'Probably an idea not to wait for something quite so drastic.'

Hal stood. 'Perhaps we should stop making assumptions about each other all the time. And, talking of which, tell him I don't use whores. Never have. Never will.'

Sam knuckled his forehead. 'Good to know.'

Hal laughed walking away.

CHAPTER 6

Noah

When he opened the door to their bedchamber, he found Sam sitting on a chair in front of the open casement doors looking out at a vast sky awash with stars, their light glossing the calm black water. He did not move until Noah rested the hot weight of a hand down onto his shoulder. 'Made a bit of an arse of myself, didn't I?'

Sam covered the hand with his. 'Afraid so.' He turned to look up at him. 'I hope you don't mind but we talked awhile after you left?'

Noah smiled. 'Stomped off in a big-girl flounce more like. And you'll have made a better fist of it than I did.'

Sam blinked. 'Not all that difficult, in truth.'

Noah barked a laugh. 'Agreed. A low starting point.'

Sam cleared his throat. 'Well, Hal now understands

where the bastard concerns came from. I gave him Susannah's letter to read and then a rather more succinct version of what happened than I gave you.' He leaned his head back against Noah's solid form. 'Forgive me for laughing, though the goat was amusing.'

'Well, you would have laughed harder had you known I'd not one clue about what to say to him.' Noah bent to kiss the top of his head.

'Don't worry about him. He's not a fool, though he rather thinks you believe him one.' He grinned. 'I've learnt somewhat more than I wish to know about the prevention of bastards, edifying though it is. How adequate such things are I have no idea, but it must be reassuring to know he thinks of it. Oh, and he wanted me to tell you he doesn't use whores. Though, looking at him, I imagine he would have little need to.'

'Christ.' Noah sighed. 'I'll speak to him tomorrow. Who's the girl? Did you find out?'

Sam leaned forward to stand, turning to face him. 'Her name is Marianne Carlisle. Her father is James Carlisle, Commander of Militia at Fort Charles.'

'Christ,' Noah said, again.

Sam was restless, still. Noah lay quiet, hoping he would find sleep. When eventually he sat up, moving his legs to leave the bed, Noah reached for him, placing his hand on his shoulder to gently force him back. 'Tell me. Better to speak of it, Lad. What you've learnt today can't be easy to come to terms with. Not for anyone.'

Sam sighed. 'I think perhaps it's the horrible understanding that something you knew to be so utterly shameful you could scarce bear to think of it, is actually far worse even than that. What it meant for Susannah. The price she paid for it—'

'She got an adored daughter from it. You both did.' He closed his eyes. 'Marriage was naught but a smokescreen for me until Hal was born and love for him poleaxed me. It was the same for you. I know it.'

'Damn it, Noah. You don't have to be so bloody kind to me.' He turned to stare at him in the feeble light from the waning moon. 'I think I'd rather you be angry. It's what I deserve, after all. My God. What if Hal had done such a thing? Or Michael? You'd have been completely enraged.'

Noah sat up high against the pillows, beginning to feel something of that rage now. 'What the hell do you want from me? To use my tongue as a hairshirt? I'm not your fucking father, Sam. Your morals back then are nothing to do with me—'

'*What*? My fucking morals! I wasn't a degenerate. I was a foolish, selfish boy who made a horrible, cruel mistake. A devastating mistake ...'

Noah took a long breath. A long sigh. 'Which is exactly what I've been saying to you.' He hesitated for a moment. 'But no one in their right mind would wish it hadn't happened, would they?'

Sam shook his head. 'Why, then, do I feel I want to weep?'

Noah gathered him in then. 'Weep if you need to. It's only me here.'

'Christ. There really is nothing to be done, is there? Nothing to wish any different? Only that I might have been kinder to her.'

'I'd be grateful for it, Laddie. For the past can't be changed however much it might need to be. Just thank God this doesn't.'

CHAPTER 7
Susannah

I stood alone, holding the taffrail in the chill wind, the racing slate-grey sky suggesting no relief from it nor from the storm-whipped sea. Many days had passed since we sailed from the Thames down into the North Sea before turning west along the English Channel and out into the Atlantic, making for Lisbon to take on provisions and an additional cargo of wine destined for Fort Charles in Port Royal.

Three days before we left, we learnt the maid's body had been found in the canal in St James's Park. Tom Monkton had come to us with the news. She had been strangled. The search for further victims proved fruitless, thank Jesu. Raphael would cross himself now, experiencing such gratitude. I sighed, though I could not hear myself above the wind. There seemed nothing to be done then, other than accept Penny had been taken. Next, we learned three ships of interest had sailed from the Pool of London since the girls' disappearance, two going to Jamaica and one to Virginia. It had been decided to get us a passage to Jamaica. This was done quickly for there were only a handful of ships about to sail there before the winter storm season began, ending such journeys until next spring.

So here we were on the Linden, a sleek three-masted East Indiaman. Just as when we sailed to Southampton in the summer to fetch Penny home, palace influence had been at work to secure us such a last-minute passage, this time also supplying us with letters of introduction under the King's seal to ensure colony officialdom would come to our aid. And once again, we had the best cabin in the aftcastle Though this was a merchantman, carrying a cargo of porcelain tableware and fine textiles, the captain was a former navy man and ran his ship on naval lines. Bells sounded for each watch, day and night. We were never at a loss to know the hour, just as with church bells in London.

I wrapped my thick cloak more tightly around me, trying to stop the wind taking it, watching the endless line of foam topped waves receding to the horizon where it was hard to tell where was sea and where sky. Raphael stayed in the cabin while I was on deck. We made a point of being apart as much as possible now. I knew how it had happened and why. And I knew it was my fault. I had pushed him away because, of course, the best way to hurt myself was to hurt him. And Jesu I wanted to hurt myself. I had allowed my child to be stolen. I had allowed her to come to harm. I

81

had been here before though, punishing myself through hurting others and had vowed then never to let it happen again. So much for vows.

It had started in Cheapside in the days before we took ship. I have no memory of how I passed those days. I know Raphael spent hours in his workshop making sure everything was prepared for his extended absence. Lucia would remain to take his place. She seemed to feel little urgency to return to her husband in Florence, which occasioned no surprise from Raphael. Yet I could not summon sufficient energy to question him about it. Why his mother appeared so sanguine about living apart from his father? Though I knew he had never been faithful to her. Perhaps enough was enough?

The first night he had tried to hold me in his arms again, I had pulled away. I was tired, I told him when he pressed me to know what was wrong. On the next few nights, we slept with our backs to each other as far apart as was possible, reminding me of our time together in coaching inns before we married. Only it was Penny's spectre lying there between us and not my living breathing girl. At dinner, we were courteous but distant. He would ask after my health and press me to eat more. I would enquire after his progress in the workshop. His mother would look from one to the other of us, worry etched on her face. Wherever we were then ... and now, I had brought us to it and had no idea how to get us back or even if I wished to.

Once onboard ship, things had become more difficult still. We shared a cabin and a captain's bunk bed beneath the aftcastle windows and keeping any distance between us there proved almost impossible. This very morning, I had woken at dawn to feel his arousal pressing into me. Barely awake, I had moved back against him as I always would, often eliciting a gentle entering from behind. A dreamlike coupling when neither of us seemed fully awake. This time it elicited a 'your pardon' and his back turned towards me instead. Jesu, I wanted him. Just another part of my punishment.

'Susannah?'

I had not heard the sound of his approach over the tumult of sea and wind. I was already clutching the rail tightly with both hands to keep my footing, having been so lost in thought as to be unmindful of the worsening weather.

'What in the name of God are you doing? Do you wish to be washed overboard?'

I turned to look at him, realising my face was numb with cold. 'I don't know.' I was unsure which question I answered.

He propelled me across the slippery deck to the cabin and removed my sodden cloak and outer clothing, wrapping me in his banyan and drying my hair on a towel as best he could, while my teeth chattered. He wrapped a quilt around me. 'What were you thinking?'

'Yes. Yes, I was thinking. I lost track ... of everything.'

He took my face in his hands, pushing back damp

strands of my hair. 'Are you all right? You seem confused.' He guided me to the table, making me sit before sitting opposite and pressing a glass of wine into my hand.

There was hot food – probably cold now – laid out. This was why he had come to find me.

'You must eat.'

Jesu, I was so utterly tired of hearing it. I drained my glass, the alcohol quickly pulsing through my blood. 'Would you had shown as much concern for my child as you do your own. Then perhaps we would not be making this infernal journey.'

All colour drained from his face. 'Would you care to repeat that. I don't believe I can have heard you correctly.' His voice was ice.

'You heard me perfectly.'

He stood. 'Would you had been a better mother to your daughter that she might have been with you that morning, instead.' He took a stride towards me.

I rose to move back away from him. 'Would you had not left my daughter in the company of a murderous kidnapper.'

'Perhaps, had she not spent more time with that family than she did with you, had she even known she had a mother at all for– No. No. Damn you. I won't do this, Susannah.' He took a long breath, his nostrils flaring, then bowed to me before going outside.

By now pressed hard against the cabin wall, I slid down until I sat on the floor. I closed my eyes, holding my hands to my belly where the tiny scrap of life that was our child swam in velvet darkness. I swore to him then, I would be that better mother. I would care for him and protect him from all harm. I promised to find his sister so they could be together. How she would love him. And so, I told him all there was to know of her. Every last thing I could think of. Everything. Then I told him of his father ... and my overwhelming love for him.

Feeling calm at last, I looked up at the great stern windows and saw the storm had passed and in the dark of the moon, the sky was aglitter with cold bright stars. When his hand came down on mine, I almost leapt from my skin and shrieked, feeling my heart about to explode, for I had neither heard him return nor felt him sit beside me on the floor. 'Jesu. Raphael.'

He pulled me into his arms. 'Forgive me for startling you.'

'How long have you been here?'

'Long enough. Every word of love I've just heard you say, I feel for you. Why have we done this to each other?'

I shook my head, not looking at him. 'No, it's all me. I swore I'd never do it again, but I can't seem to help myself. I hurt myself by hurting others. It's what I do. Hurting you is the worst thing I can do to myself. It makes me hate myself even more. And I deserve to be hated.'

'Susannah. I let you push me away. You didn't do it alone.'

'What choice did you have ... other than to force me.'

He held my face to make me look at him, then he smiled. 'You once said that would be impossible.'

I smiled a little then, too. 'I remember. And it's true, it would be. So maybe that's the answer.' For we both knew I could never be anything other than an eager participant in any such attentions from him.

'Maybe it is.' Still holding my face, he moved in to kiss me.

It was then I realised how cold he was. His face his hands. 'My God, Raphael. You've been out on deck without a cloak? Why didn't you go to the captain's cabin?'

'I did for a time, but I was poor company, I think ... and the stars are spectacular over the sea tonight. Worth the chill.' He stood and helped me to my feet. 'Let's not ask forgiveness for the things we said, *cara mia*. We didn't mean them. They were nothing but foolishness and a spiteful wish to hurt. We had the ammunition, so we used it.'

I was surprised how clearly I could see him in the starlight. 'You did nothing wrong that morning, I swear it. But I know you blame yourself, that's why I said–'

He put a finger to my lips. 'No, *cara*. Let's just love each other and find some peace now.'

He took off his coat and waistcoat, putting them over the back of a chair. I moved to him, untying his cravat. 'I love you so much, Raphael.' I wanted very badly to ask for his forgiveness, but his eyes were fixed on mine, and I knew I must not. I untied his banyan, slipping it off my shoulders and placing it over his clothes upon the chair. I shivered a little in the sudden chill.

He wrapped his arms around me. 'I can't do much to warm you. Not out here, anyway. Get under the quilts.' He sat down on a chair to take off his stockings.

I watched him until he looked up at me again and pulling my shift over my head, stood naked before him in the starlight.

'Susannah. Holy Christ.' He lifted his shirt over his head and shed his breeches almost in a single move-ment and with one step forward, he pulled me into his arms. 'I want you now, *amore mio*. Can I have you? Or shall I take you?'

Sometime later, we lay side by side, close and warm in the small bed bathed in silver light that seemed brighter than ever. I turned on my side to look at him. 'Let's never stop touching. I think that is when the madness finds a way in. I need you to touch me if you don't want a wife who has lost her wits.'

'That doesn't sound too onerous a task. I won't forget it again.' He reached up to stroke my face. 'Though don't be too hard on yourself, you have cause for it.'

'I know you believe we'll find her.'

'I do.'

'Because of your faith?'

'*Si*.' He crossed himself.

'I don't know why it gives me hope, but somehow it does.' I tried then to understand. Was it just a child-like trust in him because I love him? I know the strength of his faith impresses me in the same way one can be impressed by any skill or talent one does not oneself possess. I was impressed with his skill as a jeweller but that did not seem the same thing at all. Why, though? Because he had learnt it, had practiced it, honed it until he excelled. Just as I had with portrait miniatures. But had he not learned faith and practiced it, too? As I had, of course. Yet he had excelled, and I had not.

Was it simply his Catholicism; so ancient and arcane? I closed my eyes. Well, whatever the reason, I trusted his God where I could not trust my own. I ran my hand down over his chest. 'I am glad you have such faith, Raphael. And I'm grateful for it. Mine only brings me to question why God allowed it to happen, even though we are taught to believe he is merciful.'

He turned on his side to face me. 'We believe we cannot know or expect to know. We believe in God's mystery. Less demanding for the mind. Simply trust and give thanks, politely, of course.'

I smiled, knowing this mockery was artifice. He wore his faith so lightly it had taken me a while to understand how deep it went. 'Well, perhaps we lost some of the more useful consolations along with the relics and indulgences. Even when prayers are not answered there's just more mystery.'

He smiled. 'Precisely.'

I moved closer to kiss him, and he rolled me over him. Religion proved somewhat less interesting after that.

CHAPTER 8
Raphael

I woke to find her eyes on me. It was just coming light, and her hair was haloed in dawn citrine. I placed my palm on her cheek. 'My beautiful wife.'

'I love watching you sleep. You look ... so innocent.'

We both looked down at my state of morning readiness and I grinned. 'Which, I fear I can make no claim to be, *amore mio.*' Her hand moved down onto me, and I closed my eyes. 'Shame to waste it, no?' I opened them to meet her steady, grey gaze.

'Indeed, it would. I believe I told you some weeks ago about my particular cravings?'

'You did.' I moved over her. Just hours before catastrophe had found us. And how little of each she had allowed herself, since. And I had not even realised what she was doing or why, God help me. I had thought her angry with me, and deservedly so. I even feared she might grow to hate me. Listening to her tell our child that she loved me so completely felt like a benediction. 'Forgive me, *cara*. I'll make it up to you, I swear it.' And, without any false modesty, that is precisely what I did.

When we lay side by side once more, the sun had risen high enough to shine directly onto our sweat-glossed bodies. I knelt, reaching over her to open one of the large casements a crack to allow a little cooling air into the cabin. Now, looking down at her I could see what I had been unable to the night before. I swung my legs off the bed and stood before it, holding my hand out to her. 'Come.'

'Why? I'm not sure I can stand, my Raphael. You have quite exhausted me.' She stretched, languorous as a cat, and rolled to the edge of the bed. 'In a good way, of course.'

I smiled. 'Glad to hear it. Come, I wish to look at you.' She allowed me to help her from the bed and I turned her towards the light. 'Christ.' I ran my hands down over her breasts and slight swell of her belly. I closed my eyes for a moment and pulled her to me. 'Your body is already changing. I can see you are with child.'

'Yes.' She cupped her breasts. 'I am already a little sore.' She sighed. 'It will get a lot worse so I must not complain now, must I? I'm sure you know all of this.'

I gently replaced her hands with mine. 'What do you think?' Then it occurred to me she might imagine such knowledge came from my time with Valentina when nothing could be further from the truth. There had been little contact between us at my father's insistence. I questioned again how he had come to dominate me to such an extent. How had I allowed it?

'In some detail, I would imagine.'

I nodded, trying to smile as I leant in to kiss her, relieved she had taken it no further. 'Piss first and then I must feed you, *cara mia*.'

'You or me? The piss?'

I located the pot and set it on the floor in front of her. 'No preference.' I knew she hated using the heads, shared with the whole crew. Decidedly unsavoury places, especially for a woman, with sailors often waiting there. The captain had them cleaned daily but men were filthy creatures and a pitching ship helped no one. 'How can we be shy with each other now?'

She smiled. 'We can't, but you may go first.'

I shrugged. 'Takes me back to that flea-infested coaching inn. I think best not to watch me, or it might take rather longer than is good for either of us.'

She laughed. 'Old Basing. Close your eyes then no one can see you. Penny used to do–' She moved away to find clothes for the day, opening cubbies and drawers as noisily as she could, making me smile. I opened a window to dispose of the pot's contents.'

'Wouldn't do if the wind were in the wrong direction.'

I donned my breeches and shirt from yesterday. 'I'll see about breakfast.'

'Thank you.'

'I love you, Susannah.' I wasn't sure whether her thanks were for breakfast or privacy.

After our meal, I helped her dress, tying-off the laces on her bodice. I was pleased she seemed to have found her appetite again, but her silence now worried me. I placed my hands on her shoulders and turned her to face me 'There's something wrong, *cara*. Tell me what it is?' She took my hand and led me back to the table. When we sat, she reached for it again, holding it and stroking it with her thumb. I began to have an idea what she was about to say. Christ help me. 'Valentina?'

'I think you need to tell me now.' She chewed her lip. 'You also need to explain why you didn't when I'd bared my soul to you?'

I shook my head, watching her. Had we not enough misfortune to contend with? This need not be aired now. There would be time later when, please God, Penny was safe. 'Why now, Susannah? Why must we talk of it now?'

'Why must we talk of it now? Listen to yourself. We should have talked of it as soon as I told you about Penny.'

Gesu Cristo, I heard the thunder of anger pulsing in my ears. 'Should have? Why?'

'Why not?' she said, sharply. 'I must confess to you, yet you feel no obligation to do so to me?'

'I didn't ask for your confession nor am I obliged to make one to you.'

Her face flushed; she clenched her fists on the tabletop. 'You're my husband. You had a child, and I have no right to know anything about it?'

God help me. 'A dead child. You want to talk of a dead child now?'

She leapt to her feet. 'You vile brute. How could you say such a thing to me?'

I closed my eyes. Indeed, how in the name of God could I? When the door slammed behind her, I put my elbows on the table and clutched my head in my hands. Why not just tell her the whole filthy tale? Did I really think I can hide what a prick I was then by being a worse one now? I stood. When I opened the door, she fell back into my arms. She had been leaning against it. 'You waited outside?'

'I wondered how long it would take you?'

'Take me to what?'

'To look for me. I'm not a complete fool.'

I crushed her to me. 'Forgive me–'

'Don't be tiresome. No need for that.' She spoke gently, pulling away to look at me. 'I never expected it would be easy for you.'

'Christ's blood. It won't be that.' I had not thought of it much after arriving in England. It had seemed like something from a different lifetime. Perhaps even one that did not belong to me. When I knew my mother had told her, I had gone over it all again thinking of ways to soften it a little, to make it more palatable. I would not attempt that now. She would have plain truth.

This time we lay on the bunk. The sky had clouded over, and the first squalls of rain began to strike the windows. I crossed my arms beneath my head. Where to start?

'Begin with the worst. The rest won't be so hard after that.'

I sighed. 'It is all the worst, *cara*. And it is all hard. I got a married woman with child, a woman whose husband knew it could not be his. And they died. Her and the child.' I tilted my head back. I was going to weep. Jesus Christ I was going to weep, for I knew in that moment what the worst was. 'I didn't love them. God forgive me. I didn't.' How could I know then what that meant? But I understood it now. I lay still and let the tears fall for I had little choice. Susannah held tightly to my hand but did not try to comfort me. I was grateful for it.

Eventually, I fetched a towel and dried my face. She sat, now, with her back against the window, and I joined her there. 'Mamma said it was in Rome?' She nodded and then I told her all of it. The husband, a captain of dragoons, who fought for whoever paid the most. Valentina so often alone and available, though there were many servants to consider – in a sumptuous villa close to the Tiber not far from Castel Sant'Angelo – so we were discrete, and in all honesty, I found I could only tolerate her in small doses, anyway. 'She was rather vain and empty-headed is the truth of it. Christ, I didn't even particularly like her.' Yet more to be ashamed of.

'But you enjoyed her company for other reasons.'

I sighed. 'Yes. She was very beautiful, and I desired her. I was flattered by her attention and somewhat surprised and grateful she desired me, too. But, still, I was much relieved when it was time for me to return to Florence. By then, I was more than a little glad to escape her.'

'Until she arrived at your door.'

'At my father's door, which was a very different thing. He saw her without me. I knew nothing of it until all decisions had been made. That probably tells you all you need know about him.' I was twenty-one and very far from being a child. My God, how raw it all felt still when I talked of it. It forced me to face once again how much he had controlled me. Yet, for the first time, I questioned why he had wished to. Did he fear if he did not, I might become a threat to him? To his authority?

'Jesu. What decisions were made?'

'After the confinement Valentina would return to Rome and her husband, and the child would be left behind. My child this was, yet my father agreed he would arrange for it to be fostered out. My opinion on the matter was not sought.'

'And you wished to keep her?'

'My daughter? Yes. Christ, I did. When I tried to argue with him, he said in all likelihood she wasn't mine anyway, I was just conveniently out of Rome.' I remembered his mocking tone, implying doubt at my ability to even get a child, regarding me as this older woman's dupe instead. Why?

'You didn't believe that?'

I shook my head. 'And I was right. My mother told you, I think. She knew she was mine.'

She brought my hand to her lips and kissed it. 'You never saw her?

'No.' But Holy God, I imagined her. 'She lived at first ... but not for long.' I crossed myself, bringing my fingers up to my lips before commending her soul to God, as I always did when I thought of that brief flicker of life. I had to finish this quickly, now. 'Valentina died of childbed fever a week later. Her husband fetched her back to Rome and Papà took care of the child.'

'So, you had a grave you could visit?'

I looked away. Something else I knew nothing of until it was too late. How cruel it seemed now, yet then I had not truly questioned his right to do it. 'My father claimed her stillborn. I don't know what they did with her. Threw her in the Arno for all I know.' Mother of God, I sounded so bitter. I needed this to stop.

'You would have loved her, Raphael. You wanted her.'

'Yet she was not loved, was she, in those precious few minutes of her life? Valentina didn't want her. Mamma said she never looked at her or touched her.'

'Your mother loved her because she was yours. I know she did. Love happens like that when you hold a child.'

'I've never thought to ask her. I will.' I hoped it were true, for it might bring some small comfort. The sun had broken through again and I could feel it hot on my back, our shadows stretching out across the cabin floor. 'Let's get some air.'

Susannah nodded and hopped down. 'I still don't understand why you didn't want to tell me.'

'Because I should never have touched Valentina. If I hadn't, she'd have lived, and a child wouldn't have been born to survive but minutes. So, *amore mio*, I'm ashamed. I bedded a woman I didn't much like, and she died because of it. And a child died too.' And it must seem to her I never learned from it, knowing of my behaviour at the English court.

She put her hands on my shoulders and held my gaze. 'Why do you think you must take all responsibility for this? She knew what she did ... what she wanted from you just as you did from her–'

I pulled away. 'She lost her life. I didn't.'

She shook her head. 'Sometimes women need to take responsibility for their actions, too. Do you really think you were the first she took to her bed? It was ill-luck–'

'I can only take responsibility for myself and my own actions.' I pulled her into my arms and kissed her. I could talk of it no more.

CHAPTER 9
Susannah

LISBON, PORTUGAL 1676

We leaned against the port rail, Raphael's arm around my waist as the ship moved ever closer to the sheltered harbour of Lisbon in the mouth of the Tagus. We had crossed the Bay of Biscay with no more of the autumn storms we had been warned of and so had made good time. The Linden would remain in port overnight while fresh water and provisions were loaded for the crossing to Jamaica together with casks of port destined for the officers of Fort Charles and the naval yard.

'Captain Dunt suggests we stay ashore for the night.' He turned to me. 'It certainly has some appeal. What do you think?'

Oh, Jesu, yes.' I clutched his arms. 'We must. A night in a proper bed where the room stays still. And I can bathe ... in a tub. With hot water.'

He hugged me. 'Well then, that's what we'll do. Dunt said he would send a messenger ashore as soon as we dock to make the arrangement, should we wish it.'

'We do wish it. We wish it very much indeed. Go. Tell him straightaway.'

He knuckled his forehead and bowed. '*Signora.*'

I watched him stride away dressed in a white linen shirt open at the neck and grey breeches, feet bare, his black hair loose about his shoulders. My eyes filled with tears at the sight of him. How could he be mine? My husband whom I loved so completely it made me afraid. And then, of course, I remembered why we were here and knew I had no right to such happiness. To such love. What sort of mother rejoices in her own happiness while her child suffers? I rarely allowed myself to contemplate what that suffering could mean – I truly feared it might stop my heart – but would do so now as punishment for my frivolity. Here was that abys, and I would look into it as unflinchingly as I now gazed into the sea's depths.

His hand gripped my shoulder almost painfully. 'Stop. You think this will help her?'

I lifted my head to look at him. 'How? How do I stop?'

He held my face. 'You live this. You live my hands on your face in the sunshine. You live sailing into Lisbon and walking on land again. You live making love in a featherbed and waking in my arms.' He kissed my forehead. '*Cara*, we're doing everything we can to find her. Inflicting more pain on yourself does nothing. Changes nothing. Can't you see that?'

I closed my eyes and placed my hands over his. 'I'll try, I swear.' We stood side by side then, looking out over the city's panorama spread before us, terracotta roofs climbing high up over the hills with the Castle of São Jorge perched above them. Naval ships flying the Portuguese flag were docked before a wide piazza, flanked by stone towers in front of stately buildings the colour of sand in the harsh white midday light. The whitest light. The blackest shadows. Even the sky seemed bleached of colour. Further seething merchant wharves spread along the waterside to both left and right, upriver, and down towards the sea. I turned to him. 'The girls must have been on one of the London ships that left before ours. Both were due to come in here. We should ask in sailors' taverns. Maybe someone spoke of them?' I touched my hair. 'Penny must have stood out. What were the ships' names?'

He looked at me, coolly. 'The Ferdinand and the Green Forester. I can visit taverns if you wish, but it would not be appropriate for you, Susannah.'

When at last the Linden was tied up at the dockside and a gangway in place, we collected our belongings and left the ship in the company of a Sub-Lieutenant Charles Grant who carried our box and would guide us to The Tamarind where a note had been sent ahead to secure our accommodation. He was a particularly large black-haired Scot with a barrel chest and the broken nose of a fighter. 'Perhaps the lieutenant might accompany you on your tavern visits this evening,' I said, as we walked down long shady alleyways behind the grand waterfront properties, the air alive with the scent of spices. Cloves. I could smell cloves above the rest. And birdsong. Birdsong was everywhere.

'Well, if Sub-Lieutenant Grant is willing, I would value his company.' Raphael turned to him. 'I see you have some knowledge of the city, which would prove of great service.' He glanced at me. 'We are hoping for information about passengers aboard the two English ships which called in here ahead of us. Sailors' haunts seem a good place to start.'

'Indeed. I would be most happy to oblige you, Sir.'

He stopped beside a close-planked wooden gate in a high brick wall, opening it and guiding us into a spacious courtyard shaded by the spreading branches of a huge tamarind tree with a covered well in the centre. A blue door beneath a vine-covered arch led inside the cream stucco building.

'The Tamarind Tavern. It is quiet and comfortable, I believe.'

I assumed the hostelry itself was at the front. I looked around the peaceful court with its terracotta pots of scarlet geraniums and purple bougainvillea cascading down from first floor balconies and smiled. 'It's perfect.'

We were soon shown up to our room, which pleasingly had one of those small wooden balconies I had seen from below. The bed boasted white linens and white muslin drapes, looking made-ready for a wedding night. I glanced at Raphael and found his eyes on me. He smiled and, God help me, I blushed which made him laugh.

Sub-Lieutenant Grant eyed us, appearing decidedly uncomfortable. 'I'll return at sundown Signor Rossi.' He bowed and left us alone with the *proprietária*. A slim dark-haired woman with large brown eyes, dressed in soft grey much enlivened by a cherry-red apron.

The woman gestured to the room. *'Você está feliz com isso?'*

'Si, señora. Muy feliz.' Raphael smiled. *'Tal vez un poco de agua para bañarme, por favor.'*

'Sim, senhor. She hurried away.

'I didn't know you spoke Portuguese?'

'I don't, it was Spanish. I asked for water to bathe.' He looked around, his eyes coming to rest on the bed. 'I think it will do rather nicely.'

'For what, pray?'

He moved face to face with me, without touching. 'I have several things in mind, believe me, *amore mio.*

'I don't doubt it for a moment.' I glanced at the bed again. 'It looks dressed for a maidenhead not a wife already with child.'

He touched me now, holding the back of my head while he kissed me. 'I'll take with child in preference. Not that I've had a virgin to make the comparison.'

I raised my eyebrows. 'I remember you thought you were getting one with me.'

He snorted. 'You'll recall, too, I was somewhat alarmed by the prospect. And I seem to remember what you lacked in experience you made up for in rather wild enthusiasm.'

I put my arms around his waist. 'Do you, now? Were you completely shocked and horrified by my wantonness?'

'Oh, very much so.' He kissed me. 'Couldn't you tell, *cara*?'

I laughed. 'Though bedding virgins is overrated, in my opinion. If the couple love each other then it's distressing. If not, it's unlikely to lead to it.'

'Yet it must be done.' He smiled. 'Just not by me, thank Christ.'

'No, you get a woman with child instead. That involves pain too, believe me it–' Then I realised what I had said. 'Raphael, forgive me, I beg you. How thoughtless of me.'

He placed his palm on my face. 'I think women must suffer too much.'

'More of God's mystery? Though St Paul seemed rather delighted by it all, did he not?' I was destined not to hear my husband's views on St Paul for the hot water arrived then, together with a strange round tub made of oiled wood, soft as satin. The maids filled it and added something sweet-smelling to the water before leaving us alone. 'And the bride shall come fragrant to the marriage bed.'

He eyed the bath speculatively. 'Can we fit in together, do you think?'

'We can try.' I tilted my head, studying the problem. 'Perhaps if I sit between your legs?'

He licked his lips. 'Or vice versa?'

I stood still while he undressed me. I liked the silence between us. I liked the building of need. When I stood naked before him, he helped me down into the water. 'Will I ever stop desiring you like this? Is it the child? Or am I truly wanton?'

He turned his attention from the tub back to me. 'How is it wanton to desire your husband?' He began to undress. 'And why would you think it might stop?' He sat on the bed to remove his stockings and I could not find breath to answer him as he stood to shed his remaining clothes, his desire rather more visible than mine.

I held my hand out to him and somehow, we managed to fit in together without the water overflowing, while I straddled him. It did not take long for either of us. When we were back to ourselves, we went about the practical business of washing. He washed my hair while I sat between his legs. 'We can stand outside on the balcony to dry it.' He lifted my wet hair to kiss my neck before we stood to change places. How could we not kiss, naked and face to face? And so, it began again.

Out on the balcony in breeches and shift, he brushed my hair while bees flew between bougainvillea flowers. It felt like a kind of Eden. 'Is it wrong to feel so happy?'

He sighed and handed me the hairbrush. 'How does your being happy harm Penny? Or worsen her

situation in any way? It makes not the remotest difference. Inflicting pain upon yourself doesn't lessen hers.'
He crossed himself. 'I wish I could understand how
you arrive at such thinking?'

I brushed his hair rather vigorously, making him
grin. 'In my irrational, inferior woman's mind, you
mean?'

He removed the brush from me and took over the
task himself. 'We should eat soon if I am to go out at
nightfall.'

'Fuck me and feed me, is that it?'

His eyes widened at my choice of words. 'I believe
you requested such.'

I gasped a breath. Out of the blue, I feared I might
weep, which made no sense when I had just claimed to
be so happy. 'Raphael.' I held my hands out to him.

He swept me up and carried me to the bed,
holding me on his lap. 'Christ. You're rather heavier
than when I last did this.'

I snorted. 'Well, it's your fault.'

'The fucking or the feeding?'

I laughed and cried a little at the same time. 'Both.'
I held his face. 'I love you more than I can ever put into
words. I want to be happy cocooned with you always,
whatever catastrophe happens outside. Will you help
me stop trying to sabotage it?'

'It's simple, *cara*. 'Stop judging yourself and take
happiness where you find it ... and trust in God for
everything else. Now I shall go down and see about

food, he pulled on his shirt as he went but remained barefoot.

I moved back out onto the balcony, in full shade now, and sat on the floor, my back pressed against the sun-warmed wall, listening to the hum of bees, and drinking in the scent of bougainvillea. 'I shall find you my little love. I shall find you and fetch you home.

CHAPTER 10

Raphael

I waited for Grant in the courtyard behind the taberna. The last of the light was still leaching from the sky but the yard was already bright with candle lanterns. The well was in constant use now, so the scullery maids and kitchen porters needed to see their way. I sat on a stone bench flanked with tubs of geraniums almost glowing in the lamp light. I had left Susannah stretched out on the bed, languorous as a cat after a fine dinner taken from numerous small dishes. Some indeterminate as to their ingredients but all equally delicious. Then we had sated our desire once again. Rather well, truth be told.

'Signor Rossi.'

I looked up, startled from my thoughts. 'Raphael, please.' I stood.

'Then I'm Charlie. We should head to *As Bagunças*. More sailors' haunts there than anywhere.'

He was out of uniform, of course, and had dressed

plainly as I had myself. We would still stand out in such places, but it might be as well not to appear particularly wealthy. 'Look out for cutpurses.'

He tapped his chest. 'On a lanyard. No bugger'll gets hands on it there.'

'Then watch out for whores.' We walked out onto a wider street leading from the docks into the city. This part was lined with tabernas, all doing a lively trade.

Charlie gestured with his head towards a dark alleyway that ran up the side of one such hostelry where two women waited below a lamp just bright enough to reveal their presence. 'What say you? Make a braw start to the evening, no?'

'Not for me, thank you all the same.' As we got closer, I was able to discern they were well past first youth and more disreputable looking than many of their calling.

He nodded. 'Well, I wouldna either had I such a wife waiting in ma bed.' He nudged me before approaching the younger of the two, then turned back. 'I dinna suppose you have the language?'

'Spanish, only.' I saw then it would not be needed for the woman pointed at her mouth then towards her lower regions, followed by a hand gesture to convey it was a question. A port city always finds ways to accommodate its babel. Grant pointed to her mouth. *Cristo*. Then pantomimed counting coins on his palm. An arrangement was obviously arrived at when she knelt before him, without any suggestion they should move further into the shadows. Perhaps she hoped such signs of activity might drum up further trade? I was about to turn my back when the sight of her plucking-out her teeth froze me to the spot. Wooden? Her mouth was now entirely concave and the smile on Grant's lips revealed this as altogether pleasing to him.

I did turn my back then, the whole notion of it leaving me a little queasy. I had never used the services of a prostitute but tried not to be judgmental about those who did. A coin for an orgasm. What was a man's fist for but to slake such base need? But then I had never had difficulty finding a willing woman to bed when I wished for one, so what was it if not pejorative?

Minutes later he was back at my side, still buttoning his breeches. He shook himself like a dog. 'Where's the best place to start, Charlie?' I had no wish to hear about what had just occurred. But, alas, it was not to be.

'If I'da known her teeth'd been pulled the lass woulda had more coin.'

Holy Christ. 'She seemed content enough.' I took a long breath, looking up and down the crowded street. Sailors here from everywhere it would seem. Lascars. Moors. Women, too. Fishwives and mussel-sellers wheeling barrows to the tabernas, shouting at *flaneurs* to make way. Serving wenches on their way to their places of work. And whores aplenty, of course. Everywhere raucous shouts and laughter. The air was cool now and heavy with the smell of fish and ale ... and something else that transported me to the steps of the Duomo in Florence. Lemons. Baskets of lemons in the afternoon heat. I cannot for the life of me think why they should have been there like that. I shook my head to clear my thoughts. 'Is there an establishment that English sailors are known to prefer?"

Unfortunately, he did not yet wish to move on to the task in hand. 'Like a cunny that sucks. You wouldna turn such as that down, now wouldya?'

Oh, believe me, I would. 'May we proceed Sub-Lieutenant Grant?'

He straightened his back 'Of course, Sir. A taberna where sailors from English ships congregate, is it? Let me see.' He set off deeper into the city. 'Follow me. I think I know the very place.'

And follow him I did from one hostelry to the next. All frantic with sweating men, downing their ale, and puffing on their pipes, the air blue with tobacco smoke. Much dicing and card gaming all accompanied by a ceaseless shouted clamour. I smiled at serving wenches and pot boys, asking about sailors from the London ships. Drinking sweet Portuguese wine. Taberna after taberna where no one remembered sailors talking of any passengers never mind of small girls. No one. Charlie asked any idle whores the same questions about their customers. Occasionally availing himself of their services at the same time. It seemed a kind of sexual incontinence. But then could not the same have been said of me at the Whitehall court?

In the next place – somehow, we were now back close to the docks again – I engaged the rather pretty red-haired young woman in conversation when she bought our wine to the table. Her hair stood out against all the other wenches with their dark buns and olive skin like mine. She wore hers loose down her back and when I tucked a stray curl behind her ear, I saw she had freckles and smiling, ran my finger along her collarbone. I could have her now, should I wish it. Christ. What was I thinking? I rose and pushed my way through the throng, almost choking on tobacco smoke. How much had I drunk? Too much, clearly, especially as I had no idea where I was or how to get back to the ... the. *Merda.* I could not even recall the name of our *hospedaria.* I found a stone bench and collapsed down upon it, putting my head in my hands.

Charlie Grant dropped down beside me and seemed to struggle to keep his balance for a moment. 'I told the lassie 'bout your wife. That she was bonny. Ye left the poor lass without a word.'

I raised my head. The lass? Who was he talking of? 'Scusi?' I tried to gather my drink-addled wits. 'Can you ... will you direct me to my lodgings, Sub-Lieutenant?' And he did, holding tight to my arm, though I never once had any idea where I was. He steered me through the gate into the courtyard, and I stumbled inside and up the stairs with no notion which room was mine, until I saw one with light showing beneath the door. Good enough. I grasped the handle and turned it.

CHAPTER 11

Susannah

I had not expected him to be gone quite so long, for the midnight bells had just sounded from St Marco's across the street from the Tamarind. Hidden in shadow on the balcony, I had watched him leave as night fell and there had seemed little point in my dressing again, so I lay naked and uncovered in the heat trapped inside the room from the afternoon sunshine. The candles were all alight, waiting for him. I wished I could snuff them as I could not find sleep with so much light.

The street outside was quiet now, with only an occasional shout carried on the breeze from the less salubrious streets and alleyways where Raphael, no doubt, used his potent charm upon serving wenches and idle whores alike. Or, indeed, upon anyone susceptible who might have the information we sought. Charles Grant was a polite, well-educated young man from Edinburgh, with the physique required of a bodyguard. Ports could be dangerous places when drink was taken. I just hoped my husband had been circumspect with his own consumption.

The door opened then, under sufficient force to hit the wall with a resounding crash. 'Oops. *Perdonami*, if will.' Then his own language, walking very carefully across the floor, muttering, before sitting down beside me on the bed. '*Sembri essere nudo.*' His hair was loose around his shoulders. His ribbon long gone, I imagined.

'Naked?' I looked down at myself in mock surprise. 'Yes. So I am. I wonder how that happened?'

He sniggered and touched his nose. '*Probabilmente io*. Probably me.'

At least he remembered how to speak English. 'I imagine so, yes. You should undress and come to bed. You need to sleep it off.'

He grinned. 'Undress and come to bed with you?'

'Yes, Raphael. You're very drunk. You need to sleep.' Jesu. I hoped he would not vomit.

'Undress. Bed with you?'

I sighed. This was getting tiresome. 'Dear God. Well, no help for it I suppose.' I wriggled around him and saw his eyes trying and failing to track my progress, though he managed to squeeze my breast as I passed. 'Ow.' I slapped his hand away and bent to remove his shoes and stockings.

He rested a heavy hand on my head. 'Susannah?'

I looked up at him. 'Yes?'

He smiled. '*I tuoi capelli non sono rossi*. Your hair ... Susannah. My Susannah?'

Red hair? Had he been in another bedchamber tonight? 'Of course I am. Who else would I be?' Someone with red hair, perhaps?

He shook his head. '*Scusi*? What?'

Had he found out anything useful? I chewed my lip. I would get no sense from him now. About anything. I stood to take off his coat, then his waistcoat and cravat. 'Stand.' He did as asked, though wobbled somewhat. When I removed his breeches and stooped to pick them up, his hand returned to my head guiding it towards his crotch. I pulled away. 'I think not.' Just what had he been doing tonight?

He managed to struggle out of his shirt himself and I saw he was in no condition to enjoy what he wanted from me, anyway. I fetched him a cup of water from the ewer and watched him gulp it down, hoping again he would not vomit. He lay down then, with studied care and fell almost instantly asleep. There would be snoring. I stroked his damp hair back from his face and kissed his forehead. 'I love you, my Raphael.' I rose then, finally to snuff out the candles. All save one.

I woke at dawn to find him sitting on the edge of the bed. 'Are you all right?'

'Holy God. I'm not even sure I'm alive.'

I moved to him, kissing his back. 'I hope you are, my love, for what would I do without you?'

He turned around. 'Must ask forgiveness. Not entirely sure why, yet. Or of any of it, in truth.'

'You did nothing.' That I know of. 'You were drunk, and I helped you to bed. That's all. Well, you did invite me to take you in my mouth.' I smiled. 'More the idea of it, I think.'

'*Cristo.*' He moved back to lie beside me, clutching my hand. 'I'm sorry we didn't have our blissful night away from the ship.' His belly roiled, noisily. He clutched it. 'Forgive me.'

'I was the one who asked you to trawl the taverns–'

'But not to get arse-fucking ... *ubriaco* ... drunk. Oh God. Oh, Christ. *Porco Dio.*' He clutched his belly and fled.

There was a garderobe with a close stool at the end of the passage. Though I imagined he might be some time, I had not expected to sleep again. I woke with a start when he moved to sit beside me on the bed once more and reached out to him. 'How are you now?'

'Purged.' He closed his eyes. 'Christ's wounds.' He was quiet for a minute or two, his eyes closed. 'What can I have drunk to cause the raging shits?' He shook himself and droplets flew from his hair. 'I found a girl down in the kitchens who gave me water. The well here is fed by a spring coming down from the hills. Apparently, they cask it and sell it to ships at a premium over other suppliers because of its quality. Anyway, I must have swallowed a whole bucket of it. Emptied another over me to wash.' He managed a faint smile. 'So, I believe ... hope I'm just about recovered.'

'I wondered why your hair was wet.' I sat up then and moved in to kiss him. His mouth tasted cold and sweet. His cool hands moved down over me, one caressing my breasts, the other slipping between my legs. He pushed me back onto the mattress. The last thing I had imagined was for us to make love then. Yet how quickly I was lost in him when he moved inside me. Jesu help me. It was where I needed him to be, and I wished it would never end. If I could have stopped time then, in such oblivion, I would have done it. Just my hands on his body and the feel of him inside me would last me for eternity.

We must talk now, *cara*.'

I opened my eyes and then narrowed them in bright sunlight. 'What?' He sat beside me on the bed and when my eyes grew accustomed to the glare, I saw he was dressed in very fine clothing indeed. 'You look like a Florentine prince.'

'I think it helped,' he said, gnomically.

'Helped what?' He had been back to the ship to dress and our box had gone, though he had laid out clothes for me. I looked at them ready to find fault but, irritatingly, could not. Too clever by half. I sat up higher against the pillows. What on earth was the hour? And how long had he left me alone?

He fetched a cup and a plate of pastries and put

them down on the table beside me. '*Pastéis de nata.* They're very good. Eat some. And coffee.'

'Raphael. Where have you been and what have you been doing?' I picked up a tart and took a bite. My eyes widened. 'They are good,' I said, spitting crumbs.

He grinned. 'Not on my best coat, *cara*, if you please.' He bushed imaginary specks from his sleeve.

I carried on eating until the plate was empty. He watched in silence. 'Are you planning to speak, at all?'

He passed me the coffee dish. 'It is somewhat convoluted, but I'll try to explain as simply as I can.'

I gave him a wide-eyed look. 'Did you know a woman's intellect recedes as her belly expands when she's with child?'

He frowned. 'I hadn't heard that, no.'

'Well, you wouldn't. I just made it up.'

He laughed. 'Forgive me. I meant succinctly.'

I patted his arm. 'I'm teasing. I knew what you meant.' I drank my coffee, my eyes on his face. 'Have you discovered anything? Just tell me that first then I can hear the details.' His expression told me there was something and hope soared. How could it not?

When he took the empty dish from my hands, his smile confirmed it. 'Yes, *cara*. They were seen on the Ferdinand walking together on the deck. They appeared to be under the care of a man and woman who were passing as their parents. They looked well fed and adequately clothed. The man who saw them discerned nothing untoward about the family. He only noticed them because of Penny's hair. Just as you said. He's Portuguese. Such yellow hair is a rarity here.'

As mine must have been to him. I closed my eyes, trying to take in the enormity of it. It was such a momentous thing. For, until now, we had faced the possibility that she had not gone to Jamaica at all and could instead be in Virginia of even remain in England, still. I covered my face with my hands for a moment. Penny was alive and unharmed as far as it was possible to know. Thank Jesu. In port so no longer seasick? Or had her time at sea made her accustomed? I shook my head, smiling. 'So, who saw them?'

'The *proprietário* here, believe it or not. He sold water to the Ferdinand then went on-board because of some dispute about payment.'

'How on earth did you discover that?'

He grinned. 'Well, without the shits I wouldn't have done. When I woke again this morning, I thought it worth finding out if the water business here had any contact with our ships. Especially as we had nothing from last night.' He shook his head. 'A complete waste of time.'

'Apart from giving you the lucky shits.'

He snorted. 'Quite so. Didn't feel so lucky at the time, mind you.'

'I'm sure.' I touched his sage green satin coat with its gold lace. 'And this?'

'For the harbour master. I wanted to see the passenger manifest. I needed names'

'I expect you dazzled him.'

He leaned down to kiss me. 'I believe I did, *cara*. He called me *vossa Excelência* and was pinkly deferential. They are traveling under the name of Berringer. James and Elizabeth Berringer and their daughters, Catherine and Jane. I doubt they'll keep those in Jamaica, but we can pass them on to Fort Charles and the Lieutenant Governor anyway. And perhaps I might go on a more successful tavern crawl. I believe Port Royal particularly well served by such establishments.'

I smiled. 'With Noah to protect you.' I had tried not to think of facing Sam. He barely knew Penny was his daughter and now I must tell him she was lost. I longed to see him and dreaded it too.

'Well, at least whores should prove less of a distraction for him.'

He gave me a fuller account of the previous evening, including his encounter with the red-haired serving wench. 'But you didn't touch her?"

'No more than I've told you.'

'But you could have?' Of course he could, though I knew he would have no wish to, thank God.

He nodded. 'I have had many such encounters and that's how they generally ended. I'm not proud of it.' He shrugged. 'But I've never had a whore.' He was quiet for a few moments, clearly thinking. 'Yet it's still a transaction, is it not? Pleasure for pleasure or payment for it. Perhaps I've no right to feel more virtuous than the man with the coin?' He stood, holding his hand out to me. 'Come. I'll help you dress. We should get back to the ship.

I rose, enjoying the feel of his eyes upon my naked body. 'May I ask you something?' He handed me my shift and I pulled it on.

He looked a little wary. 'Please do, *cara*.'

I hesitated, uncertain quite how to word the question brought to mind by the serving girl. Perhaps it was for another time? 'No matter, my love.'

He moved away and sat on the windowsill close to me. 'How I found my way back into a woman's bed after what happened?'

I perched next to him and grasped his hand. It wasn't a difficult question to guess, I suppose. 'Only tell me if you wish to.'

He sighed and turned to face me. 'The answer is, for a very long time I didn't.'

'What?'

He smiled that slow smile. 'I was celibate. I never touched a woman again until London. I know you'll find it difficult to believe, but it's what I did.'

I pulled him into my arms. 'Jesu.' This truly made me understand how much what had happened with his child had devastated him.

He laughed. 'Doesn't sound like me, I know.' He kissed me. 'Don't pity me too much, *cara*. I took care of myself extremely generously.'

I punched him lightly on the arm, though my heart ached for him. For the guilt he had insisted belonged to him alone. 'Well, of course you did. Yet in—'

'Yet in London I lost all such inhibitions? And you

wonder why this should be.' He moved away to hold my gaze. 'I know you disapproved of me then.'

I found it hard not to question why what kept him celibate for four years no longer mattered to him. 'I don't know what to say to you–'

'It's simple. I was tired of it. I gave in to temptation, again. Women wanted me and I wanted them.' He shrugged. 'I was as careful as I could be ... but, God forgive me, I was tired of it.'

'Careful?'

He tilted his head, eyebrows raised, waiting for me to understand.

'You mean you didn't ... so I'm the only one who's had your seed?' It seemed rather wonderful that part of him had been only for me, until I saw his eyes slide away. 'Who?'

He met my gaze again. 'Frances.'

I closed my eyes. Of course. She was childless and the King's mistress. Two things that tended not to go together. 'So, she's barren?'

'It would seem so.'

'Well, then, I pity her.'

He put his hand on my belly. 'Yes. She's saddened by it. Poor Frances.'

How strange I could listen to him talk of her like this and not mind any more. He was mine so completely now, and always would be. I stood. 'I should finish dressing.'

CHAPTER 12
Raphael
PORT ROYAL, JAMAICA 1676

After sailing through turquoise water past miles of white beaches with verdant hills behind, lush greenery flowing down like liquid right to the sand, we stood together at the taffrail again looking at a port our ship was about to enter. Rounding a headland into the harbour, we passed Fort Charles and beyond was the close-packed sprawl of Port Royal. I had not expected the sheer size of the place. I put my arm around Susannah's waist. She was tense with anxiety. It was nearly December. Was Penny still here? And we must now tell Sam what had happened.

'Jesu. How shall we even find them?'

The harbour was crowded with ships tied up at long wharves disappearing into the distance, with many more at anchor further out. There was little doubt some were privateers. I had heard of the so-called forced trade, where merchants sold to the

Spanish and pirates returned the same goods for a share in the profits. With the Royal Navy yard close beneath the fort, I wondered whether the English thought it their business to intervene. Small boats wove to and fro – some with a single sail, others moved by oars alone – across blue-green water aglitter under the fierce sun. Fortunately, we had shade where we stood but Susannah would need protection once she moved out into the open for any length of time. 'We shall keep asking for Bartholomew and the Mirabel, it's all we have.'

She wrapped her arm around my waist. 'We need Sam and Noah. Then we can start searching for her. They'll know what to do.'

I pulled her into my arms and kissed her. 'They will. It feels the sort of place where coin likely changes hands to oil the wheels of it.'

Down on the dock, assailed by a quotidian stink probably ubiquitous to all such ports in the heat. I began to identify some of what went into the mix. Fish and spices, rum, and smoke from cooking fires, underlaid by sweat and human waste. Now lost in the melee of porters and cargo and the general throng of humanity, with our boxes and possessions heaped around us, it was difficult to know where to start. I think we both appeared rather tired and very be-wildered.

An African porter with a single gold earring and a

yellow bandana halted his handcart beside us. 'Help, Sa?'

In no time he had our boxes loaded and made enquiries along the waterfront until he learnt where the Mirabel might be found, should she be in port. What we would do if she were not was something to consider if and when we must. The porter traded Susannah's silk shawl for a yellow parasol – earning himself a healthy commission I felt sure – and she sat in the cart, at his suggestion, looking a little more relaxed now we appeared to be making some progress. I tossed my coat, waistcoat, and cravat in beside her for it was, unsurprisingly, extremely hot.

The wharf teemed with people, many appearing of Mediterranean origin and more African of all skin-shades ranging from my own to deepest blue-black. Some were clearly slaves, down from the plantations inland with cargos of sugar and molasses, others, sailors and cargo hands. And some certainly looked to be pirates judging by their cutlasses and plethora of pistols tucked through their belts. I heard English and Spanish spoken, and the strange cadences of African tongues.

We walked on past rows of wooden buildings, warehouses, and taverns too many to count. There were numerous brothels, too, with an assortment of women and girls of all ages and colours and states of undress, taking their ease outside on benches whilst equally diverse – no doubt newly disembarked – men took their pick even at this hour of the morning.

Looking beyond to the mountains, they were now dark under massing clouds, the mist of rain already rolling down the slopes.

'Sa. Sa.' The man pointed. 'Mirabel.'

And there she was, tied up at the dockside, bulging nets of crates and barrels winched up from her holds and lowered down onto the wharf, where they were quickly loaded onto mule carts overseen not by Noah but, to my stunned surprise, by Hal. I cupped my hands around my mouth 'Hal.'

Susannah turned to look. 'Hal. Jesu, it's Hal. It's truly him.'

He jogged over to us, grinning and obviously just as astonished to see us. 'What in Christ's name are you doing here? My God, Papa and Sam will be mighty pleased to see you.' He frowned, suddenly. 'You know they–'

I nodded. 'We know they're together.'

His smile returned and he grasped me in a bear hug, before helping Susanna down into another. 'I'll take you to them right away. I was only really in town for provisions which are already on the pinnace. We must get your boxes onboard. We have a house in Hayes Bay beyond the headland.' He gaped at us again. 'God. How the hell can you be here?'

The porter walked along behind us with the hand-cart as we made our way to Hal's boat, Susannah on my arm under her yellow parasol. The pinnace turned out to be one of the ubiquitous single masters that plied the harbour. Hal handed the man a gold coin after the boat was loaded and he departed, appearing content. 'I've only English and Portuguese. Would they serve?'

He shrugged. 'Gold or silver possibly. Pieces of eight or reals are best here.'

I stood back a little to scrutinise him properly. Holy God, he looked different. Tanned and muscled, his hair bleached almost white by the sun. I had smiled noticing how many female heads turned as he passed by. 'You look well. I hadn't realised your papa took you with him.'

He grinned. 'Neither had he to start with.'

I smiled a little at that. 'And was he pleased to see you?'

'Yes.' He blinked. 'But not immediately.'

I laughed until I caught sight of Susannah staring out across the harbour, looking desolate. I pulled her close. '*Cara*. Don't. We're here. We'll find her now. I know we shall.'

Hal looked at us, serious suddenly. 'What's happened? What's brought you to Port Royal?'

Susannah took a shuddering breath. 'Penny. My daughter ... our daughter. She's been taken. And brought here. We must find her.'

'Christ blood! What can I do?' He shook his head as though to collect his thoughts. 'I'll get you to Papa.'

Susannah clung tightly to my hand while Hal sailed the small craft out of the harbour and through chop around the headland where Fort Charles crouched glowering, its guns turned seaward. We soon arrived in calm water off a sweeping white-sand beach, with a wooden jetty leading towards an expansive single-storey house wrapped around by a covered porch.

As we approached the landing, Noah came towards us, shading his eyes against the glare obviously aware Hal was not alone but unable to yet see who was with him. He was just as brown, muscled, and pale-haired as his son. The moment he recognised us, he turned towards the house, cupping his mouth to call Sam. By the time the sail was furled, and we were tied-up, they stood together waiting for us to disembark both looking worried knowing, of course, we were here for a reason. And it would have to be significant to bring us on such a mammoth journey.

Hal helped me up onto the wooden pier and Noah grasped Susannah's hand and hauled her up, giving her a quick hug before passing her into Sam's arms where she burst into tears. While Sam hurried a distraught Susannah up to the house and Hal unloaded our boxes, Noah walked beside me. 'You already know it's bad?'

'I do, Raphael. Much as we're glad to see you, you've not come all this way on a social visit.'

I sighed. 'Perhaps we'd better tell you together.' He led me up the steps onto the porch where Susannah sat on a sofa held in Sam's arms. I sat beside her, and she moved into mine. 'We must tell them now, *amore mio*.'

'I can't,' she said against my chest. 'How can I tell Sam such a thing.'

He looked suddenly pale behind his tan. 'Holy Christ. It's Penny, isn't it? In the name of God, tell me what's happened.'

'She's been kidnapped.' Then I told them everything. How I had seen her in the park, the searches, the maid's body in the canal and all Tom Monkton had told us of Spiriting. Lastly, I spoke of what I had learnt in Lisbon.

Susannah pulled away to look at me. 'Raphael, you must stop blaming yourself for leaving them. I can hear it in your voice that you do. You stopped and spoke to the maid–'

White-faced, Sam turned to me. 'Christ, no. How could you even think of blaming yourself? He moved to Noah and sat beside him. 'What should we do? Where do we start?'

Noah frowned as he pondered. 'The harbour master first to find if the Ferdinand is still in. Then the Lieutenant Governor and the militia commander at Fort Charles.' A slight woman with honey skin and a red kerchief covering her hair, stepped out from the house carrying a tray with a platter of fruit and a jug of wine, placing it down on the table.

Hal stood. 'I'll see to it, Pearl.'

She nodded and made to leave without a word.

Noah stopped her. 'Could you prepare a room for our guests.'

She gave him an amused look. 'Done it a'ready. Soon as dem boxes come in.'

Noah barked a laugh and shrugged. 'Of course you have, Lass.'

The wine was cool, which surprised me. 'Then, if these are the people to see, should we not do so immediately?'

Noah emptied his glass in one gulp. 'Indeed, I think we should go now.' He put his glass down and stood. 'Come Hal, let's be on our way.'

I rose. 'I must come with you. I need to.'

Susannah got up and took my hand. 'Then I shall.' She pulled out her miniature of Penny kept in her pocket. 'I have this we can show them.'

I held her close. 'No, *cara*. You must rest for a while, I think.' I put my hand on the swell of her belly.

She sighed, resignedly handing me the portrait. 'Very well.' She tilted her head. 'You know too well how to sway me, Raphael.'

I smiled. Then looking at Sam, I realised I was seeing myself as Penny's father when, in truth, he was. 'Forgive me, you should go–'

'No,' Noah said. 'Sam doesn't go to the town. It is safer he shouldn't be seen there.'

Sam gazed at him, unsmiling. 'I do believe Noah puts it around he has an idiot brother hidden in an outhouse or some such.'

Noah met his stare. 'The true idiot would be the one who showed his face to the English.'

Tension between them on it, then.

Sam looked up at Susannah. 'I'll keep Sukie company.'

She held me for a moment. 'I trust in your God, my Raphael.' Then she sat beside Sam once more.

Noah moved inside and quickly returned, carrying two swords, passing one to Hal. Then he handed me a dagger. It gleamed malignly in the sunlight. I buckled it on somewhat reluctantly, noticing how both Bartholomews' hands moved instinctively to their sword hilts. The touching tell of the expert swordsmen, which Susannah had once pointed out I lacked.

Noah, having read my reluctance, seemed a little vexed by it. 'Raphael, Port Royal is a den of thieves and cutthroats. And we're likely to stir it up when we start asking the sorts of questions we'll need to. I realise you probably don't know how to use one of those but as long as you remember to do it before one's used on you, you should be fine.' He turned to Susannah. 'Don't be concerned. No harm will come to him, for any who try will have to get through us first.'

Sam tilted his head. 'I've seen them practice, Raphael. You have nothing to fear, believe me.'

CHAPTER 13
Susannah

We stood at the porch rail watching Noah and Hal use the oars until the wind filled the sail and Noah moved to the tiller. How ironic we two should be left behind when the search for our daughter finally began. We watched until the little boat rounded the headland, hard to see in the glare off the water, though I thought I could still make out the gleam of Raphael's black hair. I kissed my fingertip and turned it towards him just before the boat went out of sight.

Sam sighed, glancing at me. 'What can I do for you, Sukie? Will you rest in your chamber for a while?'

I grasped his hand. 'No. I'll stay with you.' We returned to the sofa at the back of the porch and sat close together in silence for a while. I looked around, truly taking in my surroundings for the first time. A mismatched group of well-used chairs and couches placed near the double doors leading into the house. A battered table at their centre. Beyond the porch rail, the sea sparkled almost blindingly with the soft woosh of waves breaking on the shore the only sound. An idyllic place, and we had arrived with such evil tidings to shatter their tranquillity. My God, Sam had deserved his peace after all he had gone through earlier in the year.

I finished my wine and he refilled both our glasses. He looked as brown and vigorous as the others, but his face was pinched in a way I suspected it had not been yesterday, and he seemed to find it hard to meet my gaze.

He looked at his glass but did not drink. 'So, you know about Noah? What we are to each other.'

I nodded, smiling a little ruefully. 'I was rather foolishly blind to it for quite some time.'

He sighed. 'I should have spoken to you about it. I can't explain why I didn't ... even to myself.'

Silence again.

'Sukie, I don't know what to say to you ...'

I touched his face, lightly. 'I know. I feel the same.'

'Please God they find her. It doesn't bear thinking of.' He looked at me properly at last. 'What did you mean you trusted Raphael's God?'

I sipped my wine. 'You know he's Catholic?' I watched him nod. 'It took me a while to realise how strong his faith is. It's given me something I couldn't find in my own.' Jesu, we were so awkward with each other. I could not remember ever feeling like this with him before. We had to get past it somehow. 'I've always known how much you love her, right from the first moment you saw her.' He still seemed unable to speak. 'Sam, please.'

He drew a sharp breath. 'Christ. The day I told you how well you looked.' He gazed intently at me. 'How have you forgiven me? Noah was certain you had. How?'

Anger flared. 'Forgiven you for Penny? You can't mean–'

'Holy God, no. Why would I say such a thing? Why would you think it of me? I mean how could you forgive me the rest of it. The ugliness of it.'

I pulled him into my arms. 'Because getting her was all that mattered. Can't you see that?'

He kissed my cheek, holding me tight for a while. 'Well, perhaps it is easier to forgive someone else than to forgive yourself. I won't ever do it, I know. But I thank God for our daughter, of course I do. How could I not, when I've loved her all her life.'

'My letter must have shocked you.' I shook my head. 'I was so happy when I wrote it. Happy with Raphael.' I touched my belly. 'Happy we'll have a child. Before this unspeakable thing.'

He took a sharp breath. 'Your happiness didn't summon it. Please tell me you know that?'

Jesu. How well he understood me. 'It made me hate myself for a while, but Raphael helped me through it. He made me see how inflicting suffering on myself would change nothing for Penny. In a way it's a kind of selfishness. Hating myself makes it about me.

And it was easy to do when I pushed him away. When I hurt him to hurt myself.'

'You've done it before. So, I'm glad you see it now.' He smiled. 'I knew Raphael would be good for you.'

'And his God will help him find Penny, though I have considerable faith in Noah too. He saved your life, after all. So, I trust them to find our daughter.' We held each other still. What else could we do?

Pearl appeared silently onto the porch, again carrying a tray which she set down beside the empty platter, Hal having singlehandedly consumed the fruit. She placed a tureen and ladle down together with two bowls, a basket of bread, and a dish of butter. 'Mebe you serve your guest a spot of fish soup, Sam.' Her voice was soft and deep.

He stood. 'This is Susannah Rossi, Pearl. My dearest friend.' He turned to me. 'Pearl is our housekeeper. She keeps us in proper order just as much as she does the household. I can't think what we'd do without her.' He gave her shoulder a quick squeeze.

She smiled up at him and then at me. 'With a chile comin you needs eat little bits a lot of times then you no get sick.'

I returned her smile, recognising what a truly beautiful woman she was. Small and slender with skin hardly darker than Raphael's and large amber-brown eyes, the red of her bandanna matched her sculpted lips. 'Thankfully not with this one. Just endless hunger.' Jesu, and not just for food, of course. I felt heat on my face, thinking of it.

135

Sam's eyes were on me. 'Then I must feed you, Sukie. Pearl's fish soup is a truly wonderful thing.'

Pearl glowed, ladling it into our bowls. 'So, if you've a boy this a girl, or de other way.'

I moved to the table and sat. 'Girl.' I looked at the soup, feeling no inclination to eat but resigned that I must.

'We have a daughter,' Sam said, quietly.

Her eyes widened and then she frowned, staring at us. 'Why she no here?'

I nodded to him, and he told her all that had happened to Penny while I forced soup down my throat, thinking it the most repellent thing I could ever do whilst listening to such horror about my child.

Her eyes brimmed with tears, and she hugged me. 'I pray for you. And your chile.' She crossed herself and was gone.

We finished our meal in silence and returned to the sofa. 'I think you've been lucky with her.'

He held my hand. 'She knows about us. That's why she's here. She had too much unwelcome attention where she was before.' He rubbed at his face. 'I wonder how they're doing. It is hard not knowing.'

I squeezed his hand. 'Is it really dangerous for you in the town or is Noah being overly cautious?'

He looked away. 'It's probably wise. I do know things I shouldn't, unfortunately.'

'So, it was true.' I watched him nod. 'I didn't think it was. And you could still be in danger?'

He sighed. 'Port Royal is the sort of place where all

information has value and there are people here who collect it and then seek out buyers. Even the Governor started out as one of the forced trade's biggest operators. He was a privateer and a raider not just of Spanish ships but their ports as well. He bought his three sugar plantations with the proceeds. Now he is a Knight Bachelor and Lieutenant Governor of Jamaica.' He shrugged. 'It's that sort of place, too.'

I watched the sea, but it remained stubbornly empty of pinnaces. 'Do you and Noah make many trading voyages?'

He shook his head. 'The Mirabel is mostly Hal's affair now, while Noah deals with cargos and such.'

'So, what on earth do you do with your time?'

He smiled, ruefully. 'I paint, believe it or not. Seascapes. Portraits of Noah and Hal. And the servants. The slaves.'

'Will you show me?'

He tilted his head. 'Why not. But first I'll show you to your chamber.' He stood, taking my hand to lead me into the cool gloom of the house.

We passed through a large parlour – furnished with another eclectic assortment of comfortable-looking chairs and sofas – kept cool by closed slatted shutters allowing air to circulate. Beyond was a long gallery with walls the silver of driftwood in the dim light.

'I've made myself a studio at the other end of the house next to our room.' He pointed behind us. 'Though I paint on the porch whenever I can.' At intervals along the passage, doors led off to the front and rear. He opened one at the end where two sets of full-length glass casements were open with their slatted shutters closed behind them against the heat. He pushed them out onto the porch, showing a view over the sea and, on the other wall, up the beach where verdant jungle flowed down to the white sand.

Our boxes had already been unpacked.

'This was Hal's before he moved to the front.' He raised his eyebrows. 'Let's just say afternoon trysts were rather too evident from the porch and Noah wasn't impressed.'

'Ah, I see.' It was a lovely chamber. I made a big effort not to dwell on the reason we were here. Not to allow my imagination to feed me all too familiar nightmare scenes. But, Jesu, it was hard. I took a deep breath.

Sam's arms closed around me. 'Christ, Sukie. I'm so sorry this terrible thing has happened.'

I hugged him tight for a few moments before pulling away. 'So, show me your work.' I watched him blink away tears.

He took his own deep breath and moved back out onto the porch, where we passed by the living area, going on towards the equivalent corner room at this end of the house. He led me in through open doors to the room beside it. I halted. On his easel was a fine if somewhat startling nude of Noah, not far from completion. He coloured and reached to take it down. 'Forgive me.'

'Leave it. It's wonderful.' I raised my eyebrows. 'I had no idea you could paint like this.' Noah looked like a man content after his needs had been well met. I knew that look rather well. Those half-closed eyes. Sam's blush deepened and he removed it from the easel, placing it on the floor facing the wall.

'Neither had I.' He pointed to a stack of canvases and panels propped against the wall. 'Be my guest.'

They were all outstandingly good. I selected one of Hal perched on the porch rail with turquoise sea behind him. 'My God. He's spectacular, isn't he. He must turn some heads.'

'Oh, he does, believe me.' He placed it on the easel. 'Hence, the Mirabel. Noah thinks he needs some focus in his life. He seems skilled at it, too. Well, he never comes back with an empty ship which must be a good way to judge it, I imagine.' He moved to the doorway, his eyes scanning the sea. 'How is Papa? It's been a while since I've had a letter, of course.'

I clutched my head. 'Jesu, Sam. I have one for you. How have I forgotten? It was in my box.' I hurried back out and up the porch to find it for him.

He followed me. 'You have other things on your mind.'

I found the letter on a cabinet beside my hairbrush and handed it to him before picking up the brush. It had my hair and Raphael's caught in the bristles. A sudden memory tore at my heart. 'Penny is so taken with his black hair. She loves to brush it. She would hold hers against his and laugh at how they could be so different. His mother showed her how to make Schiac-ciata cakes. She loved watching him eat them.' I pressed my hand hard on my chest, feeling like my heart would break. 'Jesu.'

He held me tight in his arms. 'We'll get her back. I know we shall. We must.'

'Yes.' I had to believe it, otherwise I would shatter.

I felt him tense. 'There's a boat, Sukie.'

CHAPTER 14
Raphael

I watched Susannah standing on the porch with Sam, knowing how much she had wanted to come with us. Holy God, I of all people could understand how being shut out of something she was at the very heart of felt. Yet I could do nothing else. I touched the dagger at my waist. Port Royal was a lawless place, Noah had made that starkly clear.

We rounded the headland and returned into the harbour again, which appeared even more crowded than when we had arrived on the Linden. Noah and Hal manoeuvred the pinnace skilfully up to the wharf and Hal jumped ashore to tie-off the lines. 'Where first?'

'Harbour Master,' Noah said. 'I know the man well so we shouldn't have any difficulty getting the information we need.' He led us to a single-storey stone building at the end of the wharf closest to Fort

Charles. Inside it was gloomy and surprisingly cool – though probably only in contrast to the extreme heat outside. We passed several clerks at a long wooden counter, very little different to the one in Lisbon, making entries in registers to record ships newly arrived and those about to leave, their cargos, passengers, and ports-of-call. Noah knocked on a door at the end of a corridor and opened it without waiting for a response. 'Hector, I need your help my friend.'

Short and rotund with coat buttons straining across his paunch, he stood to shake hands. 'Noah. Hal.'

'This is Raphael Rossi,' Noah said.

Once we were all seated, I quickly told him of the Ferdinand and how my daughter had been seen onboard. 'We need to know if it's still here.'

'She's not. Sailed yesterday bound for Barbados with a mixed cargo. Can't recall its exact nature.' He turned to a clerk at the other desk. 'Pass me yesterday's log.' Taking it, he began turning the pages until he found what he sought. 'No passengers.' He returned the book to his clerk. 'Farley, fetch the one for when she come in. Should be 'bout a week back.'

'Will do.'

Hector turned back to us. 'Let's find out just who was onboard when she arrived.'

Farley returned from the storeroom with another large volume, placing it down on Hector's desk.

Once again, he flipped through the pages until he found the entry. 'Two families.'

He turned the book around so I could see the names. The Berringer family were listed. 'So, they either left on another ship or she's still here.' I looked at Noah. 'But how do we go about finding her?'

'I can put the word out for you. Describe your girl to me, if you would, Sir.'

I pulled Susannah's miniature from my pocket. 'I can do better than that.' I handed it to him. 'My wife painted her.'

He smiled. 'Well, she's a pretty little thing ain't she, though?' His face became serious again. 'I must say I'm surprised she weren't taken on to Barbados. There's a big market trading bonded servants there.' He scratched his head underneath his wig. 'Though seeing her, she was probably ordered special, like.' He stood. 'As I say, I'll ask around.'

After thanking him and taking our leave, we stood outside in a patch of shade.

'Commander of militia,' Hal said. His father stared, frowning. 'I know his daughter. If the idea is to get her description out to as many people as possible, he's our best bet.' He gestured to the portrait still held in my hand. 'May I?' I passed it to him. 'She's so like Susannah. It's lucky for us she is so distinctive. Her colouring will turn heads here.'

'Just as ours does, I suppose,' Noah said.

I looked up at them. 'Maybe a little more than just your colouring, gentlemen.'

· · ·

The walk up to Fort Charles was an arduous one with little shade and unpleasantly steep. Then, to make matters worse, we were kept waiting for a considerable time whilst the commander was located.

Eventually, though, he appeared and showed us into his office, waving away our letters of introduction after a perfunctory glance. The King's seal was enough. 'My apologies sirs, allow me to offer you refreshment.' James Carlisle was tall and broad-shouldered in a fine militia uniform of navy and scarlet worsted augmented by considerable quantities of gold lace, his sword gleaming silver at his side. Hal might be acquainted with his daughter, but he clearly had no knowledge of it for he had shown no reaction to his name.

When the wine was poured, once again I told my story. 'So, we now know she was on the island but, of course, have no idea whether she's still here or has been put onto another vessel.'

'Hector Paine will ask around for us. Perhaps your men might do the same and keep an eye out for any sightings of her, too?' Noah said.

I handed him Susannah's miniature. 'As you see, she'll be noticed.'

'Indeed, she shall.' He rubbed his face, already showing dark stubble as, I knew, was mine. 'It is a filthy evil business, so just the sort of thing to find rife in Port Royal.' He tilted his head in thought. 'What I tell you now is likely little more than malicious gossip I shouldn't wonder, but there have long been rumours that a certain Barnabus Rifkind has irons in this grisly fire.'

Noah leaned forward. 'Rifkind? I've heard the name. Never met the man, though. He's one of the big planters, isn't he?'

'He is. Second only to the governor himself.' Carlisle drained his glass. 'He calls himself a sugar baron.'

Noah sat back. 'Does he now? Perhaps we should pay him a visit as well as the governor, then?'

'Morgan's up at one of his plantations in the hills. Spring Garden, I believe. His aide at the Governor's House will likely be of more use to you, anyway. Name's Edmund Trelawny. Tell him I sent you to ask for his help. He has a keen interest in all criminal activity in Port Royal. Not an interest shared by Morgan who is himself a well-known and highly successful past practitioner of such. And I use the word past without complete conviction, though it wouldn't do to let such speculation get back to him. So, I'll trust in your discretion, gentlemen.' He raised his eyebrows and watched us all nod our agreement. 'I shall issue instructions for each patrol to be given your daughter's description before setting out. Let's pray it proves useful in locating her.'

There seemed little more to be said, and with our wine finished, the commander rose from behind his desk to show us out. Opening his door, he halted, finding a young woman – clearly the daughter Hal had spoken of – waiting outside. 'Ah, Marianne. These gentlemen are just leaving.'

Her curtsey gave him little choice but to introduce us. She was very like her father and more than a match for Hal in eye-catching good looks, with glossy dark hair and lively chocolate brown eyes. I smiled when she appraised me quite openly while I kissed her hand, '*Signorina*,' before her eyes moved on to Hal. It was clear, save to her father, just how well they knew each other, though neither acknowledged it, of course. It was also clear how little Noah approved.

We were soon on our way down the hill with the intention of visiting the Governor's House – two-stories and stone built – to speak with Trelawny. This gentleman, receiving us in Morgan's office seated behind his desk, turned out to be every bit as helpful as the commander had told us, giving us a general outline of how Europeans were brought to Jamaica and sold on around many different islands, where they were much in demand as house servants.

'Many planters desire white servants but don't wish to pay for such, so they take bonded men and woman who have been transported as criminals now the number of those buying their passage with seven years servitude has dwindled to near naught. Hardly surprising after it became widely known they would often not receive the promised final sum to start their new life in the colonies and land had become too expensive, anyway. So now non-criminals must be acquired by other means—'

'Kidnapped, you mean,' Noah said.

'Well, yes. I don't suppose they volunteer. As I said, they are highly prized and so more expensive because they have no criminal background. And some, including children, are stolen to order which I imagine is what has happened to your daughter, especially as she has such a distinctive appearance.'

My mouth felt suddenly dry as ash. 'Why would a fair child be so desirable?' Then I wished I had not asked such a question because I truly did not want to hear his answer.

'Many reasons. Fair skin is highly sort after, and pretty servant girls are often seen as something of a status symbol.'

I shook my head. 'She's only eight years old. How can she be a servant? What could she possibly do?' Another question I did not wish to hear the answer to, I quickly realised.

'Anything she's asked, I fear. We must pray she'll be nothing more than an indulged pet for the lady of the house or a companion for another child.'

I know I was not alone in imagining what else might be required of her. 'Can you tell us what we should do now. Who might help us find her?'

'There is a man I know to be involved in this trade called Suliman Mendes da Costa. You must see him, I think. And also, Barnabus Rifkind who is rumoured to be his backer.'

'Barnabus Rifkind. We've heard his name already. We'll pay him a call. Where might we find him?' Noah said.

'Cinnamon Hill in St Andrew parish. It is a little way up into the Blue Mountains. Perhaps an hour's ride.'

Hal leaned forward in his seat. 'But how do we get them to tell us where she is when it's not in their interests?'

He shrugged. 'I'm afraid I can't say. If you're lucky and Mendes da Costa is not involved, he might help in order to damage a rival. Who would use them if the merchandise could be found and reclaimed, as it were?' He shrugged again. 'If not, then coin, perhaps?'

'Where might we find this man?' I asked.

'I suggest leaving a message at the Crossed Swords tavern. Perhaps say you wish to meet him to discuss a business matter with an hour when you'll return tomorrow.'

After calling at the insalubrious tavern, I was happy to leave the port when Noah decided we had time enough to get back from Rifkind's plantation before nightfall. We hired horses and rode up into the mountains through a pristine aromatic jungle of mahogany, cedar, and palmetto palm, along tracks which, though humid and airless, offered shade, at least. Once out into the cane fields there was a cooling breeze, making it just about tolerable. There was no sign of them being worked here. Everywhere seemed deserted. Perhaps the crop was not yet ready for cutting?

The plantation house was approached through an imposing gateway and surrounded by a well-tended park where a few fat sheep grazed, incongruously. Built from cream stone it was encircled by a covered porch much as Noah's house was, though the entrance was very grand, with marble colonnades topped by a carved portico to double-height doors. A slave appeared to silently relieve us of our horses. As we mounted the steps, the door opened, and we were ushered inside by a black footman in a full livery of cream and gold, topped by a white wig.

'Please wait, Sas. I see if master free.'

Two wide staircases rose before us to form a gallery above the light and airy hall, its walls lined with black and white statuary like chess pieces massed ready for a game on the black and white marble floor tiles.

Tall doors opened and the footman returned to show us into the drawing room, decorated in pastel shades with a mahogany floor and furniture upholstered in floral fabrics with many tall plants in great terracotta pots grouped together, filling the air with their verdant scent. Their fronds and branches reaching up to the high, dark, wood-panelled ceiling bringing a strange kind of dappled light to the room, occupied by a lone woman. Tiny, very young and startlingly pretty with black curls falling to her waist, she had full lips and honey-brown eyes. Somehow, she brought to mind both Valentina and Frances.

Might this be Rifkind's daughter? We all bowed to her.

She remained unsmiling. 'I'm Isabella Rifkind. My husband is at the crushing mill today. Might I be of some assistance to you?' She gestured to silk upholstered sofas. 'Do sit. I shall order tea.'

Yet she made no move to do so.

She spoke in English but with a Spanish accent. After formally introducing us all I sat, finding her eyes upon me. What harm would it do to tell her of Penny's plight? I smiled. 'We came to see your husband, having learnt he is a leading figure on the island, hoping he might use his influence to help locate my daughter.'

She blinked. 'I see.'

I stood to show her the portrait miniature.

'What a lovely child.' She looked up at me. 'She was kidnapped?'

I glanced at Noah, a little startled by her directness. 'Unfortunately, that is so.'

Her eyes slid away, plainly having read something of my surprise. 'Why would you be searching for her otherwise?'

I lowered myself beside her on the sofa. 'Indeed. My wife–' I closed my eyes for a moment, and thinking of Susannah's suffering, found I could not speak of it. I bit my lip quite hard. 'We now know Port Royal is a place where such things flourish. I hadn't realised it was common knowledge, though. Have you always lived here?'

Her eyes went soft, and she smiled then, bringing

her face vividly to life. 'I come from Costa Rica. My family have a cattle farm there.'

I looked at Noah. I had very little notion where Costa Rica was. In truth, I had absolutely no idea. Was it another island?

Noah raised his eyebrows. 'Between Nicaragua and Panama.'

I raised mine, little better off. Hal met my gaze and shrugged.

Noah glanced from me to his son and shook his head, slightly. 'The narrow strip between north and south America.'

'Ah. I see.' I quickly returned my attention to Isabella Rifkind. So, how long have you lived here, *Signora*?'

'Six months, only.'

And she already knew of Port Royal's reputation as a kidnapper's port? Surely that implied some particular knowledge of the practice through her husband who, as we had already been led to believe, had some involvement. I touched her arm. 'Then, you must miss your family very much, I'm sure.'

'Very much.' Her eyes shone with unshed tears.

I thought her probably of an age with Hal. Her husband, of course, was considerably older. Enough to provide her with such opulent surroundings ... and to acquire such a reputation. Yet she was alone here. 'When do you expect your husband's return?'

She shrugged. 'He returns when he returns. I am not kept informed about it, *Señor* Rossi.'

A quick glance showed Noah and Hal were watching me closely. 'We would be most grateful if you could pass on what I told you of my daughter when you see him. I hope he might contact us if he can help in any way.'

Noah stood. 'I've taken the beach house in Hayes Bay, should he wish to.'

I stood also and bent to kiss her hand. 'Thank you for your time, *Signora* Rifkind.' We bowed again and left her, still sitting on her sofa

'And thank you for the refreshments,' I murmured.

We let ourselves out as the place now seemed entirely deserted, though our horses were brought round by the same silent slave who had relieved us of them earlier. Perhaps Cinnamon Hill worked only for Barnabus. Isabella could be safely ignored. I mounted. 'Poor girl seems lonely and somewhat bewildered.'

'What she seemed was somewhat taken with you, Raphael,' Noah said, riding down the track beside me.

Hal laughed. 'That's why she looked bewildered. You stunned her with your charm.'

'I did no such thing.' I found myself affronted by such a notion. 'I pitied her, so I was kind to her. I had no intention of charming her.'

Noah turned to me, his pale blue gaze steady. 'I know you didn't intend it. I could see that. Yet it is what happened, nonetheless.'

We rode on in silence then, back to Port Royal to return our horses to the livery stable and pay a second

visit to the Crossed Swords to see if our pirate had responded to our message. I found I liked the place even
less, though the man had left word agreeing we should
call there at noon tomorrow. Now I must return and
tell Susannah we had nothing. I prayed she had not believed we would return with Penny.

The next day was a repeat of the one before it, leaving
in the pinnace though this time feeling my wife's now
thoroughly resentful eyes upon my back. She had, of
course, allowed herself to believe Penny could be with
us when we returned, though she denied it. Yet I saw it
on her face and in the depth of her distress.

Today she had been quietly determined to accompany us, appearing ready to do me bodily harm when I
denied it to her. She had not seen that grim tavern or
its unsavoury patrons. It was no place for her. Feeling
particularly cowardly but prepared to tolerate it, I allowed Noah and Hal to go inside without me. In
truth, they had little need of my presence for would I
not be more hindrance than help when they must protect me should the need arise?

Hal stepped out closely followed by his father.
'Nothing. Not there, and no further messages.'

I took a long breath, realising I had been holding it.
'*Porco Dio*. What now?'

Noah squared his shoulders. 'We wait and return
in an hour. What else can we do?'

We began walking back towards the Fort Charles

end of the docks with, I assumed, some destination in mind. 'Where are we going?'

Noah looked down at me. 'There is a rather more wholesome tavern a little further along where we can get food.'

Hal laughed. 'Not a huge improvement on the Crossed Swords, though the fish stew is at least edible.'

It turned out to be more of an improvement than Hal had suggested, particularly as it boasted several serving wenches, all large and plain, but it had always seemed to me the presence of woman whatever their appearance improved the ambience of a place. So, we passed the hour with rum and fish stew. Hal and I somehow found ourselves discussing the merits of John Donne's meditations and his anti-Catholic polemics, which I had read in translation in Florence and, unsurprisingly, found less impressive than he. We did agree on the holy sonnets, though.

'*Death be not proud, though some have called thee mighty and dreadful,*' Hal quoted.

I smiled. '*For thou art not so, for those, whom thou think'st, thou dost overthrow.*'

Noah scowled at us. 'Sweet holy fuck. Let's get back to that shithole. It's preferable to listening to you two. God's blood. Don't I have to hear enough of this sort of prattle with you and Sam?'

Hal patted his father's arm. 'Well, you knew where Costa Rica was, which is more than we did.'

'At least that is knowledge with some use to it, Lad.'

Hal and I looked at each other as we rose, and Hal rolled his eyes. 'There is such a thing as wilful ignorance, Papa.'

Noah then called him something extremely obscene in Italian. I set off back towards the shithole, chuckling to myself, before I was asked to translate. I stepped into the gloom, completely unprepared for the sight that awaited me. Holy Mary mother of God. Then I felt Noah and Hal arrive behind me.

CHAPTER 15

Susannah

Again, we watched them sail out towards the headland in the pinnace. I had begged to go but Raphael refused me and would brook no argument on it. I understood why Sam could not, but I knew I was forbidden simply because I was a woman and with child. His woman and his child. Yet, as Penny's mother, I had more right than anyone to search for her, surely?

I now felt at a complete loss as to how to occupy myself. Anger at being left behind and fear they would learn nothing useful once again, plagued me. 'Go to your painting, Sam, if you wish it. Don't feel you must keep me company all day. I think I might take a stroll along the beach.' I truly did not wish to be a burden to him.

He studied me, carefully. 'You'll need your parasol.'

I realised then, he thought I wanted to be alone,

which was probably the last thing I needed. Still, perhaps he did wish to paint? Jesu. I should just go for my walk. I moved to kiss his cheek. 'I'll fetch it.'

In all honesty, I had not planned to do it. Yet, when the opportunity presented itself, how could I not take it? I had walked along the beach beyond the house towards the headland where Fort Charles squatted so menacingly – or so it appeared to me in my current state of mind – when I came across a track leading into the lush jungle that hugged the shore. I followed it for a while, enjoying the wonderful cool green light and relief from the fierce sun. The calling song of cicadas made a constant background drone and large ungainly jewel-coloured butterflies floated slowly through the foliage. I caught a sudden flash of an iridescent hummingbird in the blossom of a flame tree. The air was thick with its scent against that of warm earth and vegetation.

After a time, the trail joined a wider one rutted by cartwheels, and I wondered if it might lead to Port Royal. When I heard the unmistakable clop of hooves and rumble of wheels, I moved back off the track to allow the cart to pass but, instead, it stopped. The driver was a large black woman, her skin glowing moist in the heat, with a small girl sitting beside her. They both wore faded red cotton shifts with matching cloths wrapped round their heads. I realised how outlandish I must look to them in my fancy lemon muslin with my silly yellow parasol and flaxen hair. They both grinned at me, so I smiled back.

'You goin' town, Mam?

And there it was. The opportunity. 'Er, yes. I do believe I am. Might I beg a lift from you?'

She reached across to pull me up beside the child. 'Course ye can. It a fair walk there, sure enough. This Sugar. I's Lena.'

The wagon bed was full of ripe mangoes, enveloping us in a sweet intoxicating fragrance. I pointed to myself. 'Susannah. This is so kind of you, Lena.'

The little girl laughed. I realised, with a pang, she must be around Penny's age. 'You sounds funny, missus.'

'I'm from England.'

Lena made a noise in her throat that plainly conveyed her views on England and shook the reins to encourage the mule on its way once more.

Sugar told me they came from a small coffee plantation up in the mountains and how the slaves had mango trees behind their cabins. Their master allowed them to barter the fruit for cloth and even the occasional small luxury. 'He good to us.' She touched my gown. 'I's get this kind. It pretty.'

'The colour would suit you very well.'

When her mother made that disparaging sound again, I looked away.

They dropped me off down by the harbour and it was only then I questioned how I might return to Sam's house and, even more alarmingly, what he would make of my disappearance. Jesu. It would worry him a very great deal. Of course it would. How could I have been so foolishly reckless? I scanned the dockside for a sight of two fair heads standing high above the crowd but to no avail. I knew they were returning to a tavern called the Crossed Swords to find the man they had been told of yesterday, so I must go there now to ask if they had already done so. I did not wish to think what Raphael would say when ... if I found him. I took a breath, feeling panic rising. What would I do if I could not find them?

I walked with purpose towards the first tavern I came upon. The Crossed Swords. I could scarcely believe my good fortune and lifting my chin, I stepped inside, looking for a serving wench who would likely be a touch less hostile towards me. There were none, naturally. The room was entirely full of men. And disreputable looking ones at that. *Damn.* The eyewatering stench alone nearly caused me to turn and leave. Stinging fumes of rum. Sour sweat. And an overflowing privy somewhere close by. I fought hard not to retch. Yet, somehow, I managed to arrive at the counter without making eye contact with anyone while attempting to inhale as little that of fetid stink as possible. The serving man hurried to me, scowling. I held up my hands in an attempt to forestall him. 'I'm looking for my husband and his two friends. They're both large with yellow hair like mine.' I pointed to it.

He pointed to the door. 'I care not. Out.'

A chair scraped on the floor behind me as someone got up. 'Now, is it a husband you be wanting, Lady?' Hands grabbed me by the shoulders, turning me to face him. 'I'd be happy to offer me services.' He was dark and balding with greasy, sallow skin. Several gold teeth were revealed. And the gaps between them.

It could almost be that the stench of the place emanated entirely from his person, so foul was it. He thrust himself against me, lewdly. 'I have a husband. I am looking for him.' Jesu, my voice shook. I tried to remove his hands, which had by now found their way to my breasts.

He squeezed. 'Well, until that time, Lady, you have me don't you, now? I shall swive you good, so I will, just as a husband ought.' When he moved in to kiss me, I spat at him. Then he got really nasty, hustling me backwards his arm across my throat, until I was pressed against the wall. Then, just like that, I was no longer there. I was somewhere far away from myself. And preternaturally calm.

I became aware – quite impassively – of other patrons finding this all terribly entertaining and already making wagers on his chances of a successful rape. Needless to say, the consensus was in his favour. 'Please don't. I'm with child.' Someone had spoken those words, but I doubted they were mine. How could they be?

He yanked my thin muslin gown down, uncovering my breasts, which elicited some whistles and general hoots of admiration. 'And that should matter to me, why?' He rubbed his crotch and then began to gather-up my skirts, moving his mouth down onto my breasts. It was at that moment I crashed back into myself. And it felt like a physical blow, making me gasp for breath. In the name of sweet holy Christ, how could this be happening to me? And what could I do now?

'Perhaps you would be so good as to remove your person from the vicinity of my wife,' said a deep voice with a rather pronounced Italian accent. This was followed by the sound of blades withdrawn from scabbards. The man raised his head and turned around. Two sword tips arrived on his chest.

My husband's hands arrived upon mine, righting my gown. His eyes flashed with fury, though all seemed directed at me. Jesu, could he not spare even a tiny portion of it for the brute who had attacked me? Reality seemed to have shifted again for I could make no sense of it. 'Thank you, Raphael, I–'

He grasped my arm so tightly it verged on pain and began tugging me away. 'Outside. Now.'

'Let go.' When I tried to shake him off, his grip tightened. 'You're hurting me.'

He marched me out and into the deserted alleyway beside the tavern, and once again I found myself pinned against a wall. 'Raphael? What in God's name is wrong with you?' I was truly alarmed now. Jesu, had I not already been through enough? Had he quite lost his wits?

He held my upper arms and shook me, slightly. I bit my tongue. 'Would you care to explain why I find you in a tavern with your gown down around your waist, a man slobbering over your breasts and lifting your skirts, his cock out ready to have you. Explain it to me, please.' He shook me again. My head banged on the wall.

It was either tears now, or anger. I lifted my chin and kicked him as hard as I could. Though, hampered by my skirts, there was little power behind it. He moved, pinning my legs with his. '*Piccola puttana, dovrei battere il culo crudo.*'

More Italian invective was spat into my face. Why did he bother when I barely understood a word? Though I was sure most of it was threatening and none of it was complimentary. 'I don't have to explain myself to you.'

He remembered English again. 'Oh, but you do. I am your husband. How could you risk such a thing? Risk our child?'

'Ah, I see. Just as with Valentina, your child is your only concern.' I knew this to be so completely untrue, I almost laughed until I saw the effect it had on him. I had been here before. I wanted to touch him but was quite unable to move, he had me so tightly pinned. I held his gaze. 'Forgive me. You know I don't mean that.' I turned my head away, my cheek pressing against the wall, closing my eyes so I could no longer see the hurt in his. 'I know I was foolish to come here. I know I was foolish to go inside that stinking place ... and I know I frightened you badly. Jesu, I've never been so afraid in my life. And I'm sure I've frightened Sam, too.' I bit my lip, hard. 'So, I'm thoroughly ashamed of myself and if I could turn time backwards I would, and then do none of it.'

He groaned, gathering me in. 'Christ, Susannah. What if we hadn't arrived when we did? Christ.'

When I crashed back into the reality of it once more, I began to tremble ... and then I began to weep.

Noah led us to a quiet square where a low wall around a fountain afforded us somewhere shady to sit while Raphael held me until I was able to compose myself. I was now horribly aware they were all here with me rather than waiting for the man who might have knowledge of Penny. So, instead of helping, I had done the exact opposite. God help me.

Raphael turned to Noah. 'I shall take Susannah back. Perhaps you and Hal might wait without me?'

'I'll find a carriage for you first.'

After we watched them walk away, I gasped a shuddering breath. 'I don't know what to say to you. I am so ashamed ... and mortified by my stupidity–'

'No, *cara*. This isn't a civilised place. Of course, there are parts of London and Florence, too, where such things happen but they are not places we know of or would ever go to. Well, not alone, anyway. This sort of vice and cruelty is unknown to us, I think. So, it's not expected.'

I shook my head. 'I should've expected it when Penny was taken the way she was. When that maid was slaughtered. I know how base men can be. How can I not? No. I'm simply a fool.'

Hal waved then, calling us to follow him. We

found a two-seat open pony carriage waiting for us near one of the piers far away from the Crossed Swords, thank the Lord. 'I don't know if I shall recognise the track back to the beach.'

Noah squeezed my shoulder. 'The man knows it. Go back to the house and rest. You've had a shocking ordeal, Lass.'

I looked away. 'I was at fault. My own folly.'

'No, Susannah. Perhaps we should have made it clearer to you what sort of a place it was.'

'Why should you when you had no expectation I would ever go there?'

We took our leave then and Raphael kept his arm around me while we retraced my earlier wagon journey. Neither of us spoke. I could think of nothing to say to him, and it seemed he felt the same. When the carriage stopped, he helped me alight, and we walked down the jungle track that would take us back to the shore close to the house.

He looked around him as we walked, hand in hand. 'This must be how the Garden of Eden looked, I think.' He stopped to comfort me with kisses, which let us both say what we could not with words.

I held him tight, glad to lose myself in him for a while. I pulled away. 'Now I must ask Sam's forgiveness, then I want to bathe. And then, my dearest Raphael.' I touched his face. 'Then I want to make love.

'I believe all can be arranged, *amore mio*.'

• • •

I lay in his arms, our bodies cooling in the breeze from the open casements. He raised himself on his elbow to look down at me in the afternoon light, the sound of the sea splashing rhythmically over the beach was all we could hear above our breathing. 'Can you forgive me, *cara*?' He moved to kiss my upper arms. 'My fingers have marked you.'

I felt his heat inside me still and the resonance of my release like a struck bell. 'Without your love I think I'd die, Raphael.'

'I feel the same.'

He had washed me himself, removing all physical traces of my attacker from my skin just as he had removed him from my mind with his body. I sighed. 'Now we must go outside and wait for Noah and Hal. Please God they've seen this wretched man.'

He moved away from me, stretching. 'Food, too, I think.'

I smiled. 'Of course. I believe I've learnt my lesson. I'll obey you in all things from now on, you have my word.'

He raised his eyebrows. 'Is that so? I rather think you will until you disagree with what I ask of you.'

I laughed. 'Well, I didn't say I wouldn't have to agree with it first, did I?'

He rolled over me again, his face serious now. 'But you'll obey me about Port Royal, Susannah?'

'Oh, indeed, but should you insist I go there ever again I must warn you the outcome might be somewhat different.'

'You understand why I was so angry?'

I touched the bruises on my arm left by his fingers and then I touched his face. 'Because you knew what could have happened and not just from one man. You knew what I'd risked–'

He sighed. 'I was angry with myself, too. Christ, what could I have done without Noah and Hal?'

'I must admit, I was rather glad to see their swords.'

Later we learned they had nothing beyond a message to return again tomorrow. I truly found myself close to despair.

CHAPTER 16

Noah

Noah went in cautiously in case Sam slept. He had written a long letter to Michael and a short one to Margaret. God's wounds, that woman was hard to write to. He would maybe add more over the next few days before leaving them with Hector Paine to find a suitable ship ... if and when. He put his candle down softly but sat on the bed when he saw Sam's eyes were open. 'Did I wake you?'

Sam sat up higher against the pillows. 'No. I was waiting for you.'

Noah tilted his head. 'Were you now.' He moved to kiss him, but Sam ducked away. 'I want to talk to you first.'

'I shall hold you to that *first*, Laddie.' The unnecessarily heavy emphasis on the word, made them both smile.

Sam ran his hands through his chestnut hair, loose

about his shoulders. 'I'm sure you will. Now, what exactly happened in Port Royal. I know Susannah was attacked in some way that made her wish to bathe immediately and pass the gown she wore to Pearl for one of the kitchen girls.' He bit his lip. 'God. She wasn't raped, was she?'

Noah drew a quick breath. 'A hair's breadth from it. If we hadn't arrived when we did ... well.' He sighed. 'He was already lifting her skirts, poor lass. There'd have been plenty more takers, too. I thought Raphael would swoon when he saw her. He was very angry with her when he got her outside. I didn't know he had that in him.'

'With her? Why with her? He couldn't think she consented–'

'Christ, no. Angry she had come to the town. That she had gone in there, looking as she does, offering herself on a plate to a room full of scum.' He shook his head. 'My God, he threatened her with some very unpleasant punishment for it.'

Sam took a sharp breath. 'He did what?'

'In his own tongue. She wouldn't have understood much of it. It was coarse and explicit, and I imagine rather satisfying to say. Presumably, you heard no screams from their chamber, so I don't expect he went through with any of it?'

Sam raised his eyebrows. 'I didn't hear anything like that. Nothing unpleasant, anyway.'

Noah barked a laugh. 'That room does seem to be a tad lacking in privacy.'

'Open casements.' He eyed theirs, dubiously. 'She was in a bad way when they arrived back. Very tearful. Christ knows why she thought about my distress at finding her missing. How could it matter compared to hers after that? Though, in truth, I'd been worried sick. I very nearly rode into Port Royal to find you. I even had my horse saddled ready before deciding against it. I didn't want her to return and find me gone.'

Noah stood and began shedding his clothes. 'Sense prevailed then. Thank the Lord for small mercies.'

Sam watched him. 'Remember the open doors.'

'I will if you will, Laddie.'

'Well, I can certainly try.'

CHAPTER 17

Susannah

I looked at Raphael sleeping still, naked in the heat, his hair a black shadow on the white linen of the pillow. Then, as though feeling the caress of my gaze, I watched the first stirrings of his morning arousal beginning its tentative rise. Jesu, I was tempted. Yet, feeling such an unpleasant mixture of nausea and acute hunger, I knew I must eat first. 'Damn,' I said, under my breath, before slipping from the bed and retrieving my shift from the floor.

I moved silently through the house and out along the open-sided covered passageway leading to the kitchen block, which smelt enticingly of freshly baked bread. A sleepy-eyed slave girl handed me a roll, slit to insert a goodly dollop of butter. My mouth watered as I carried it onto the porch, intending to return to my husband as soon as I was finished. I moved to the rail, looking out across the lucent sea, calm and flat as glass in the still early morning air, watching ungainly pelicans fold their wings to drop like great arrows into the water while terns waited to rob them of their catch. I laughed, watching one trying to snatch a flapping fish before it was transferred from a pelican's long beak into its throat pouch.

'Sukie?'

I whipped around, startled. 'Sam.' I had been entirely unaware of his presence there on the sofa in deep shadow. I took another bite and moved to sit beside him, noticing he was hardly more decently dressed than I, in grey breeches and nothing more. Though my shift must have been all but transparent with the light behind me. I had never seen him so scantily clothed. Why would he be anything other than completely beautiful? Fine-boned. Broad shouldered. Browned by the sun. I held up my roll. 'Hungry.'

He grinned. 'So I see.'

I took another bite and offered it to him. 'You finish it. It's good.'

He held up his hands. 'You need it more, I'm sure.'

I looked at it and shook my head. 'It usually only takes a few bites to feel back to myself. I've had enough.' He took it from me and ate the rest with some relish, I was pleased to see.

His fingertips grazed the burgeoning swell of my belly. 'You were more unwell ... the last time?'

I nodded and grasped his hand, bringing it to my lips. 'The only thing that matters now is getting her back. Our daughter.' I searched his face. 'Sleep was difficult?'

He nodded. 'In truth, I've too little to occupy me here.' He held up a drawing block. 'Only this and my painting.' He closed his eyes. 'God forgive me. I faced death not six months ago and I complain of my lot now. And with Penny's terrible plight.' He snorted. 'I do occasionally rather disgust myself.'

I leaned in to kiss his cheek. 'Well, you shouldn't, my dear. Be kinder to yourself. You taught me that, did you not?' I took the sketchbook from him and flicked through it. Studies of this view in many different lights and weathers. Many of Noah and Hal; one rather fine one where they fought with swords. I looked up. 'They look lethal.' I turned the last page to find a drawing of a sleeping Noah, every mark made with love.' I blinked. 'It's beautiful. Has he seen it?'

He shook his head. 'I drew it just before I came out here this morning.' He shifted his position to turn towards me. 'He told me what happened yesterday. I'm so sorry. It must have been ... terrifying.'

I chewed my lip. 'It wasn't real at first. I simply didn't believe it could be true. Such a thing couldn't possibly be happening to me. I looked at it from outside of myself, like it was a dream. A nightmare, but someone else's. I'm not sure if you can understand? It sounds too strange. But I wasn't afraid until I fell into the truth of it, when I realised what was about to happen.'

'I understand it completely. I was sentenced to a

horrible death. How could that be real? I wanted to laugh at the absurdity of it, until I held my father in my arms and felt his tears on my face.'

I blinked away my own tears then, remembering the horror of that day. Thank Christ we had got him away. 'Well, I was a fool. Raphael thinks me too sheltered to understand the risks which, in truth, I probably am. It simply never entered my head when I walked in there what could happen to me. He was quite angry with me at first.'

'So I heard. Noah thought it just as well you didn't understand what he threatened you with.'

'I do believe I'd rather not know.'

'Perhaps it would be better if you did, *cara*.' Raphael stepped out onto the porch. 'Maybe it would give you pause for thought next time.'

He sat beside me, putting his arm across my shoulders. Like Sam, he was dressed only in breeches and also astoundingly beautiful. And, most importantly, mine. I smiled. 'But, as I was never subjected to any of it, why ever should it?'

He laughed, shrugging. 'Possibly I might not be so lenient again.'

I patted his thigh. 'There'll be nothing like it to punish, you have my word.

Sam tilted his head, studying me. 'May I paint you? I should like to very much. And Raphael too.' He gestured towards me. 'I want you as you are now, Sukie, with your hair down around you.'

'Why not.' I looked down at myself. 'But perhaps a

little less *déshabillé*?' I stood. 'Which is something I must rectify now.' I held my hand to Raphael. 'You, too, my love.'

We walked hand in hand through the silent house. He closed the chamber door, leaning against it, watching me as I untied my shift at the neck, letting it fall to the floor. He smiled, undoing his breeches, and dropping them where he stood. We stood still, looking at each other. Wanting each other, until I moved to the bed and lay down, closing my eyes. I heard his foot-steps on the wooden floor and knew he stood over me.

'Look at me, Susannah.'

I opened my eyes and looked. 'Raphael.'

'Tell me, *amore mio*.'

We watched them sail away for the third morning, only this time I had no desire to be with them. I reached for Sam's hand and squeezed. 'Please God, they see this man today and get some news of her. Every day that passes is another when she has to endure–'

'Stop. It doesn't help imagining.'

'So, you don't at all?' I found that hard to believe.

He sighed. 'Of course I do. But I try not to ... I can't allow myself to dwell on it.'

I sighed, too. 'Raphael stops me. He always seems to know when I'm doing it. And he's right. Torturing myself makes not a jot of difference to her.' I took a deep breath. 'Well, at least I can hope she is no longer aboard ship. How can she have withstood such a crossing? Yet the man who saw her in Lisbon said she looked well, so maybe she'd got over her sickness on such a long voyage.' I sat on the sofa and picked up his drawings again. There was one of me now, and one of Raphael. I studied it. 'This is astonishing.'

He sat beside me again. 'You like it?'

I smiled. 'How could I not. It's him. Not just his likeness either, it captures his power.' I shook my head. 'Or whatever it is that draws people to him. Women, anyway.'

'I meant it about painting you both.' He stood and held his hand out to me. 'Come. Let's make a start. It's not as though either of us have anything better to do.'

I took his hand and he led me to his studio once again. There was a battered old sofa against one wall. 'Shall I sit there?'

He nodded. 'Just be comfortable.' He lifted an already sized panel onto his easel and began to load his palette from paint bladders. He smiled. 'Will you unpin your hair for me?'

I did as he asked. Soon my thoughts began to wonder, thinking of Raphael and the others in Port Royal waiting in the Crossed Swords for this Suliman Mendes da Costa. Would he come? Of course, I saw the place where they waited, smelt it too, and then watched myself walk in there the day before. Feeling heat on my face thinking of my idiocy. Christ, what had I been thinking? I frowned, picturing all those men who had seen me only as a body they could use.

'What are you thinking of, Sukie?'

'Nothing much.'

'Well, whatever it is it's making you frown.'

I sighed. 'Those men. Why are they like that? So base and cruel.'

'A lot of them are transported prisoners sold here as indentured labour. When their term's up, they're inevitably drawn to Port Royal and most remain there. Without the means to return to England, they've little choice. I wonder if you know pardons are offered for sale to anyone so sentenced. £10 will set you free, if you have such a sum.' He snorted. 'Can you guess who gets the revenue?'

I rolled my eyes. 'The King, I imagine.'

'Portsmouth.'

'Louise de Kérouaille? Why does that not surprise me.' I gasped, putting my hand on my belly. 'Jesu.'

He put down his brush and hurried to me, dropping to his knees. 'What's wrong? Have you pain?'

I smiled. 'No. No, I felt him move. Felt his flutter for the first time.'

He moved up to sit beside me, looking relieved. 'A boy, you think? Like Pearl said.'

'I feel so different to how I did with Penny.' I shrugged. 'I'd like a boy for Raphael.' I wondered whether to tell Sam of his daughter but knew I must not. That was his to share, should he choose to. 'He's been a wonderful father to Penny, and he will be to this one.'

Sam pulled me into his arms. 'Forgive me for not being so.

'You always loved her. And she loves you. You were part of her life and that's what matters.'

He held me away to look at me. 'I won't be when you take her home again.'

He put heavy emphasis on when. I nodded. 'When I take her home.' I rested my head on his chest. 'I talked to Raphael about you. I was sad to think that once you knew she was yours you'd never see her. He said we couldn't know it for certain. So now you will, Sam. When we find her, she'll be with you as your daughter.'

'Did you tell him all of it?' He watched me nod. 'Well, he must think rather badly of me then and quite deservedly, of course.'

I stroked his face. 'He doesn't at all. He understood. He pitied you ... pitied both of us.' I saw him frown, uncertainty in his eyes. 'He's had his own difficulties in the past too, you know that. Things that shame him.'

He lifted a strand of my hair and ran it through his fingers. 'Frances Stuart. He told me of her. He had to when she was the reason he was released from the Tower.'

'There were many, many others besides her.' I sighed. 'And something in Florence, which he didn't tell me of for quite some time. His mother spoke of it, thinking I knew. It was the day Penny was taken.'

'I can hardly bear to imagine how that day must have been for you.'

I shook my head. 'There I was thinking of

Raphael's secret, angry with him because he'd kept it from me when I'd been so open with him, and I knew how much it had helped me that I had been. Yet he hadn't allowed me to help him. I'd gone to the Foyles' lodgings thinking of what I would say to him and felt only annoyance when I discovered Penny wasn't there, I was so eager to get back to speak my mind to him. Anne Foyles was distracted by her new son and hadn't even noticed their absence. Raphael told me he'd seen them in St James's Park earlier, so I went there to find them. When I couldn't, I began to feel alarmed. I walked to the canal, calling. I walked and then I ran until no breath remained to call.

'I still don't know why I went to Frances Stuart. I ran in through the Park Gate and saw Richmond House there in front of me. The King was with her. Everything was done then. Men were sent out to search. She sent for Raphael and Papa. Your Papa, too.' I gasped a breath. 'I barely remember those next days.' I had not dared to take my mind back there until today. It felt like somewhere dangerous. Somewhere I must not risk setting foot for fear it might send me mad.

'Holy God, Susannah.'

I stood, trembling from reliving it all so vividly, and walked out on to the porch. I spotted the boat immediately. 'They're coming back.' He caught me before I fell to my knees. 'Pray God there's good news.' We waited for them outside, Sam's arm around my waist, watching them tie up. 'Raphael looks unhappy.' I closed my eyes.

'Christ, they all do.'

I leaned into him. 'I don't know how much more of this I can endure.'

'Yet we have no choice. What else is there for us?'

I stepped away from him then, into Raphael's arms. 'Nothing?'

He held me close. 'Not entirely nothing. A tenuous report of a fair-haired girl seen boarding a ship heading to Santiago de Cuba.'

I gasped and pulled away to look at him. 'That's a great deal more than nothing.'

Noah snorted. 'Not if you'd seen the fucking man. A sly little cunt.' He looked at me, shamefaced. 'Forgive me. The bastard lied to us and found it amusing, knowing we must act on what he told us.'

'Or it was a performance to make us think he lied, so we wouldn't act upon it.' Hal said.

Noah shook his head, appearing exasperated. 'Why bother with such deviousness. What would be the point?'

Raphael arms tightened around me. 'Or he was told to make us uncertain. Something makes me think of Rifkind. Everything we know points to him being underhand and capricious enough for this.' He sighed. 'Yet, we must still go to Cuba, I think.'

Noah threw himself down onto a couch. 'God's wounds, I believe we must.' He rubbed his face and looked up at Hal. 'We'll scrape up a cargo tomorrow and get her victualled. It's a good day's sail.'

'Where is Santiago de Cuba?' Hal asked.

'Southeast part of the island.'

I clutched at Raphael's arms. 'I'm coming, too.'

CHAPTER 18
Susannah
CUBA 1676

So here I was again, standing beside Raphael as we sailed into yet another harbour. This time Santiago de Cuba, passing through a narrow strait between two headlands – the hill on the left topped by another castle fort – widening into a long bay taking us around an island to arrive at the docks. Beyond the town of crowded single-storey buildings spread over sloping ground coming down to the shore, was a range of dark hills with greenery striped by crevices of bare rock. Many ships were anchored in the bay and the long wharves sported the usual forest of masts.

Though the voyage had been a short one, it had not been pleasant with Noah and Hal constantly ill-tempered with each other. Sam, exasperated by them, spent most of his time with us. Well, with Raphael on deck while I rested on the bunk at my husband's insistence. I felt horribly guilty that everyone had insisted we should have the captain's cabin but there was nowhere else I could be suitably housed.

Sam moved to stand beside us now, eyeing the Bartholomews darkly. 'Christ, I'm not sure how much more of this I can take. Noah is so dammed critical, and Hal does all he can to provoke him.' He tilted his head. 'It's especially vexing knowing how much they secretly enjoy it.'

I patted his arm. 'I must admit Noah's dark muttering and Hal's sneering have started to pall, somewhat.'

Raphael frowned. 'Well, I hope someone has an idea about what we should do now we're here.'

Sam scanned the docks area while sailors tied-up the lines. 'Ask everywhere we can. Show her portrait. What else is there?'

Noah appeared beside him. 'Harbour Master. Always the place to start finding out about a ship and its passengers. I have his name and a note from Hector Paine in Port Royal to introduce me.'

Sam looked sceptical. 'If we don't know the ship's name, how can we find out about its passengers?'

'We look at the logs for ships arriving.' Noah snapped. 'We know roughly when that would have been according to when the sighting of the girl took place. Christ, Lad, allow me to have some notion of what I'm doing.'

Sam gave him a hard stare. 'And allow me, if you please, to see this whole thing as a wild-goose-chase foisted on us by a perfidious charlatan.'

'Perfidious, is it? Well, there's a prick's word if ever I heard one.'

Sam smiled, unpleasantly. 'You do seem rather intent on falling out with everyone, Noah. As for perfidious, perhaps you'd like me to define it for you?'

Noah took a step towards him. 'I know what it means you f–'

Raphael put a hand on each man's arm. 'Please feel free to use the cabin if you must continue this, just don't do so in front of my wife.'

They both gave him rather nasty looks but stomped away, nevertheless. I hoped they might use it to apologise to each other rather than come to blows. 'Noah is rather tetchy. I hope it isn't because we're commandeering his ship for our search. And his time, too, of course.'

He pulled me to him. 'No, he's just anxious to find Penny for Sam ... and for you. But he knows there's something wrong with this trip. You heard what he thought of the man who supplied the information. He doesn't like being made a fool of.'

I looked out at the stretch of warehouses and cargo sheds, the many taverns ... and the heaving crowds of men around them knowing, suddenly, I could not leave the ship. I shuddered, thinking of what happened in Port Royal. 'I shouldn't have come. She's not here. I'd know if she were.' I shook my head. 'I can't leave the ship. I can't go down there.'

He studied my face. 'No. I see that. I'll stay with you.' He led me to the starboard rail where we watched ships out on the water, some on their way into the docks furling their sails as they slowed, others leaving, sails filling and pennants flying as they found the wind.

He put his arm around my waist, holding me close, his hand on my belly. I closed my eyes for a moment, enjoying the feel of him pressed against me. 'Have they had enough time?'

'They've had all we'll give them.' He took my hand, then, and led me back to the cabin. It was empty and there was no evidence any violence had taken place there, everything appearing undisturbed. We sat at the table. 'Let's leave it to Noah. There's a cargo to unload and I'm sure they'll find one for the return voyage.' He sighed. 'I'm not sure what we can do. Where can we go for information next?'

I fought despair. 'Not that man again.'

'No. Not him. But who?'

CHAPTER 19

Noah

Noah opened the door to the aftcastle cabin and gestured impatiently for Sam to go inside. The space that had once been theirs. Christ, so much had happened between them there.

With a look of disdain, Sam did so. Then, after studying Noah's face, he sighed eyeing him with some sympathy now. 'I know there's something wrong? Would it help to tell me what it is?'

Noah's eyes widened and he frowned. 'There's nothing wrong with me, Lad. It's those around me who're the problem. You suggesting I've no clue what I'm doing. Hal behaving like he's nothing whatsoever to learn from–'

'Damnation, Noah, stop trying to silence any view that differs from yours–'

Noah grabbed his shoulders. 'That's not what I'm

doing at all. I'm trying to find your daughter, Sam. That's what I'm doing. Do you want me to stop?'

Sam smiled slowly, tilting his head back to meet Noah's gaze. 'Ah, I understand, now. You're doing it for me. You think it's your responsibility to do this for me. And you haven't been able to yet, and its eating at you.' He touched his face. 'You're not God. This isn't all on your shoulders.'

Noah closed his arms around him. 'So why do I feel it is?' He shook his head. 'Who else's, then? This is my ship. My crew. I know these islands and their ports. If I don't take responsibility for finding your little girl, who will?'

'We all want the same thing. All of us, Susannah most of all. You griping at Hal and snapping at me is just wearisome. No one blames you for our lack of success or expects any more from you. We're just grateful for what you've done.'

Noah bent to kiss him.

They kissed for a while until Sam moved away a little. 'You know that first day you went into Port Royal, Susannah said she trusted you to find Penny because you'd saved my life.' He smiled. 'And she trusted Raphael's God.

Noah snorted. 'Has his own, does he?'

'He's a papist with a particularly strong faith, I believe.'

Noah raised his eyebrows. 'Can't say I've noticed it.'

'Susannah has and she knows him rather better than we do, I think.'

'Well, Lad, I'll try and mend my ways, and I'll have a word with Hal. Though I think he needs to change his attitude, too.'

'Stop finding fault with him all the time and he will.'

He sighed. 'Perhaps I better apologise to everyone, then.'

'Can't hurt, can it?'

Noah barked a laugh and kissed him again.

That evening they all sat around the table in the cabin. Everyone was in low spirits, though Noah had tried to put things right with all of them. Susannah and Raphael had shown surprise when he offered the explanation for his ill-temper, both saying they felt nothing but gratitude towards him, just as Sam said they did. It was more difficult to judge with Hal, who had watched him with raised eyebrows and a scornful expression. Yet, in the end, he admitted he had been trying to bait him. Christ. *Why?*

But, of course, the not unexpected news that they had found nothing in the port: not from the harbour master, nor anywhere else they had tried, indeed, that no one had seen a fair-haired girl at all, explained the despondent mood. Yet it would be days before they could trust they had left no stone unturned. Days they must remain in port.

Noah spoke first. 'I think we're all agreed this was a waste of time. We shouldn't have come here. Mendes da Costa can't be trusted. But did he intend to mislead us?' He turned to Raphael. 'I know you think he did.'

'I do. The problem is who do we turn to instead?'

When nobody answered, Noah looked at Sam.

He met his gaze and cleared his throat. 'Trade to all the main islands. Check with Harbour Masters, looking for passengers with children. Ask in taverns. Just as we did today. We know if she's left Jamaica then it has to be after the Ferdinand arrived.'

'Did you ask in Port Royal whether any children have left on another ship since then?' Susannah said.

Noah frowned. 'No. But it's something I can rectify when we get back.'

'How do we know the records are accurate?' Hal's nostrils flared. 'These are kidnappers. Smugglers. Hector Paine was surprised they hadn't taken her on to Barbados because of the bond servant market there. How do we know they didn't?'

Raphael stared at Hal for a moment. 'Yet they listed her into Lisbon and into Port Royal. Why stop?' He answered his own question. 'To leave a trail only as far as Jamaica, perhaps? She was taken from St James's Park. Richly dressed. And who knows what she told them about herself? They would expect her to be searched for. They may have wanted to leave a false trail or simply a dead end.'

Susannah's eyes were on him until she turned to Noah. 'Jesu. What can we do?'

He looked around the table, his eyes finishing on Sam. 'We do as Sam suggests. Trade around the islands and search. There is nothing else.'

CHAPTER 20

Raphael

PUERTO RICO 1677

The Christmas festive season had passed us by unmarked and a new year had stolen upon us, unawares. What a contrast to the year before when I had first met Susannah at the Twelfth Night Ball at Whitehall Palace. Holy God. So much has happened since then.

Our first port of call after sailing from Port Royal again, was Puerto de San Juan on Puerto Rico, a journey of around five days. Noah's estimate proved surprisingly accurate, considering all the factors not in our control. We sailed into the bay of San Juan through the entrance passing Toa Baja and on by the hill-top citadel of Castillo San Felipe del Morro, arriving at the wharves at mid-day in overpowering heat, the air still and heavy with moisture on the coastal plain. The backdrop was of a central mountain chain, dark with dense forest like a giant moss-covered boulder. Was this how arriving in Hell felt? Fanciful, I know.

The dockside had the usual array of low taverns and brothels though none so far had rivalled the profligacy of Port Royal with both such establishments. I sighed, unable not to wish myself back in Jamaica with Susannah yet guilty for it too because, in truth, we had as much chance of finding Penny here as anywhere. All that was needed was one report of a fair-haired girl, which might then lead us to her.

I watched while Noah and Hal oversaw the unloading of the cargo in their usual efficient manner before Hal left with one of the merchants to secure a cargo for our four-day voyage on to Barbados, which seemed in many ways a better proposition because of the indentured servant market there. I shuddered at the implications of this, but they had to be faced. Noah beckoned to me, and I steeled myself to leave my patch of shade on deck to join him down on the wharf, in the fierce white sunshine. His hair was dark with sweat, his shirt clinging to him. 'Harbour master.' It was not a question. I knew we would do exactly as we had in Jamaica and Cuba. What else was there?

The man's office was cool and gloomy, with closed shutters beneath a wide porch roof, shading them. Water was fetched for us while we waited for the same logs to be brought out, listing ship arrivals, their cargos and passenger manifests. No children. We showed Penny's enamel miniature and Kitty's water colour portrait Susannah had done before we left, then watched

the usual blank faces full of regret. We stood. Elsewhere, regret would not be so forthcoming, but it
would again take us days to satisfy ourselves we had
missed nothing. Days before we could leave for Barbados. Weeks were passing and we still had nothing and
all the while I remained parted from my wife.

On our last night in Puerto de San Juan, I took out my
rosary and Mamma's letter from my pocket to read it
again, as I did every night, to prepare myself for sleep.
Noah still sat at the table writing in his ledgers, though
Hal already snored softly, stretched out on a thin mattress on the floor. I unfolded her letter, turning it towards the light from Noah's candle lantern. It had
waited for me at the harbour master's in Port Royal,
passed on from the governor's office where it had arrived just before we sailed. All had been explained as
soon as I saw the Richmond seal and found an en-
closed letter from my mamma.

Richmond House
Whitehall Palace
November 16, 1676

My dearest Raphael
   Your mother was anxious to write to reassure you
about your business interests at court and to pass on
some items of family news she has had from Florence.
I have sent my letter as part of diplomatic communi-

cations between the King's agents and the Lieutenant Governor's office. It will cross the channel and then travel overland to Lisbon where it will take ship to Jamaica at some point. I have little notion how long it will take but as it goes within the diplomatic pouch, I feel sure you will receive it eventually.

Now to you, my dear. I hope all goes well and you have made progress with your search? I even dare to hope you may have already found the poor child by the time you receive this.

I pray this might be so. I pray, too, for Susannah's continued good health and the safe delivery of your child.

Be assured of my fondest good wishes, always
Frances.

Post Scriptum. The King has found a replacement for Castlemaine in the person of Hortense Mancini, Duchess of Mazarin. He is already most attached and showing it in all his usual ways.

Now I opened Mamma's letter.

Cheapside, London
November 14, 1676

My darling Raffaello
Your duchessa—

'Not my duchessa, Mamma,' I murmured, as I did each time I read those words.

—has very kindly agreed to get a letter to you for me as it is, of course, too late to send one by ship from London because of the winter storms season.

I hope you are not worrying about the workshop and our business at court? I know you have much greater concerns to occupy you, yet perhaps it is worthwhile to tell you how things are going to, at least, set your mind at rest. The duchessa has taken me under her wing at court, introducing me to many of our patrons there. They have all been most complimentary about your work and seem more than open to what Giuseppe and I are producing now. The duchessa is already wearing some of my pieces. She truly is a good friend to us. (Yes, I do know what you were to each other before your marriage, but it seems to have been nothing but advantageous to our business, so I will say nothing further on the matter. It's not for me to judge you, anyway.)

Which leads me to something I must tell you of your father. He has brought Fulvia Ferranti to live in my house. She is there as his wife. Your sisters told me of it, and both have refused to see him while he lives in sin with her. Raffaello, I hope you will understand that I must now stay in your household, even after you return with your children ... for I know you will, my darling. Both of them. I hope you can forgive me for this, but I cannot live with your father again.

Both Sir Richard and Lord Carter call on me often and Lieutenant Monkton does his best to keep me up to date with the search for those behind the kidnapping and their motives. Was the poor child stolen for someone or was it misfortune? Signor Monkton remarked how Signor Bartholomew's tenacious help would have been of much value to their efforts–

I had told Noah of this and though he made light of it, I do believe he was gratified. I know he admires Tom so this reciprocation would mean a lot to him. We had speculated endlessly about the motives behind Penny's abduction. Neither of us believed for one moment it had not been planned with her as the target. The question still was why?

–but I know he will be doing the same for you now, and thank God for him ...

Noah interrupted my reading. 'I do wonder whether to lease another ship for him. This must be difficult. Working so closely with me again,' he said, quietly.

I looked up and saw his gaze fixed on his sleeping son, his eyes soft. 'Sam told Susannah he had taken over many of the voyages,' I whispered.

He rubbed his face. 'He was just starting to get some regular contracts in place for return cargos, too, but they've had to be abandoned just as those out of Port Royal have.'

'Can you resurrect them after we've found Penny?' I refused to doubt that as our outcome.

'We can certainly try. But no matter. This is what we must do until we have her.' He turned back to Hal. 'I'd hoped he might think I have a little still to teach him–'

Hal sat up, then, yawning and rubbing his eyes. 'Of course you do, Papa.' He grinned. 'We might get a touch rancorous with each other from time to time but I don't hold it against you ... well, not much anyway.'

Noah smiled, ruefully. 'Nor I you, Lad. And forgive me for waking you.'

Hal lay down again and turned onto his side. 'Not for long, believe me.'

This very quickly proved correct when he began to snore softly almost at once. Soon Noah had unrolled his own mattress beside him and fallen rapidly asleep, also. I lay there on the bunk in the starlight, holding my rosary, murmuring my decades, and longing for Susannah. Sleep would come when it came, and I would dream of her.

CHAPTER 21
Raphael
BARBADOS 1677

It was now February. With no involvement in the esoteric business of cargos or sailing the ship – plotting her course with longline and astrolabe – time passed remarkably slowly, leaving me too much at the mercy of my imagination resulting in an unpleasantly vivid dream on our first night at sea on the way to Barbados.

I had arrived back at the house with Penny beside me, overjoyed to be taking her to Susannah whom I somehow knew had already given birth to our son. I stood on the jetty and looked down to find Penny was no longer beside me, nor indeed was the pinnace tied-up there. I walked up to the silent house, making my way along the porch to our chamber, which was deserted and littered with debris blown in through the open casements. All the other rooms were the same. Even the stables were empty with vines already taking hold. Everywhere had the melancholy feel of long abandonment. I called out, my voice echoing in that terrible forsaken place and knowing I would never see Susannah again, began to weep. I woke to find my face wet with tears.

A sense of vague disquiet brought about by the dream, was amplified by the continuous presence of another ship – a three masted East Indiaman – just far enough away for us to be unable to ascertain what she was, though Noah was convinced she was a privateer. That she shadowed us for the entire voyage made it seem likely she was spying but for who we had no notion nor, indeed, why this should be so. But I could not help thinking it proved our trip to Barbados had raised a red flag for someone who knew of our business.

The sighting of a sail on the horizon had brought us brief excitement that first day and Noah had climbed the rigging himself to view her from the crow's nest with his spyglass. I had looked up at him, shading my eyes against the sun's glare, with absolutely no intention of joining him up there. And that is where the ship stayed until we arrived in Carlisle Bay and Bridgetown, when she dipped below the horizon and, to our knowledge, we did not see her again. Though we could not be entirely certain she did not come into the extensive docks herself later as, of course, she had never come close enough for us to identify her. There was certainly no shortage of privateers tied up there.

I had not expected the sheer size of the place. The

ranks of ships tied up at the great docks with endlessly strumming winches and forests of masts. For I had not realised how much sugar the island produced. It saw the largest trade of all the British colonies, Noah told me. The wharves looked every bit large enough to accommodate it all.

We walked along a dockside, almost rivalling Port Royal for its abundance of tavern and stews, though lacking something of the sinister, feral quality that so epitomised the Jamaican capital. Our first task was the customary visit to the harbour master, asking our questions and showing our portraits, with the usual result, unfortunately.

I found myself battling a feeling of hopelessness and its accompanying jaded acceptance of failure. I looked at the others, wondering if the same feelings lurked there behind their eyes. Yet I could not bring myself to ask for fear that I alone entertained such dismal thoughts. I who should be Penny's staunchest advocate in our search.

Next, at the harbour master's suggestion we paid a visit to the governor, Sir Jonathan Atkins, to see what we could learn of the Bridgetown indentured servant market. The single-storey stone-built house was shaded by a long wooden porch and a copse of Flamboyant trees in full scarlet bloom. We were shown in by a liveried footman and left to wait in a marble-tiled hall. 'Well, if he doesn't know of the market himself, he will surely know where to direct us to find out.'

Noah scrubbed at his face. 'I think we must attend

one of these abominations ourselves, anyway, so we can ask about Penny. I imagine the same people come there fairly regularly either on their own behalf or to buy European servants to sell on elsewhere.' He shrugged. 'Other islands.'

Hal stood. 'I'm going to start asking round in the taverns. I'll meet you at the King's Head down by our berth. Midday.' He strode away without looking back.

When Noah sighed, I wondered whether he too was finding it difficult to keep optimistic. Then I watched him straighten his back and square his shoulders, as though to keep going by sheer force of will. Well, if he could do it then so could I.

Inside the governor's gloomy wood-panelled office redolent with the scent of Flamboyant blossom wafting in through the slatted shutters, we sat in gold brocade-upholstered chairs, with generous glasses of claret in our hands. Sir Jonathan Atkins was a slight man with lustrous fair hair tied at the neck of his gold-lace embellished crimson uniform. He had pleasant, even features and a shrewd look in his dark blue eyes.

I handed him our portraits and bonafides before telling him Penny's story, in words I had honed and polished to their best essence like fine gems where each could now be no more nor less than it was. 'So, Sir, as you will understand, we feel it likely she was taken for a particular person but, if this is not the case, the market here would seem the next most obvious place to search for information.'

He steepled his fingers, leaning back in his chair

behind his desk. 'I see. I must say, I concur with both your conclusions. Yet, bearing in mind your wife's connections with the King, would your daughter have been chosen simply to fulfil a commission? I do wonder whether such connections might prove rather more relevant than they would at first appear to. Though, of course, if she were taken without any prior knowledge of who she was they would soon learn it from her. Perhaps, then, disposing of her more anonymously through the market might pose less risk of King's agents discovering her whereabouts?'

'Can you tell us how these markets work?' Noah asked.

'Well, naturally, the legal and illicit auctions are kept entirely separate.' He looked decidedly uncomfortable. 'Officially, the British Government is unaware of the illicit trade. Let's just say this stance comes from above. In truth, quite high above.'

'So, the illicit ones are for kidnap victims?' How convenient it was not acknowledged, leaving them with no obligation to attempt to close it down and access to lucrative bribes for not doing so, no doubt.

'Actually, not only them. Many women are sold through illegal channels. Jamaica and Barbados don't accept them at all. Puerto Rico and other Leeward Islands do, I believe. You'll need to see Sheldon Fanning who operates these proceedings.'

I glanced at Noah. 'If possible, we'd like to attend one.'

He shrugged. 'You must speak with Fanning.' He

sat back in his chair. 'There used to be a good supply of migrants out to the colonies, willingly selling themselves into indentured servitude with promises of land or coin after their five or seven-year term was served. This largely dried up once it became known how often such promises were reneged upon.' He lifted his glass but set it down again without drinking.

I recalled we had already had a similar conversation with the lieutenant governor's aide in Jamaica.

'For a time, indentured prisoners filled this gap, particularly when they were royalist prisoners of war Cromwell disposed of in this way. Some were quite high born and none, of course, criminals in the accepted sense. That's all changed in recent years, and many are more than a little unsavoury. Now the whites who managed to acquire their own smallholdings – which are gradually being bought-up by the large plantations – are becoming overseers or servants on these large estates and the fields are worked exclusively by African slaves.' He shook his head. 'Many plantation owners are becoming absentees now, though some still live at least part-time on the island. Not too good for society here, as you might imagine.'

'My heart bleeds for him,' Noah said, dryly, as we walked away.

We located Sheldon Fanning, as directed by Sir Jonathan, in rooms above the Royal Oak tavern tucked away in a shady square two rows back from the waterfront. Making our way to his office we saw a large room with something of the look of a theatre about it, with a raised dais at one end and steeply tiered semi-circle of seating. The auction room, I imagined. Two stout black women were in there moping the floor. I wondered if that meant another sale was imminent? Could we really be that lucky? I found it a little hard to believe, the way things had been going.

Fanning was tall and fleshy with thick greying hair. He wore a single hefty gold earring with a rather brash gold chain around his neck. His clothing was too fine for his dingy office, smelling of rum and to-bacco smoke ... and something else vaguely putrid. A man who liked to display his wealth upon his person, then, but cared little for his surroundings. I left Noah to introduce us. We had decided not to tell him about Penny, posing instead as buyers for indentured men, with the intention of trying for women and testing his response as a way to access the illicit auction.

'Well, gentlemen, you're in luck. We have an auc-tion tomorrow. A few slaves being sold-on and a newly arrived shipment of indentured prisoners.' He looked at us, avidly. 'What did you have in mind?'

I studied my fingernails. 'In truth, we need inden-tured women for indoor work. My wife finds negros in the house a little unnerving.' Not remotely true, need-less to say. I hoped Susannah would forgive me such a lie spoken in a good cause.

He frowned. 'All too common, Sir. But unfortunately, it is against the law to sell white women in Barbados. So, I'm afraid I can't help you.'

I matched his frown. 'Well, we must look elsewhere in that case, for my wife must be indulged with this. She's with child, you see.' I shrugged a *what can you do.*

Noah cleared his throat. 'I understand such women can be bought in Puerto Rico. Perhaps we must travel there then, but it's deuced inconvenient.'

We made as though to rise.

He held up a hand to halt us. 'A moment, Sirs. I should warn you women sold on the Leeward Islands can only go to men assigned to become their husbands. It's considered immoral for single women to live as such.'

'Well, there must be something to be done.' I looked up and held his gaze. 'Especially with money no object in the matter.'

He watched me in silence for a long moment. 'Ah, is that so. Perhaps, in that case, I might be able to assist.' He steepled his fingers. 'I can't stress enough that I tell you this in the strictest confidence.'

We both nodded, looking suitably eager.

Pray God, at last we might get somewhere. 'So, what can you do for me?'

He smiled, revealing several gold teeth. 'You're in luck. Not only have I acquired a selection of white indentured female prisoners, but I also have one or two specials. None criminals that is. They're extremely hard to come by, so not cheap as you can imagine.'

I sat forward. Not Penny, surely? 'How old might they be, these specials? My wife is also in need of a nursemaid and would like her young.'

'Oh, they're young all right ... but old enough if you know what I mean.'

Noah smiled and looked at me. 'Sounds promising, no?'

'It does, indeed. What must we do to view these women?'

'Come here at noon tomorrow. The auction of negros and prisoners will take place in the yard at the back and then we move to a private chamber up here for our other business.' He stood. 'I trust I shall see you there, gentlemen?'

'You will, Mr Fanning. Have no fear of that. Good day.' I bowed.

Noah followed suit and we left.

'Fuck me. I need a damned drink, Raphael. Let's find Hal.'

At the King's Head, he waited for us at a table towards the back, well away from the windows where it was cooler. We soon had a bottle of the local strong rum colloquially known as Kill-Divil. It was rough and powerful ... and exactly what was needed. I drank, watching Noah tell a frowning Hal about our meetings with Sir Jonathan and Fanning.

'The women are all supposed to be unmarried before they can be transported for indentured servitude, but I don't believe that's true. When you see some of the brutal punishments for often petty crimes reserved especially for women, it's hardly surprising they'd forsake a husband and children rather than hang or be burnt to death. The Leewards rule that each must be sold to a man who will take them as wife.'

Hal shook his head. 'Christ's wounds. So, the authorities think they protect their morals when men they're forced to marry are then free to rape them?'

'That's marriage for you, Lad.'

I snorted. 'Well, it certainly wasn't like that for me. If there was rape involved, I was more the victim of it.' Our laughter relieved the tension. 'And I'm sure indentured servitude is grim for everyone.'

Hal drained his glass. 'But not as grim as slavery, I'll wager.'

After a night onboard ship, we arrived at the Royal Oak in good time and with a plan in place. We would part company during the auction and try to engage those around it in conversation to find out whether they had attended another recently and, if so, who they had seen sold there. We were all taciturn when we stepped out into the yard behind the tavern. None of us had seen human beings sold before, nor had any wish to do so now. My belly roiled at the prospect. We spread out.

First to be brought out were a dozen or so negro men. Naked, shackled hand and foot with the two sets of manacles attached together by an additional chain. *Dio cane*, why could they not afford them the small dignity of clothing? I wanted to cover my nose as the yard filled with the rank odour of human fear and neglect. They had clearly all been through this ordeal before, knowing to face away from the buyers at the start. They were of all the different hues of skin colour I had noticed before, from deepest black to copper. Some had flogging scars on their backs, many with other signs of past injury. Most looked malnourished and resigned to their lot, their heads down. One or two were little more than gangling boys.

On a sharp command from the overseer, they turned around and held out their hands. Most were missing a finger or two. I closed my eyes for a moment. Cutting cane at the speed required of them would take its toll. When I opened them again, I felt bile rise in my throat. One of the two youths had been castrated. He had no genitals at all, just gruesome scars. Who would do such a grotesque thing? Holy Christ, he was the first to be sold and for the highest price. Why? Then I wondered what would become of those who were not wanted.

Negro women were brought out next, bare breasted with skimpy rags of skirts, wearing leg irons only. For some suckled infants and most held a child on their hip, often clutching another by the hand. Many of the children were light skinned suggesting white fathers. Most of the overseers making their purchases would no doubt use them at the first opportunity. I bit my lip hard, feeling my eyes prick with tears. Noah's face looked carved from granite. I could not see Hal at all. Had he left? All these women sold for high prices. Worthwhile it would seem to acquire future hands and the prospect of breeding more, of course.

The prisoners, when they shuffled out manacled in the same way as the male slaves, seemed only pathetic. Dressed in rags. Emaciated, with bearded narrow faces and hollow eyes. If starvation had an odour, it was immediately added to the already foul miasma. I wondered what use could be found for such as them and it seemed not much, for the few sold went for very little. Again, I wondered what would happen to those left behind. I turned to the man next to me, dressed in a leather jerkin with a bullwhip through his belt. He had purchased two of the women. 'What happens to those left over?'

'Arab traders take them for a pittance.' He spat. 'Most don't survive long.'

Finally, after waiting some time in the now deserted yard with a score or so of others, some of whom knew each other and conversed in whispers, the auctioneer from earlier appeared again to lead us upstairs. Hal had returned. None of us spoke. Once again, we spread out. Holy Mother, I wondered what horrors we were about to witness now.

First the female prisoners were brought out onto the dais one at a time. They were clothed plainly and not chained. The first women, neither old nor young stood looking straight ahead with the same look of resignation on her face I had already seen many times that day. She sold for a modest sum to a fat man who had examined her teeth before making his purchase, just as he would a horse, I imagined.

The next few were a little younger. Plain of face. Hair scraped into tight buns. Too thin. The last one, though, was pretty but only because she was so young. Her black curls were loose around her shoulders, and she had been given a green gown cut low enough to reveal too much of her breasts. Poor creature was shaking with terror. Fanning stood off to the side of the dais, looking pleased with himself. He had clearly saved her for last, and it appeared to have paid off. Several men moved down to study her more closely. I glanced at Noah when one seedy-looking fellow lowered her gown sufficiently to uncover her breasts completely. Her eyes were tightly closed. No one seemed to find this untoward, though Fanning intervened when he began to lift her skirts.

Hands off, Summerton. 'Pay for her first, if you please.'

And pay for her he did, substantially. He would ensure he got his money's worth, I felt certain. Poor girl.

Finally, the two 'specials.' The first looked little more than a child. Perhaps fourteen? She hardly seemed present, standing swaying with her head bowed, wisps of auburn hair hanging across her face. Was she drugged? It seemed more than likely. None of the men touched her but she fetched a good price.

Holy God. She had been stolen from someone who grieved for her and would never stop suffering her loss.

The second girl marched out, her eyes defiant, in a fine sapphire gown now somewhat despoiled by capture and imprisonment. Tall and slender with wavy brown hair hanging to her waist, she stood facing the viewers, hands on hips. 'I've been stolen from my father's ship. These criminals have no rights over me.' She gazed around the spectators. 'I am not for sale so no man here may buy me—'

Fanning slapped her face hard, so she staggered down to her knees, where she panted with shock. 'Oh, but they can my chick and trust me they will. I believe a better class of fellow might though if you still have teeth. But there's many a stew would take you without.'

Laughter rumbled around me while my heart pounded, and bile rose in my throat. Noah talked to the grinning man beside him. He had remembered our plan, whereas I found myself quite unable to speak. Once again, Hal had disappeared.

Fanning grabbed the girl's hair and dragged her back to her feet. Her face was awash with tears. 'Who thinks they're up to taming this pretty shrew?'

Needless to say, many did. She struggled still when they dragged her away until Fanning punched her in the belly. I do not believe I have ever felt such visceral hatred or truly wished to take someone's life before. God help me.

· · ·

We did not speak or look each other in the eye until we were able to sit around the table in the cabin, a bottle of brandy open before us. Glasses filled. Glasses drained and filled again.

I emptied mine a second time. 'I've seen evil today. I knew of its existence, of course, but this is the first time I've truly witnessed it for myself. Fanning. That castrated boy–'

Hal leaned forward. That's when I left. Who did it to him? His last owner? Why?'

Noah shook his head. 'Arabs did that. I've seen it before. It's done to boys so they can serve women in the haremlik. I imagine he sold so readily here for similar reasons. Perhaps working in a household amongst women. Posing no threat to them.'

I shook my head. 'Why could they not just geld him if that was their purpose. Though, heaven forbid, that's bad enough. God forgive us, it's done in my country to provide castrati voices for the church. Why maim him like that?'

'Christ knows, Lad, for I do not.' He banged his fist down onto the table, hard. 'So, what did we learn? Please God, something useful to give this hellish day some purpose other than to enlighten us to the full extent of human depravity?'

Hal shook his head. 'No one knew of children. Well, none younger than the first girl this afternoon. I asked the women sweeping Fanning's office. They see everyone sold there.'

Noah sighed. 'I had the same response.'

'So, Penny and Kitty were never there.' I crossed myself. 'Well, I thank God for it but–'

'We've learnt fuck all of any use.'

Hal nodded, angrily. 'Jesus Christ. I wish we'd never come here.'

Noah gazed at him, contrite, placing a hand on his arm. 'Forgive me. I shouldn't have taken you with us.'

'Don't be absurd, Papa. I'm not a child.'

Not a child. No. But probably the same age as that poor girl. That spirited girl who would be broken now. And we could do nothing for her.

Noah stood. 'I shall see Atkins about those two lasses. This is a British colony. It's his duty to do something about them and I shall see he does.'

I should accompany him I knew, but I simply could not. It felt weak and cowardly, but I could not. I was more than grateful when Hal rose to go. When the door closed behind them, I rested my head upon my arms on the table and wept. Impressive, no? And what about all those others. The prisoners and the slaves. No one could even hope to do anything for them.

Hispaniola 1677

So here we were now into March, making ready to leave the port of Santo Domingo on Hispaniola. That all these islands had such a look of each other was becoming disorientating. Central mountain chains and verdant forest down to turquoise sea. Harbours full of ships. Waterfronts full of warehouses, taverns, and brothels. Sailors. Slaves. Pirates. Whores. And, once again, we had nothing to show for our time in the place though, thank Christ, we were at last about to embark on our homeward journey to Jamaica. The thought of returning to Susannah almost overwhelmed me with longing, even though I had failed her.

I found Noah in the cabin, sitting at the table writing in his log. He looked up when I closed the door behind me, indicating I was alone.

After giving me a dirty look, he sighed. 'Where is he? He knows full well I want to get underway as soon as possible now the cargo's finally all on.'

I nodded somewhat ruefully, sitting down at the table. 'He does.' I couldn't help smiling. 'He promises he won't be too long.'

Noah made a disparaging noise through his teeth. 'The same one, I presume?'

'He wanted to say farewell properly was how he phrased it.'

He shook his head, his disgust even more apparent. 'Well, I must be grateful she's not a whore and just hope he doesn't leave a bastard behind.'

I knew we both thought of Penny. 'Bastards can be wanted and very much loved.' God knows I would have loved mine. I lay on the bunk, hoping we could soon get underway, fizzing with impatience, yet I believe I dozed for a while.

Finally, Hal's head appeared around the door. 'I'll see to the cast-off.'

'About bloody time,' Noah called, following him out. 'Let's get this fucking ship under way, then.'

And so, I began to count the days until home. I had no idea what our plans were now. We had not discussed it. We had not discussed anything since Barbados. We had gone through the motions in Santo Domingo. Harbour master. Taverns. All of it. Diligently. I had already decided I would not sail again, though had said nothing to Noah. Our child would soon be born, and I would not leave Susannah again. I sighed. We had promised each other never to be parted when we married but had now spent more time away from each than we had together. Yet what choice had there been for either of us?

CHAPTER 22
Susannah
JAMAICA 1677

I sat on a blanket in shade cast by a flame tree with branches arching over the sand, watching Sam's head bobbing above the water as he swam out, strongly. The detritus of our luncheon lay spread around me, and I finally stirred myself to pack it away into the basket. Two wine bottles lay empty. Sam had consumed most of it, which probably explained his lack of inhibition, stripping-off and plunging into the sea. I envied him the chance to cool down. I watched him turn and begin to swim back towards the shore. God, I longed for Raphael to return and how I prayed he might have Penny with him when he did.

When Sam waved and called out to me, I struggled to my feet for I could not hear his words. Standing at the waterline with wavelets ruffling over my bare feet, I waved back. 'Are you all right?'

He grinned. 'Just find myself in need of breeches.'

I laughed. 'Didn't seem to worry when you went in.'

'I fear I was a touch inebriated. The water has sobered me somewhat.' He frowned, standing in water that came to his waist. 'So, I'd be most grateful if you would hand me my breeches, Susannah.'

I fished in my pocket and pulled out a small handkerchief. 'This do you?'

He barked a laugh. 'I think, perhaps it's a touch insulting.'

'I've seen a naked man many times. Just come out and let the air dry you off.' I turned and began walking back. I heard the wild splash as he complied, dashing past me and onto the blanket to cover himself with his shirt. He looked not a little shamefaced. 'Don't be embarrassed, Sam. I'm not.' I replaced the handkerchief in my pocket and pulling out the letter, held it out to him. 'This came for Raphael.'

He took it. 'Francis Stuart. Are you going to open it?'

'That's what I've been pondering. You open it.'

He broke the seal and handed it back. 'I think you must read it first, though.'

So, I did.

Richmond House
Whitehall Palace
December 28, 1676

My dearest Raphael

I shall send this once more in the diplomatic pouch and trust the governor's office will forward it to you. As before, I have no idea when it will reach you but have some confidence that it shall. Firstly, thank God, I can tell you everyone is well. Your mother asks me to send her love and let you know the studio has worked at full capacity over the festive period. I assume this to be a good thing.

Please tell Susannah, her father also sends his love. He is, of course, anxious for news of Penelope – as are we all – and for word of his new grandchild. They all await letters eagerly as soon as there are ships to bring them. Sam's papa is well and sends his love. He tells me how glad he is to know Sam and Susannah have had time together again.

Well, now to court news. And first to a rather wonderful scandal. The King's affair with Hortense Mancini came to an abrupt end when he discovered she was dallying elsewhere. Not usually so much of a problem, of course. This time, however, all that changed because of whom she dallied with. Mancini was having a full-blown Sapphic liaison with his own daughter, the Countess of Sussex. Later he was reconciled with the girl, blaming her behaviour on her mother's influence. I rather feel Castlemaine would be somewhat affronted by that. I do believe men take a kinder view – or is it more a prurient interest – in such encounters between women. Needless to say, no one has yet thought to seek Anne's husband's opinion on the matter.

The other seasonal distraction was rather different, if no less entertaining. The King and Prince Rupert staged a particularly fine pageant at Windsor where the siege of Maastricht was recreated in its entirety, enabling Monmouth to show-off all his cunning, skill and courage in tunnelling in to raze it. I have to say it was thrilling but I cannot help but wonder at the cost. Charles and his son had a fine time of it, of course. A risk in December but the weather was kind. A lovely crisp clear day. And it made a change from hunting.

Do get word out when you can, dearest Raphael. There are many of us waiting on it.

Your loving friend, always
 Frances

Post Scriptum. One last oddity. Louise was seen leaving York's privy chamber. There was, of course, much speculation about another of the King's mistresses betraying him rather too close to home. Yet I do not see Portsmouth being quite so foolish. That is something Charles could not forgive, I think. I wonder what it means though? Something tells me it must be significant but how I have, as yet, not the least notion.

I rolled my eyes not sorry to be absent from court, in truth, more wondering how I could ever steel myself to return there. 'Read it.' I handed it across to him. He snorted a few times looking contemptuous and I thought he probably felt much the same.

He looked up, passing it back. 'Christ. I don't know what to say. Sitting here looking out at this.' He gestured towards the sparkling sea. 'Whitehall seems a fetid place. Mancini must be thoroughly without scruples. Anne Lennard is hardly more than a child. Dacre is an empty-headed buffoon, not fit to be her husband.' He sighed. 'I'm glad the King has forgiven her.'

'He wanted to marry Hortense once, didn't he?'

Sam nodded. 'When he was at the French court. Cardinal Mazarin wouldn't see his niece married to an exiled king. Louis wanted her too, until her uncle overstepped himself and fell from favour.'

'Didn't she marry someone awful in the end?'

He shrugged. 'I do believe he treated her fairly unpleasantly.'

I folded the letter and replaced it in my pocket. 'So, she's written to him before.'

He smiled. 'I'm sure it was perfectly innocent. Just as this one is.' He reached for my hand. 'Come now, Sukie. You can't doubt him, surely?'

I smiled. 'Of course not. I just wondered why he's never shown it to me.'

'Well, you can ask him when he returns which should be any day now, I hope. They seem to have been gone a ridiculously long time. Now, if you would walk away somewhere, I'll dress so we can get back to the house.'

I raised my eyebrows. 'Just get on with it. I won't look.'

He gave me a hard stare. 'Very well.' He stood, holding his shirt, and making no attempt to cover himself. 'I do believe you are looking, Susannah.' He held my gaze. 'Seen all you want?'

I tilted my head, studying him and smiling. 'It's strange to think I've never seen you naked when we've made a child together.'

He looked away before pulling on his shirt and bending to step into his breeches.

When he offered me his hand, I stood placing my palm on his face. 'Forgive me, I shouldn't have said that.'

He pulled me into his arms. 'There's nothing to forgive. You'll never need to ask my forgiveness for anything.'

He collected up the rug and basket and we walked back holding hands.

Still discussing the court's dissolute absurdities, we mounted the steps to the porch where Sam placed our lunch basket onto the table. It was then the man stood up, startling us. Neither of us had been aware of him after the glare of the beach. I quickly realised how very young he was when he moved out of deep shadow. He had shed his coat and waistcoat though still wore his cravat with his red hair neatly tied at his neck.

Sam stepped by me to seize his hands. 'Michael?

What in God's name are you doing here?' He made as though to hug him, but the young man's expression checked him. 'Forgive me. You've no idea who I am, of course.' He grinned. 'But I feel I know virtually all there is to know about you since the day you were born.' He turned. 'This is Noah's son, Michael.' Then he gestured towards me. 'And this is Susannah. Susannah Rossi.

Michael smiled a smile I recognised both from his father and brother, though there was little else to see of them in either his stature or his countenance. His large eyes were a rather startling pale blue-grey with a dark outline around the iris and they were quite beautiful. He kissed my hand. 'Mistress Rossi.' He looked again at Sam. 'My apologies, Sir. You still have me at something of a disadvantage.'

'Of course. Forgive me. I'm Sam Car–Bartholomew as I'm known here.'

I recognised Sam's discomfort. 'Sam is living as Noah's half-brother for the moment. He had something of a brush with English justice last year, which meant he had to leave the country with some haste.'

Michael's face became quite red, and he looked down at his feet. 'My mother has told me Papa came here to start a new life with another woman.' He looked up at me. 'Am I correct in assuming you are she, Mistress Rossi?' His eyes dropped to my rather prominent belly.

Whatever I had expected him to say it had not been that. I reached out to touch his arm. 'No. No, not at all. My husband is away on the Mirabel with your father and brother.'

His colour intensified alarmingly. 'Do please forgive me–'

I smiled, reassuringly. 'An easy mistake. Pray don't let it concern you.' This wasn't going to be easy to explain. I looked at Sam, who shrugged.

Michael cleared his throat. 'I've already been told both my father and brother are away. Might you know when they are expected to return?'

Sam stuck his head through the door to the house, calling for wine to be brought out. 'Soon we hope. They've been away for some time. I think we'd better explain.' He pointed to the sofa where Michael had been sitting earlier. 'Please.'

Pearl arrived on the porch with a jug and glasses. She picked up the basket, frowning at the two empty wine bottles. 'Noah axe me see you no drink too much, Sam.'

He laughed. 'What a shame he's not here then, so I could tell him to mind his own business.' He poured wine for us all.

I sat opposite Michael on another shady sofa. Sam sat beside me. 'I suppose we must tell him what they're doing?' I shook my head, suddenly fearing I would weep. 'Perhaps you would?'

He nodded and drained his glass. 'Of course.' So that is what he did.

I squeezed his hand when he had finished. 'I think

Michael also needs to know she is your daughter, Sam, and not Raphael's.'

Michael chewed his lip as colour swamped his face, again. 'I see.'

Sam sighed. 'But you're wondering why he's doing this ... sailing all over the Caribbean searching for her. It is for Susannah and Raphael too, of course it is. But mostly it's for me. To get her back for me.'

'For you? I don't understand.'

Sam stood. 'I think you must ask your father to explain–'

I gestured for him to sit down again. 'No. You can't leave it like this when we have no real idea when they'll return. You must try to explain.'

'Saying what? When Noah hasn't prepared him for it at all.'

'Yet he told Hal, didn't he–'

Michael now looked extremely wary. 'Told Hal what?'

Sam drew a long breath. 'That we love each other. Your papa and I love each other.'

Now it was Michael's turn to stand. 'Love each other? I don't understand,' he said again.

Poor boy. He appeared completely bewildered.

Sam closed his eyes. 'We live together here ... as a couple–'

'Holy God. Hal knows this yet he remains here with you?'

I squeezed Sam's hand hard, seeing his distress.

'Michael, I know this is hard for you to make sense of–'

'Hard for me to make sense of? That my father lives a life that goes against God? No. That's impossible for me to make sense of.' He shook his head. 'I must return to Port Royal.'

Then, I fear, my temper quite deserted me. 'You'll do no such thing. You'll remain here until your papa returns when you'll explain yourself to him. I don't believe you can truly be such a coward with a man like Noah Bartholomew as your father. I refuse to believe it, for he is one of the bravest men I know.'

He bowed. 'Madam. Your housekeeper has already shown me to my chamber. Please excuse me.' He walked away into the house.

'Don't be too hard on him. Noah said it took Hal a few days to come around.' He took a long breath. 'Though Hal's not very religious. I have a feeling that will make rather a difference this time. I believe Michael is shortly to go to Oxford to read Theology with a view to becoming a minister.'

I squeezed Sam's hand. 'Ah. Well, I can certainly see how that might be difficult to reconcile. Let's hope Noah can resolve it.'

CHAPTER 23
Raphael

Susannah waited for me at the porch rail with Sam at her side, as always. With eyes wildly scanning for Penny, they quickly knew the outcome of our voyage, and I felt again the weight of their dashed hopes. I mounted the steps and grasped her into my arms, running my hand over the great swell of her belly. Her body had changed so much in the weeks I had been away, and it saddened me I had not been with her to witness it. To watch our child grow. 'Forgive us another failure.'

Her eyes brimmed. 'I'm just grateful to all of you for keeping going the way you have.' She glanced at Noah and Hal.

How are you, *cara mia*?' I kissed her. 'Christ, I've missed you so much.'

'And I you, my love.' She wrinkled her nose. 'You need to bathe, though.'

I grinned. 'I do. We all do. Pearl will have water brought.'

I caught a movement out of the corner of my eye then, when a figure stepped forward from the shadows close to the house, his red hair glinting in the sunshine. Michael Bartholomew? It had to be. How had he found a ship?

'Good day, Papa. Hal.'

Noah gasped a breath before pulling him roughly into his arms. 'What the fucking Christ are you doing here?'

Hal shook his head. 'He said that to me, too. Not very welcoming, is it?'

Michael broke away from his father to grasp Hal. 'No, it's certainly not.' He stepped back. 'And yes, you definitely both need to bathe.' And then he was back in his father's arms.

'We must talk, Michael.'

'Get cleaned-up first, Papa. It can wait.'

Hal grinned. 'Come and scrub my back, little brother. Make yourself useful.'

Michael punched his arm and set off after him towards the front of the house. 'Never going to happen. Believe me.'

We walked away along the porch hand-in-hand to the sound of their laughter, and it felt wonderful to step inside our chamber, dim behind closed shutters. 'How long has he been here?'

'Several days.' She looked away. 'Sam told him

about them. He found it difficult. He's kept away from Sam. I hope Noah can do something.'

'He'll come around. Hal did.'

'That's just what Sam said. He also said when religion is a factor, as it is with him, it might not prove so straightforward.'

'Well, I believe Our Lord instructed us to love one and other. I don't think you can go far wrong with that, even when the pope talks of sin.' I grasped her hands and kissed them. 'Christ, I've hated being parted for so long, especially for absolutely nothing. *Merda. Fanculo–*' I had intended to continue my expletives further, but the servants arrived then with my tub and water. We waited in silence until they had filled it and the door closed behind them.

Susannah sat on the bed and watched me shed my clothing, dropping it to the floor until I stood before her naked. 'I never want to see another island or stinking docks or a filthy tavern or foul brothel.'

'So, you won't go again?'

I shook my head. 'I'll tell Noah I need to be with you now.' I saw such despair on her face. I sat beside her and held her close. 'Noah isn't giving up. There are many more islands, and he intends to search each and every one of them. He's a very determined man. Obstinate even.'

'Well, thank God for it.'

I climbed into the hot water then with some relief, sighing contentedly as I reached for the soap.

She lowered herself to her knees beside me to take

it from my fingers. 'Let me help you, Raphael. I need to touch you. I want to do this for you. I know I look a little ungainly.'

I sat up, leaning across to kiss her. 'You look entirely beautiful, *cara*.' I moved back then and abandoned myself to the feel of her hands upon me.

When she was satisfied my odour was acceptable again, she smiled, ruefully. 'Now, my love, I must ask your assistance to regain my feet.'

I quickly jumped out and did as she asked, easing her down onto the bed again before towelling myself dry and tossing it onto the heap of my soiled clothing. 'Now, *cara*, I want to look at you.' I pulled her to her feet and unpinned her hair, burying my face in it, already aroused as I began to undress her, pausing only to kiss her.

She ran one hand down my back, her other found my cock. 'Jesu, Raphael. I want you so intensely. Surely it must be improper to feel such a thing now?'

I pulled her shift up over her head and stood back to gaze at her. She closed her eyes. 'Holy Christ, *amore mio*.' She took my breath away. My wife, heavy with my child. I felt I would weep with love for her ... for them both.

She chewed her lip. 'I know I look like a great whale–'

'No, Susannah, you look entirely beautiful.' I moved to her taking the weight of her breasts in my hands, before moving them down over the dome of her belly. 'My child. I can scarce believe it.'

She placed a hand over mine. 'Oh, he's there all right, writhing and kicking day and night.' She looked down. 'You had hiccups this morning, didn't you, my poor little love?' She saw the wonder on my face. 'You'll feel it all if you have your hand there when he's awake.'

I led her to the bed. 'Lie down, *cara*.' I lay beside her, moving close to cup her face while I kissed her. 'Roll onto your side facing away from me.' She did as I asked and I moved behind her, kissing her neck and caressing her breasts. I smiled as she moaned when I slipped inside her. 'Tell me if I hurt you, *amore mio*.'

She sighed. 'Jesu, no. It's just wonderful to feel you again.'

She lay on her back with my hand resting lightly on her thigh, then gasped smiling as she moved it up onto her belly. 'He's awake. Perhaps he felt your small intrusion into his space?'

I traced the distinct outline of a tiny foot with my finger. 'Holy Christ. My son.'

'Well, possibly a daughter but I think a son.'

I watched the movements, utterly enchanted by it. 'Our child, Susannah. Boy or girl, I don't care. As long as you're both safe.'

'That's of some importance to me, too.' She took a long breath. 'I'll be glad to get it over now. Just a few more weeks, I think.'

I moved up onto my elbow to look down at her. I

prayed she couldn't read the fear on my face. Yet she would know I felt it and why I did, of course. 'Are you very afraid, *cara mia*?'

She chewed her lip. 'Yes, and so are you.' She sighed. 'It won't make any difference, though. When it starts it can't be stopped, not until I get the child out. In a way it's a comfort to know it will finish then. The pain, that is. To know there is an end to it.'

I pulled her into my arms, barely able to contemplate the idea of her suffering. 'Does knowing what it will be like make you more afraid or less, do you think?' Her laughter surprised me.

'Both. But like I said, it won't make any difference.'

I closed my eyes. Fearful to ask the question. Fearful of her answer. 'Would you like me with you?'

She looked startled. 'Well, in truth, yes, I would ... and I'm very impressed you've offered.' She studied me. 'Why, though, when it's not expected of a man?'

'Well, your papa was there when you were born. And if you can go through it, I can damn well have the guts to stay with you while you do. Also, might it not be better to know what's happening rather than imagine it which is, of course, what I would do?'

She ran her hand down my back. 'For you, I think it would be. Now, my love, perhaps you'll help me dress. We should join the others.'

CHAPTER 24

Hal

Soaking in the tub, Hal regaled Michael with tales of their trip around the islands, describing with enthusiasm all the conquests he had made along the way. And he found it helped subdue those other darker memories he had no wish to dwell upon. 'They like our colouring here. Your hair will prove a particular fascination I'm certain.'

Michael frowned, giving his brother a dirty look. 'Are you truly happy living here ... with them?'

'With Papa and Sam? Of course I am. Papa tries to interfere too much in my life but that's just him. He means well, I know ... well, mostly he does. And Sam tries to keep him reasonable in as far as he can.'

Michael looked away. 'How can you stand seeing them together?'

Hal sighed. 'Papa's happy. Please don't tell me you

grudge him that? I like Sam and I'm glad he makes him so. Can't you be, too?'

'But it's sinful. The Bible tells us sodomy is an abomination.'

'The bible tells us lots of things. Pass me that jug so I can wash my hair. 'Fornication is also an abomination, I believe.' He poured water over his head. 'Which it most certainly is not in my opinion. Far from it, in fact.' They were silent for a while until Hal stood up and Michael handed him a towel. 'You should talk to Raphael ... who more than likely is indulging in such pleasures of the flesh as we speak–'

'Holy God. With his wife in that state, poor lady.'

Hal laughed, quickly pulling on a clean shirt and breeches. 'You really know nothing of men and women, do you? And I meant you should talk to him about faith. He's a Catholic. I believe Susannah has more confidence in his God than in ours.'

'A Catholic?' He shook his head. 'There can be nothing to learn there.'

'Well, I see we must open your mind, Brother, not to mention part you from your virginity as quickly as possible. How long will you stay?'

'Not long.' He sat on Hals' bed and closed his eyes.

Hal frowned, realising all was not as it seemed. He sat beside him. 'Do you want to tell me about it?' What in God's name could have made him come all this way?

Michael stared intently. 'I've lost my faith, Hal.'

'But you've just been citing the bible at me.'

'Habit. I don't believe a damn word of it anymore.'

Hal laughed, finding it hard to credit. He must be exaggerating, surely? 'What? Not even the good bits? The love and forgiveness.'

'Especially not those.' Tears brimmed and he swiped them away, angrily. 'There is no love or forgiveness.'

Hal found himself extremely worried. What in hell could have brought him to this? He squeezed his shoulder. 'Something's happened to you. Tell me.'

Michael took a long slow breath, seeming to pull himself together. 'No. I don't need to do that, but I can tell you what my plans are now. What I intend to do with my life. That's why I came here. I wanted to tell Papa myself.'

'Not a minister, then?'

'Christ no. A physician. I'm going to read medicine at Caius. But first I'll do a year at Leiden to learn anatomy and dissection.'

Hal watched with relief as his anguish seemed to fall away when he talked of it. He still wanted to do good in the world for he would not be Michael if he did not, of course.

'Well, that sounds a magnificent plan. I'm very proud of you, Michael, and Papa will be too, I know. Now, let's go out and join the others.' He would try to get an opportunity to tell their father what he suspected. Perhaps he could induce him to talk of it for he surely must.

CHAPTER 25
Noah

They sat side-by-side on the bed, Noah stripped down to his breeches, a small heap of malodorous clothing on the floor at his feet. 'Is he reconciled to it at all, do you think?'

'He's very polite when we do see him, which is mostly at mealtimes. He speaks when spoke to. Otherwise, he's in his room or out riding in the hills with one of the stable lads.'

'Christ. Well, I'll have to talk to him. It won't solve itself, clearly.'

'Talking to Hal will help, I'm sure.'

'Not certain Hal's my biggest supporter at the moment.'

Sam laughed. 'And he thinks you find him falling short all the time when, in truth, you both think the sun shines out of each other's arses.'

It was Noah's turn to laugh, and he leaned in to

kiss Sam on the forehead.

'Perhaps you need to talk to him, too?'

'Perhaps I do.'

After the water was poured, Sam lay stretched out on the bed, his arms folded behind his head, while Noah finished his ablutions. 'Was it as grim as your expression suggests?'

Noah sighed. 'In terms of trade, it was reasonable, I suppose. I'd already realised how good Hal is at finding cargos.' He frowned, remembering. 'So, I left it to him while I asked around about your girl. Now that was grim. All those endless blank faces, some caring, many not but all knowing absolutely bugger all. Again. And the people-auction in Barbados was a circle of hell. I saw things there I wish could be unseen.'

Sam swung his legs off the bed and sat facing him. 'God, Noah. You must feel like you're trapped in some hideous Sisyphean task straight out of hell.'

'There's a possibility I might feel such a thing, had I a single fucking clue what it was?'

Sam laughed and stood, bending to kiss his lips. 'Forgive me. It's from Greek mythology. Sisyphus was punished in Hades for his wrongdoing by being condemned to roll a heavy stone up a hill, which rolled down again every time it neared the top. He had to repeat it for all eternity. So, laborious and futile.'

Noah grinned. 'Endless, indeed. For, I refuse to stop until I've been to every bloody island. Then I shall begin again until we find her.'

Sam fetched a towel and handed to him when he

climbed out of the begrimed water. 'I wish I could tell you to do differently, but I can't.'

Noah hugged him. 'I know you can't. She's your child.' He put his hands onto Sam's shoulders. 'Now, assuming I've passed your exacting standards of cleanliness, perhaps you'd care to show some pleasure in my return?'

Sam tilted his head, smiling. 'I believe I might be persuaded.

The towel dropped to the floor.

In his studio, Sam sat on the sofa while Noah riffled through the work he'd done while he was away. He looked without speaking for a while, overawed by the skill of it all. How, in the name of Christ was he able to do it? There were many of Susannah, of course. One large painting of her in a diaphanous blue gown, the swell of her child plain to see, her bright hair cloaked around her. He lifted it, taking it to the light. He shook his head. 'You should show this to Raphael.'

'I plan to give it to him.' He stood. 'There's one of him I did from a drawing Susannah particularly liked. He pulled it out from another stack leaning against the wall, handing it to Noah.'

He took it from him. 'Holy God. What will he make of it?'

'Susannah thought I'd captured what draws people to him. Women, she said.'

'I'd say he's rather drawn you too, hasn't he, Laddie?'

Sam laughed and shrugged. 'I can't say I'm not fond of him. He's been good for Susannah.'

Noah snorted. 'Come. Let's take these outside for him.' He picked up Susannah's portrait, too.

Sam followed him.

Out on the porch, they lounged on a sofa in companionable silence for a while until Hal came out to join them, a silent Michael beside him. Hal was barefoot, dressed in a light shirt and breeches, his damp hair loose around his shoulders, just as they were. 'God, it's good to feel clean again. Seawater is all very well but after a while it leaves you feeling crusted with salt.'

'Is that why sailors are called old salts?' Sam murmured, his eyes closed, head resting back.

'Fucked if I know, Lad.

Hal flung himself down on to a battered couch, gesturing for his brother to sit beside him. 'Didn't know they were.'

Noah snorted. 'Doesn't surprise me.'

Sam laughed. 'Well, you didn't know what a Sisyphean task was, Noah.'

Now it was Hal's turn to laugh. 'And that definitely doesn't surprise me.'

Noah gave them both dirty looks, which unfortunately made them laugh again. He closed his eyes for a moment, immensely pleased to be home. Yet seeing

Michael staring out at the sea, unengaged with the rest of them, filled him with disquiet.

Hal caught his eye. 'Talk to him,' he mouthed.

Noah nodded.

Susannah and Raphael walked out onto the porch then, hand in hand.

Sam leaned forward. 'I believe Noah has decided Raphael should have gifts.' He pointed at the canvases leaning against the wall.

Susannah smiled as she sat down. 'Give him his first.'

Sam fetched the painting and handed it to him.

Noah watched them both look at him, their expressions remarkably similar. Waiting for his reaction.

Raphael closed his eyes for a moment, before clearing his throat. 'Well, it's extraordinarily flattering.' He shook his head, smiling, his hair sweeping his shoulders. 'What can I say? *Grazie mille*. You're a very fine artist.'

'You most certainly are, Sam. And, my dearest Raphael, there's nothing flattering about it. It's you.'

Noah thought he looked truly uncomfortable. Did he really wonder if this was some sort of mockery?

Sam bent to squeeze his shoulder. 'Believe me it's nothing more than a good likeness.'

Susannah kissed Raphael's cheek. 'Perhaps you might be more comfortable with the other one.'

Again, Sam retrieved it. 'Hope you approve.'

Raphael's eyes widened. '*Santo Dio. È meraviglioso, amore mio*. You're simply beautiful.'

'Sam wishes us to have them both.' She turned to him. 'Perhaps you might paint Penny when we have her back.' There was heavy emphasis on when. 'Then we can hang them all together at home.'

Raphael pulled her into his arms. 'Indeed, we can, *cara.*'

CHAPTER 26

Raphael

The next morning the letter arrived. I was astonished to find Barnabus Rifkind had written to me. It was a brief request to see me alone, with no indication of the reason for it. I handed it to Susannah, who had just finished dressing.

She sat on the bed, looking up when she had read it. 'What can he want? Has he some news of Penny? Please God he has.'

I crossed myself. 'Why does he wish to see me alone, though? He's very insistent.'

Her concern was now plain. 'Will you go? Is it safe to?'

'I think I must. How else will I find out what he wants?'

Outside on the Porch, joining Noah and Sam at breakfast they, too, showed some disquiet.

Noah looked pensive. 'Going alone feels risky, to

me. Especially when you know nothing of what he wants from you.'

Sam tilted his head, frowning. 'We already know he's a disreputable character. Isn't it foolhardy to trust him?'

'I must, though. I've no choice when it may be about Penny.'

Sam frowned, still. 'But why would he have to pass whatever this is on to you alone? It makes no sense.'

I shrugged. 'Yet, I have to go.'

In the end it was agreed that I would.

I set out after breakfast. Susannah came with us to the stables where a groom had saddled two horses, for Noah wished to accompany me as far as the Cinnamon Hill cane fields. We rode up through the jungle, appreciating the dappled shade, though my thoughts were too occupied with the coming meeting to take in much of my surroundings. And I could tell how troubled Noah was by his posture while I followed him along the trail. I moved to ride beside him as soon as the track widened out sufficiently.

'Why you?' he said. 'He hasn't met any of us. So, what does he know of you to make him summon you? And why alone?'

I shrugged. 'Well, I imagine I'll find out when I meet him.'

He stared at me for a few moments. 'His wife was

rather taken with you I seem to remember. Perhaps she has something to do with it?'

I snorted. 'Seems unlikely if it's about Penny. And what else could it be?'

'Well, if she told him of our visit and he wanted to speak to one of us, I'm sure she would have suggested you, Raphael.'

We halted when we arrived at the edge of the first field. 'Turn back here.' I sighed. 'Looks damnably hot out there.'

He looked up at the sky. 'It's around noon, so we haven't timed it too well.'

I sighed, again. 'Well, the sooner I go the sooner I can return. I Just hope it proves worthwhile.'

'Should it not be, I shall be very tempted to go there myself and run the whoreson through.'

I laughed. 'Why not?' I touched my horse with my heels to encourage her forward out into the heat, the air thick with smells of hot sugarcane and dust. And with a small wave, I started off towards Cinnamon Hill, praying I would find news of Penny there.

The house was a hive of activity when I arrived this time, looking very different to my previous visit. It would seem, then, that my surmise about how the household viewed Isabella Rifkind's importance was proved correct. Yet surely, she must complain to her husband of it? Perhaps he did not care?'

I was shown into the same large airy drawing room

as last time and asked to wait. After a rather impolite amount time, the door opened, and Rifkind walked in. He was uncannily similar to how I had imagined him. Of medium height and heavily built, his florid face could only be described as pugnacious. He looked like a vicious fist-fighter, who relished his ability to win by whatever means. I stood. We bowed to each other. His expression seemed wary with a suggestion of something suppressed. Glee? I found myself disliking him with a fierce intensity. I smiled.

'Sit, Rossi.' He pointed at the sofa I had just risen from, rubbing his hands together, vigorously. 'I have a proposition for you. If you agree to what I'm sure you won't find a burdensome task, I shall be in a position to assist you with the matter of your wife's daughter.' His voice was something of a surprise. Soft and sibilant, with an accent I couldn't place. Perhaps a local one? Though his tone had a dangerous quality to it. That sense of something supressed, again.

His smile more resembled a snarl. *Cristo*. 'What can you possibly require from me, Sir? And I fail to understand why you should expect something from me in return for offering help to find *my* daughter.' I put heavy emphasis on 'my'.

That sinister smile again. 'Well, I'm afraid that's not how I do business.'

My eyes widened. 'Business. Holy God. This isn't business. My daughter was kidnapped!'

'And I know where she is.' He studied his fingernails. 'So, there we are.'

My heart swooped. *He knows where she is?* Thank Christ. I crossed myself. 'Then, Sir, it is your moral duty to tell me at once.'

He grinned, unpleasantly. 'Oh, I shall, believe me. But first a small task.'

I sighed. *Gesù Santo.* 'Very well. What do you wish of me?'

He watched me intently. 'I require you to relieve my wife of her maidenhead.'

Whatever I had expected it had not been that. How in the name of God could it have been? I found myself quite speechless while I watched him enjoying my astonishment, his eyes hard and glittering. 'How dare you suggest such a thing. Have you lost your mind?' He laughed. Dear God. I heard his glee exposed starkly, then.

'As I told you. This is business. I'll sell the girl's whereabouts to you, and this is my price.' He tilted his head one way and then the other, studying me. 'From what I know of your reputation at the English court, Rossi, you're a serial womaniser. So, I find your reaction ... well, unexpected.'

'I left that life behind when I married. I love my wife. Christ, man, I made vows to her before God, and you expect me to break them? Why? Why would you do such a repugnant thing? Both to me and to your own wife.' And then I felt a horrible conviction he had always viewed his wife's innocence as a commodity. He had saved it to trade.

'You needn't take long over it, but you will do it,

believe me.'

My heart sank then, for I knew it to be true. What choice did I have? 'Have you told her?'

He touched his wig, limp in the heat. 'I have, Sir. She awaits your pleasure now, in her chamber.' He gestured to the door. 'I'll show you up myself.'

My thoughts reeled. I still could not understand why he had chosen me for this. He must know of my marriage, as he knew of so much else. There was much here I could not comprehend. One thing I knew for certain, however, this man was a damnable brute. I followed him from the room and up the wide sweep of the staircase to the galleried landing. He opened a door, gesturing for me to enter. The first thing that struck me was the whiteness of it, like walking into a cloud. Even the flowers were white. And the sky outside the window. It was like a stage set for a sacrifice. Blood must be spilled here. Even in the heat I felt chilled.

She was already in bed her face as white as the pillow behind her, her hair falling in a mass of dark curls. She looked like a terrified child. I closed my eyes. How in the name of Christ could I do this awful thing? I turned to Rifkind. 'Why are you doing this?'

He grinned. 'I do it because I can. And don't get any ideas of cheating me. I shall know it's been done. Isabella will suffer for it, if not. And your wife shall never see her daughter again.' With that he left us alone.'

I took a long breath and turned to her. She was

weeping, silently. What could I say? My heart filled with pity for her. 'I wish this wasn't happening. I'm so sorry he's done such a thing to you.'

She shook her head. 'Forgive me. It's all my fault. Mustafa watched us together when you visited with your friends. He saw I liked you.' She covered her face with her hands. 'I should have known he would watch. He spies on me for Barnabus.' She said her husband's name with a great deal of animus.

I moved to the bed to sit beside her, gently prying her hands away. 'Don't blame yourself. Your husband is the only one at fault.' What, in the name of God, could I say to her now? I held her hand, knowing what I had to do and completely horrified by it both for her and for me. I pulled her into my arms, as though to comfort her. 'Will this man watch us now?' I whispered into her ear.

She moved her head to murmur into mine, 'Yes. I believe so. That's how my husband will know what we do.'

Porco Dio. Did he want to see me hurt her? Was that what this was about? Because she liked me? *Fanculo.* The man was a twisted bastard. I held her close, speaking louder. 'I won't hurt you.' Was that even possible? How the devil was I supposed to know? But, Christ, I was going to try. I stood up and took off my coat and waistcoat, smiling at her. She needed to relax ... as did I, of course. I climbed into bed beside her in only my shirt, after closing the white bed drapes, though they were so diaphanous they would afford us little privacy. Where would we be watched from? Would it be Rifkind or the man who had done so before? *Dio Santo*, I detested him. I wished fervently for Noah to run him through. I even imagined him doing so in full grisly detail. Yet should I not imagine Susannah to get this done. Had I not done so once before? But how could I bring my wife into this bed?

'Just do it and go,' She whispered. 'I don't care.'

I moved to her then, whispering again, too. 'No. I won't do that. I refuse to do what he wants.' Yet what a temptation it offered. Though was it truly what Susannah would wish of me when her own experience had been so difficult? I closed my eyes and kissed her then. 'Do you understand what will happen?'

She moved her head away. 'He told me. It doesn't matter. My mother told me, too. I know it's an unpleasant thing for a woman ... with a man.'

'Isabella, it's not. Perhaps only a little so the first time. Then many women enjoy it as much as men do.'

'Does your wife?

I smiled. 'She does, very much.'

She was beginning to look slightly less terrified. 'What must we do now?'

I took a deep breath and pulled off my shirt. 'This, I think.' I touched her nightgown. 'May I?'

She nodded. 'I have no idea what to do next,' she said, shakily.

My eager cock knew what to do, to my shame. Cocks, of course, are blind and quite without conscience.

I laughed a little, helping her pull off her gown. 'Neither have I, entirely, believe it or not.' I saw her puzzlement. 'I've never made love to a virgin before.'

Her eyes widened. 'Not your wife?'

I shook my head.

'Didn't you mind?'

I laughed again. 'In truth, I was mightily relieved.' I touched her face. 'So, you're not the only one feeling some trepidation.'

She smiled for the first time. She was a very pretty girl. 'May I kiss you?'

'If you wish it.'

I did so, tentatively. Her lips were soft but unresponsive. Christ, this was going to take some time. I kissed her again for longer, running my fingers down over her throat. Gradually, through kissing and stroking, I felt her relax and begin to respond a little. When I bought my hand gently to her breast she stiffened, making a small cry, though she soon responded more fiercely to my kisses. So, slowly, with my fingers at last working between her thighs, I brought her to where I felt ... hoped ... she needed to be. God help me. And then I broke the marriage vows I had made to my wife before God, in the hope of bringing her daughter home to her.

Later, she lay in my arms, our bodies hot and slick with sweat. I knew I had hurt her, but it had seemed to be but briefly. And I also knew I had given her pleasure. 'How do you feel? Was it as you expected?'

She sighed. 'I'm a little tender ... but it felt–' She

smiled. 'It took me quite by surprise.'

'Good.' I felt certain Rifkind would be displeased she had appeared to enjoy it. Strangely, she felt familiar pressed against me. Her body was so like Frances, her face and hair like Valentina, and that had made it easier for me. Somehow, it had seemed less transgressive when I felt I knew her. Unfortunately, when she moved in so diffidently to kiss me, I had her again as gently as I could, and that seemed very transgressive indeed.

She lay watching me as I dressed. 'Thank you for being so kind to me, Raphael.'

I thought that something she saw little of in this house. '*Prego, carissima*. You deserved nothing less.' Now I hoped Rifkind would tell the truth about where Penny was, if indeed he even knew it. I wondered, then, whether my kindness would anger him, causing him to deceive me. I prayed it would not. I kissed her forehead. 'Go with God, Isabella.'

I made my way down the stairs and into the drawing room, finding it deserted. When I rang the bell to summon a servant, I was unsurprised to be kept waiting for a considerable time. Finally, a black footman appeared with a letter on a silver tray. He held it out to me without comment. I broke the seal. George Meeker, Golden Ridge, Holetown, St James, Barbados. Nothing more. Please God, it was the truth. I placed it in my pocket. 'Have my horse brought round.' Now I must tell Susannah what I had done to get it.

. . .

To my surprise, I met Noah and Hal on the trail. 'What's this? I can find my own way home.'

'You've been a while,' Noah said. 'I was concerned. What did he want from you?'

Reticence seemed to have no place with this. 'I assume both you gentlemen are acquainted with a maidenhead?' I looked from one to the other. 'Well now, unfortunately, so am I.'

'What the hell, Raphael?'

'Rifkind told me where Penny is ... if it's true. Now I need to tell my wife the cost.' We rode back to the house in silence through the verdant forest alive with birdsong, though again I barely noticed my surroundings. I should tell Susannah first and she must decide how much the others should know.

I left my horse with a stable boy, though Noah and Hal were taking care of theirs themselves. I presumed in order to give me privacy to speak with my wife. I climbed the front steps up to the porch and made my way round to the back. I saw her sitting with Sam at the far end near the entrance to the parlour. When I reached her, she stood, and I held out the note. 'I don't know whether we can trust it. Holy God, I want to. Though that the man who gave it to me is as about as despicable as it's possible to be, casts some doubt on it.'

She scanned it, her eyes quickly returning to my face. I saw her uncertainty very clearly. Her joy at the possibility we had found Penny was overshadowed by what she sensed from me. 'What's happened? Why did he want to see you?'

I held out my hand to her. 'Come. I'll tell you.' We walked along the porch to our chamber at the other end. I closed the doors behind us.

She sat on the bed. I sat beside her and took her hand in mine. She searched my face. 'For the love of God, Raphael, tell me what he wanted.'

So, I told her. I left nothing out, including the choices I had. 'I don't know if I made the right ones, but they felt the only ones I could make.'

She looked down at the floor, silent for some time. Then she looked at me, her face deathly white. 'For you. Right for you. You really are a conceited bastard.'

Christ. Now I saw the extent of her fury, my own burst forth. I replied in the same harsh whisper. 'What then would you have had me do? Refuse? Really? When I did it for your daughter Do you think I wanted–'

She pulled her hand away. 'Yes, that's just what I think.' She gestured to her belly. 'Look at me. Of course you wanted her. Twice only? Do you expect me to believe that?'

Porco Dio. I truly could not believe she would say such a thing to me. 'Indeed, I do. What–'

'What would I have had you do? How about what he asked of you and no more. What about that, pray?'

I took a breath.

'Do not speak! I have not yet finished–'

251

'You asked me a question.' I spat. 'Perhaps you'd do me the courtesy of allowing me to answer it, *Signora*. You of all people expected me to do that to her?' Christ, I thought she would strike me. I stood.

'How dare you? This is too much, even for you. You did it because of me?' She laughed, cold as ice. 'No, Raphael. You did it for you. Because you wanted to, and you enjoyed it. That you wanted her to enjoy it, is pure conceit. Vanity. The court swordsman thrilled to have another chance to show off his skills.'

I sat down on the bed again, closing my eyes, my heart still thumping from anger, as it drained away as quickly as it had arrived. 'Is that what you really think of me, Susannah?' I asked, softly.

'Yes, it is. And because of it, we can't trust what he's told us. But Noah and Hal will have to sail to Barbados again to find out, anyway. Jesus Christ. Well, you can damn well go with them, you bastard.'

I tilted my head back to stare at the ceiling for a moment. 'As you wish.' I took off my coat and boots and returned to the porch without looking at her.

Thankfully the living area was deserted, Sam had tactfully removed himself, so I dropped down onto a sofa to ponder her words. Yet I could not imagine doing as she said I should. If she expected it of me then she wished me a different person. I sighed. And Christ, I had enjoyed it. My cock had, anyway. There was no denying that and nothing to be done about it either. Was it really arrogance about my prowess? I thought rather I had been reckless for wanting to defy him.

And it was not the first time I had allowed such reck-lessness to influence my behaviour. Please God, Rifkind had told the truth. I closed my eyes until after quite some time, I heard soft footsteps approaching. Susannah. I sat up straighter, watching her. When I saw she had been weeping, I held out my hand to her. She took it and sat beside me, and I wiped away her tears with my fingertips.

She squeezed my hand. 'I hope you know I didn't mean any of those things. I also hope you can forgive me for saying them. I simply cannot bear to think of you with another woman. But I understand you had no choice.'

I held her close. 'No, *cara*. Some of what you said I deserved. It's true I have a ... what? A need to please a woman? And, in truth, it's not something I think I can change ... or, perhaps, even wish to.'

'Oh, Raphael. How could I ever want you to change? None of this was your fault. Rifkind wanted you to rape her and you'd never do that. You couldn't, I know. I spoke from jealousy and not for the first time as I'm sure you'll recall.' She moved away and patted my cheek. 'I won't go into your second time with her ... I can't say I don't wish you hadn't but–' she shook her head. 'No matter. I would ask you to bathe though, my love, if you don't mind.'

I knew I should regret that second indulgence but even now, God help me, I could not. I tried to tell my-self it had been for Isabella when I knew this to be not entirely true. 'I love you, Susannah.'

253

CHAPTER 27

Noah

'I know we weren't supposed to hear but ...' Noah scrubbed at his face. 'Did he do right, do you think?'

'What else could he do? She'll understand that. She's just very angry now.' Sam grasped his hand. 'Michael's horse is back, finally. Time for you to speak to him.'

Hal had passed on what he knew on their ride up to Cinnamon Hill. 'But how can I help him with his faith when I have so little myself? You'd be better for that ... or Raphael.'

'Yet you're his father, Noah. So, it must be you, I'm afraid.'

'Christ's wounds.'

'Just listen to him. Something has brought him to this. You need to find out what it is if you can.'

Noah stood up from their bed. 'I know I do.' He took a breath. 'Let's hope he's in his room.' In truth,

Noah hoped he was not. Sam knew it, of course, and gave his arm a squeeze.

When Michael opened the door, he appeared decidedly displeased to see him. 'I'm tired Papa. Might you excuse me this evening?'

Noah moved passed him. 'Sorry, Lad. We really do need to talk. And now's as good a time as any.' The door to the porch overlooking the stables was open. Michael had clearly been sitting on the bench out there. Noah gestured towards it. 'Let's sit.'

Michael did as asked. 'There's nothing to talk about. Hal must have told you all I said.'

Noah sighed, knowing Sam would do this so much better. 'He did. A physician, is it? Well, I'm very proud of you, Michael. Very proud indeed. I want you to know that.' He reached out to take his son's hand. 'But Hal also said he believed something has happened to you. I think you should try to tell me what it is, even if it's difficult.'

Michael held his forehead, looking close to tears. 'Forgive me. I really don't think I can.' He stood and returned inside the room, sitting on the bed.

Noah followed and sat beside him again, his heart aching for him. 'I only want to help. You know that.'

Michael looked up at last, searching his father's face. 'Nothing is as I expected here. I knew I'd find you with someone—'

'Just not with Sam?' Christ. Why had he interrupted him? Sam had told him to listen. Why was he always such an imbecile?

Michael shook his head. 'No. I hadn't expected that.'

He couldn't seem to help himself. 'Has it made this harder for you?'

He watched his son nod. He closed his eyes, almost afraid to speak, especially remembering what had happened with Hal the year before, when he had asked such a question. 'So, it's a man?' he said, softly.

Michael stood, his face twisted into an ugly grimace. 'A man?' He shook his head, tears now streaming down his face, though he seemed quite unaware of them. 'Someone like you would think that, wouldn't they? See their own filthy perversion everywhere they look. Well, I'm not like you.' His voice rose to a shout. 'I'm not. I'm damn well not!'

Noah managed to grab him and pull him into his arms, holding him tight until he felt him begin to calm himself. 'I know you're not. I know it, of course I do.' He stroked his hair. 'Hush now. Hush, Lad.'

He struggled out of his father's arms, appearing overwhelmed with despair. 'But what if I am, Papa? Oh, Christ, what if I am?'

Noah pulled him down beside him on the bed once more, his arms tight around him, wondering how he could bear it. 'Try and tell me what happened if you can. I know it's difficult.'

All fight seemed to leave him, and he slumped against his father. 'I trusted him, loved him even.' He met Noah's eyes, then. 'He was a mentor. A friend.'

Noah groaned. 'And he–' He squared his shoulders and took a deep breath. 'He raped you.'

Tears spilled down Michael's face again as he nodded. 'He said he thought I wanted it,' he whispered. 'But I'd told him to stop. I'd tried to escape him. Why would he think it?'

Noah clenched his jaw. 'It's not true, Michael. He didn't care what you wanted, only what he did–'

Michael clutched him. 'Christ. He said he knew I did because I ... I–'

'Hush, lad. Hush now.' He rocked him gently, feeling him shake as he wept. 'Of course you did. It's what cocks do. He knew that perfectly well. Christ. I'd like to geld him. Christ's fucking wounds, maybe that's just what I will do. I'll take you back to England and after that I'll finish him.'

Michael pulled away. 'Perhaps best not, Papa.' He found a damp smile from somewhere. 'He is a rather well-respected cleric.'

Noah took a long, calming breath. 'Well, the fucker shouldn't be respected.' His nostrils flared. 'You're right of course. But I shan't forget, and neither will Hal. One day he'll stand before me, and I'll remind him of what he did.'

Michael's eyes widened. 'Please don't tell Hal. He'll think me such a gullible fool.'

'He won't. Of course he won't. Now tell me all there is to know about this man.'

And that is what his son did. Speaking of this tutor who helped him and a small group of others at school to prepare for reading Theology at Oxford. Noah saw his relief at passing the burden of it on to someone else. It was what fathers were for, after all. When it was done, Noah stood. 'Come. We'll find wine and then have a talk with Sam. I think he might be able to help a little.'

Michael shrugged. 'Whatever you say, Papa.'

He had truly placed himself in Noah's hands and his relief at doing so was plain to see on his face.

Later, when Sam came outside with Noah, he moved to the porch rail with his back towards them while Noah refilled their wine gasses and then sat down beside Michael, patting his arm, reassuringly.

Sam turned to face them, though he was in silhouette against the brief fiery sunset behind him, now the sun had suddenly dropped below a bank of cloud low over the sea. 'Your papa asked me to talk to you, but you must wish it for yourself not just to please him.'

Noah snorted. 'You think I'd force it on him.'

'Perhaps, if you think he needs to hear it.'

Noah shrugged. 'Michael, feel free to say should you not wish Sam to tell you what happened to him.'

Michael smiled, tentatively, looking from one to the other. 'Go ahead, please.'

Sam moved to sit beside Noah. 'From what your papa told me, I imagine this man has played each of you against the others trying to show you were chosen because of what you were when, in truth, he's abused all of you knowing you'll never admit it to each other.'

Noah leaned forward. 'Have you spoken to any of them about it.'

'I asked Stephen Fletcher if Reverend Garland had done or said anything that troubled him. He said absolutely not which is, of course, what I said when he asked me the same question.'

Sam sighed. 'He attacked all of you when he lured you to his house. No doubt he's been doing it for years, relying on shame and doubt about yourselves preventing you from speaking out.'

'Tell him what happened to you—'

'Noah, I'm about to, if you're able to stop interrupting me. Is that possible, do you think?'

Noah shook his head, exasperated, but managed to stay silent, tapping his foot on the wooden boards.

Sam stared at him until he stopped. 'I'm telling you this because I want you to understand the difference between my experience and yours. This is a private thing but I'm going to tell you a little of it because I think it might help you.' He cleared his throat. 'I was raped when I was fifteen. The circumstances aren't important. But I wasn't given a choice about it just as you weren't. The difference being I found it wasn't altogether unwelcome, and I never asked him to stop. When I didn't, he ceased forcing me because he no longer had to. The next day I was angry at his impertinence, of course I was. That I wasn't given that choice. Yet later I was even grateful for it because of what it showed me about myself. Now, I think your experience was very different no matter what this man tried to convince you of.'

'Christ, it was. It's hard to describe just how much. At first, I was affronted … angry. I expected he would stop when I told him to, it somehow felt unreal when he didn't. I couldn't believe it was happening to me. I tried to fight him off but he's a big man … heavy. Strong. Finally, I begged him to stop.' Michael looked away. 'He would never have tried such a thing with my brother.'

Noah laughed, rather cynically. 'Hal was rusticated from Oxford for mutual pleasuring with a lad in his rooms–'

'Jesu, Noah.' Sam shook his head. 'That's just a schoolboy thing and up to Hal to speak of it.'

Imbecile, yet again. He held up his hands. 'Of course.'

'It's all right, Papa. He wrote to me of it at the time and how he told everyone it was because he'd been caught with a whore.' He smiled a little. 'I never quite understood why he thought that better.'

'Better for his reputation, perhaps? More adult.' Sam said. 'And then, of course, he found he had no need of such services.'

Noah saw Michael appeared a little puzzled. 'Young ladies swoon at his feet, Lad.'

Sam laughed. 'And he's more than happy to assist them up.'

CHAPTER 28

Susannah

I lay beside my husband watching him sleep in the dawn light, grateful again for his boundless capacity for forgiveness. Of me in particular. I admit it had been hard to contemplate this beautiful young girl, seemingly a combination of Frances Stuart and Valentina Gentileschi. Sometimes I wish he could be a little less honest. I paused on that thought for a moment. Did I, really, though? When it meant I could trust him implicitly to tell me the truth, however unpalatable. He had given me his word on it after Valentina. Anyway, Hal had already said how lovely she was after their visit and that Raphael had charmed her. Something else that seemed innate in him. Of course, my interest in her appearance came in some part from thinking of my own. Though that I carried his child, enchanted him. When his son chose that moment to kick as though trying to break out from a prison cell, which I suppose he was to some extent, a rather loud grunt escaped me.

Raphael bolted upright and clutched me. 'Susannah, what's wrong. Have you pain?'

I took his hand and placed it on my writhing belly. 'Just your son being a brute.' When I saw such naked love in his eyes, I truly thought I would weep, my eyes quickly filling.

'Are you hurt? Don't cry, *cara*.'

'I'm hurt because I hurt you when I love you so completely. Why did I wish to hurt you like that?'

He stroked my hair. 'Forget it now, *amore mio*. I have. Truly. Let's just pray we bring Penny home soon.'

I looked down at the great rise of my belly. 'She'll be so thrilled with him.' How could I not think of all that might have happened to her, especially after his experience the day before. I knew he thought of it too. But it could not be spoken of between us for if it were, it would become real. I prayed once again for my little girl.

We left our room together to go to breakfast with the others. I wondered what they had overheard of our conflict the day before. And what, indeed, they knew of the price exacted for the name of the man in Barbados. There was an awkward silence when we seated ourselves. I looked at Sam and read his concern. I lifted Raphael's hand and kissed it. Sam smiled and looked away.

So did Noah, turning to Hal. 'We'll go into town and start victualling the ship and see if we can get a bit of cargo together, yes?'

Hal nodded and then spoke to Raphael. 'Will you still come with us?'

Noah rolled his eyes. 'Christ's wounds, Hal. Why can't you think for a single moment before you speak?'

So, they had heard me telling him to go.

Raphael met my gaze. 'Yes.'

'No. You can't,' I said in some alarm, resting my hand on my belly. 'You mustn't leave me now.'

'One of us should be there for her. So, it has to be me.'

'Why shouldn't I go?' Sam said. 'She's known me all her life. She'll feel safe seeing me. I'm her natural–'

'No.' Raphael watched him, carefully. 'It's me she calls Papa. So, I must go. I need to. I left her in that fucking park.'

I saw Sam about to speak again and shook my head, slightly. I understood why Raphael wanted to do this, feeling responsibility for Penny and a debt towards his own daughter, too. I just prayed they would return in time for my confinement. 'Then you should, my love. Though I can hardly bear to be without you.' I glanced at Sam, again. 'But I won't be alone.'

Sam tried to smile. 'No, Sukie. Of course you won't.' He turned to Raphael. 'I'll take good care of her. You have my word.'

I could see how hard he found this. Raphael was not the only one feeling an obligation to make recompense to Penny, when neither of them need ever think such a thing. Raphael nodded, about to speak again when Pearl arrived out onto the porch accompanied by a tiny, extremely pretty dark-haired girl. I knew immediately who she was. When Raphael stood, I felt suddenly faint. What could she want? Why had she come here?

'Isabella? My God.'

'Raphael. I wanted to leave my letter for you, but this woman said I must speak to you.'

He took it and broke the seal and reading it aloud. 'Duncan Hilliard, Bissex Hall, Bathsheba, St Joseph, Barbados.' He looked at her again. 'But this is a different name and a different plantation.'

'It's the other side of the island,' Noah said.

'He lied.' She closed her eyes as though she did not wish to see all of ours locked upon her face. Then she glanced down before directing her gaze up at Raphael again. 'He found your being kind to me extremely amusing and hoped your wife would enjoy reading all about it when he wrote to her after you'd left for Barbados. He said you were stupid and naive to trust him. He'd always planned to mislead you.'

She turned to me. 'Your husband was kind to me when he had no reason to be, so I had to do something for your daughter. There is one servant I trust. He went into Barnabus's office and risked looking at his private ledgers.' She pointed at her letter. 'The little girl went there, to that man who wanted her to replace his dead daughter. She was in our house for a few days. My husband said she was going to her natural father. That's what she believed, too. It's what I believed, then.

Sam gasped. 'My God. *What?* But I'm her father.'

She looked at him and then at all of us. 'I should have known it wasn't true.' She blinked away tears. 'Forgive me, I thought I must keep it secret when you called on me.'

I clutched at Raphael, staring hard at Isabella. 'You saw Penny. You saw my little girl. Oh, dear God. How was she? Was she ...?' I could no longer speak.

She looked directly at me for the first time. 'I only saw her briefly. She seemed happy and eager to meet her father.'

Three of us groaned.

'I had to do something. I needed to for Raphael.' She looked at him with such longing. I found myself suddenly able to pity her. I reached out to touch her. 'Thank you.' Jesu. I loved my husband. I thanked God for him. Then, well ... I swooned. I knew nothing of it until I came back to myself, lying on my bed, Raphael looking down at me anxiously.

He stroked my face, trying to smile. 'How are you now?'

'I worried you. Forgive me.' I thought about all we had just learnt for some moments and, of course, understood what his gentleness to Isabella Rifkind had done for us. Penny would come back to us because of him. When I closed my eyes, tears spilled. He lay down beside me and pulled me into his arms. 'Raphael, if not for you we wouldn't find her, and I was angry with you for it. How can I ever forgive myself?'

He kissed me. 'I think I might not appreciate you pleasuring a young man either, however necessary.' He sighed. 'Though it's not the same at all, is it? It's generally a very pleasing first experience for a man but rather less so for a woman, sadly.'

'Yet mine brought me Penny.' I gasped. 'You didn't–'

He kissed me again. 'Of course I didn't, *cara*.' He sighed. 'She'd been sent out as a wife with very little idea about it. And, considering what sort of man he is, I doubt he's finished exploiting her.' He searched my face. 'Though all that really matters now is that we know where to find Penny and why she was taken. If he's masquerading as her father, it must mean she's being well cared for, surely?'

'Please, God it does. How can they have told her such a thing? That this man is her father. How can a man buy a child for such a wicked purpose? Take someone else's to be his own.'

'Christ knows. He's experienced the grief of loss himself and then, seemingly without conscience, makes another suffer the same.'

I sat up. 'I must talk to Sam.'

We found him still seated where we'd left him next to Noah, though Isabella and his sons had gone. We sat down opposite them.

Sam's eyes were fixed on me. 'You look better. We were worried about you, Sukie.'

'The lads have gone with the girl, to see her back. We're a little concerned she might come to harm when Rifkind suspects her, which he will surely do when Penny arrives here.' Noah shook his head. 'I'll give it some thought. Perhaps we can find somewhere safe for her away from him.'

'Sam.' He turned to look at me. 'She needs to know who you are. We'll tell her when we get her back.'

He nodded. 'That she thinks this man her father means she won't be afraid of him ... if he's been kind to her.'

I took a long breath, holding his gaze. 'We have to believe that he has.'

'He paid an extraordinary sum for her, so the girl told us. Though if he's another like Rifkind, he can afford it quite easily, I imagine,' Noah said.

Sam looked at me in a rather guarded way, now. He did not understand why I wanted Raphael to go to Barbados instead of him. 'How long will it take you to get there and back, Noah?'

'With good weather and a kind wind around eighteen days or so. We can be ready to sail in two days if we push it.'

I looked down at my belly, placing my hand there, silently instructing its occupant to remain where he was at least until then. Jesu, it sounded a long time. I hoped it would not be too long.

Raphael's hand joined mine and I knew he added

his own plea. 'I'll do my utmost to be here, *cara*. I swear it.'

How little that would be in his power. Sam sighed but said nothing.

Two days later, I watched the pinnace sail away towards the headland once again, with Sam and Michael beside me. I could not allow myself to doubt it would be for the last time. Sam gave my hand a squeeze. He felt it too. They would bring her home this time.

Michael ran down the steps onto the beach. 'Walk, I think ... and perhaps a swim.'

'He seems better. Happier.'

'He is. He talked to his papa. Got things more into perspective.'

'You said he plans to be a minister?'

'Ah, that's all changed. He's set on becoming a physician now. He's off to Leiden for a year. Then Oxford.'

'Noah must be very proud of him.'

'He's proud of both his sons.' He ran his hand through his hair, glossy and loose about his shoulders. 'Perhaps he doesn't always make that clear enough to one of them.'

We watched him go a little distance, splashing through the foaming wavelets before I gestured to a couch. 'Come. I know you need an explanation from me about Raphael.'

He took my hand. 'Let's take a stroll up the beach ourselves before it gets too hot.'

We walked in companionable silence, stepping barefoot through the cool frills, until we arrived at the low tree branch stretching out across the sand where we ate our lunch that day. He nodded towards it. 'We can sit here for a while in the shade.'

I did so and he lowered himself beside me beside me, grinning. 'I think it dips nearly as much for you as for Noah.'

I punched his arm, softly, laughing. 'Why, how terribly ungallant of you, Sir.' I looked down at myself. 'Admittedly, I'm considerably larger than I was with Penny. Though I was sick for much of the time with her, now I just eat.'

'I was teasing, Sukie. You look very beautiful.' He stroked my face. 'You should have let me go with them. You need Raphael with you.'

'Has he told you about Valentina Gentileschi?'

He shook his head.

'He won't mind if I tell you now, I don't think.' I hoped he would not. I told him as succinctly as I could. 'He finds it difficult to bear that his daughter was not loved in her very brief life. Valentina wouldn't touch her. Raphael's mother held her, though. I told him she would have loved her because she was his. His father had insinuated she wasn't, but his mother knew the truth of it.'

His eyes were full of compassion. 'So, this is what you learned from his mother that day?

269

I nodded.

'Christ, it sounds utterly wretched.'

'It was. So, when we married, and Penny became his stepdaughter it felt like a benediction to him. That God had forgiven him. He made a vow to always take care of us. It's why he blames himself so much for leaving her in St James's Park, though I wish he wouldn't ...' I shook my head. 'Yet it can't have helped I once blamed him for it–'

'Oh, Sukie.'

'It was on the ship travelling out here. He was concerned I should eat. I said it was a pity he didn't care as much for my child as his own. Sometimes I wonder how he keeps forgiving me the way he does. Jesu. I expect everyone heard what I said to him about Isabella.'

He lifted my hand so his lips and kissed it. 'Well, I heard you say something about him claiming it was about you. It wasn't too difficult to decipher what that meant.'

'Rifkind wanted him to rape her. To hurt her.'

'As I did you.'

I snorted. 'Well, you certainly didn't rape me, Sam. I seem to remember I was a rather eager participant. Somewhat more so than you if I recall.'

He smiled a little. 'As it turned out.'

'And neither of us understood quite why.' I held his gaze. 'What made you flee?'

He sighed. 'I don't know. I was fifteen. I didn't understand what I felt or why I felt it. I couldn't face you I suppose. What could I have said to you?'

'You didn't really want to do it all, did you? I didn't understand that then.'

'Neither did I.' He looked away. 'I felt a certain amount of pressure. I'm not sure how to explain it–'

'Other boys?'

He looked at me, eyes wide.' How on earth would you know that?'

'My husband was one, once.'

He smiled, ruefully. 'Of course he was. And I'm sure you've discussed it all thoroughly ... as I have now with Noah. And I never did say anything about it at school. Other things happened to me later. I didn't talk of those either.'

I held his gaze. 'For a long time, I thought, somehow, it'd been my fault–'

His eyes widened. 'Christ, Susannah. Why?'

'Raphael put me right on it. He actually found it amusing.' I remembered how he told me he imagined it was me in another woman's bed, after first seeing me at court.

He raised his eyebrows. 'Well, I'm sure he did. I saw the way he looked at you. There was little doubt what he was thinking.'

'So, I discovered.' I sighed. 'What would it have been like if we'd married, I wonder? Would we have been all right, do you think?'

'I think we would. More so than most in such a marriage because of our feelings for each other. Friendship and love.'

I caressed his face, where leaf shadows danced. 'Better than Noah, I'm sure,' I said softly.

'Holy God, yes.' He chewed his lip. 'But I would have strayed because I had no choice.' He shrugged. 'Maybe you would, too? But I do believe we'd have been honest with each other.'

'Yet I didn't know about you. Not until Raphael told me. After I came home with Penny I was away from court for a while. Still, when I returned, I heard no rumours about you.'

'You wouldn't by then. I kept that part of my life well away from court. I didn't like the ugliness of it there. The ever-present sense of violence underlying it all. I learned that very early on.'

I leant against him, and he put his arm around my shoulders. 'I think, my Sukie, we are both considerably better where we are now, though.'

I smiled. 'With the ones we can love fully.'

Michael came into view then, approaching our tree. His hair was darkly wet with some strands already drying against it, glinting like fingers of flame in the sunlight. I turned to Sam.

'I need to paint him.'

I laughed, for he had read my mind. 'Just as he is now, I think. We should walk back.' I watched him beside us, dressed only in his breeches. 'You're lucky you don't have skin like mine with your hair colour. The sun only needs to touch it for a moment, without my parasol.' I twirled it. 'And I go a most unpleasant shade of puce.'

He ran a hand down his muscled arm, already starting to tan. 'Papa says it's a Viking thing.' He shrugged. 'Not sure that makes a lot of sense. Wouldn't Norsemen more likely be as fair-skinned as you?'

Sam laughed. 'Noah if fond of the Norseman tale. He'll find proof of it anywhere he can, however unlikely. Though he is from Yorkshire where there was a big Viking presence, of course.'

'Well, he and my brother certainly have the stature. Not sure about me, though.'

We stepped up onto the porch. Yet he was very young still. While he would never have their height, he would be broad of shoulder and strong. Much the same as Sam, I thought, comparing them. 'Sam wishes to paint you.'

He shrugged. 'Why not. I've nothing else to do.'

We moved down to the area outside Sam's studio, and he helped me make myself comfortable on a couch before disappearing inside to fetch what he needed. I sighed. 'Eighteen days. It sounds interminable.' I placed my hand on my belly. 'Please God, it's not too long.'

Michael, standing at the rail looking out towards the headland, turned to look at me. 'Papa has never told me how he came to be in Port Royal? Why did they choose this place?'

Sam came out and began setting-up his easel. 'Stay where you are, Michael. I've painted Hal in just that spot. Sit up on the rail.' Michael did as asked.

'Perfect. As to why we're here. Well, it's because of me.'

So, as Sam painted, between us we told him the events of the year before, which had culminated in Sam being sentenced to the traitor's death. I wiped away tears, remembering the despair of that day. 'But Noah never gave up, thank God. He kept fighting for Sam until he was able to uncover what had really happened. And, of course, once the real murderer was revealed the King had no choice but to release him and Noah had him away from the country within hours before fresh charges could be brought against him.'

Michael stared from one of us to the other. 'So, you're both godchildren to the King?'

Sam grinned. 'We are. Though much good it did me for a time there. Port Royal is a bit of a double-edged choice. It's lawless but also full of spies looking for information to sell. Noah thinks it safer for my presence here to be kept secret.'

Michael frowned. 'I think I must get down from here for a while. My arse had gone completely numb.'

'Forgive me. Of course you must. We'll take a break.' He dropped his brush into a jar of turpentine, wiping his hands on a rag. 'You'll be pleased to know you lasted considerably longer than Hal. He was squirming after only five minutes.'

Michael laughed and seeing me about to get to my feet, offered me his hand and together we joined Sam to look at his painting. Colour flooded his face. 'It's very flattering.'

So, another like Raphael who could not see himself. Still, I supposed he had always felt himself in his father and brother's shadows and had not yet realised he had moved out from them. I still had no explanation for my husband. 'No. It's a true likeness, I promise you.'

Sam tilted his head. 'I can see your Papa in you but there's something finer about your bone structure. Your high cheekbones.'

I nodded. 'Give it a year or two and you'll be turning heads too. I think I might like to paint you then, myself.'

Sam touched his arm. 'Forgive us thoughtless artists. I can see we're making you uncomfortable.'

When Pearl chose that moment to arrive outside with a tray of wine and fruit, Michael's relief was clear and, he fell upon the fruit as though starved. Sam poured wine for us all.

I took a sip. 'Eighteen days.'

Sam sat beside me. 'Well, whatever happens, they'll be here. I know they will.'

I had to believe it, too. I had no choice.

CHAPTER 29

Noah

Noah watched Raphael gaze back towards Port Royal as they sailed out of the harbour into the open sea. He understood how reluctant he was to leave Susannah. And he would do everything in his power to get him back to her as soon as possible. Yet how little would rest in his hands. The wind. The tide. How long it took to find the child. Hal came to stand beside him, looking up at the men running sure-footed along the yardarm and high in the rigging, as though on solid ground, hastily unfurling the remaining sails to speed the ship forward.

Hal followed his father's gaze. 'Should he have come?'

Noah turned to him. 'Not for me to say.' Perhaps he had been reckless and not for the first time. 'I can understand why he feels it's his duty to fetch the girl home and also to be there for his wife's confinement.

He hopes to do both, of course. But I imagine he feels he can take a more active part in this one than in the other.'

'I wonder which one Susannah truly wished for?'

'She will hope for both, too.' Noah sighed. 'In truth, I think she wanted him with her. Perhaps it was even what they both wanted.'

'Well, she did tell him to come with us as a punishment because of–'

'You know we weren't meant to hear that. Don't mention it to him again, for Christ's sake.'

'I'm not a complete idiot, Papa. I spoke without thinking. I won't do so again.'

Noah punched his arm, lightly. 'I know, Lad.' He scratched at his stubble. 'Perhaps they both chose what they least want as a kind of penance? A pact with God?'

'A sacrifice, you mean?'

Noah raised his eyebrows. 'Yes.' That was exactly what he meant. Once again, he appreciated Hal's acuity. Even though he wished for a little more circumspection on occasions.

Raphael turned and looked at them as though he sensed they talked of him. He walked slowly across the deck to join them, unsmiling. 'I did vow not to do this again.' He shrugged. 'But I must fetch her home. I've no choice. Though I think I might tolerate the tedium with certainty at the end of it this time.' He crossed himself.

Noah squeezed his shoulder. 'We have to trust the

information we have. The girl put herself at considerable risk to get it for you.'

Raphael sighed. 'She did. Yet Rifkind is such a twisted whoreson, a part of me can't entirely trust anything that originates from him. I pray, though, this time it's the truth.'

Sensing a different tension in the ship as the wind picked-up and veered a little, Noah left them then to shout instructions to the boatswain at the helm and then up to the men high in the rigging.

He turned back to watch Raphael talking still with Hal, both dressed in breeches and shirts, their hair loose to their shoulders. They drew women to them like bees to nectar, though they differed in appearance about as much as was possible. Christ, what did a man do when he was desired? Well, he knew what he did. What he had done in the past. Different stakes, of course, but momentous in their own way. Both he and Raphael had found security ... a refuge in love, but Hal was still out in the world swept along by it all.

He watched the men carry out his orders up in the rigging and felt the ship settle herself, once more, taking-up the wind and filling her sails. When he looked around again, Hal had departed, and Raphael stood alone staring out over the sea. He walked back to join him again. 'Where's he gone, then?'

'Some shifting of cargo. Not sure what or how.' When Noah made to go after him, Raphael caught his arm. 'Can he really not handle it himself?' Hal was designated first mate on this voyage, so cargo was his job.

Noah stopped. He sighed. 'He can, I believe.' He met Raphael's gaze. 'And I should let him?'

Raphael smiled. 'I don't wish to interfere, but I think you should, Noah ... if you can.'

Noah sighed again. 'I've gathered from what you've said of him, your own father is somewhat over-bearing?'

Raphael snorted. 'You could say that. My father saw me as a possession, deserving of no free will–'

'Holy God. You don't think I'm like that with Hal, surely?'

'No, not at all. But you can be, perhaps ... a little too watchful? And too eager to pounce on any missteps?'

Noah looked up at the sky. 'My father was indifferent to me. Didn't try to teach me or guide me in any way. I learnt about ships from others, never from him. Christ, are we all destined to do the opposite of what was done to us?'

Raphael laughed, wryly. 'Well, I'm indifferent to mine now and have decided my children will most definitely have free will.' He was silent for a few moments, still looking out over the cerulean, glittering water. 'Perhaps it's just a question of loving them and trying to give them what they need rather than what we do.' He shrugged. 'But, in truth, what do I know of it ... yet?'

'Quite a lot, it would seem. I'm very proud of Hal. I know I should make more effort to see he knows it.' When Raphael made to move away, Noah placed a hand on his shoulder to restrain him. 'I'll do my up-most to get you back to Susannah in time for the birth, you have my word.'

Raphael smiled. 'I know you will, Noah.'

'I understand why you feel the need to be there.' He smiled, ruefully. 'Though there's little to be done beyond waiting and drinking too much.'

Raphael tilted his head. 'I've promised to stay by her side so a little more than that, I imagine.' He closed his eyes for a moment. 'If I can be there at all, of course.'

Noah raised his eyebrows. 'Is that an Italian thing? It's certainly not done in England. It's best left to women in my view, like it always has been.'

Raphael smiled, again. 'In my country, too. But her papa was there when she was born.' He shrugged. 'It's what we want ... what we've decided.'

Noah watched him walk away. He understood how close they were and wondered if he realised how hard it would be. Christ, he had found it so just hearing Margaret's cries when all he had felt for her then was a sort of respectful affection and guilt that it could never be more.

CHAPTER 30
Raphael

I lay stretched out on the bunk with the long casements ajar, letting in a little cooling air in the late afternoon as the ship rode the wind. Though we all shared the cabin, the Bartholomews had insisted, as they always did, that I should take the bunk. Any arguments against it on my part fell on deaf ears. I sighed. We were nine days out now and should arrive in Bridgetown within a matter of hours. I cannot say I had any desire to see the place again. It would be forever tainted by memories of the auction and sights I tried never to revisit.

Now I found my thoughts uncomfortably divided between Susannah back in Jamaica and Penny. I prayed for them both. Holy Christ. I sought only the end now. Some sort of resolution. Please God let me return home with her before Susannah's confinement. Yet it felt somehow too rapacious to ask for so much. I picked up my rosary. A few decades would calm me. When I opened my eyes, I found Hal sitting at the table. I had not heard him come in.

He cleared his throat. 'You were praying?'

I moved off the bunk and slipped my rosary into the pocket of my coat, hung over the back of a chair, and sat down across him. 'I was.' I smiled. 'Thank you for not interrupting me.'

'Do the beads help?'

I enjoyed how direct he was, always. It was charming, though I knew as he got older, he would become more guarded. Everyone did in the end. 'They do. They help me quieten my thoughts ... and so feel closer to God.'

'What must you do with them?'

I took it from my pocket again. I kissed the crucifix and quickly crossed myself. 'This first and then pray the Apostles' creed. You'll know it. *I believe in God, the Father almighty, creator of heaven and earth.* Only we say it in Latin.'

He nodded. 'I do.'

I smiled, touching the large bead above it. 'Here the *Pater Noster* ... the *Our Father*.' I counted three small beads. 'Pray three Hail Marys and on the chain the Glory Be.' I saw his question. '*Gloria Patri, et Filio, et Spiritui Sancto* ... again, you've probably heard it.' Another nod. 'Then the praying of the decades – ten Hail Marys – the first of the five mysteries on the large bead.' My fingers moved. I grinned. His eyes were starting to glaze over. 'Well, I'm sure you get the idea.'

He looked sheepish. 'It does sound quite complicated.'

'I can barely remember when I didn't know it, so it has the comfort of the familiar for me.'

'What are the mysteries about.'

'The Crucifixion of Our Lord. There are another four sets, but these are the most important.' I dropped the rosary back in my pocket. He gave me a rather searching look. 'You have a question?'

He cleared his throat and ran his hands through his loose hair. 'I find it difficult to reconcile your religion with ...' He studied his fingers. 'How you were with women.'

I laughed, wryly. 'It's not unheard of, believe me. Far from it. Don't forget confession and absolution through penance. Though I went quite some time without it.' And I have never confessed Valentina.

'God. What do they make you do?'

I smiled. 'Repent and pray, usually ... sometimes a disconcerting amount of praying.'

Hal went to stand at the window. 'We should be at the harbour quite soon.'

I moved to stand beside him. 'Please God.' I crossed myself.

He turned to me. 'May I ask you something, Raphael.'

When he asked permission, it usually meant it would be even more personal than usual. 'Please do.'

'How did you know the right thing to do with Isabella Rifkind?'

In truth, it felt rather more about luck than my ability to make the correct judgement. 'I didn't know if it was right or not. Maybe I was simply doing what felt right to me and this time it happened to turn out well.'

He frowned. 'Well, it seems quite brave to me, considering the stakes. I mean, knowingly to defy Rifkind.'

Susannah had thought the same to start with. I sighed. 'Something like that can't be wholly altruistic, can it?' When there are mutual benefits, it's not always possible to know how much these weight your decisions.'

'I see what you mean ... though I don't see anything wrong with that.' He pointed to a hump of land on the horizon. 'Barbados. I better get on deck. I followed him out, feeling hope and anxiety in equal measure.

Later, when we sailed into Bridgetown harbour again, I felt all sense of optimism leach away, the sight of the waterfront oppressing me. It seemed a place built on suffering. Yet, in truth, they all were. The difference here was that we had witnessed some of it first-hand.

As always, Noah soon had us at the wharf with men up in the rigging to furl the last of the sails and over the side to tie up the heavy rope lines. The light was fast dropping away like water streaming from a dipper. There and gone. We would spend another night onboard, before setting out for Bathsheba on the other side of the island. I feared sleep would prove elusive for all of us this night. And so, it did. Noah sighed and grumbled as he tossed and turned. Hal chose to lose himself – surprisingly discreetly – in the age-old way of men, which made Noah mutter darkly under his breath about the privacy of the deck, while my fingers moved silently upon my rosary.

As usual, Noah called in on the harbour master to log our arrival and learn the whereabout of the nearest livery stables while I sat beside Hal on a wall in the shade. In truth, I knew he remained with me as much as my bodyguard as for company and was grateful for it. Docks could be dangerous places but not so much in the presence of Hal Bartholomew.

Noah strode out, rubbing his hands together. 'Right. Now for horses. I only have a vague idea of the route for Bathsheba, but the man was confident the stable owner would be able to give us more details on it.' He moved off up a shady alleyway away from the wharf, making several turnings until we arrived at the livery. This time Noah left the arrangements to Hal while he made sure of directions and found out everything he could about Bissex Hall plantation. In no time, it seemed, we were mounted and on our way. Barbados's interior proved quite different to Jamaica's.

More barren and flatter, though cooled by a constant wind off the sea, which compensated to some extent for the lack of shade.

During the voyage, I had read Ligon's *Barbados: A True and Exact History*, which gave me some understanding of the impact of sugar on the island in respect of its landscape, flora, and fauna, with so much forest cleared for planting. I now knew the numbers of African slaves needed to work the fields exceeded Europeans on the island and much about the empty often sybaritic lives of the plantation owners. Though the unspoiled landscape sounded idyllic, it was its very fecundity that had brought about its downfall. And how could I not think again of what we had seen at that nightmare auction where mankind was reduced to a commodity with less value than the crop their labour produced, with such unthinkable profits achieved only by their enslavement.

We were able to ride three abreast for a while, giving Noah time to tell us what he had learnt. 'This Duncan Hilliard is the biggest producer on the island, though Bissex Hall is one of his smaller plantations, he favours it for his home because it's on the cooler, more scenic East coast. He has something of a reputation as a strict owner, tough with his slaves and with his overseers. His wife and daughter died of smallpox some years ago. It doesn't seem to be common knowledge that he has a girl living with him there but there have been rumours of the existence of a child or children from an earlier liaison.'

I turned to him, sharply. 'You don't think he may have Kitty Foyles too?' I could hardly dare hope for it. We had never ceased to ask about her, showing her small watercolour alongside Penny's miniature though, sadly, her dark colouring was not in her favour when asking if anyone remembered her.

We were silent for a while, listening to the steady clop of the horse's hooves along the hard, sun-baked track. All around us, looking down towards the coast, were cane fields as far as the eye could see, like an undulant green inland ocean. I heard its susurration on the wind. Some were hives of hellish activity. Men, ant-like in the distance, cutting rows at what appeared impossible speeds, machete blades flashing like signals. Mule carts were loaded. Fires burnt, smoke soon lost against white-hot sky. While further on, fields remained benignly deserted beneath the scorching ball of the sun.

Noah wiped sweat from his brow with his forearm. 'It seems rash to even dare hope for it.' He glanced at me. 'Whilst you were with Susannah in your chamber, we asked Isabella if her servant had seen the child's name in the leger with Penny's, but sadly not. She'd asked him to look because you'd mentioned the girl to her.'

The track began to climb up into a range of low hills covered in scrub, Aloe, and a few Bay Leaf trees and Bearded Figs. The air grew hotter. Noah led us into the shade of a copse of large Bearded Figs, their profusion of ariel roots cascading down from branches, where we dismounted to drink tepid water from our leather bottles. He turned a full circle, surveying the panorama below us. 'Christ's wounds. This really is a sugar island.' The air was tainted by the acrid smoke from more fires close by. Was there a hint of sweetness behind it, or was that just fanciful?

After giving ourselves some minutes to cool down, we mounted once more and resumed our journey towards Bathsheba. 'I imagine Rifkind will have written to Hilliard telling him we're searching for Penny. Even though he tried to conceal her whereabouts on Barbados, perhaps it might occur to him he made a mistake telling us the right island ... or does he enjoy taking such a risk?'

Noah glanced at me. 'He'll be ready for us. I'm sure he'll hide her away so finding her probably won't be easy.'

I thought for a few moments. 'I think you and I should go to the house and Hal stay away for a while.' I turned to him. 'Perhaps have a look around outside? There may be outbuildings where he could conceal her. It would be easy enough to have her cooperation if she believed bad people were coming to steal her away from her papa.'

'Makes sense,' Noah said. 'He certainly won't want her to see you, Raphael. Though she doesn't know us, I'm sure Hilliard is already well aware of our appearance, but there's little we can do about that.'

I felt a touch more confident now we had some sort of plan in place, however rudimentary. 'Let's hope he hasn't sent her away altogether.' Yet to risk that he would have to place her in the care of someone he could trust explicitly. And would he be able to see her go from him when he knew we were searching for her? I prayed he would not. The cold expression on Noah's face suggested he was reviewing methods for persuading the man to reveal her whereabouts, should this prove necessary. I did not doubt his readiness nor, indeed, his ability to do so.

We parted company from Hal in a valley before the track rose again to approach the plantation house visible on a rise beyond. I rode side by side with Noah up to the large house with its own ubiquitous wraparound covered porch. It was, perhaps not quite as grand as Cinnamon Hill but not by much. As expected, we were met by slaves who relieved us of our horses and were then ushered inside by the usual liveried footman; white-wigged, ebony-skinned, and impassive. In the mahogany furnished drawing-room with its open casements, a cooling breeze stirred pale diaphanous drapes, offering a panoramic view of the beach below with large, jagged rocks like weapons dropped by the gods along its length, white breakers shoulder-charging against them.

At the sound of footsteps on the polished boards, Noah and I stood. Hilliard was short and stocky with thinning fair hair and a pink shinny face. He looked surprisingly amiable, though his button eyes were hooded and wary. There seemed little point in dissembling. 'My name is Raphael Rossi. I'm here for my daughter.'

Hilliard's face darkened. 'Your daughter, Sir. Why, pray, would you imagine your daughter is here?'

Noah tilted his head, eyeing Hilliard coldly. 'No need for denial. We know how you acquired Penelope Rossi and why. Tell us where she is.' Noah moved forward. 'For if you do not, Sir, things will not go well for you, you have my word on that.'

Hilliard bristled. 'You threaten me, Sir? You enter my home and threaten me?' He moved towards a bell-rope.

Noah swiftly blocked his way, looming over him. 'Indeed, I do. Make no mistake. It's no idle threat.' His hand went to his sword hilt. 'Do not call out. I can and will hurt you.'

I stepped up beside him. 'Return my daughter so I might take her to her mother, at once.'

His face turned puce. He flung his hand towards me in a disparaging manner. 'Not your daughter, Sir. Never yours.'

I moved close to him, smiling. 'My wife's daughter and my stepdaughter. A child you purchased and then tricked with lies—'

'I *am* her natural father.'

I felt his spittle wet on my face.

'Her mother has kept it from you ... Penny knows it, though. She wishes to be with me. And you cannot prove otherwise. You—'

'Oh, but we can.' I took a breath. 'Penelope's father is Samuel Carter, godson to King Charles II of England. His father is Admiral Lord Rupert Carter, close friend to the King. My wife is goddaughter to the King also. And, believe me, he knows they are Penelope's parents. Will you challenge him on it, Sir? Will you challenge the King?' I watched the scorn of disbelief quickly followed by horror cross his face when he understood.

His shock was quickly subsumed in the bluster of contempt. 'The King? Absurd, Sir.'

'You wish to test it?' Yet I hoped he would not for, in truth, what proof did we have? None without waiting for an exchange of letters with London which, of course, would take months. 'You know my daughter was taken from St James's Park. You know she was finely dressed. She must have told you something of her life? Do you truly doubt it?'

I saw defeat in his eyes then. He looked away yet seemed to find his resolve again. 'I do, Sir. Indeed, I do.'

He was nothing if not tenacious.

Hilliard lifted his chin. 'She is no longer here, anyway. When I learnt there was a search for her, I sent her to another of my plantations.' He shook his head. 'The girl is my natural daughter. You have been lied to.'

I glared at him, my heart pounding with rage. 'You cannot believe she has no such connections? Why would we claim it so if it were not the truth? You expect to steal her from those who love her with impunity when her parents are under the King's protection?' Well, perhaps Sam less so of late. 'You lost a child and inflicted the same agony on my wife. We didn't know where she was. If she were alive or dead. My wife – I staggered slightly, almost overwhelmed by emotion, then stared hard at him again. 'You're not worth a single moment of my wife's torment.'

CHAPTER 31

Hal

Hal rode along the outer edge of the field closest to the plantation house until he came to a track leading inwards, presumably where the cart loads of cut cane would be brought out. Still there was no sign of life anywhere in heat that made the air shimmer, the only sound the ceaseless calling song of cicadas. So, the cane could not yet be ripe enough for cutting. When he arrived at a ramshackle cabin the colour of driftwood at the far side of the field, he dismounted, holding his horse's bridle, waiting in the shade of a copse of aromatic trees.

There was a small garden plot at the front where a rangy black woman, dressed in a blue calico shift with a grey kerchief around her head, knelt to weed around the staked beans, pouring a wooden dipper of water from a pail onto each meagre plant. He continued to watch from the shadows until she struggled to her feet and moved away down a narrow path swinging her bucket. How far was the well? Yet, he had no choice but to act then for lying on the covered porch that fronted the little house was a small girl, playing with a pair of lean grey and white kittens. That this was Susannah's daughter he had no doubt, for she looked as much hers as he did his father's son. He tied his mount to a tree branch before stepping out into the light.

He smiled. 'Ho there, Penny.' She looked up, returning his smile a little uncertainly, politeness vying with caution on her face. Again, he saw only her mother.

'I give you good day, Sir.'

Hal bent to pluck two or three sturdy stems of what looked like ryegrass – who knew here – with heavy seed heads and moved onto the porch to sit cross-legged beside her, his jackboots dusty from his ride. He handed her a stem and began to move one in a way to attract the kittens' attention. They were soon chasing and pouncing, while Hal and Penny knelt side by side, laughing at their antics. He put his blade of grass down and sat again.

Penny did the same to sit beside him, companionably. She lifted a strand of her hair and knelt up to place it against Hal's. 'See, we have the same hair.'

He smiled, taking the strand, and running his fingers along it.' We do. Though yours is finer.' He tucked it behind her ear. 'My name is Hal Bartholomew. I've come from your mama. She want's you back with her, Penny.'

Her eyes widened. 'Is Mama here?' She looked ready to leap to her feet and run.

'No. She's in Jamaica ... the island where you landed before you came here. Raphael is though.'

'Papa?' She stood, looking uncertain, glancing around her. 'He's here. Where? Why hasn't Mama come, too?'

'Your papa is at the big house with mine. Your mama really wanted to come but she couldn't. She's to have a child.' He smiled. 'He may already be born, your brother or–'

'A brother ... my brother?'

'Yes, Penny. Sam Carter stayed with her, though he wanted to come here too.' Hal could see she found what he said difficult to take in. He stood and picked up one of the kittens, which was busy trying to steal a stalk from the other, who growled determined to re-tain it. 'Will you come with me to the house and talk to Raphael? He loves you very much and wants to get you back to your mama as quickly as he can.'

'But what about my Papa here?' Her eyes filled with tears 'He loves me, too. How can I leave him?'

Hal put down the kitten and lifted Penny into his arms instead. 'Sweetheart, this man is not your papa–'

She leaned away. 'He is. He explained it all to me. Raphael is my step-papa because he is Mama's husband now.'

Hal lifted her hand and kissed it. 'Penny that's quite right, of course, but Sam is your natural father not this man. He stole you. Your mama didn't know where you were. She was sick with worry for you. It's taken us until now to find you.'

She now appeared truly bewildered. 'Sam? ... but Papa ... he said Mama knew where I was. That she was happy for me to spend time with him.'

Poor little girl. She had been snatched from St James's Park yet had accepted this man as her father and it seemed he had not harmed her apart from by such cruel deception. Christ, how she had been hood-winked. Not difficult, he supposed, with such a young child. And what of the other little girl? He would leave such questions to his father and Raphael. He set her down. 'Come. Let's go to Raphael, now.'

She grasped his hand. 'Papa,' she whispered, smiling. 'I should like that.'

Then he noticed the woman who had been watching over Penny, standing in the gloom inside the shack. She must have used another entrance, and she clearly had no intention of trying to prevent him taking her. He raised his hand in surreptitious thanks and saw the suggestion of white teeth in the shadows. Hal lifted Penny up onto the horse and mounted be-hind her. With an arm securely around her, they made their way along the track towards the house, for he had no intention of relinquishing her. They would return her to Susannah ... and Sam. No one could prevent it, now.

. . .

The slaves who took his horse, stared at Penny wide-eyed to see her with him. He lifted her from the saddle and carried her inside. A footman opened the door to the drawing room without a word. When he walked in, all three men turned. He made straight for Raphael, handing Penny to him. And she clung to him, tears rolling down her face. 'Papa. Papa.'

Raphael's face was wet, too, as he lowered her to the floor, dropping to his knees in front of her. '*Piccola amore mio*. How we've missed you. Your mama will be overjoyed.' He crossed himself before holding her to him, his hand cupping the back of her head.

Hal watched his father turn to Hilliard who stood seemingly transfixed by the sight of Penny held in Raphael's arms. Noah moved to loom over him again. 'Where is the other child? Is she here?'

It was Penny who answered. 'She's gone home to her mama and papa. Pa–' She pointed at Hilliard. 'He said she only came to keep me company on the voyage.'

Noah shoved the man hard in the chest, sending him sprawling down onto the sofa behind him. 'Where is she?' Hal came to stand beside him and there was a susurrus of blades unsheathed before two sword tips appeared on his chest. Noah moved his up to Hilliard's throat, pressing hard enough to draw a bead of blood. 'I wouldn't recommend making me ask again, Sir.'

'On my life, I swear I don't know. Only Rifkind does.'

CHAPTER 32

Raphael

In the end Noah and Hal tied him up and we took him with us, uncertain what else to do with him. No one tried to stop us, which at first surprised us but then did not. Hilliard was not well thought of and by the look of some of their expressions, he would likely not have fared well had we left him to their mercies. None showed any desire to come to his aid, either, with the overseer clearly away from the plantation. Slaves would see nothing defensible in stealing a child when their own were stolen with impunity.

We had all removed our coats and folded them into saddle bags in the still heat of the afternoon, even the wind off the sea seemed to have died. My hair, tied at my neck, felt heavy and damp. I pulled the string from it, letting it fall loose around my shoulders. Penny rode in front of me, having attached herself to me like a limpet as the closet link to her mother. I understood, for I felt it myself, my eyes fixed on her hair, one arm around her holding her close. 'Will I have a brother now?'

I kissed the top of her head. 'It's possible but I hope not quite yet. I want to be there with Mama when he comes if I can.'

I was not prepared for her next question, though it was entirely logical. 'Was Sam with her when I was born?'

I sighed. 'No, Piccola. He didn't know about you then.'

She turned around to look at me. 'He thought I was her sister?'

I smiled. 'He did. Everyone did then.' I knew, of course, this was not entirely true though Susannah had believed it so at the time. Her father, and even Frances Stuart and the King had been quite aware of Penny's parentage, just as I told Hilliard.

'Does he know now?'

'He does, and he's very happy to be your papa.' It was then the coincidence of it struck me. Penny's natural father lived in the Indies as did the man who had claimed to be him. Did Rifkind know this? Had Susannah's letter to Sam been intercepted? Could someone have thought Penny knew where he was? 'The people who took you in St James's Park, did they tell you why they wanted you?'

She leaned back against me, and I tightened my arm around her. 'They were taking me to my papa. They asked me if I knew where he was, but I didn't.

Then they told me the name of the man here. He was my father and wanted to see me.'

I kissed the top of her head, again. 'Well, we can talk about it all once we're safely aboard the Mirabel and on our way back to Mama.' I felt her head bounce a little off my chest as she began to doze and moved my arm up a little higher to hold her steady, wondering how I could ever let her out of my grasp.

We had crossed the ridge and were heading down towards the plain to pass by Holetown and go on to Bridgetown and the harbour when Noah held up his hand for us to stop. For a moment I could hear nothing beyond the wind and the susurration from the cane fields ... and then I heard it. The sound of distant hoof beats. We were pursued.

He pointed to a group of baobab trees a little way down the slope not far from the trail. 'We'll hide ourselves in there, until Hal and I can take them from behind.'

Hilliard was tied to a sturdy shrub and gagged, while our horses were tethered a little further in. I held Penny's hand, watching the track from the shadows of the great trees which had additional trunks seeming to support each main branch. Noah and Hal held their horses' bridles, tense and waiting, while the hoof beats came ever closer. Christ, could we really fail now when we were so close to escape? I saw Penny appeared alarmed. 'Don't be afraid, *piccola*.' I gestured towards Noah and Hal. 'We have giants to protect us.' She smiled, her eyes fixed on Hal.

Noah held up his hand. 'Quiet.'

We watched two burly men on scrawny horses pass by at a loping canter. Hilliard's struggling reaction told us they were his rescuers. Noah and Hal mounted in unison then, their faces set and grim. And, once again without a word, they walked their mounts out onto the track drew their swords and launched themselves after the men like two marauding Vikings raiders coming on them out of the sun. So, when Hilliard's henchmen turned at the sound, they were forced to shade their eyes to see who approached, giving the Bartholomews some additional moments of advantage.

Penny's eyes were on Hal, still, and I turned her towards me, my hand on her head. 'Don't watch. All shall be well, you'll see.' I, though, could not turn away. The outcome now would seal our fate. I was acutely aware of the man tied to the tree behind me. He would serve as a hostage should it come to that. I prayed it would not. So, how could I not pray his men would be overcome?

The Bartholomews were now upon their adversaries. At the last moment, Hal turned his sword and used its pommel to strike his opponent's forehead, causing him to catapult over his horse's rump and hit the ground hard. Then he was on him, vaulting from his horse, leg over saddle swell, his sword ready to pierce his throat until the man got his own weapon up to parry the blow. Meanwhile, Noah was battling his foe, both on horseback still, driving him back down the gradient, using his superior strength and reach.

I released the breath I hadn't known I held. 'All shall be well, *piccola*,' I said again, feeling some confidence in those words now, watching Noah and Hal fight with such skill and – it has to be said – complete lack of scruple which even I knew to be the only way to fight to win. As such thoughts occurred to me, Hal proceeded to kick his opponent viciously in the genitals before administering a coup de grace down into the back of his neck and quickly running to his father's aid. Needless to say, Noah looked to be in very little need of such assistance. The silence of it all surprised me. Grunting gasps and heavy breathing only, in air hazed by the dust of their struggle, with no energy to waste on bloodcurdling screeches when fighting was to the death. The horses had made more noise, snorting and whinnying, hooves clattering on the track as they were forced to twist and turn.

'Are they dead?'

I had just sufficient time to realise what a shocking thing it was for her to have to ask, when I was able to reply. 'It would seem so.' I heard a groan from behind me. What would the Bartholomews do with him now? The sound of his rapid breathing revealed the same thought had occurred to him. Holy God. I now watched Noah make certain of his kill by stabbing the supine man directly through the heart. Hal collapsed down where he stood onto the dusty track, putting his head in his hands, before turning away to puke. Had he ever killed before? I had certainly never witnessed death by violence and the shock of it left me numb and strangely detached from the scene. I tried to pray though only managed to rather feebly commend the dead to God.

Noah squatted beside Hal, resting his hand on his shoulder. 'All is done now, Lad. We're safe.' He stood. 'Now let's clear them from the road.'

I reached for Penny's hand, without allowing her to look behind her. 'Come.' I led her deeper into the green shade beneath the trees, suddenly fearing I might puke too, but determined not to for her sake. 'We'll soon be at the ship. 'I hope you won't be seasick, *il piccola mio.*' No surprise it had come to mind.

'I wasn't after a while before. The woman said I'd become used to the ship's movings.'

I smiled. 'Then I'm sure it will be so again.'

In the end, Hal came to find us, white-faced and sweating. I wanted to ask what they had done with Hilliard but could not in front of Penny. 'The horses wait for us on the trail.' His eyes did not meet mine.

We made it back on board safely and Noah had us under way in record time. There was a collective sense of relief when the Mirabel sailed out of the harbour and into the open sea on the cusp of nightfall. In the cabin, I laid Penny down onto the bunk and watched her sleep for a while, until I had to wake her for the evening meal. Noah arrived followed by two deckhands bringing us food – a stew of some indeterminate meat, bread, cheese, and a large jug of small beer. None of us had much appetite, Penny barely able to keep her eyes open, managed to get down a little of the stew before I moved her back onto the bed, where she dropped back into sleep almost immediately.

Noah sighed. 'Poor little lass. I suppose we must ask her what happened to her, but she'll need a good sleep before we inflict it on her.'

Hal scrubbed at his face. 'Christ. I'm not sure I want to hear it.'

Noah frowned. 'Then don't.'

They glared at each other before Hal stood and left the cabin. My God. Why in the name of heaven did they not talk to each other rather than hoard resentment until it festered and erupted? I sighed. Fathers and sons. Hard eyes turned on me in the lamplight, brows lowered. I smiled and held up my hands in mock surrender. 'Not my concern.'

'Indeed,' he stood, too, and strode from the cabin. And not to find his son, I felt quite certain. I was self-aware enough to know I had little room to judge. I'd had a less than adequate relationship with my own papà and had to take some share of the blame for it. After the table had been cleared and the others had still not returned, there seemed nothing left to do other than climb carefully up beside Penny and hope for the oblivion of sleep.

She stirred a little as I lifted my rosary down from its nail above the bunk. 'Is Mama all right, do you think?'

'Yes. I believe she is,' I whispered. 'I think we'd

know if she were not, *piccola*.' Sleep found me easily then, my beads still clasped in my fingers.

I had not heard the men return but woke in the dead of night to see their sleeping forms lit by starlight, bright in the dark of the moon. A sound had woken me. My first thought was that Penny wept in her sleep, but I quickly realised the quiet strangled sounds came from Hal. Noah slept on. Christ. I prayed for him then, which felt woefully inadequate, but it was all I had. Killing was a Mortal Sin as, I'm sure, was condoning it. Not for the first time, I was grateful my religion offered me the sacrament of absolution through penance. Hal, of course, had no such blessing. Yet was not killing without any choice in it ... kill or be killed ... was this not exempt from such judgement?

I woke again to find myself alone in the cabin, though breakfast had been left on the table for me. Well, bread, cheese, and small beer. Why had no one woken me? And more to the point, why had nothing woken me? But I had slept deeply and felt refreshed, so I should perhaps be grateful for that at least. I made a hasty meal before taking myself out on deck into air alive with shouts and the rattle of rigging. There was a stiff wind filling the sails, with sunlight glaring off the chop. I shaded my eyes and quickly spotted Noah at the helm. Scanning further, I saw Hal sitting cross-legged propped against the mainmast with Penny, giving close attention to a section of his hair, which fell loose about him.

I smiled and walked to them. 'What's this, Penny?'

She had plaited two or three strands and was busy hooking a small, downy seagull feather through one of them.

Hal looked up returning my smile, rather ruefully. 'I think my colouring not quite right for a red savage, Raphael. Perhaps you would prove a more satisfactory vi ... subject.'

I laughed. For I knew he had been about to say victim. 'Maybe you need one or two more feathers, *il piccola mio*?'

She jumped to her feet. 'I'll ask Morris. He has hens below.' It had not taken her long to find her way around the crew.

We watched her skip away on her errand as though her ordeal had never happened. I crossed myself thanking God for his mercy before sitting down, my back against the other side of the mast. I cleared my throat. I had to say something. He, of course, was under no obligation to answer me, but *I* felt an obligation to at least ask. 'Are you all right? I'm afraid I overheard you last night.'

He stood in a single motion and moved across the deck to the starboard taffrail. Reluctantly, I followed him. 'Forgive me. I only wish to help if I can.'

He closed his eyes. 'Did Papa hear me, do you think?'

'You barely made a sound. I only woke because of Penny.' *Cristo santo.* Did he really believe Noah would not have gone to him if he had? But then, would mine? Noah, though, was not remotely like my father.

His face was grim. 'Is there any way to find forgiveness for it ... taking a life, in your religion?'

What could I say? 'I think, perhaps, killing in self-defence is not a Mortal sin.' I hoped it was so. And also, for praying it would occur, as I had? 'I could see you hadn't done it before.' And that his father had. I touched his arm. 'Neither of you had a choice. You know that Hal. We would have all died and Penny would've been taken again. But I can understand how shocking it must have been for you.'

He gave me a hard stare. 'To see my father cut a man's throat in cold blood? Yes, admittedly, that was something of a shock.'

I swallowed. I had wondered what they had done with Hilliard. Now I wished I did not know. 'He would have bought another child–'

'You can't know that.'

We both turned at the sound of running footsteps. Penny approached carrying a bunch of brown feathers gathered like a posy clutched in her fingers, her blue skirts over white petticoats billowing out behind her mirroring the sea-swell we sailed upon. 'It seems a risk that could not be taken.'

Hal nodded. 'Tell her Papa called for me.' He walked away without looking back.

I swept Penny up into my arms. 'Hal has ship's duties, so it seems you must have a new patron for your ministrations.'

'Then, Papa, you must sit down at once.'

I sat.

. . .

Later, in the cabin for our main meal, Noah looked from me to Hal, eyebrows raised at our pagan hair, before turning to Penny with a grin. 'Nicely done, little sweetheart.'

She blushed. 'They both have very pretty hair.'

I was stricken then with a memory of seeing her with her friend in St James's Park that terrible day, both with daisy crowns woven into their hair. I turned away. Holy God. Where was poor Kitty now? We could not give up trying to find her before we returned to London. How would we face her parents if we had not tried? We must leave word with the authorities everywhere possible for one thing seemed certain, she would not have been sent home.

I pulled Penny onto my knee and glanced at Noah, who nodded. '*Piccola*, what happened that day? How did they take you from the park?'

She looked up at me with such complete trust, my eyes pricked with tears. 'Mistress Berringer came for us in her coach.'

'Why did she do that? Had you met her before?'

'No, but she said Mama had sent her for us.' She relaxed back against me. 'She lied, didn't she?'

I sighed, glancing at Noah and Hal. 'I'm afraid she did.' And then we listened as she told us her tale, while my anger soared at the scale of the deception inflicted upon them. I could see it reflected on the others' faces, too. Little girls such as Penny and Kitty had never learned not to trust, nor that it could ever be necessary for them not to do so. Penny had arrived at St Katherine Dock believing Susannah wished her to visit her father in Jamaica. Gentle hints that she wished some time alone with me after our marriage, which she had told them of herself, made her feel it was the right thing to do. She was dutifully following her mother's wishes. That she told them I was her stepfather made the notion of a real father waiting for her easier to foist upon her.

Noah made an angry sound through his teeth. 'That pair must be found and dealt with.'

I had little doubt what that would mean for them. *Good.* 'And after a time, you were no longer seasick.'

She nodded and smiled. 'Just like I'm not now.' She chewed her lip. 'When we arrived in the Indies, they took me to a house without Kitty. Master Berringer said she would return to England. I asked when I could go back to my mama, and he said she would write when she wished me home.'

I stroked her face. 'You know none of it is true, don't you, Penny? Mama wanted you with her always and so did I. She was very distressed when we found you gone.'

She turned to look at me. 'I cried because I missed her, but I thought her happy without me.'

'Oh, Penny. How could she ever be happy without you?'

Later, when she had at last settled into sleep, we went out on the deck silvered by starlight, keeping within earshot in case she should call out. 'They took her to Cinnamon Hill but where did they take Kitty?'

Noah looked up at the rigging, casting an expert eye over it, even in such poor light. 'I intend a visit to Rifkind. He sits like a great black spider at the centre of all this.'

Should I tell them of my musings on the coincidence that Sam, too, was in the Indies. If it was too fanciful one or the other of them would point it out to me, I felt sure. 'Is it possible Susannah's letter to Sam was read before it left England? Did they wonder if Penny knew who her father was and where he could be found?'

Noah turned to me, sharply. 'You mean, did they think they could find out from her?'

'Interception would give them the Bartholomew name and Port Royal. Having her captive could prove useful for prising him out. Could this be about Sam?'

Noah closed his eyes. 'Christ wounds, I hope not. That would mean he's no longer safe in Jamaica.'

Hal touched his arm. 'Or it could simply be this Hilliard bought a child and Penny was the one delivered to him.'

'Well, it's something we must find out for certain,' Noah said.

CHAPTER 33
Susannah

I watched the sea as I always did. My first task at dawn. The same when the light died to the sound of birds roosting in trees at the front of the house. The pelicans made their last dives into the darkening, brooding swell. Terns still flying in a last hope of an easy stolen meal. The sky was streaked a dark crimson purple like old, spilled blood when Sam arrived beside me.

'The wind's getting up.'

I had been unaware of it until he spoke. 'The sky looks disturbed, too. Bruised.' The Pelicans had now stopped patrolling just offshore and waves began to break more noisily up onto the beach. We both turned at the sound of footsteps behind us.

Pearl placed a large candle lantern down onto the table. 'Clive's goin to put up dem storm shutters. Looks like we's in for a big blow. You want eat out or in?'

I looked at Sam, deferring to him. He smiled. 'Your choice, Sukie.'

'Let's stay outside while we still can.'

Pearl moved quietly away to fetch our supper. Eventually, we carried our half-finished plates indoors when debris began to blow up onto the porch. Leaves and twigs to start with, followed by larger branches and palm fronds. Finally, when a small green coconut ricocheted off a closed shutter like a cannon shot, it seemed time to defer to local knowledge and get under cover.

Sitting at the polished mahogany table inside, somewhat windblown, I found I had lost what little appetite I had, for how could I not think of the Mirabel sailing in this? As, I saw, did Sam. 'Have you known such storms before?'

He pushed his barely touched plate of griddled flying-fish away. 'Once or twice.' He reached across and grasped my hand. 'We'll be safe here.'

Both of us were not thinking of here, of course. After all, we had loved ones onboard ship. And our daughter, too ... I prayed.

He walked me to my chamber through the long gallery the ashen colour of driftwood in candlelight, hugging me once inside the room amidst the howl of the wind and the clatter of seemingly much larger and heavier debris against the house now. He kissed my forehead. 'Will you be all right?'

I looked to the rattling, pounding shutters. 'Might you stay for a little while?'

He blinked. 'Of course. In truth, I would prefer not to be alone, either' He took a long breath. 'They'll be safe. Noah's a fine captain.'

'And they're bringing Penny home, aren't they?'

When he closed the door, I moved into his arms. He placed his palm on my face. After a few moments there was a light tap on the door, and it opened to one of the girls coming in to help me prepare for bed. Sam moved away to take his leave. 'Come back, yes?'

He nodded. 'If you wish.'

The girl hummed as she unlaced my skirts and bodice. Was this because she was fearful? Or because she was not? Jesu. I missed Raphael. I tried to send thoughts out to him, carrying my love. Please God, keep them safe.

Sam returned after the girl had gone and climbed into the bed beside me. We held hands, silent in the clamour. 'Try not to be afraid.' I knew he was not talking of the house but of the ship that held our hearts. 'Noah is extremely capable, you know. He first went to sea when he was thirteen years old, so I imagine there is very little he hasn't experienced before.'

I turned my head on the pillow so I might face him. 'I've witnessed him in action, don't forget. He's very determined.' I watched him smile in the flickering candlelight. I made one of my involuntary harrumphs as a foot made its own determined effort to secure my attention. My hand arrived to pat and comfort.

His came to join mine.

I knew we both thought of Penny doing this very same thing. 'She was probably even more brutal than this one.'

He turned on his side to face me. 'I just saw Pearl go into Michael's room, rather furtively.'

I wondered why he seemed so pleased about it. 'Really? Well, I'm surprised at you, Sam. Not sniggering male delight at a young man losing his virginity to an older woman, surely?'

He narrowed his eyes, looking affronted. 'Christ, you know me better than that, surely?'

'Forgive me. I do. Of course, I do. But I was a little surprised by your expression.'

He sighed. 'Let's just say something happened to him that makes this a very good thing, I think.'

I stared at him. 'Too good perhaps, then? Could Noah have something to do with it, do you think?'

'Well, I could see him mentioning it to her. He's a pragmatic man. But Pearl's not one to do anything she doesn't wish to.'

'I'm sure she isn't. I suppose you can't tell me what happened to him?'

'That's for him to do.' He took a breath. 'But I can tell you about something that happened to me a long time ago. If you wish to hear it, of course?'

I held his gaze. 'Tell me.'

'When I stayed with a school friend in Richmond one time ... in truth, it was right after I'd abandoned you.' He bit his lip. 'Anyway, the first night I was there a man came into my room. I never did know who he was.' He blinked. 'Well, he forced himself on me–'

'Jesu, Sam.'

He smiled. 'Rather to my surprise, force soon became unnecessary, but I can't say I wasn't rather cross about it.'

I watched him close his eyes. *Why bother with insouciance? I know you too well.* 'Hmm. So, may I infer something similar happened to Michael?'

He met my gaze again, raising his eyebrows. 'So it seems I've told you, after all.' He tilted his head. 'Let's just say similar but far from the same, poor boy.'

It had clearly been his intention I should know. Perhaps leaving me such an easy guess assuaged his conscience? 'Then a good dose of woman has been prescribed?' I frowned, suddenly understanding. 'Don't tell me this man tried to make him doubt himself?'

'Oh, indeed he did. He's done the same to many other boys, I'm sure. He tells them he knows they want a man because he's able to pleasure them which means nothing, of course. So, they don't tell each other because he's left them with too much shame.'

I rolled my eyes. 'Well, they are rather easy to please.' When Sam's eyes widened in surprise, I wanted to laugh. So did he, I saw. We looked away from each other for a few moments. 'Yet, my dear, you were only somewhat cross with your man?' Considerably more than that, I knew.

He raised himself on an elbow, trying to be serious

again, looking down at me. 'All right. He led me somewhere I needed to go, not that he was aware of that to start with, was he? Neither was I, of course. But would it not have been a touch more civilised to woo me a little first?'

I sat up to raise my pillows. Jesu, it was difficult to get comfortable. Sam moved to help me. It seemed almost dreamlike it was him beside me and not Raphael. The ceaseless commotion of the wind added to the sense of unreality. Sleep felt very far away. My child clearly felt the same for he moved around restlessly, never seeming able to settle. 'I'm trying to think of a situation where a woman might react to rape in the same way you did.' I closed my eyes. 'Perhaps one at court, believing she had ensnared the man who treats her so rudely ... even seeing him as a conquest. But then that implied she wanted it as, in truth, you did. So, is that rape at all?'

'Perhaps not, but it's certainly extremely bad manners.'

I chuckled. 'I once told Raphael it would be impossible for him to force me. It's hard to explain how we arrived at such a topic. Let's just say it was rather silly. But my argument was that he would have no trouble overpowering me should he wish, but he couldn't coerce me because I would never wish to refuse him however much I might say I did. Yet I also know just saying I didn't wish it would be enough for him to stop. If that makes sense.' Something clattered loudly on the roof above our heads. I clutched his arm. 'Please God, let them be safe.'

'Raphael will look after her, I'm sure.'

'They'll look after each other. She was always trying to take care of him ... she's such a kind little girl. I'm pretty sure that comes from you. There's an unpleasant streak of vindictiveness in me. And temper. Like Grandmama, maybe?'

He laughed. 'It's true Sylvia's can be a force of nature. I wonder, though, if Penny isn't more like my mama than either of us? I've thought of it quite a lot since I knew she was mine.'

'Well, I know she would have recognised her the moment she saw her. Known she was yours; I mean. Like Lucia did with Raphael's child.'

Sleep took us in the end. I'm sure I held his hand though when I awoke, I was alone.

I found him outside on the porch working again on Michael's portrait. He was perched up on the rail again, his loose hair ripping around his face like streamers of flame in the stiff breeze coming off the sea. The servants had cleared the debris left by the storm from around the house, though the air was redolent with the bitter smell of sap from vegetation ripped apart by the wind, the beach strewn with detritus as far as the eye could see. I shielded my gaze against the glare, staring out to sea. Where in the name of God was the Mirabel now? Please let her be safe. I went to Sam and placed my hand on his shoulder.

He turned, bending to kiss my cheek. 'You look a touch pale, Sukie. Pearl will be out with breakfast shortly. You should eat.'

Michael stretched and yawned. 'I'm starved. I feel like I haven't eaten for a week.'

Sam raised his eyebrows. 'What can you have been doing to work up such an appetite, I wonder?'

Colour spread across his face. 'Didn't sleep very well,' he muttered. 'Damn storm.' His face broke into a wide grin when Pearl and two of the kitchen girls stepped out onto the porch carrying heavily laden trays. 'You're a life-saver, Pearl.'

Sam and I glanced at each other, battling to keep our faces straight.

Pearl pulled a chair back from the table. 'Susannah. Eat. You be needing your strength, soon now, me think.'

I looked towards the empty sea. 'Not quite yet, I hope.'

One of the girls turned to me, pointing excitedly up the coast away from the headland. 'There be a ship aground someways yonder, Mistress–'

'Hold yous blather, Rose. Get dem trays back to kitchens now.'

Sam took the chair next to mine. 'What do you know of it, Pearl?'

'Pah.' She waved her hand, dismissively. 'One

foundered aways beyond. Folks say some cargos washing up. Nothin bout us, for sure.'

Sam reached for my hand. 'I'm certain she's right.'

A pain clutched my belly then, like the cruel tightening of an iron band around my middle. I struggled to my feet and blundered away from the table. A sudden liquid rush ran down my legs, splattering onto the wooden deck boards. 'No. Jesu, no.' This couldn't happen now. It was too soon. Raphael had not yet returned. I turned to Sam, whose look of stunned horror made me want to laugh ... or cry. I could not quite decide which. Pearl's hands found me then. 'Come. We clean you up, then you must get some food in you.' She glanced at the wet floor before turning to Sam. 'That jus mean the chile, he come. Will take him time I spec. Like always.'

'Penny took three days,' I said, gloomily.

'Christ. You never told me that,' Sam said.

I held my back. 'Why would I? It was nine years ago.'

Michael stood and took my arm and, with Pearl holding the other, they walked me to my chamber. We stopped outside my door. 'What a pity you're not further along in your physician's training.'

He smiled, ruefully. 'Reading only, so far.' He rested his hand on my belly. 'I understand the process ... but so do you, of course. I'll leave you in Pearl's care.' A look passed between them, which told me Pearl's visit to him the night before would not be her last. She closed the shutters behind him and efficiently cleaned me up and dressed me in a clean shift.

I clutched my belly as another pain came. 'He definitely means business.'

'Nothin for it now but wait on him.' She patted my arm, reassuringly. 'You want a tray in here or back out?'

'I'll come out. I'll be stuck in here long enough later.'

She nodded. 'I'll send a lad to tell Ma Gala we'll be needing her. She'll see you right. Better than dat town woman.' She made a drinking gesture. 'And there's Michael, too.'

'That's good.' Though I was uncertain just how useful he could be.

Sam was alone on the sofa closest to the house, sipping coffee. He looked somewhat surprised to see me. I noticed the floor had been scrubbed. I sat beside him. 'Did you think I'd pissed myself?'

He raised his eyebrows. 'Elegantly put. But, in truth, it crossed my mind. Michael explained it all to me. He even brought me an anatomy textbook book with some rather unpleasant illustrations to complete my education.' He gestured to the book on the couch beside him.

'Should I look?'

'No. You don't need to, anyway.' He shook his head. 'Once again, I saw that look of incredulity when he understood I hadn't known Penny was mine.'

'It was for the best; we both know that.' I gasped a

breath as pain gipped me again. They were getting worse. He put his arm around me and after a few moments, I was able to relax against him. 'I hope he gets here soon.'

'How much time do you have?'

'Many hours ... or perhaps even days.' God help me. I never thought I would pray it might be days. Though I tried to resist, how could my thoughts not go to the ship foundered up the coast. What if I had lost them both?

'It's not the Mirabel, Sukie. Noah would never allow that to happen ... and neither would Raphael's God, perhaps.'

Michael came out of the house. 'Raphael's God?'

'It's a long story. But what else have I to do?' The pain that seized me then served to remind me that I did indeed have something else and was, in truth, already doing it.

CHAPTER 34

Raphael

How could it be May already? I marked-off the days as we sailed back to Jamaica, praying Susannah had not yet given birth.

I had discovered Penny enjoyed playing chess and was rather good at it for one so young. Sam had taught her when she was very small. Hal showed her how to play Ombre and various disreputable English gambling card games. He also taught her an impressive game-face, which I found somewhat disconcerting. For some reason she seemed to find it especially easy to win against me, much to Hal's amusement. By our seventh day out, he appeared more light-hearted. I'm sure Penny's company relaxed him. I even wondered if Noah had talked to him, but their ongoing reserve suggested this was unlikely. I decided I must put it in Sam's hands when we arrived back. Poor Sam.

On the eighth day, I watched the sky darken through the aftcastle windows. As it looked like we were in for a storm, I left Penny and Hal to their cards and went out on deck. Noah was up in the crow's nest with his spyglass. Just seeing him up there made me dizzy. I moved to the starboard rail and looked out over the grey angry-looking sea, with the wind already whipping white tops on waves beginning to rise alarmingly. I clutched the taffrail, hoping the storm wouldn't slow our journey.

I startled when Noah arrived beside me. 'Wind's in the right direction, at least. Let's hope it doesn't blow us past Jamaica.'

I crossed myself. 'Please God, not.' I watched him frowning up at the sky. 'How worried are you?'

His eyes ran over the array of sails, which were being adjusted as we spoke by men who seemed just as surefooted up in the rigging regardless of the wild weather. 'We should be able to ride it out, but I'd like to get us into Fishermans Bay to drop anchor there, if we can.' He turned to me. 'You should get back under cover. It's going to get ugly out here very quickly. Send Hal out, can you? He's needed.'

A squall of rain hit us before I made it into the cabin. Hal was already preparing himself to go outside. 'This is all we bloody need,' he muttered, gloomily.

Penny moved to hug him before he left, and he swung her up into his arms. 'Stay with your papa. You'll be safe in here.' He met my gaze. 'Where is he?'

'He was heading for the helm.'

He nodded, looking grim ... and hostile. So, definitely no reconciliation between them.

The sky had darkened further, and the cabin was full of shadows. I found the candle lamps and lit them with a flint and steel, placing them on hooks where they were safer in rough seas. Penny looked pale and I hoped she would not find herself seasick again. Poor little girl. I rubbed my hands, trying to seem cheerful. 'Chess, I think.' I hoped it would keep her mind occupied. Mine too, of course.

We played for a while and that she seemed on course to beat me suggested she was being distracted rather more successfully than I. Though after a time she began to lose interest, too. The rain hit the windows hard as the wind tossed the ship making it pitch and roll, alarmingly.

Hal returned then, soaked and wind tossed, his hair dark and plastered to his skill. 'Help me get the shutters across. We might lose some panes.'

I stood to help him lift the heavy boards and fasten them in place with wooden batons. 'Do we hold our course still?'

'Just about but we've furled most of the sails now and Papa has lashed the wheel. He still hopes to get us to shelter in Fishermans Bay.' Penny chose that moment to vomit onto the floor. When she began to cry, Hal picked her up and laid her gently down onto the bunk. 'I'll send someone in to clean up and bring you a bucket for her.' He kissed her forehead. 'Rest, little one. We'll be through the worst of it soon, I'm sure.'

After a while, I lay down beside her and clasped her in my arms, while the ship tossed like a cork in a maelstrom. It felt like being caught in a nightmare, so much so I was unsure if I were awake or asleep. Yet I clutched my beads, still, and told my decades, asking God to let us live. For how could we get so close to Susannah, and all be lost like this now? I crossed myself, kissed my beads, and told God I trusted in his mercy.

The silence and the gentle rocking of the ship woke me. Some light crept in around the great shutters; enough for me to see the sleeping forms of Noah and Hal sprawled on the floor. Penny slept, still, and I stroked back strands of bright hair from her forehead, my heart overflowing with love for her.

Her eyes flew open then, and she threw her arms around my neck. 'Will Mama be all right?' she whispered.

'I'm sure she will.' Please God.

Later we stood out on deck, enjoying the fresh air after the stale cabin. Noah looked exhausted as he issued orders to unfurl the sails when we left Fishermans Bay to begin our sail around the coast towards Port Royal. 'You did well to get us here last night. It can't have been easy.' An embarrassingly stupid remark. I still felt rather shaken by the whole experience.

He gave me a hard look and scrubbed at his stubble. 'It wasn't. It was touch and go for a while.'

'Well, I'm extremely grateful for your expertise.'

Penny tugged at my hand. 'Will we be there soon?'

Noah's face softened and he squatted down in front of her. 'A few hours yet, sweetheart. We can't use all the sheets ... sails because of a cracked foremast.' He smiled. 'But the storm was lucky for us, too. We got here sooner than we would have without it. And you'll be with your mama before you know it.'

She flung her arms around him. 'Thank you.' She turned to look at the damaged mast and seeing Hal there directing the temporary repair, set off towards him.

Noah rose. 'She's rather taken with him.'

'He's good with her.'

He shook his head, blinking. 'She's so like her mother. I didn't think I'd see anything of him in her. But she has Sam's eyes.' Tears spilled and he swiped them away, impatiently.

I squeezed his arm. I had never seen him so affected. 'I know. When I first noticed it, I was surprised I never had before.'

He shook himself, clearly trying to find sure ground. 'Forgive me. The night took its toll more than I realised.' He tried to laugh. 'So, I'm a touch overwrought.' Yet tears fell again, and he struggled to speak. 'It just brought it home to me, is all. Who she is and what it means to get her back.'

I had to bite my lip hard, for I felt it too. The enormity of it and how close we had come to disaster. Christ. Noah had killed for her. So had Hal. I wished he could see his father now. Perhaps then he could understand. 'Susannah and I will never forget what we owe you, Noah. And neither will Sam.'

He grasped my shoulder briefly and took a long breath. 'Well, I've a ship to sail. Best get to it.'

It seemed but moments before Hal arrived beside me while I struggled with emotion, still. 'Where's Penny.'

'Feeding hens.' He watched his father talking to the boatswain at the wheel. 'Is he all right?"

'What makes you ask?'

'He looked odd ... the way he stood.' He shook his head. 'In truth, I don't really know.'

If I tell him, will it help them or make things worse? I sighed. 'He was distressed. He wept a little–'

He looked incredulous. 'Papa wept? Why?'

Suddenly I was angry. 'Holy Christ, Hal. Ask him. Just damn well talk to him.' I turned on my heel and walked away. I found Penny in the galley breaking eggs into a bowl under the watchful eye of the cook, Morris, who fished out pieces of shell as necessary, which appeared to be rather often. 'Are you all right in here?'

'Yes, Papa. I'm helping.'

Morris, understanding the question was really more for him, met my gaze and nodded slightly. 'You is indeed, my lovely. And very grateful I is for it, too.' The crew had truly taken her to their hearts. They all knew of her ordeal.

'That's good then. I shall be in the cabin should you need me.' Inside, I sat at the table and closed my eyes, longing for Susannah with such intensity it felt hard to breath. Was she safe? Was the child already delivered? I knew I would feel every minute of every hour that passed until we arrived at the house. I took the beads from my pocket and began to pray again.

CHAPTER 35

Susannah

I was at the stage now when walking seemed to help so I paced the porch, sitting when I needed to. Sam remained outside his chamber, sketching the debris on the beach though, in truth, I believed his eyes were more often on me. Did I make him uncomfortable? I stood and walked slowly back towards him. I had to stop to grasp the porch rail, clenching my jaw through the pain, though I whimpered a little. I hoped he had not heard. When his arms closed around me, I knew he had, of course.

'What are you doing, Susannah?'

'What do you think I'm doing? I snapped.

'Would you not be better lying down for a while, finding some comfort in your chamber?'

I pulled away from him. 'No, I would not. And what the hell do you know about it, anyway? I narrowed my eyes. 'If seeing me like this offends you, I suggest *you* go to *your* chamber.'

He reached out for me again, but I moved away. 'Forgive me. I just want to help you ... though I've no idea how to.'

I covered my face with my hands, surprised to find it wet with tears. I tried to swipe them away and looked at him again. 'There's nothing you can do for me, Sam.'

He took my hand and led me to the sofa outside his chamber. 'Sit, then, at least.'

'Very well.' I doubled over for the next pain, and he kept his hand on my back. When it passed, I took a deep breath. 'I need to watch the sea. I have to.'

'Of course you do. Of course, Sukie.'

Pearl came out onto the porch with a jug and two glasses. 'Lemonade. Is cool from well. She poured two glasses and handed them to us. 'Mebe on your side, Susannah. Rest your head on Sam's lap?'

I finished my drink, which tasted like chilled nectar and, with Sam's help, did as Pearl suggested. And it did help for a while. He took the clip from my hair and began stroking my head. I closed my eyes, finding I could let the pains wash over me. 'Forgive my anger.'

His fingers stroked and massaged. 'I really wasn't trying to get rid of you.'

Somehow, I dozed.

I awakened to Sam's gentle shaking. 'The pinnace, Sukie. Jesu, I think it's the pinnace.'

He helped me struggle to my feet, and we moved to

the rail. I shaded my eyes against the sun, now much lower in the sky. How long had I slept? A pain seized me then with some brutality. 'I hadn't forgotten,' I hissed through my teeth. Though, blissfully, I had for a time while I slept. Sam's arm was tight around me, keeping me upright. 'Can you see Penny? Christ, Sam. Can you see her?'

I felt his tension as he tried to see, despite the glare off the water. He leaned forward. 'I see Noah and Raphael.' He clenched his jaw.

I moaned involuntarily when another pain crushed me hard. Jesu they were getting stronger and closer together. 'Is she there?' I managed to gasp.

'Holy God. Oh, sweet Jesus, I see her. She's with them, Susannah. She's in Hal's arms. They have her.'

We clung to each other, both weeping while the boat closed in on the jetty. I tried to pull myself together, in as much as a woman well into the throes of childbirth could. 'Help me to stay upright. I don't want to frighten her. I won't make a sound. I shall smile and kiss her and hug her and then, I shall retire to my chamber and stifle my screams against my husband's chest.'

'After he's bathed, I presume.'

I laughed. Not quite sure how I had.

CHAPTER 36
Raphael

I walked along the Jetty up to the house, holding Penny's hand. Susannah was on the porch with Sam's arm around her, her loose hair a bright cloak. She had wept. They both had. But she made no move to close the distance between us. And she was holding herself very still. It had started, then. I looked down at Penny, radiant with joy at the sight of her mother and released her hand. 'Go to her, *piccola.*'

She rushed up the steps into Susannah's arms. Sam still held her, but hugged Penny too as best he could. I ran up the steps and took my wife from him. 'I have you.' Sam dropped to his knees, clutching Penny tight, then. I searched Susannah's face. Her jaw was clenched, holding in the pain she would not allow Penny to witness. 'How long?'

Sam looked up. 'Breakfast time.'

'Is it very bad, *amore mio*?' I watched her let go and give herself to me.

She fell against me. 'Yes, Raphael. I'm afraid it's quite difficult now.'

Noah and Hal were with us. Our boxes were carried away by servants. Michael arrived and talked quietly with Pearl, their eyes on Susannah.

Pearl took charge of Penny whose eyes were also fixed on her mother, looking confused and a little afraid. 'I help you bathe an into fresh tings, chick. Then you see mama.'

Penny looked up at her. 'Is it the child coming?'

'Him is. Your mama be fine. You see.'

Susannah took a step toward her, bending to kiss her. 'I am. I promise. Now, go with Pearl, sweeting.' When Penny disappeared inside the house, she allowed herself to groan. 'I do believe I'll lie down now.'

Noah was quickly there, sweeping her up in his arms. 'I think it's time, Lass. Now, if you'll pardon the reek of me, I'll take you to you chamber.'

I quickly turned to Sam. 'How has she been?'

'She slept a little with her head on my lap this afternoon. Not good, though.'

I hurried away after Noah to sit beside her on the bed after he gently placed her down. Her eyes were tightly closed. I looked up at him. 'Thank you. For everything.'

We grasped hands. 'I should get back to Sam.'

I nodded, watching him go. Susannah had moved

onto her side though her eyes were still shut. 'Is there anything I can do for you, *amore mio*?'

She opened them, managing a small smile. 'Bathe.'

I laughed. And right on cue, servants arrived with the means to do so. 'Well, then, I shall.'

She pointed to the floor beside the bed. 'There. I want to see you. I want to know you're truly here and I'm not dreaming.'

I stood and bent to kiss her. 'You're not dreaming, *cara*.' She closed her eyes again. I quickly stripped off my travel-crusted clothing and lowered myself into the water. It seemed so long since I had last been in this room. So much had happened ... and this the most momentous of all. I watched her closely for a time, hoping she had found sleep once more, before picking up the soap. When I looked at her again though, I found her watching me. I stood and reached for a towel, drying myself off before finding clean breeches and a shirt in the armoire. I sat beside her again and she reached up to touch my wet hair. Then she drew her knees up and keened almost silently. Holy God. It broke my heart. In truth, I had not expected quite this ... brutality. I gripped her hand tightly. 'I love you, Susannah.'

'I know. There's nothing to be done now. Only this. Go out to the others for a while.'

'You shouldn't be alone.'

'Pearl will come to me.'

I stood. 'If you're sure it's what you want, *cara*.'

She nodded, gasping again.

I bent to kiss her. 'Very well.' I walked out onto the porch feeling more cowardly than I had ever done in my life. Pearl was there just about to go in to light the candles. Night had descended suddenly as it does here. Like it rose up from the depths of the sea to coat the sky in the same inky blackness. I missed twilight. That slow tidying away of the day.

She touched my arm. 'Eat now. It be a long night, me think.'

'Where's Penny?'

'Sleeping. One of the girls be wid her. She no left alone.'

'She's not too worried about her mother?'

Pearl shook her head. 'She knows what must happen afore the chile come. She sleepin content, now.'

I watched her slip inside the chamber before going to the table and pouring myself a large glass of red wine. Then, very much as an afterthought, I loaded a plate with bread and cheese, though I had no appetite. I lowered myself onto a sofa and closed my eyes. When I felt sleep circling, I fought it off, angry with myself. How could I sit here dozing while Susannah went through such a thing? '*Porco dio.*' I gulped down my wine.

Sam stepped out onto the porch from the parlour. 'How is she?'

'Pearl's with her.' I chewed my lip. 'I think I was not quite prepared for it ... for the ...' My words slipped away.

'Yes.' Sam sighed. 'I watched Penny sleep for a while. It felt so strange knowing she's my daughter.'

Now it was my turn to sigh, for I understood I must tell him about Noah and Hal. 'Has Noah told you anything of what happened?'

'Very little. He bathed, collapsed onto the bed, and fell deeply asleep.'

'He had a hard night.' I shook my head. 'He and Hal saved our lives for the second time last night. But what happened on Barbados – Christ that place seems cursed for us – well, what happened there has made things difficult between them. They need to talk to each other.'

He closed his eyes. 'Tell me something new. They exasperate me, Raphael. They're so alike yet they don't see it. They both hoard their resentments like misers with treasure.'

'Well, try and get it out of him tomorrow and tell him to speak to Hal. If he won't tell you than I shall because you need to know.' I rose to refill my glass and pour one for him. 'Forgive me for pushing this onto you. But I've seen them both weep and that's not something I can dismiss.' I touched my chest and smiled. 'From me, yes, but not from them.'

'Holy God. Very well, Raphael. Leave it with me.'

I was more than happy to do so. I just hoped it would remain there and not return to me. Hearing footsteps, I turned away. Pearl. I stood. 'She's not alone, is she?'

She shook her head. 'Ma Gala wid her. De birthin woman. Give likkle poppy syrup. It help her.'

Sam took a sharp breath. 'Poppy syrup? You mean she's dosed her with opium?'

Pearl laughed, holding her thumb and forefinger close together. 'Likkle spoon. Pain there, no so mithering.'

It sounded excellent to me. 'Should I go to her?'

'No yet. Ma send girl when she done.'

I nodded, resuming my place next to Sam. We sat in silence for a while.

It was Sam who broke it. 'Can you tell me a little of what happened on the island? I think I must have an outline if I'm to know how to press him on it, should I need to.'

What he said made sense. So, I did exactly that. The men on the road. Noah and Hal riding at them out of the sun and cutting them down. Hilliard's fear. 'I kept Penny turned away, but I'll never forget her asking me if they were dead. It seemed such a terrible thing for a child to have to ask.'

He had visibly blanched. 'But they had to do it, or they would have killed you.'

'They would. And taken Penny again. Hal had never killed before. Taking a life shocked him–'

'And Noah has?'

'It looked that way to me, yes.' I sighed. 'One last thing. I know from Hal what happened to Hilliard and what that particular killing did to him. He hasn't told Noah, of course.' I held his gaze. 'And I know what made Noah break down.' A girl appeared in front of me. I hadn't heard her bare feet on the wooden floor. 'Am I to go in?' She nodded before gliding away, silently, into the parlour. I stood, feeling afraid and ashamed because I was. I crossed myself.

Sam looked up at me and smiled. 'You must trust in your God still, Raphael. Sukie sets much store by him.'

I smiled, too. 'She told you.' I shook my head and walked away.

The room was bright with candlelight and Susannah rested against pillows. Her eyes were closed but she opened them when I stepped inside. 'Did I wake you? I moved to sit beside her and clasped her hand. 'How are you now, *cara mia*?'

'I wasn't asleep. Ma Gala gave me medicine. It's taken me away from it enough for it not to overwhelm me. Does that make sense?'

'It does and I'm so glad for it.' I moved around the bed to lie beside her, pressing close. I felt her tense as a pain came and she moaned a little. I stroked her face.

'Where's Penny? Is she all right? I want to see her.'

'She's sleeping. Sam sat with her for a while. She's exhausted. Noah's sleeping, too. Last night was ... well—'

'I know.' She placed her hand on my face. 'I know. I was so afraid for you all. You should sleep yourself.'

'I will when you do.'

'Then tell me about Barbados. I want to know everything. How did you get her away?'

'Do you really want to hear it all now. It's not a pleasant tale. We were lucky it ended the way it did, but it could have so easily gone the other way, if not for Noah and Hal.'

After some moments to let a pain pass, she gave me very a direct look from those opium-dark eyes. 'I need to know what happened to Penny before I see her. I need to know everything she saw. Everything that might have frightened her.'

'Yes, of course. I can understand that.' So that is what I did. I told it all, including what Sam now knew and what he did not. She closed her eyes, her jaw clenched and not from pain this time, though they still came. Harder and more often now, it seemed to me.

'I'm glad you said what you did to Noah. I shall give him my thanks, too, when I can, and so will Sam. We've put them through so much.' She shook her head. 'Hal did it all for his father ... and because he's a good man.'

She struggled to sit up higher, and I held her close to help her. 'Is that any better?'

She shook her head. 'I need to stand up, I think.'

I scrambled across the bed to help her, pulling her into my arms when I got her to her feet. 'Do you want to walk?'

'I'd like to go out onto the porch.' She pointed at the side doors. 'Not at the front. I don't know who's out there. It might make them uncomfortable.'

'As you wish.' I opened the door and we moved outside, looking across the silvered shore to the sea, ruffled into diamonds of star light. Though the air was warm, the breeze felt wonderful. 'Does this help, *cara*?' She nodded. One of the ubiquitous couches had been placed against the wall, this one more battered than those at the front, but it was soft and yielding. She curled-up on her side with her head on my lap and we both slept a little. Though she whimpered from time to time – each sound awakening me – though I don't think she was aware. We both woke with a start when Pearl touched her shoulder. I moved to help her up.

'Stay here, Raphael. The midwife wishes to see me.'

I leaned back, looking up at the stars. Whatever the astronomers now knew, for me they would always be the lights of God. I wondered how long it was until dawn.

A little later, Pearl leaned out and beckoned me. 'She axe for you.'

Susannah sat on the side of the bed, and I sat beside her, taking her hand. It was then I saw the chair. '*Cristo santo*. What in the name of God is that? It looks like something from a torture chamber.'

She snorted. 'That's not a bad description. It's a birthing chair.'

The door from the house opened and a small black woman with a deeply lined face crossed the room towards us. Her eyes, however, were fixed on me. 'You go now, Mister.' She pointed at the chair. 'Her ready.'

I remembered Susannah's father saying how he had disregarded the midwife at her birth, but her mother had begged him to stay with her. This had to be Susannah's choice. 'Do you want me to go?'

She tightened her grasp on my hand. 'Jesu, no. But this is the hard bit. So don't stay unless you're certain. If you stay, I'll need you to help me. Last time I had my mother and grandmother.'

How could I refuse? 'And this time you have me. What do you need?' She moved into my arms.

The midwife scowled, making a disparaging sound through her teeth. 'This ting no for a man. What good he be to you, chick?' She made that sound again. 'You want more poppy?'

Susannah moved away and sighed. 'I should like a great deal more of it, but I shan't have it. I must keep my wits about me.' She turned to me and found a smile from somewhere. 'Just in case my husband swoons.'

CHAPTER 37

Susannah

When he said he would stay, I was almost overwhelmed with gratitude. He listened carefully to Pearl who explained to him what would happen now. The rhythmical waves of pain that would bring us our child. The brief respites between them to gather strength again. Ma Gala seemed to have decided the best way to deal with his presence was to ignore it. So, I sat in my torture-chamber chair and did my best to push our child out into the world, with my husband holding my hand and wiping away the sweat that streamed from me. He had helped me take-off my shift when it stuck to my body, soaking wet. Childbirth is not for the demure. Yet it was easier with Raphael beside me than it had been with my mother and grandmother.

When I cried out, which I did. Often. When I told God I could not do what I must (for what choice had

I?) Raphael spoke to me softly in his own language and though the meaning was mostly unknown to me it was of no matter, for all I heard was his love.

I don't know how long it took, but it was fully light when it was done. When our son was born into Raphael's hands, I saw so many emotions cross his face. Disbelief. Utter joy. Understanding of who this tiny creature was and what he would mean to him for the rest of his life. For both our lives. We wept. I had never loved him more.

Women washed me and dressed me in a clean shift. Our son was taken from Raphael's arms and tended to by the midwife. 'Yous have fine boy.' She turned to me. 'He good man, chick. Good man is good father.'

How could I not laugh at his expression? He had not expected that from her. 'He's well, then? The boy.'

She frowned at him. 'He a healthy chile.'

I knew why he would ask such a thing. His fear. The girls helped me to my bed and handed my son to me at last. 'Jesu, Raphael. See how beautiful he is?' Somehow everything felt heightened in that chiaroscuro of stark white sunlight and darkest shadows yet distanced at the same time. Like I had become a passenger in someone else's life.

He lay beside me on the bed. 'Susannah ... I have no words.' He shook his head. 'How can this be?'

'Paolo. We have him.' I reached for Raphael's hand. 'Thank you for staying with me, my love. It meant so much to have you there when I needed you.'

He shook his head. 'I don't know how you'll ever

understand what it meant to me. To see him born. To take him from your body into my hands. It was a holy thing. A true gift from God. It felt like forgiveness, finally.'

'I understood. And I thanked God for it, too.' We both turned at the sound of the door opening a crack. A small face peeped in. I held out my hand to her. 'Penny. Come and meet your brother, little one.'

She jumped up on the bed and scrambled close, beaming. 'He's so tiny.' She turned to Raphael. 'He has your hair, Papa.'

I ran a finger over it. 'He does. Though it'll probably fall out.' I touched hers. 'Yours did. You were such a funny bald little thing for a while.' When I passed our son into his father's arms, he looked down at him with that same look of stunned disbelief. 'Perhaps it's easier for me to accept he's really with us as I was more aware of the process of getting him here then you were.'

'Oh, I was quite aware, *cara*. Believe me.'

I leant across to kiss his cheek. 'Yes. Forgive me. Of course you were.' I returned my attention to Penny, kneeling on the bed, watching us. 'Now, let me hug you, little one.' I held out my arms for her to fall into and then closed them around her. 'Oh, I've missed you so much, my sweeting.' We clung to each other, both our faces soaked with tears. I would need to talk to her about it all but now was not the time. I held her back from me for a moment, so I could see her face. 'You do know I didn't send you away, Penny–'

She nodded. 'He lied. He was a bad man and he lied to me.'

I held her tight again. Perhaps it was better she had thought she was following my wishes. That she believed I would send for her must have made it easier. 'Well, it's over now and we're all together again. We can go home soon when Paolo's a little bigger.'

'Then Kitty can see him.'

I met Raphael's eyes. Something else we would need to speak of to her, for it seemed impossible to believe those wicked people had returned her home. I prayed we might find her before we sailed.

When Sam arrived, we must have looked quite a family group, with Paolo in his father's arms and Penny in mine. I was so glad to see him. After Raphael handed him our child, how could I not think of him holding Penny in the same way, looking so intently at her just as he did at Paolo now? When he looked up, I knew he thought of it too.

Back in Raphael's arms, our son opened his eyes. '*Buongiorno figlio mio.*' Paolo began to squirm and whimper, then. 'And it is your mamma you need now, I think.'

Sam came to me, kissing my cheek. 'I should check if Noah's awake.'

'Talk,' Raphael said, passing our boy to me.'

Sam bent to hug Penny, then he was gone.

I untied the ribbon at the neck of my shift while Paolo kicked and waved his arms. 'Poor little love. I think he's just discovered hunger for the first time and

345

found himself rather unimpressed with it.' I eased him onto my breast and watched him take some moments to realise what he must do. I closed my eyes feeling my first milk let down to flood his mouth. It was a sensation I had somehow forgotten.

Raphael smiled. 'Ah, now he *is* impressed.'

Penny touched his hand and laughed when his fingers opened like a starfish. 'It must be very strange being so new. Did I feed from you like this?'

'You did. Though it had to be a secret. Grandmama hired a woman to do it. So, we hid ourselves away while she nursed her own child and I nursed you.'

Raphael tilted his head. 'I've never understood the concept of a wet nurse. Why a woman would pay someone to do it for her? My sisters made a kind of sling from a shawl and tied their infants to them, so they could feed whenever they wished. Papà told Giana she looked like a peasant.' He shrugged. 'She asked him if that was not what his grandfather had been. She looked so innocent when she asked it. She wasn't, of course. Mamma said indeed it was. He had been a shepherd. Papà muttered something about damn women and left in a huff. Needless to say, there was much amusement.'

'Perhaps we can make such a sling for him. I must say, I like the idea of it.'

'Then we shall.'

Penny lay down between us with her eyes closed. The little one too, looked sated and ready to settle again. 'Now we must await the result of his first feed,' I said, dryly.

Raphael laughed. 'His first shit.'

Penny giggled. 'Whatever will he think of that, Papa?'

'Well, I'm sure he'll find a way to let us know, *piccola*.'

CHAPTER 38

Noah

Sam walked in smiling and stood beside the bed. Noah sat up higher on the pillows. 'I wondered where you'd disappeared to.'

'I went to see Susannah. They have a son, who I suspect will be the very image of Raphael. Penny was with them. I must paint them together. They make a lovely family.'

'But she'll always be yours. That'll never change.' Noah raised his eyebrows, watching him pull off his shirt and begin unfastening his breeches. 'Is this an invitation, Lad?'

'It's whatever you want it to be.'

'Invitation it is, then.'

Afterwards, they lay side by side. Sam took a shuddering breath. 'It's so good to have you safely home.' He looked up at the ceiling. 'But now, it's time to talk.'

Noah sighed. 'Why? I'm sure Raphael's told you–'

'He told me you saved their lives in the storm ... and on the island.'

Noah moved away and swung his legs to the floor. 'I sailed my ship. That's what I do, for fuck's sake. I fought men who would have killed us ... so did Hal. There was very little choice on either occasion.'

'You killed them–'

'Christ's fucking wounds.' He moved back onto the bed and glared at Sam. 'What should I have done, then? Let them kill us? Let them take Penny?' When Sam laughed, Noah moved over him, holding his wrists, and forcing his arms above his head, feeling ready to explode with rage. 'What's funny? You think it's fucking funny, you cunt?'

Sam no longer smiled, his nostrils flaring. 'It's funny you can come out with such absurdities. And you're actually hurting me, Noah. Will you please let go of me and get off before you crush me to death?'

Noah was instantly contrite, rolling away. 'Forgive me.' He scrubbed at his stubbled cheeks. 'God. I'm losing my mind.'

Sam moved to cup Noah's face. 'And I think you need to tell me everything. Not just what happened but what you felt.'

'Oh, you do, do you?' God's blood. He supposed he had better get it over with, for Sam was not about to let it go. His nostrils flared. Fuck. 'Very well if I must.'

Sam lay on his side watching him while he spoke, never interrupting him or touching him even when the odd humiliating tear arrived unbidden on his face.

After he had finished, Noah shook his head. 'Holy God. I'll never forget how Hal looked when he'd killed that whoreson. He went white. And I'd asked it of him. When I had to get rid of Hilliard, he looked at me as though he no longer knew who I was.'

Sam spoke at last. 'I'm pretty sure that's exactly what he felt.'

He gazed at Sam, intently. 'You do see, I had no choice? 'Well, no. I had a choice about allowing Hal to witness it–'

'Do you really think he'd have let you send him away?' Sam left the bed and began to dress again. 'Now, however much you don't wish to, you must say all this again to Hal.'

'And what makes you think he wants to talk to me?'

'I'm sure he doesn't. Any more than you did to me. But if you take a moment to think about it, you'll see it must be done.'

Noah scowled. 'Sam. Sometimes I find you unbelievably ... insufferably–'

'Right?'

'No. Smug. A smug little shit.'

CHAPTER 39

Hal

When he called out a sleepy yes in answer to a knock on his chamber door, his father was the last person he had expected to see. Or, indeed, wished to see. He sat up higher against the pillows, trying to collect himself, still sleep addled. He shook his head. 'What can I do for you, Papa?'

Noah cleared his throat. 'I hope you slept well. I'm sure you were in need of it. Just as I was.'

Hal narrowed his eyes. What on earth did he want? 'I did indeed. Though you woke me. But no matter.'

Noah sat on the bench in the window appearing decidedly uncomfortable. 'Forgive me, then. But I think we need to talk.'

Oh, Christ. 'No, we don't. Not at all. What is there to say, anyway?' He found sudden inspiration in the hopes of diverting him. 'How is Susannah, Papa? Has the child come?'

'Yes. Yes, she has a son. They're both well. Sam saw them this morning.'

'That's wonderful news. Now if you would forgive me, I must dress–'

Noah waved his hand. 'Go ahead. But I'm going to talk, so you might do me the courtesy of listening.'

Hal shrugged. What else could he do? After a time, he closed his eyes, for whatever he had expected his father to say it was not this. It seemed all the things he had thought him indifferent to had, in truth, cost him too much. Yet why had he chosen to expose himself like this?

'I hated putting you through it, Hal. But Christ, there was no one else. And I didn't know we'd be forced to kill.'

'I know that, of course I do. Yet, when you seemed to take it so much in your stride, I felt weak because I couldn't.'

Noah bit his lip and moved to sit beside Hal on the bed. 'I was your age, perhaps a touch younger, when I killed for the first time. We were off Tortuga, a risky place to pass close by, but we risked it. More than foolishly when you consider we had a hold full of rum. My father was always a risk taker. Probably his single principle. Perhaps that's why I try to avoid them when I can.

'Well then, we were boarded by pirates, of course. My father died almost immediately from a cutlass blow to his neck. We fought though, all of us. We fought for our ship. And thank Christ we prevailed. I killed seven men that day and tossed their bodies into the sea without compunction. It meant nothing to me. Though later it came to haunt me. Those men I killed. I had a friend on board, then. An Italian.' He closed his eyes, suddenly wistful. 'When I woke from yet another nightmare, he made me see they weren't worth my anguish. We'd killed defending ourselves and what was ours, while they took lives from greed. From wickedness. He was right, of course, and I never thought of them again. Or dreamt of them.'

'Oh, Christ, Papa. That's why you were a captain so young.' Hal wept then in his father's arms, his face soon covered in snot while his father rocked him like a small boy until he was able to compose himself again. He moved away drying his face on his forearm and clearing his throat. He held his father's gaze. 'I wish we'd talked sooner so I might have better understood.' Why had he been so ready to think badly of him?

'I've been pondering that. I wonder now if I couldn't face it square-on until we knew for sure it was over and we were safe. The storm confirmed that.' He sighed. 'And the honest truth is, I wouldn't have done so now if Sam hadn't insisted. I didn't think you'd want to talk to me.'

'Well, I didn't but I'm truly glad for it and I shall tell Sam so. I feel I'm starting to understand you a little at last.' He studied his father carefully for a moment. 'I saw you talking to Raphael yesterday morning, after the storm. You seemed distressed. I'd wondered if there was something wrong?'

Noah shook his head. 'Strange how things find a way in somehow, even when you fight against it. When I looked at the little girl and saw Sam in her, I realised what bringing her home truly meant. To Susannah ... and Sam. And why we'd had to do it all, of course.'

'You saw a cause worth killing for.'

Noah moved to him once more and they hugged. 'Breakfast.'

Hal grinned. 'Agreed. So, if you might excuse me while I dress–'

'For Christ's sake, Hal, just put your fucking clothes on. You haven't got anything I haven't seen before.'

Hal smiled, leaving the bed. 'Once again, Papa, I must admire such a delightful turn of phrase.'

Noah frowned, shaking his head. 'Sometimes you sound just like Sam. Do you two get together to practice or something?'

'No. We're just civilised.'

Outside on the porch, Hal was surprised to see Pearl coming out of Michael's room. She nodded to them before hurrying away. His father was less so, he noticed. 'What? You know about this?'

'Well, I told her he needed to bed a woman as soon as possible. I never actually suggested it should be her, though.'

Hal snorted. 'You truly never cease to amaze me. You really think it's your place to say such a thing?

How do you imagine Michael will feel if he finds out it was a pity fuck?'

'A pity fuck? Christ. That's a new one on me. But it wasn't that, anyway, was it? The lass chose it for herself.'

'After you told her he needed it. And why are you acting as Michael's pimp when you behaved like my grandmama trying to preserve my maidenhead.'

'Wasn't your virginity that concerned me, Lad. Bit late for that by then.'

Hal laughed. God's blood. They were doing it again. 'Well, I can't deny the truth of that. So, I'm willing to concede you're probably looking out for our best interests ... mostly.'

His papa looked somewhat incredulous. 'You are?'

He rubbed his hands together. 'Now, get your breakfast, Papa. I think I'll have a quick word with my brother first.'

Noah grasped his arm. 'Christ. Don't tell him I spoke to her.'

Hal looked at his father, sternly. 'Now, do you really think me such a fool?'

Noah barked a laugh. 'I can't seem to help myself, can I?'

Hal punched his arm, lightly.

After Noah walked away, he tapped on Michael's door and went in without waiting for a response.

Michael bolted upright. He had been sprawled naked on the bed. 'Fuck.'

'Hal raised his eyebrows. 'So it would seem.'

He frowned, pulling a quilt over himself. 'You startled me. Don't you knock?'

'I did. Don't worry we saw her go, so I knew you were alone'

Michael left the bed to pull on his breeches. 'We?'

Hal grinned. 'Papa and I.'

Michael sat back down and sighed. 'I suppose he told you what he'd said to her?'

Hal frowned, narrowing his eyes. 'She told you? I'm surprised. Well, doesn't it bother you she came to you out of pity?'

Michael looked startled. Why should it? She came back because she wanted to.'

'Really? It's been more than once?' How in God's name had he managed that? 'I tried for her several times without any luck.'

Michael grinned. 'I think she finds me interesting for some reason. She seems to enjoy talking to me.'

Hal felt suddenly uncertain. 'So, she comes to you just to talk?'

Michael rolled his eyes. 'Don't be absurd, Hal. We talk afterwards. Mostly about the medical books I'm reading.'

They talk about medical books? Michael has a woman like Pearl in his bed and they talk about medical books? 'How long has it been going on?' Hal was suddenly unsure he wanted to hear the answer. Why had he assumed it had only been last night?

'Since the first night you sailed.'

He took a deep breath. 'Dear God. So, while I've

been risking my life rescuing Penny.' He shook his head. 'While I've fought-off whoresons and battled to save the Mirabel from foundering, you've been here swiving Pearl?'

Michael made a disparaging sound. 'Crudely put, Brother, but that about sums it up.'

Hal began to laugh. What else could he do?

'I don't see what's so funny about it.'

'No matter. Let's get breakfast. I think we're both in need of it.'

CHAPTER 40
Noah

Noah found Sam in his studio, sizing canvases. He spotted the portrait of Michael straightaway, lifting it and carrying it to the door to look at it more closely in brighter light. 'Sam, this is grand. He looks so carefree.' He turned to him. 'It makes me want to weep.' He grinned. 'Though I shan't, of course.'

'Slippery slope and all that?'

'What?'

Sam laughed. 'How did it go with Hal?'

'Well, I think. He says he's grateful to you for it, anyway.' He placed the portrait back against the wall. 'We saw Pearl coming out of Michael's room. Did you know about them?'

Sam nodded. 'I saw her going in the night before last. So, it seems she must have liked him. Good.'

Noah looked down at the painting again. 'Judging by the way he looks there, I'd say it's been going on somewhat longer than that, Lad. Have you breakfasted?'

'No. I waited for you.'

'Let's go, then. I'm ravenous.'

Hal and Michael were already eating when they joined them. Noah gave his older son a knowing look, while his younger one tried to disregard them. 'I've just been admiring Sam's portrait of you, Michael.' He raised his eyebrows at Hal. 'I couldn't help noticing you looked rather a lot happier than when you first arrived here.'

Michael's face flamed.

Pearl chose that moment to arrive out on the porch with fresh platters of corn biscuits and ham. She took in Michael's blushes and his father and brother's grins and shook her head. 'Why you behave like silly children? Shame on you.'

'They're a pair of buffoons. Ignore them, Michael. After a while you'll barely notice they're there.' Sam smiled, seeing Raphael approaching.

Noah stood to hug him. He looked tired. Dishevelled. Bemused. Happy. 'How are they?'

'Sleeping. Penny, too. I probably should but hunger won the day.' He sat and began to load his plate.

'Pearl tells me Susannah took opium during the birth. Did she think it helped her?'

All eyes turned to Michael with various expressions of incredulity.'

Raphael finished chewing and swallowed. 'I believe she did. It certainly appeared so to me.'

Michael seemed to realise he had caused some consternation around the table. 'Forgive me. It's just that Susannah has a rather singular experience of the efficacy of opium in childbirth as she had her first child without it.' He slapped his forehead with the heal of his hand. 'Forgive me, again. I should explain my interest.'

'I think you probably should.' Noah said, dryly.

Michael chewed his lip for a moment. 'Pain relief in childbirth is generally not offered by physicians. The medical books say it needs to be experienced fully for the health of both mother and child–'

Raphael appeared baffled. 'Holy Christ. Why? What man would choose to see his wife suffer more than she must?'

'That's just it. Men don't see, do they? Physician's do, but they've already accepted all they've been taught. They use laudanum to relive pain, of course, but have been trained not to use it in childbirth. Religion can be significant. Original sin. The need for women to suffer.'

'So, you're telling me had Paolo been born in London, nothing would have been done to help her?'

'Quite possibly, as with her first child. Though some midwives go their own way with simples and physic and even opium when they can get it. But physicians are fairly united about it. It's interesting that in ancient Athens, obstetricians – physicians who care for women in childbirth – were often women and there are lots of descriptions of herbal medicines being used.'

Sam stared intently at Michael. 'And you'd like to see physicians change their thinking?'

'Of course I would. I shall be one in what's becoming known as the age of enlightenment. Many, particularly in the Dutch Republic, are starting to question the old teaching by means of what they call empiricism. They use the evidence of their own eyes. They dissect. They use trial and error. They find out what helps and what doesn't by witnessing it for themselves.'

Raphael took a long breath. 'Well, if it would help to talk to Susannah about her experience, I'm sure she'd be happy to do so.'

Hal shook his head, grinning. 'Well, Brother, I'm dumbfounded. I'd quite forgotten just what an alarmingly bright little fellow you are.'

'The enlightenment. I've seen it at play in England, too. The growing interest in natural philosophy. Astronomy. I imagine the King's patronage has been influential. We must admire him for that,' Sam said.

Noah snorted. 'I wouldn't have thought you had much admiration of any sort left for him.' He turned to Raphael. 'Perhaps when you're recovered, we might discus with Sam your thoughts on his continued safety here. And also, what we can do about the other child. We can't simply abandon her.'

'I'm merely a little short of sleep, Noah. Not a new experience of late and one that seems more than likely to continue for some time.' He scrubbed at his stubble. 'And I think there's one simple answer to both those questions and that's Barnabus Rifkind. We need to confront him as soon as possible. I can't believe there wasn't more to Penny's kidnapping than a contract with a man to replace his dead child. That she was brought to Jamaica and told her natural father was here can't be a coincidence, surely? And Kitty was with her, so Rifkind must know where she is.'

Noah sighed. This wasn't going to be easy. 'I agree we must confront him but I'm afraid you can't accompany us this time, Raphael–'

'Of course I can. I must. I know the child. And I left her in the park, too, don't forget.'

Sam leaned forward. 'I know her also–'

Noah narrowed his eyes, interrupting Sam. 'Here's a thought. Why don't we just tie you up and hand you to him, and save ourselves all the aggravation?'

Sam moved back and folded his arms, with a look of contempt on his face. 'You really are a complete fool, Noah. I wasn't suggesting I went there. I was about to point out it's not a valid reason for Raphael to go, any more than it would be for me. But you had to blunder in, of course. I was also going to say the chief reason why he shouldn't show his face there is that Isabella Rifkind has disappeared.'

Raphael's eyes widened. '*Cristo*. How? What's happened to her.'

'There's talk of it in Port Royal,' Michael said.

'Some say he's harmed her, others that she's gone back to her family.'

Raphael crossed himself. 'Pray God it's the latter, then.

Pearl's head appeared around the door. 'Susannah awake. I taken her breakfast. She axe for you.'

Raphael stood. 'Very well. I see the sense of what you say, gentlemen.' He looked at Noah and Hal with a sheepish smile. 'So, once again it must fall to you.'

Michael stood. 'I shall go, too.'

Noah rose, shaking his head. 'Not going to happen, Lad.' He turned his eyes on Sam. 'A moment if you please.'

Sam rolled his eyes. '*Semper ad meliora.*'

Hal grinned, again. 'That really won't help. You do know that?'

Noah looked around at the faces. All save Hal's were at least trying to supress laughter. He turned to Raphael who alone remained impassive. '*Sempre qualcosa. Che cosa?*'

'*Per il meglio.*'

A curt nod. '*Grazie.*'

'*Prego.*'

He gestured toward their chamber with his head and walked away. Sam followed without a word. Noah sat on the bed stony-faced. 'Why would you do that?'

Sam sat beside him. 'Christ. I've hurt you. Forgive me. It was excruciatingly childish of me.'

Noah scrubbed at his face with a sigh. He needed to shave. 'No. In truth, it was my fault. I began it.'

'Well, I think we both ended up looking like pricks and deservedly so. And I've absolutely no excuse for my behaviour whereas you do. Very much so.'

Noah lay back on the bed. 'Sam, there could be danger for you here now. You have the uncertainty of that, which is why it's so important we find out what's truly behind Penny's kidnapping. And if we need to move on to keep you safe, we will.' He yawned. I don't see how I can still be tired, yet I find I am.'

Sam lifted his hand and kissed. 'What would I do without you? Sleep again. There's nothing to stop you.'

He closed his eyes. 'Plans to make.'

'You'll think more clearly when you're fully rested.' Sam bent to kiss his forehead and quietly left the room.

CHAPTER 41

Raphael

When I walked away towards our chamber, Michael hurried to join me.

'Might I speak with her now? While it's still fresh in her mind.'

I couldn't dispute his logic. Though I thought her unlikely to forget the experience any time soon. For I knew I would not. 'Well, if she has no objections, then neither do I.'

At the door he stopped, grasping my arm. 'Are they often like that? Sam and Papa. Tying to belittle each other?'

'From time to time. And sometimes Hal decides to participate.'

'It sounds exhausting.'

'It is. Especially feeling as I do today.' I opened the door. She lay against pillows, feeding Paolo. Penny had gone. Unsurprisingly, she appeared a little startled to see Michael. I moved her empty breakfast tray from the bed onto the table, then bent to kiss her and my son. 'Michael wishes to ask you some questions if you've no objections.'

She frowned. 'What questions?'

I gestured for Michael to speak and listened to him repeat all he had told us earlier. Watching Susannah's face, I saw her outrage.

'All right. What do you want to know?'

'Did it help and, if so, how much?'

'It most certainly did. I know I was not offered it with Penny, but I can't believe it would be the case in London.'

'There's a consensus on it throughout most of Europe even though it is not mentioned at all in Galenic theory. Physicians have generally accepted the notion that opium slows labour and harms the child.'

'Well, it certainly didn't have that effect on me. 'Penny took far longer.' She smiled. 'So, if I ever have another child, I must ensure I find a midwife with a bottle of laudanum in her pocket?' She gave him one of her direct looks. 'So, how is Pearl?'

He turned that rather alarming shade of puce again. 'It seems everyone knows, including my father and brother, unfortunately.'

I laughed. 'I can see how that might prove a touch vexing.'

He sighed, nodding. 'I'd like to say they mean well but I'm not entirely sure they do, especially as Hal had designs on her himself, though she wasn't interested.'

I raised my eyebrows. 'Did he now? Well, it must be quite a novel experience for him to be turned down.'

Susannah snorted. 'One I'm sure you never experienced.'

I laughed, again, sitting beside her on the bed. 'That was a different life, *cara*.' Michael reddened once more. Poor boy. How earnest he was. There was something rather endearing about it.

'I should get back to my books, I think. I want to be as ready as I can be for Leiden in the autumn.' He hesitated. 'Raphael, might I ask you to try and persuade Papa to take me with them when they go to that man's plantation. I want to help. I'd like to hear what he has to say. Sometimes I can recognise the difference between what a man says and what he means or intends. It can be quite a nuanced thing. Papa can be rather too fixated on a man's physical powers if that makes sense.'

'It does, but I'm afraid I have very little influence with him not having much to offer in that way myself.'

Susannah made a choked sound of mirth. I frowned at her.

'Well, I can fence. So, I'm not completely without such skills.'

Even so, I did not imagine he would have the swordsman's touching tell like his father and brother, but he would still have considerably more ability than I did. Admittedly, a low bar. When I thought of Noah and Hal fighting for our lives in Barbados, there had been nothing civilised about it. Gouging. Kicking. Hacking with their blades. Yet, I could see how his quick mind might prove useful. 'I'll do my best.' Though there seemed little hope, knowing how Noah felt about risking Hal. He would hardly be willing to risk them both.

'I'm grateful.'

When he left us, returning to the porch, I turned back to Susannah. 'Talking of being turned down, I seem to remember some reluctance on your part once, *amore mio*.'

'Oh, but it was touch and go, believe me.'

I moved in to kiss her, looking down at my son at her breast. 'Was it? I was uncertain what you felt then. I really didn't know what to make of you.'

'What about the time you kissed me in my studio, after I'd called you a whore. Did you know then?'

'Then, I knew exactly what you felt, *cara*.'

I found Noah alone on the porch after leaving Susannah and Paolo sleeping. Once again it had somehow eluded me, though Holy God, I needed it. 'Where is everyone?'

'Michael's away somewhere poring over his books. Hal? He shrugged. 'Your guess is as good as mine. And Sam's taken Penny for a walk on the beach.'

I sat beside him on the couch. 'I'm glad he's able to spend so much time with her.'

Noah sighed. 'He needs it.' He turned to me. 'Forgive us for being somewhat rancorous this morning. It wasn't particularly attractive to witness, I'm sure.'

I waved my hand dismissing it.

He grinned. 'So how does it feel to be a father? Is it what you expected?'

I spoke in Italian for it was how the words arrived. 'God, no. I didn't expect it to overwhelm me in quite the way it has. This tiny creature who fills my heart. It's utterly joyous ... and utterly terrifying.'

'Well, don't expect that terror to ever leave you. It'll die with you.'

'I don't doubt it. Have you decided when you'll pay Rifkind a visit?' I said, in English now.

'As soon as possible. The more I go over all that's happened, the more I realise nothing is as it seems, and I can't help feeling Sam isn't safe here.'

I tried to think. 'But what if I'm wrong about Su-sannah's letter being intercepted–'

He frowned. 'How else could they know who her natural father is or, indeed, where he is? Or are you now suggesting they don't know about Sam after all?'

'No, I'm saying Susannah's letter didn't necessarily need to be read because that Sam is Penny's father is rather more well-known than she had realised at the time. Frances Stuart knows, so I'm fairly certain the King does too. He also knew Sam left with you and he'd only have to ask once to learn your destination.'

'And the Duchess of Portsmouth has unlimited access to him. And France has it to her.'

'So, if Penny were taken as a means of luring Sam

out. Then he must have information they want.' I hadn't noticed Michael standing in the doorway to the parlour until he spoke.

'They know where he is, so they can't simply want to get rid of him.'

Noah turned around to look intently at his son. 'If they did, they could easily have killed him. He's been here unprotected for weeks at a time.'

Christ this was torturous, especially after so little sleep. I thought I could make sense of it until it all slipped away again like water through a sieve. 'Unprotected. Yet they haven't tried to take him either. And why trade Penny to Barbados? It makes no sense.'

Michael sat on the sofa opposite. 'What was the result of him doing that?'

Noah frowned. 'The result was a fucking wild goose chase around the Caribbean, Lad.'

'Exactly. So, leaving Sam unprotected as you said.'

I sighed, exasperated. 'Then why didn't Rifkind come for him?'

'Perhaps he thought he'd more time?' Michael said. 'He didn't know you were going to find her, did he?'

'Yet he told us the right island.'

'A risk taker,' I said. 'A gambler.'

Michael studied his fingers. 'Then his wife ran away. And I learnt this morning from Pearl, who heard it from a pedlar, Rifkind took ship to look for her. He thought she'd fled to her family.'

Noah's eyes widened. 'He went to Costa Rica? Did this man know if he's returned?

'He hasn't. So, he won't yet know you rescued Penny.'

Noah stood and went to the porch rail, looking out across the water. 'I still don't understand why he hasn't already acted against Sam, though.'

'Perhaps he wanted to watch how the game played out ... and he had a plan to draw me into it too, for his amusement, did he not? Or he's waiting for payment first?'

Noah turned back to us. 'Now, that has a ring of truth to it. Either way, we won't be riding out to Cinnamon Hill until he returns.'

Michael looked at me. I knew this would be hopeless, but I tried anyway. 'When you do go, might I suggest you take Michael with you–'

'*What?* God's blood. Have you completely lost your mind? It's bad enough Hal's been drawn into it. But I need him to cover my back. There's no getting away from that.'

Michael rose to his feet rather abruptly. 'Well, it's good to know where I stand with you, Papa.' He walked away.

Noah rubbed at his face. 'Christ's wounds. I don't think that came out quite as I intended. I do seem to have a penchant for offending people at the moment. I'll talk to him.'

'One final thought, Noah. Might it be possible Sam knows something else he hasn't told us? I can't help wondering, as Portsmouth is so deeply involved in this, if her new dealings with the Duke of York are somehow part of it?'

'Well, I did sense there was something else when he first told me what he'd learnt at the French court. I also sensed, rather strongly, it would be better ... safer not to know what it was.'

'Even so, I think we must ask him. It's not possible to unravel this fully until we know exactly what's behind it.'

Noah tilted his head, looking pensive. 'I'm not sure he'll tell us. If knowing it puts his life in danger, he's going to be reluctant to share that risk with us, surely?'

I shrugged. 'But aren't we already at risk–' I heard voices and laughter down on the beach and very soon Sam, Hal and Penny came clattering up the steps. She ran to me, grinning, pink-faced and happy.

She flung her arms around me. 'Papa. I saw a pelican dive into the sea and catch a fish and swallow it. There were some standing on the sand. They're really big. Much bigger than the ones in St James's Park.'

I laughed. 'They are, aren't they. These must have happier lives, too.'

She climbed onto my lap. 'Oh yes. I'm sad for those ones. The rain must feel so cold to them.'

'I don't think they know any different, *piccola*. They're London birds.'

Hal grinned. 'Time for a kitchen raid, I think.'

Penny jumped down, clapping her hands. 'And me, Hal.' She chased after him, and quiet descended.

Sam flopped down next to Noah. 'You two look rather serious. What's wrong?'

Noah glanced at me and then told him all we had discussed. 'Have you any explanation for the King's brother's sudden interest? If, indeed, he is–'

'He is, unfortunately. If he's learnt what it would appear he has?'

Noah looked at him, sharply. 'Well then, perhaps you'd enlighten us.'

Sam laughed, rather sourly. 'I'm afraid I can't do that. It really is best for you not to know. Believe me.'

I drew a sharp breath. 'Surely we will be suspected of knowing regardless of whether we do or not–'

'You won't be in any danger from that, you have my word.'

Noah's eyes flashed. 'Good to hear, Lad, but hard to trust without knowing what the fuck it is.'

'I'm afraid you're just going to have to, Noah.'

Looking from one to the other, I could see this was about to deteriorate. 'Of course. If that's what you wish, I'm happy to trust you, Sam.'

Noah made a hissing sound through his teeth. 'Very well. For now, anyway.' With that, he rose and strode off to their chamber.

Sam sighed, rolling his eyes, and followed. I returned to Susannah and lay down beside her, trying to order my thoughts enough to make sense of what Sam had said.

'What were you talking about?' she said, sleepily. 'I heard your voices.'

So now it was my turn to repeat it all, including Sam's refusal to tell us what lay behind it.

Susannah lay quiet for a while before turning on her side to face me. 'I have a horrible feeling I know what it is.'

'Well then, perhaps you'd better tell me, *cara*.'

She took a deep breath. 'York is the King's heir, as you know. Think for a moment who else might have a claim?' She watched me, waiting. 'Forgive me, Raphael. I forget your knowledge of the English court is limited—'

'Monmouth?'

She smiled, nodding. 'James Scott. His eldest son. For a time, there was much speculation the King would make him legitimate. And there have always been rumours that Charles actually married his mother while he was in exile.'

'But why wouldn't he legitimise him then if it were true? To have a son as his heir would seem infinitely preferable, surely? So might not that suggest such a marriage never took place.'

'The King insists it didn't but that doesn't necessarily make it true—'

'To admit it would have made his marriage to the Queen bigamous?'

She shook her head. 'Lucy Walter died in Paris when she was just your age, poor thing. But at the time he officially acknowledged James as his son, he still hoped for a child with the Queen. And admitting a prior marriage would have caused a diplomatic furore with Portugal because, of course, James would be heir and not a son born to Catherine. So, until such a child arrived, his brother remained next in line.'

'But the King did contemplate making him legitimate at one point?'

She nodded. 'But not by admitting marriage to his mother. By then, Catherine seemed unable to have a child, which must have been hard for him considering how many he had elsewhere. And for her, of course. You can imagine how the suggestion that his first-born son should become his heir was met with considerable resistance, not only from his brother but various mistresses who had also borne him sons. And what would happen after his death had to be considered, too. York is Catholic, Monmouth protestant. You can imagine one of his greatest fears is that England should find itself scourged again by civil war. So, it's understandable he's decided on the status quo for the moment, especially as York's heir is his protestant daughter Mary, betrothed to the Stadtholder of Holland, so the kingdom's protestant future seems safe, anyway.'

'But it is possible this marriage really did take place and Sam has seen the proof of it?'

She chewed her lip. 'Yes. And it's obviously very much in the Duke of York's interests that such a marriage certificate be destroyed. I imagine he has agents looking for it and if Sam knows who has it and where–'

'They'll want to question him ... before they kill him.' I shook my head. 'And he doesn't want us to know because we would be in danger too. Yet we are anyway, though, aren't we? Torture first, no doubt.'

She was quiet again, thinking. 'That would depend on what York's agents know. Rifkind doesn't give information away; he sells it and I'm sure it will be payment in advance.' She frowned. 'So much depends on what has reached him.'

I gathered her in. 'Christ. How can I keep you safe, both of you?'

'I think we must try not to be too concerned until we know just what we're truly threatened with ... if, indeed, anything at all, yet.'

'Still, surely we must go back to London as soon as possible–'

'To Whitehall? Really?' She raised her eyebrows. 'Yet I don't believe York could go after us there right under the King's nose, could he?'

'What would the King do if he knew the marriage certificate had surfaced?' I frowned for a moment before answering my own question. 'Wouldn't he want it kept secret, but safely in his possession? It would give him freedom to choose his successor whenever he wished, depending on the prevailing opinion in the country.' I had that feeling of understanding dissipating like vapour again. 'The status quo means James and perhaps Catholicism, at least for a time, yet what if England rebels against such a thing–'

'I can't see it being tolerated for long. Yet would his brother fight for his throne ... or would Monmouth fight his uncle for it? Either way, the King has a very

difficult dilemma on his hands. I don't envy him it.'
She sighed. 'All this is just so much speculation. And
how will we ever know the truth of it? Rifkind can be
confronted but he's under no obligation to reveal anything, is he?'

I brought her hand up to my lips and kissed it.
'Coin would free his tongue, I'm sure–'

'Coin we don't have.'

There seemed nothing more to be said.

CHAPTER 42

Susannah

Some weeks later, when we learned of Rifkind's return, the time had come for the long-delayed confrontation, however little faith we had in it. What else was there? Though, in the end, it came about in an unexpected way; Rifkind having written asking to meet the Bartholomews, with a request passed on from Isabella to see Raphael. Of course, he felt he had little choice but to go, regardless of this request's provenance. Had Rifkind really found her and brought her back? If so, I pitied her.

I watched them set-off, standing with Sam and Michael on the porch overlooking the stables, a sleeping Paolo in my arms, still feeling the touch of Raphael's lips on mine. Soon there was only dust in the yard where their horses had been. I hated that he had gone with them.

Michael cleared his throat. 'Back to my books, I think.'

We watched him walk away to his chamber, entering from the porch. 'Or perhaps to Pearl?'

Sam laughed. 'Well, he deserves it. Noah seems incapable of recognising anything beyond brute strength as any sort of useful attribute.'

I thought of Raphael denying his own physical power as if there were only one kind. Not that his kind would be needed today ... or at least I hoped it would not. I looked down at our son. 'He'd be better in his cradle.'

Sam took him from my arms, careful not to wake him. 'Come. You should rest, too, until he wakes, especially while Penny's out on the pinnace.'

'That worries me as well.'

'Josh will take care of her. It's lovely to see her so happy when she's caught a fish herself.'

I smiled. 'Yes.' I followed him round to the back of the house and into my chamber, watching him lay Paolo down. 'Stay with me for a while, or have–'

'I'm happy to stay, Sukie.'

We lay side by side holding hands, lulled by the sound of waves breaking on the shore. I think we both slept a little until Paolo's stirrings awakened us.

Sam left the bed to fetch him, holding up his hand when I looked ready to demur. 'Let me. I owe you for all the time I wasn't there with Penny.'

I smiled, taking my son into my arms. 'You owe me nothing, you know that. Having her is enough.'

He watched me feeding him and stroked his dark hair with his fingers. 'He really is going to be the image of Raphael, just as Penny is of you.'

When he was done, I placed him back in his cradle myself, content to let him sleep awhile before changing his clout. I doubted that would be a task for Sam. I smiled thinking of it. Not many men would take that one on, I imagined. My husband did, though. I lay down beside him again. 'What do you suppose Isabella wants with Raphael? If that message was truly from–' When a brawny fair-haired man stepped inside from the porch, I shrieked. Sam bolted upright, beginning to launch himself towards the intruder until he pointed a pistol at his chest.

'She wishes to tell him she's with child, Susannah.'

I knew who he was then.

Sam held up his hands. 'What do you want?'

Rifkind grinned. 'Same as you've just had, I imagine. I want her. Fair's fair. Your husband had my wife, no?'

I gasped. 'You made him do it. You gave him no choice–'

His eyes went cold. 'I gave him the choice not to please her, which he chose to ignore.' He tilted his head, studying me. 'Did he tell you just how very much he did please her ... my wife? So now it's my turn to enjoy you, though I can't promise you'll have the same experience she did ... and he gave her a child, too, I'm sorry to say.'

'That's not true.'

'What a trusting girl you are. And with a man like that.' He shifted his gaze to Sam. 'Yet, you seem little better yourself. Perhaps you're well matched, after all.' He kept the pistol pointed at Sam but clearly had not realised who he was at first. 'Well, well. Samuel Carter. There are a lot of folk interested in you. You're Penelope's father, of course. A lovely little girl, what a shame neither of you will ever see her again.'

He looked from Sam to me, cocking his head again, clearly puzzled by our lack of response to those words. So, he did not yet know we had her back. *Thank God.*

'I hadn't realised you maintained a relationship with her mother still.' He gazed at my sleeping son. 'Whose is this one, I wonder?' His eyes went hard, then. 'Stand in front of the cradle. If you force me to fire, who knows where the ball may end up.'

Sam did as instructed, his hands still raised. 'You lay a finger on Susannah, and I swear I'll kill you.'

Rifkind ignored him. 'Unlace your bodice.'

I closed my eyes and did what he asked. Michael was still here in his chamber but there was no way to summon him. Rifkind had planned this well.

He placed the pistol down on the bed, looking at Sam. 'Move and believe me, I will shoot.'

Reeking of tobacco smoke, he bent down to squeeze my breast. I fought not to retch. His other hand went to my skirts, pulling them up. 'I won't take long, but I shall enjoy myself.'

Sam groaned. It was then I saw Michael move

silently into the doorway, his sword in his hand. Sam saw him too and lunged for the pistol as Michael ran forward pushing the point of his blade into the back of Rifkind's neck, drawing blood.

Sam grabbed the pistol and turned it on him. 'Do please make a move, Sir. I have a very strong desire to shoot you.'

I scrambled from the bed and rushed to my son, lifting him into my arms, hardly able to comprehend this man had threatened his life. Tears streamed down my face. When galloping hoofbeats sounded from the front of the house, I felt my knees start to buckle and collapsed down onto the bed, clutching Paolo to me. He began to whimper, and I kissed his silky hair. 'Thank Jesu.'

CHAPTER 43

Raphael

I kicked my leg up over the pommel to vault from my horse and ran up the steps onto the porch; Noah and Hal soon out-pacing me. We arrived at the chamber door to find Michael and Sam had already overpowered Rifkind. Since meeting Isabella galloping towards us on the road down from the plantation, where she had told us of her husband's intentions, my heart had pounded in my ears with my mouth dry as ash. When we first saw her horse approaching, Noah and Hal had drawn their swords until they realised the rider was a woman and then which woman.

Now I pushed passed everyone and hurried across the room, closing my arms around my wife and son. 'Susannah. Christ, Susannah. Has he harmed you?'

She shook her head, unable to speak, choked by sobs.

'He had every intention of doing so had Michael not arrived when he did,' Sam said.

Noah and Hal had a firm hold of Rifkind now, his arms twisted high up behind his back, his shirt wet with blood from a slash on his neck. Noah turned to Michael. 'Nicely done, Lad.'

Michael looked pale and not a little shocked. 'My God. He was going to rape her.'

I turned to Rifkind. 'Then, Sir, I shall cut out your heart.'

He grinned his contempt. 'If your wife can fuck Carter, why not me?' He stared hard at me with a suggestion of that supressed glee I had seen from him before. 'Or weren't you aware?'

My scornful laughter clearly took him by surprise I was glad to see before I turned my attention back to my wife still held in my arms.

Noah removed his sword belt to secure Rifkind's hands before dragging him out onto the porch and shoving him down onto a bench. 'Now, he's going to tell us everything we want to know, or I shall cut him open ready for you, Raphael, and I'll take my time over it.'

The man's grin faded. None of us were in any doubt Noah was entirely capable of doing it. Sam's life was at stake, and he would stop at nothing to protect him.

I dried Susannah's face with a handkerchief, holding her until she was able to compose herself again. 'You're safe now. God forgive me for letting this to happen to you.'

She managed a small smile. 'I do seem to make a habit of having strangers fondle my breasts and lift my skirts.'

I cupped her face. '*Sei molto caraggioso, amore mio.*'

'Not brave at the time.'

I moved Paolo back to his cradle where he kicked, seemingly content for now. 'He needs a fresh clout. I'll call a girl. We should hear what this wicked creature has to say for himself.'

The others had waited for us. While he did so, Noah had been writing notes. I looked at Sam, who shrugged.

Susannah chewed her lip. 'Perhaps we should find out what he knows about Kitty first?'

Noah nodded. 'But before we do, I must make sure he understands he has no choice about talking.' He rose, standing over Rifkind, a dagger in his hand.

Rifkind looked up, defiant. 'Why would I tell you anything when you're going to kill me regardless. There's always a choice, Sir.'

Noah nodded and reached down to tear open his shirt. Without another word, he carved a small deep slash on Rifkind's chest. The man screamed. 'Indeed, there is. And it's entirely yours to make.'

Bile rose in my throat. I held Susannah close. 'Don't stay, *cara*. I'll tell you all that's said.'

She shook her head. 'I must hear it myself.' Needless to say, Rifkind told us everything in the end. When Noah doubted him, he used his dagger. Susannah chose not to look then. Michael appeared uncomprehending. Yet I found myself watching Noah's face and not what he did with his knife, as did Sam. He appeared old beyond his years. Haggard. Cold. His eyes pitiless. Sam saw it too, looking horrified ... and yet full of such compassion for him. *Porcodio.*

Asked about Kitty Foyles, Noah used his knife when Rifkind denied any knowledge of her whereabouts.

The man gritted his teeth. 'Puerto Rico. She was auctioned there. That's all I know; I swear it before God.'

And it seemed it was, for Noah tested it. Thoroughly. Though I doubted the wretch had much acquaintance with God.

Noah told him all about Penny's rescue then, which was at first met with disbelief until he named Hilliard and described in some detail how he met his death. 'Who was behind the child's kidnapping?'

Sweat dripped down Rifkind's face leaving him blinking and grimacing at the sting when it ran into his eyes. 'I don't know. They said she was taken to lure Carter to Cinnamon Hill.'

Noah touched his finger on the point of his blade. 'What made you trade her to Hilliard, then?'

'To get you and the others away so I could have him taken.' He gasped a breath. 'I'd had fresh instructions. They knew they were here, see.'

Noah gave him a cold stare. 'What do you know about those seeking him?'

The knife was used and eventually we learned there were two groups of interested parties. In the end, we had to accept Rifkind genuinely did not know who was behind them. And, in truth, there was no reason why he should have done.

'What information have you already sold?'

Rifkind balled his fists. 'Christ. Don't cut me. Don't fucking cut me. I'm still waiting for my price. I swear it. I'm waiting.'

Noah moved the knife towards his chest. Rifkind shifted his head rapidly from side to side. 'Don't, I beg you. I've told one lot Carter is here. That's all. Want to know who else is here ... the other lot knew already. They took the girl to get him.' Tears rolled down his face. 'For the love of God, don't cut me again.' He began to weep.

I crossed myself, praying this would end soon.

Noah ignored him. 'What do you know about why these people want Samuel Carter?'

'Nothing. Why would I be told?'

Noah moved the knife close but didn't touch his chest where blood now ran copiously from open wounds. 'Holy God, help me.' More tears spilled. 'Something wanted from him. Alive. Back to England. Important people. Rich.' His voice shook while his words fell over each other in their scramble to escape.

'Did these people have names. Who did you contact to set your price?'

He panted, nodding vigorously. 'I've names.'
'Who are they.'
'Jesus Christ. How ... remember? Records.'
'Where?'
'Office.' He looked suddenly hopeful. 'I can get them for you. I can. Let me get them for you.' One look at Noah and hope left his face like a candle snuffed. He gasped a shuddering breath. 'You can't,' he shouted. 'I'll pay you ... anything. Name it. Anything.' He struggled against his bonds, death now a reality, trying to free himself. 'Friends here. Powerful. Governor–'

'Friends who'll mourn your slaughter at the hands of maroons on the road.'

Maroons. Escaped slaves. Many in Jamaica, I knew. A convenient explanation.

Sam rose to his feet. 'Noah!'

Noah gave him a black look but otherwise ignored him, his face like granite. Sam walked away and down the steps onto the beach. Christ, I wanted to follow him; glad Susannah had gone with Pearl to feed Paolo. Glad she had not witnessed that.

When Noah dragged Rifkind to his feet, finally, Hal helped him frog-march him away. Holy God. I already knew what he would do. We all did, for what other choice was there? I crossed myself and began to pray, already commending the man's soul to God's mercy. And then I prayed for Noah.

Hal arrived back with us, shaking his head. 'He sent me away. He flung himself down next to Michael

– who was white and shaking – and put his head in his hands.

Blood had pooled on the floor in front of the bench where Rifkind sat. I tried not to look at it.

Susannah returned then, holding our son. She held her hand out to me and together we returned to our chamber. After placing Paolo down into his cradle, she sat on the bed and pulled me down beside her. Placing her palm on my face. 'Jesu, Raphael, you look harrowed.'

I shook my head. 'The whole thing was unspeakable. What was done and that Noah had to do it.' I stared hard at her as though defying her to deny it. 'He had to. What choice did he have? Sam left in the end. It can't be easy watching someone you love being forced to do that for you.'

'Poor Sam. Poor Noah.' She held my gaze. 'Will he kill him?

'Again, he has no choice.' I sighed. 'I hope the plantations will go to Isabella. That her life might improve would mean some good came from it. And at least we know what we're contending with now. So, Sam may be safe here for the moment but we've no means of knowing for how long.'

She took my hand and kissed it. 'My love, he said Isabella was with child ... and that it was yours.'

My mind lurched. Holy God. I'd had no chance to ask her what she wished of me before we turned back to Hayes Bay. Please, Christ, it was not this. Yet I knew of men who thought they had done enough to stop a child, even insisting it could not be theirs because of it. 'Susannah, he lied. I know he did. He was trying to distress you.' I took a deep breath. 'They'll take him ... his body back to Cinnamon Hill, tomorrow. I'll go with them and speak to her.'

'I'll accompany you–'

'No, *cara*. They'll go after his records and we don't know who might be there guarding them, still.' And I needed to talk to Isabella alone. Susannah looked away, knowing it.

CHAPTER 44
Noah

Noah lay on the bed in full darkness now, unaware the light had gone. How could he not relive such a scene over and over? Forcing the trembling man to his knees behind the barn. Closing his ears to his desperate pleas. Watching him piss himself when the pistol found the back of his skull. Then, his last words. Garbled. Desperate. 'He'll die. He will. He will. It's too late.' Noah fired. The smell of black powder and singed hair followed almost instantly by blood and shit was like a physical assault. He had moved away then, to puke. He wanted to puke now, that stench haunting him still.

When Sam arrived in their chamber, Noah kept his back turned, feigning sleep. Sam lay down beside him, pressing close, though Noah remained unmoving. He had no words yet. He found it hard to imagine how he ever would. Yet sleep stole up unawares and when he awakened Sam was still there close against him, sleeping too. Starlight lit the room through the open shutters. He tried to move away without waking him, dry mouthed and hungry but mostly needing a piss which is what had woken him, he realised. When he swung his legs to the floor, Sam stirred beside him.

'Are you all right?'

Noah barely heard him. 'Need a piss,' he croaked.

Sam sighed and moved up higher against the pillows. 'Would it help to talk?'

Noah closed his eyes, trying to shut him out. 'I just want a fucking piss.'

'Would it occur to you I might need to? He found a wan smile. Wasted in the dark. 'Talk not piss that is.'

Noah used the chamber-pot without replying and returned to the bed, turning away.

Sam took his hand and held onto it. Hard. 'Forgive me.'

Noah moved around to look at him. Reluctant. Frowning. Christ. Why could he not just leave him be? 'Forgive you? Why?'

'For making you do such a thing.'

Noah felt himself about to explode. He scrubbed at his face, his eyes tight shut, desperate to hold on. Desperate. He took a deep breath. 'Sam. I can't talk of this now. I beg you.' Yet all he heard was Rifkind's frantic begging for his life. 'Leave me now. Please. I need to be alone for a while.' When Sam stayed, resolute, clinging to his hand again, he detached himself forcibly and fled. He stumbled down to the beach, plunging into the cold shock of the sea.

Could this be the solution? Swim out until he could swim no longer and just let the sea take him. No more stench clinging to him like a winding sheet. No more scourging himself. He swam out hard, pumping away from the shore until his arms became leaden, forcing him to slow. He had killed ... executed two men. One bound and gagged the other tortured first. Both grotesque. Both shameful. Both necessary. He moved further away from the shore but slowly now and, as his strength faded, he felt torpor begin to engulf him and with it, guilt became distant and less important. Another swimmer splashed up beside him then, startling him back to himself. Christ. Strong hands grabbed him and held on, forcing him to halt. Hal. Who else?

'Stop. What the fuck are you doing? What are you thinking?'

Noah rolled onto his back to float, closing his eyes against the stars. God, they flooded the sky. 'I don't know. I can't ...'

Hal held him tight, keeping him afloat, cursing under his breath ... almost. 'So you'll do this? To Sam? To me? ... to Michael? You truly wish it?'

'You saw what I did.' He wept then before his son, his tears lost in the swell, he hoped unseen. They trod water, black under cold hard stars. 'Hal ...'

His son grasped him. 'Josh is bringing the pinnace out. Just hold on. Christ. You fool. You fucking fool. What you did probably saved Sam's life. Do you regret it? *Really?*' Hal shook his head, seawater flying from his hair as his legs pumped, keeping them afloat. 'Think, you bloody fucker.'

And Noah did. *Sam.*

Hands propelled him into their chamber. Dripping. Pushing him onto the bed.

'He's all right.' Hal hugged his father and left them.

Sam tended to him without words. Stripping. Drying. Pulling on a nightshirt, with no resistance. Even covering him with a quilt though it was a hot night, trying to still his shivering. Sam lay next to him then, closing his arms around him, ignoring Noah's stiff resistance. Yet, how could he not be aware of Sam shuddering as he wept. He stayed, though. Sam stayed with him until, finally, he surrendered himself to his unconditional love. So, they talked in the dark of the night and Noah found himself soothed. 'It's hard to hear a man beg for his life, even such a one–'

'You had no choice.'

'I know. Doesn't help, though. At least I spared Hal this time ... until tonight. He closed his eyes. 'I shamed myself. I shamed him.'

'Jesu, Noah. Why can't you just allow us to care about you? To love you?'

CHAPTER 45

Hal

Hal left his chamber at dawn, his shoulder muscles sore from the hard swim. He wondered how his father's were. Worse, he imagined. He stopped, transfixed, watching the sun rise over the mountains, filling the sky with gold against turquoise, before moving along the porch to the back of the house to look out over the sea. The crest of the headland caught the first shafts of sunshine, with Fort Charles squatting – guns bristling – pink and benign in such kind light. The water in the bay was shadowed, quicksilver and mirror-still, the illusion of solidity broken when pelicans dived for their breakfast. He turned, intending to go through the house to the kitchens, aware his own belly awaited sustenance and was beginning to complain of it. The sight of Sam sitting in the deep shadow outside his chamber startled him. 'How is he?'

Sam yawned. 'Sleeping. He hasn't really said what

happened. He eventually told me what having to do that ... having to kill Rifkind, did to him. I don't know what he expected to feel.' He sighed. 'But what the fuck do I know about it? Christ. I can barely comprehend the courage it took.' Sam looked intently at him. 'Did he mean it do you think? To drown?'

Hal sat beside him. 'He wouldn't have gone through with it. It's not in his nature. But I couldn't just leave him swimming out like that. I was here looking at the stars. I couldn't sleep. So, I saw him go in, thank God.' He closed his eyes for a moment. 'He'd almost exhausted himself when I got to him. Luckily, Josh had just returned from night fishing so I could shout for him to bring the boat out to us.'

Sam ran his hand through his hair. 'I was trying to get him to talk. I should know by now to leave him until he's ready, but I could see how he tormented himself.'

'And you wanted to help him stop. Horses and water always with him.' Hal smiled, recognising that in himself, too. 'He's a stubborn bastard. He asked me not to tell Michael, so I won't. He finds him incompressible, anyway. So, Christ knows what he'd make of this.' His stomach chose that moment to announce itself again and he stood. 'I suppose we must take Rifkind back to Cinnamon Hill today. See what else we can discover.'

'Will his people believe you found him dead on the road?'

Hal shrugged. 'They've no way of proving we

didn't, and his wife is unlikely to want to delve into it, is she? And she won't grieve for him either; it was obvious she'd been hurt when she came to us. Nothing to see, he'd make sure of that. But the way she held herself.' Hal shook his head, his admiration plain. 'The ride out to us can't have been easy for her. Yet she rode hard.' They held each other's gaze a moment before Hal nodded and walked away.

After a detour to the kitchens for hot rolls, breadfruit and saltfish, he took his meal back to his chamber. Strangely, he was not surprised to find Michael waiting there for him. He handed him a hot roll without comment.

'Pearl told me what happened last night ... with Papa. What on earth's the matter with him?'

She must have spoken to Josh. So much for keeping it from him. 'He's better now. Yesterday was hard for him, that's all.'

'Holy God. He wanted to end his life? I can scarce get my head around it.'

'He wasn't thinking clearly.' Michael appeared so horrified ... he tried to pinpoint what he saw. Disappointment. He was disappointed in their father, and it infuriated him. His voice rose. 'Christ, Michael. Have you ever killed a man? Have you?'

His brother looked affronted. 'Of course, I haven't. I'm not a bloody savage–'

'Savage? Well then, I am for I have killed and it's an obscenity–'

'My God. You've taken a life. *You* have? Why?'

397

Hal balled his fists, fighting the urge to use them on his brother. 'Because, little brother, if I hadn't the man would have killed me without compunction. Christ, you're naïve. None of this is a game. You saw what Papa was forced to do–'

'It was nothing but savagery. That's–'

'Yes. It was hideous but it gutted him. It gutted him, Michael. Yet he had no choice. You must be able to see that?'

Michael shook his head, wildly. 'I won't believe it. There's always a choice. There has to be.'

Hal sat beside him on the bed, battling to hold his temper. 'All right. I'll bow to your greater wisdom. What were his alternatives?'

'Take him to the authorities. The man was a kidnapper. Use British law to seize his records.'

Hal laughed, mirthlessly. 'The authorities in Port Royal when the lieutenant governor is a crook himself? *Really?*'

'The commander at Fort Charles, then.'

'Who is subordinate to Morgan? There's no British law here.' He looked at his breakfast, finding he had lost his appetite. 'And don't forget who Morgan answers to.'

Michael was silent for a few moments. 'The King.'

'Precisely. Rifkind was getting instruction from London, perhaps with the King's knowledge. More likely with his brother's. This is most definitely Sam's life at stake here. Do you really think for one moment Papa wouldn't act to protect him?'

'Hal, I know it's hard for you to understand. But I feel I no longer know him. He's just so far from the person I thought he was. First finding him with Sam and now all this barbarity.' He shook his head in despair. 'And then he falls apart. The very last thing I'd ever believe possible of him.'

Hal took his time to consider all his brother had said, trying to understand it from his perspective. He blinked, surprised he had become so fiercely protective of their father that he'd found those words hard to listen to. Yet when he contemplated the difficult path he had travelled to finally get to know him, he understood Michael would need time to do the same. 'All I can say is he's the strongest person I know and if I can be half the man he is, I shall be inordinately proud.'

CHAPTER 46
Raphael

The ride up to Cinnamon Hill was hot but otherwise uneventful, thank God. It had rained heavily in the early hours, leaving the forest dripping and steaming as the sun climbed in the sky, the air reeking of mouldering vegetation. Could I really see the lush undergrowth sprouting? Surely not, though it certainly seemed so. I blinked, telling myself the vines were not creeping slowly higher on tree trunks as I passed.

The rain also meant there would now be no sign of spilled blood where we would claim to have found Rifkind the afternoon before. His body was wrapped in heavy canvas secured with ropes. The mule carrying him across its back appeared indifferent to the burden as did the stable boy leading it from another sturdy beast. We, of course, were weighed down by his presence – Noah most of all – desiring only to be rid of him.

Any conversation between us was desultory, which allowed my thoughts to go back to one I'd had with Susannah before we left. First, we had spoken of Noah's ordeal the night before, after Sam told her of it.

'Poor Sam, he feels he pushed him to it. Yet what else could he do. Hal was certain he wouldn't have gone through with it, but he was exhausted when he reached him.'

I finished dressing in a light cotton shirt and breeches before sitting beside her on the bed where she had returned to feed Paolo. 'Well, he's lucky then that Hal went in after him.'

'Will he be all right today, do you think?'

I nodded. 'He's a very resilient man, *cara*.' I saw her eyes were fixed on me and knew what truly concerned her. I lifted her hand to my lips. 'All shall be well.'

'How sure can you be?'

What could I say? Not as sure as she would like, of course. But there seemed little point in speculating. 'Let me speak to her so I can put your mind at rest.'

'And yours, too, I would have thought, Raphael?' She sounded a touch vexed.

'Indeed.' More than she could ever know.

When Noah spoke, I shook my head to clear it, his voice sounding oddly hollow in the heavy air beneath the trees. I had not noticed him bring his horse up alongside mine. Strangely, what he had to say turned out to be related to my recent thoughts, in that he mentioned Isabella. 'Forgive me, I didn't quite hear you.'

He gave me a speculative look. 'When we arrive, I'd like you to find Isabella and take her somewhere safe while Hal and I search the office.'

Sam would have told him why I needed to talk to her, of course. Though I was grateful he did not refer to it. I smiled. 'As you wish, Noah.' I studied him carefully, finding no lack of resolve on his face. I wanted to tell him how much I admired him, but I doubted he would care for it.

He clearly read my scrutiny and tilted his head. 'I'm fully restored. You need have no concerns.'

'I would never doubt it.'

He nodded, curtly, and kicked-on back to Hal.

When we moved out into the first cane field, we saw two riders approaching. Noah and Hal moved apart to cover the track and drew their swords just as they had the day before. When the small figure waved, I realised it was Isabella again. The Bartholomews lowered their weapons but did not sheath them.

She reined-in before us, her eyes round with shock when she saw the mule carrying its shrouded burden, halted further back on the track. 'Is it him? How?'

Noah nodded at her companion. A tall, striking-looking man with honey-coloured skin and a ready smile. Mulatto, I believe, is the term used for those such as him. His fine tailoring putting us to shame.

'Best introduce him, Lass.'

'This is Lafayette. He's my friend.' She looked at

each of us. 'You can trust him. You have my word on it.'

Lafayette nodded, still smiling. 'My only desire is to keep Isabella safe.'

His voice was deep and educated. I wondered what his story was. That his eyes lingered on Isabella told me something else about him. If she were with child, it was not necessarily mine.

Father and son sheathed their swords and Noah looked towards her husband's corpse. 'All you need know is we found him dead on the track yesterday and are returning him to you for burial.'

She nodded. 'Was he useful to you?'

Noah beckoned the stable boy to bring the mule up again. 'We need to see his records. He has contacts in London. It's vital we learn all we can about them.'

Isabella looked at Lafayette. 'He found the right man on Barbados for us. He knows his way around the office ... where to locate things.' She raised her eyebrows in a question. He nodded slightly. 'Lafayette is ... was my husband's amanuensis, as his father was before him.'

'Will we encounter any resistance to our search?' Noah asked.

Lafayette gave him a shrewd look. 'Not if I accompany you. The overseer is up at the crush mill today in the master's place as he didn't return last night. He'll not be back before nightfall.' With his eyes lingering on the body, he appeared decidedly content with the way things now stood.

I glanced at Noah before turning my attention to Isabella. 'I wonder if I might speak with you alone while *Signor* Lafayette shows my friends to your husband's office?'

She nodded. 'Of course, Raphael.'

Did I glimpse a touch of displeasure cross the young man's face before his ubiquitous smile reappeared once more? 'Where would you suggest?'

She looked at Lafayette. 'Your cabin? Mustafa may have returned.'

He nodded, eyeing Rifkind's body once more. 'He's done here. Just needs you to make sure he knows it.'

She nodded, too. We rode on, trailing Isabella and Lafayette in through the gate to the park and beyond to the house. Lafayette issued brisk instructions for the disposal of the corpse and the horses. Seeing how his orders were obeyed without question, reassured me all would be well for Isabella with him to support her. She beckoned to me then, and I followed her around behind the house towards a small copse of trees where a cabin stood in the shade. It looked in good repair. In front was a sturdy porch with a rocking chair. We tied our horses to the rail, and she led me inside. The place was spotless with a muslin-draped bed made up with colourful quilts, a desk, and a small table in the window with two chairs.

She poured cups of water for us, gesturing for me to sit before taking the other chair. 'How are you Raphael? And your wife and child?'

I sipped my water which was warm but fresh tasting. 'Susannah is well.' I smiled. 'We have a son.'

'You have the little girl back with you too, I know.' She crossed herself.

'Penny, yes. Thanks to you.'

'And Lafayette.' She sighed. 'I know what you wish to ask me.' Her hand went to her belly. A gesture I knew well. 'Yes. I'm with child. My husband knew of it. He knew, too, it was not his though in British law it will be regarded as such, despite its parentage.'

I waited for her to confirm what I had already guessed. She placed her hand over mine. 'Don't be concerned, Raphael, it's not yours either. My child's father is Lafayette.'

I squeezed her hand. 'I'm very happy for you. For you both.' And extremely relieved, of course.

'He's a freeman, born, as was his father. We love each other and we can marry now. He's a good man, Raphael. You taught me about good men.'

I smiled, hoping there might be some little truth in it. 'I'm sure he'll be a fine husband and the plantations will prosper in his hands.' He had struck me even in so short an acquaintance, as a particularly assured and capable young man. The sort to inspire loyalty where it truly mattered, I imagined. It seemed unlikely Rifkind had been such a one or only among his fellow scoundrels, perhaps.

She stroked her belly, absently. 'I was worried I would lose it when he beat me–'

'*Cristo.* Did he hurt you badly?'

She pulled up her sleeve and showed me old bruises made by fingers. 'I belonged to him. I ran away, so had to be punished for it. He used a horse whip on my back.'

I closed my eyes, finding it difficult to even contemplate such a thing. I squeezed her hand again. It seemed but a small comfort to offer.

'When he fetched me back, he was kind. At first, I thought it a pantomime to reassure my family but when he remained so after we returned, I began to think he had truly forgiven me. Not so, of course. Lulling me in such a way added to his enjoyment when he decided it was time for my punishment. Mustafa came with him to my chamber early one morning. He told me to take off my nightgown. I had to stand naked before them.' She pressed her lips together, clearly trying to gather herself.

I wanted to say something to help her, but no words seemed adequate.

She took a deep breath. 'I thought he was going to watch Mustafa rape me. And he must have thought the same. He'd led him to expect it, I think. My husband enjoyed his disappointment when it turned out not to be so. I was to get a whipping instead. It was Mustafa who told him I was with child. He'd seen it. He told my husband to stop. I asked him if he wished to lose his son? He knew, of course, it couldn't be his for he'd never touched me in that way. But it soon became clear he wanted no one else to know it. So, I had a little power over him at last.'

I stood and pulled her gently up into my arms. 'Isabella, I pray things will go well for you now. You deserve it after all you've borne.'

'Lafayette wanted to kill him when he saw what he'd done to me. It was he who told me my husband had lured you and your friends here so he could go after your wife. Forgive me for telling him the child was yours—'

'I understand. It meant he wouldn't search for your lover here. You kept Lafayette safe.' Even as she risked my wife. Yet what else could she have done? I would certainly have done the same in her place. Warning us was all that had been left to her. I held her away to kiss her on both cheeks. 'Now, I must return to my friends. Go with God, Isabella.'

She smiled. 'You also. I'll wait here for Lafayette.'

As I rode the short distance back to the house, I wondered why Rifkind had never consummated his marriage. Was he even capable? Would he have been with Susannah? I crossed myself, thanking God it was not something we would ever know.

I walked up the steps into the house with no idea where to find Rifkind's office. Why had I not thought to ask Isabella? The problem was solved when a footman appeared carrying a tray with a jug of wine and glasses. 'Office, if you please.' I tried to sound as though my request had authority behind it.

He looked over his shoulder. 'Follow me, Sa.'

Noah and Lafayette were seated in front of a large mahogany desk, the latter perusing letters and making copies of any that might be relevant, presumably. Copies of copies, of course. Noah pored over a ledger, noting a few names as his finger moved down the column. Hal stood with his back to me, examining the bookshelves. He turned when the footman entered and seeing me, raised his eyebrows. The question was obvious. I shook my head slightly. He smiled, nodding his understanding.

Noah looked up at the footman. 'I'll pour. And we'll need another glass.'

I took a chair before the window, glancing out over the park with its incongruous sheep. In truth, no more so than pelicans in St James's Park. 'Anything useful?' The notes and copies suggested there must be. So, I thought of a better question. 'Does any of it make sense?'

'I can't say it does, entirely.' Noah pointed at the ledgers. 'Lists of names with monetary amounts noted next to them. A few with ticks.'

Lafayette tapped his lip with his quill. 'People he had requested money from for information he would supply once letters of credit had been received.' He pointed to one of the ticks.

Hal leaned down to look at the columns. 'How will we know which of these names are relevant to us?'

'I'm copying all the un-checked ones, which must mean they're current. Some have LON against them, too. Obviously, London, so they'll take priority.'

Lafayette began another letter. 'Why can't we just take these copies? Rifkind will have no further use for them.' He looked up at me with a surprised expression. Noah, I saw, had done the same though his could more readily be called incredulous. I turned to Hal, who shrugged. I must say, I was glad not to be quite alone in my idiocy, whatever it might be.

Noah looked at each of us, shaking his head. 'Think. What happens if a reply comes to any of them? Lafayette won't necessarily know to what they refer without a copy of Rifkind's original letter. Show him one that demonstrates it, Lad.'

Lafayette sifted through the pile and pulled one out to show me. It said simply. '... *Regarding business matter. Done as asked. Carstairs.*' I nodded my understanding when he showed me the letter it referred to. '*Carstairs ... see that the brandy shipment is sent out forthwith. I shall brook no more delays with this. Rifkind.*' The replies are filed with the copies of the originals in alphabetical order.'

Noah drained his wine glass and checked the time on the long-case clock. 'We must think about leaving soon if we are to get back before nightfall.'

Lafayette put down his pen. 'I'll continue with this now I know what you seek. I can have it all brought down to you as soon as its completed.' He turned to me. 'Might I have a private word before you leave *Signor* Rossi?'

I smiled. 'Raphael please. And I'm fairly sure I know what it concerns. You may speak freely.'

He cleared his throat. 'I wish you to know how very distressed Isabella was when her lie about her child being yours sent her husband to attack your wife. When the note was sent asking you here, I had no idea that was his plan. After Isabella understood his intentions, she left immediately to warn you. I wanted to go instead but she insisted it must be her. She would not even allow me to ride with her when Mustafa was here.' He cleared his throat again. 'We had been very discrete, and she was concerned our being together would be reported to her husband on his return. We had never imagined he would not ...'

I touched his arm. 'She explained it to me, and I understand, so you need not be concerned.' With that it seemed our business there was concluded and once the papers were packed into saddlebags for us, we left to begin our ride back down to Hayes Bay. Hot gusts of wind stirred the cane under lurid light that glowed behind angry clouds already piling-up in ominous-looking columns as we crossed the fields.

'Noah eyed them, warily. 'Let's hope we can avoid a soaking.'

Hal rode beside me. 'So, she's certain the child isn't yours?'

Noah turned to look at him, shaking his head. 'Christ almighty, Hal. Just leave it for once.'

I punched his arm, lightly. 'She is. And I have no reason to doubt her.'

'Then you must be mighty relieved.' He frowned.

'It can't be easy to know what that lie might have cost, though. How close he came to—'

Noah exploded. 'Christ's fucking wounds, Lad. Raphael is fully aware, as are we. So will Susannah be in due course. Now leave it. It's done.'

Then, inevitably, it began to rain or more accurately the heavens opened and the pounding of water on leaves put pay to any further conversation ... or, indeed, confrontation.

Darkness had fallen and the rain long gone, leaving the sky full of cold bright stars by the time we were all assembled on the porch in dry clothing with large glasses of wine in our hands. Susannah and Sam had been filled in on our activities – well, Noah's activities – at Cinnamon Hill, too. Once I had put Susannah's mind at rest concerning the parentage of Isabella's child, explaining the circumstances causing her to tell her husband otherwise, she handed me a letter. Frances.

'Forgive me for opening it—'

'But you always open them, *cara*. I should be more concerned had you not, I think.'

Sam laughed. 'Understandable, I suppose. Yet I believe I opened the last one, though you read it first.'

Michael looked puzzled. 'Why?'

Noah tilted his head back against the sofa. 'God almighty, not you too. Does it never occur to either of you that some question shouldn't be asked because it's just not your fucking business?'

411

Hal looked at me and I shrugged. 'Let's just say before his marriage, Raphael shared a similar relationship with the Duchess of Richmond as you do now with Pearl.'

Michael reddened, of course. 'But isn't she one of the King's mistresses?'

'She is, indeed. Though at that time she was also Raphael's.'

As laughter seemed the best response, I laughed, and kissing Paolo, handed him to Susannah before taking the letter. Noah appeared annoyed and Susannah decidedly vexed. I ignored them both, looking down to read.

'It's nothing to be proud of, Raphael,' she snapped.

I looked up at her and frowned. 'I'm aware of that. And I'm not. Remotely.' I returned to the letter.

Richmond House
Whitehall
5th April 1677

My dearest Raphael.
I was delighted to receive a letter from you at last. (The diplomatic bag does have its uses, does it not?) I was able to pass it on to your mama for, as yet, she has not received one. She is writing to you herself and I shall again include it in the pouch with this–'

I looked up. 'There's one from Mamma?'

She nodded. 'It's waiting for you in the chamber. You'll be pleased to know I didn't open it,' she said, sharply, before turning to Sam. 'And for your information, Sam, I open Frances Stuart's letters because she often has information relevant to us here. As is the case with this one. So not because I have any doubts about my husband's fidelity, I assure you.'

Sam looked suitably chastened. 'Forgive me, Sukie. Thoughtless of me.'

I lifted her hand to my lips before continuing to read, closing my ears to Noah's harrumphing.

She continues to do well here at court, but I'm sure she'll give you a full account of it all, so I'll restrict myself to more pertinent matters. It will interest you to know I have recently had a visit from Lieutenant Monkton who informed us (fortuitously, the King was with me at the time) of the names of the man and woman who it is believed took Penny and her friend from the park. They are a Johnathan Snape and Miranda Peppin who conveyed them onboard the Ferdinand under the names you discovered in Lisbon. The King, of course, said he would have people look into it to see what might be discovered about those behind this pair.

Jumping ahead, it seemed he could find nothing. And there, you might imagine it all came to nought but, Raphael, it did not. For not long after the King had left that day, Monmouth called upon me. Strangely, he had seen the King leave and wished to know our conversation. I received the impression he also knew Thomas Monkton had visited us.

And, going quite against my instincts, I told him what the lieutenant had found out. I must say, I felt not a little alarmed when he said he would have his own people look into it, for I was quite unaware *he had any such 'people.' So, to cut a rather long tale short, Raphael, he came back to me with the names of those who pulled their strings. (Isaac Little, Richard Black and James Mortimer) They meant nothing to me, but Monmouth insisted they were agents of his uncle the Duke of York. I must say I felt complete trust that he was sincere for why would he wish to implicate his uncle in such a thing if it were not the truth? Of course, I cannot think of any possible reason why he would be. And, lastly, my dear, it occurred to me to question why James Scott had been able to discover this when his father could not?*

Give my fondest regards to dear Susannah, whom I hope is fully recovered from her confinement and you now have a healthy addition to your family. I pray also that little Penelope is safely back with you. I look forward to seeing you all when you are able to return to London.

Warmest regards,
  Your most loving friend,
  Frances

Post scriptum. Forgive me for ending on a sad note. I must tell you that, as yet, there is no news of Kitty Foyles. Though her parents have taken much hope from the knowledge you continue with your search.

I dropped the letter. 'Holy Christ.'

Susannah nodded. 'My sentiments exactly on reading it.'

I passed it to Noah, my eyebrows raised. He frowned, taking it from me. I turned to Susannah. 'Whatever I expected it was not that.' After Noah had shown some reluctance that Michael should read it, Sam had snatched it from him and, of course, Michael, read it carefully. I wondered again at Noah's blindness towards him. When we were done, no one spoke, all eyes on Sam. He looked down at his hands. Noah shook his head, clearly exasperated.

I frowned when Susannah began to talk, puzzled at first, until I understood she spoke of Monmouth. It was another reminder of the extent of their shared history.

'Do you remember when he first came to Whitehall?'

Sam looked up, smiling. 'He was extraordinary, wasn't he? Like some exotic wild creature full of energy and enthusiasm for all that was so unexpectedly available to him. I wonder if he'd had even a day of formal education up to then, but he learnt so quickly. No wonder the King was utterly bewitched by him.'

Susannah smiled, too. 'He saw his mother's beauty

in him, of course. How could he not? I think we were all a little bewitched by him.'

Sam laughed. 'And when he first discovered woman. My God–'

'When women first discovered him, you mean. What was he? Thirteen? He'd only just come to court.'

'Christ. I remember wishing I could be thirteen. I thought I would be just like him then.' He shrugged. 'But we don't always get what we want, do we?' He glanced at Noah. 'Or want what we think?'

When Susannah held his gaze, his smile faded. 'You've seen it haven't you? The marriage certificate?'

'Sukie–'

'Haven't you!'

'I can't talk of it ... what I saw or didn't see. You must know that.'

'Did you tell the King?'

'God's blood. What sort of fool do you take me for? Look, let's imagine for a moment I did see it. Would I tell him I'd seen evidence of his lie with my own eyes? If the King says it doesn't exist, it doesn't.'

'I remember you said James told you his parents had married–'

Sam leaned forward towards her. 'What would you expect his mother to say to him and he immediately asked me not to tell anyone. He'd clearly been instructed to keep it to himself and for good reason.'

Michael cleared his throat. 'Might I make a suggestion?'

Noah frowned. 'Christ, Lad–'

'Please do. I should like to hear your thoughts.' Noah's frown was turned on Sam.

'Well, you offered the hypothesis yourself that we imagine you had seen this proof of the King's marriage, so perhaps its's what we should do. That is, you've seen it. It exists. So, who wants it and how might they acquire it? These aren't difficult questions to answer, are they?'

Sam nodded. 'Go on.'

'*Cui bono*. That's what it comes down to, doesn't it?'

Noah sighed. 'Who benefits? I suppose it does. Most things do in the end.' He saw the surprised faces around him. 'What? I'm not completely bloody illiterate, you know.'

Sam patted his hand. 'Of course you're not. So, who benefits most from getting this imaginary document into their possession and how do they propose doing so? Occam's Razor supplies the answers.'

'Yes. But there are actually three parties, aren't there?' I said. 'Monmouth, York ... and the King. Yet Rifkind had dealings with only two. Which two?'

'Monmouth.' Sam said with some certainty. 'Now we know he's active in it. And York because he has the most to lose should it come to light.'

Susannah turned to me. 'But you said the King would want it so he knew it's whereabout and could make use of it if and when he wished. So, he could control its fate. And why, in the name of God, is it not in his possession, anyway?

He was in exile, I know, moving from place to place but–'

'If Sam saw it in France, he clearly hasn't got it. Perhaps Monmouth's mother did? But he doesn't need to find it himself, does he? He can let others do so and take it from them whenever he chooses.' I smiled. 'He has the most power, after all.'

Sam snorted. 'And it doesn't matter who's seen it and who hasn't by then. Once he has it, it doesn't exist. Again. Unless he wishes it to.'

Michael nodded. 'It's back to being imaginary, just as it is for our purposes now.'

Noah raised his eyebrows. 'You asked two questions didn't you, Michael? And, so far, we haven't considered the second one.' He turned to Sam. 'It seems obvious to me they believe to get their hands on it they need you. Rifkind said he'd had instructions to take you.' He sighed. 'So, whether this thing exists or not, we must leave here as soon as possible because you're no longer safe.'

Michael took a breath. 'I think it might be worse than that. If they believe Sam can lead them to this document, have you considered how they may seek to stop a rival getting to him first?'

Noah stared hard at him. 'Indeed, I have.' He turned to Hal. 'We need to get the ship victualled for Lisbon. After that we'll get Sam to his family in Florence.' He grasped his hand. 'I think it's time for a new identity, too, I'm afraid.' They looked at each other.

That it would have a huge impact upon them

seemed clear. Yet there was nothing else to be done. 'Giacomo is one of your Christian names, isn't it?' He would know the day I heard it. In truth, one none of us wished to recall when his full name had been read out in Westminster Hall before a sentence of death had been passed on him. 'What's your family name in Florence?'

'Cardinale.'

Noah took a deep breath and squared his shoulders. 'Giacomo Cardinale it is then.'

There seemed no more to be said after that. I looked at Susannah. We would go to Florence, too. She could meet my family there and they could meet mine. I cannot say I did not feel some trepidation at the prospect ... well, at seeing my father, anyway. I hoped he would do us the courtesy of removing that woman from my mother's house before we entered it. I sighed. I would write from Lisbon. Christ. Sam and Noah. What a thing to face. Such a parting. For how could it mean anything else?

CHAPTER 47

Susannah

June was already upon us, and we would soon set sail for Lisbon. My heart ached at the thought of parting Penny from Sam after Florence. Yet we had always known it would be so. And how could I forget poor Kitty? I had prayed for so long she might be back in England. That there was now no hope of this was hard to face.

Noah had written to the harbour master in Puerto Rico, telling him what we had learnt and asking him to make enquiries about her. We might hear something, should a letter arrive before we left, though time was short now. How could it not feel like abandoning her to her fate, especially when we ... they had fought so hard to rescue my daughter? But it was all we had left to us.

I looked at Raphael by the light of the night candle, though dawn was now showing through the shutters. Was he asleep? He had fetched Paolo for me when he stirred and whimpered but his eyes were closed now. Our son had taken his time to sate himself.

'Not sleeping,' he croaked.

'How did you know I looked at you?'

'Your gaze is hot, *cara*.' His eyes opened, slowly.

I frowned. 'What?

He moved higher up against the pillows and smiled. 'What did you want to talk about?'

'Tell me about them again. All the nephews and nieces.'

He laughed. I doubt you'll meet any of them. You know it'll be a brief visit before we leave for London. You'll meet Artemisia and Claudia, so they'll have their chance to marvel at this one.' He stroked our son's head. 'You do know he *is* sleeping?'

'I don't think he's going to stir again this time. It's been a bit of a battle with him. I'm fairly certain he's done now, though.'

Dawn was filling the sky when Raphael took him from me and carried his sleeping form away to open the shutters before making a sharp sound of disgust. 'Well, now he's awake. That really is the most unpleasant stench, *giovane signore*.' He turned to me. 'How can this tiny child make such a thing? And how, in the name of God does he manage to produce his own weight in shit each day?'

I laughed and stretched. 'Call a girl to clean him up.'

'I'll do it.' He laid him down onto a towel on the

floor. 'Now, before we start, may I request you refrain from pissing in my face and soiling your clout again the very moment I change it? Will you give me your word on it as a gentleman, *Signore*?' Paolo kicked, happily while Raphael did what was necessary before looking up at me. 'I'm sure he's smiling.'

'Wind, I expect. You are very good at it, you know' I moved off the bed to stand beside him as he lowered our son into his cradle. 'You enjoy doing it for him, I think.'

'I enjoy everything about him, *cara*.' We watched his eyes close again. 'We should get more sleep, too, while we can.'

'Your touch always seems to sooth him better than anyone's.'

'Does it?'

He pulled me hard into his arms then, and it felt so good to feel his body against mine again like this. The length of it. It's heat. How could we not kiss? And how could it not arouse me, especially when I felt plainly what it did to him? He moved away to look at me, smiling his smile. That smile which still mazed me just as it used to.

He lifted my hair, letting it drop back around me, and spoke against my ear. 'This is where I loosen the neck of your shift and let it fall around your feet.'

'So it is.' When he did, I closed my eyes just as I had then.

'Christ, you're so beautiful, Susannah.' He ran his hands down over my breasts and belly. 'Full and round from birthing my son. And now I do this, *cara*.' He pulled his shirt off over his head. 'And this.' He pressed my hand around himself, gasping at my touch.

I grinned. 'And I say, "Well then, the big cock." And you look completely astonished. Were you very shocked?' I kept my hand firmly around him. I could still picture his face so clearly when I had said those words, and to this day I have no notion of why I did. But our laughter at them had brought us together without any self-consciousness to mar it.

'Oh, but I was scandalised, *cara mia*. And more so when you pushed me onto the bed and had your way with me most wantonly.'

I laughed. 'I don't think so. Christ, I wanted you, though.'

'I remember.' He kissed my neck. 'Do you want me now?' he whispered.

'Oh, God, yes.' I had not expected to feel it so intensely. Our time as lovers seemed so very far away from our life now. Part of a different one, in truth. And here it was again. This desire. 'But do you want me?'

It was his turn to laugh. 'You ask me this with your hand around my cockstand?'

I bit my lip. 'It does that by itself though, doesn't it? Sometimes.'

He cupped my heavy breast. 'You think I can touch you like this and not desire you? Come, Susannah.'

He guided me to the bed, and we lay in each other's arms, kissing for a while. Finding each other like this again. Need building and building while we kissed until I felt weak with it. Desperate to have him.

'How do you feel now, *cara*?'

'You know how I feel.' He did, of course. He always had. So why could I not trust he still found my body desirable?

'I don't want to hurt you, *amore mio*.'

'You won't.' He moved over me, and I pulled him close. 'It's all right. I need to feel you inside me now.' And then, there he was. I thought I might weep. 'Oh my God, Raphael. I love you.' It didn't take very long for either of us, but it brought us together again in a way we needed more than we knew.

He rolled away. 'I've missed that so much, yet I didn't even realise I had.' He took a sharp breath and moved up on his elbow to look down at me. '*Santo Dio*. Should I have pulled out?'

I reached up to touch his face. 'I'm told we should be all right while I feed him.' I smiled. 'Which I intend to do for a very long time.'

He smiled, too, shrugging. 'Well, I'm sure he'll have no objections.'

'Whatever it takes. I've no intention of having another for a considerable time.' I closed my eyes. 'If ever.' Yet was that even feasible? Were there other things we could do to stop it? I hoped there were.

He moved down beside me again and stroked my face. 'We're perfect as we are, *cara*. 'I'll do everything I can to make sure we stay this way.'

We slept then, while the day shoulder-barged its way into existence, until our son awakened demanding his needs be met again. We smiled with our new secret knowledge of each other. Jesu, it was so good to feel this sort of oneness again.

CHAPTER 48
Noah

Noah sat at the tiller after hoisting the sail. The pinnace skimmed through the choppy, glittering water, waves splashing into the boat as they approached the point of the headland with sheer cliffs soaring above them. Either he or Hal had remained at the house each day to guard Sam while the Mirabel was made ready to sail. Michael accompanied him today to oversee the last of the cargo loading. He had proved remarkably capable of judging how the holds may be filled to optimise their capacity.

Michael adjusted the sail himself without Noah having to tell him as they rounded the promontory to enter the harbour. He certainly learnt quickly. Perhaps Sam was right, and he had underestimated him? 'This is the last one. You're sure it'll load?'

Michael shook his head, exasperated. 'What do you think, Papa?'

Noah steered them around the sandbank and towards the harbour entrance and grinned. 'I think it will, Michael.'

'Good.'

Noah laughed. The port seethed as always. It was strange to think they would leave here so soon. It seemed an age since they had first arrived. The three of them. In truth, it was a hellhole, but it was one he knew. And change was always hard. But Sam would be safe, which was all that mattered in the end. After Florence, though? He had not allowed himself to think of that. First things first. Yet how could he remain there? For they could no longer live as they did now. This place, for all its faults, had been good to them.

'Will you miss it, here?'

The lad seemed to have read his mind. 'In some ways I shall. And the house has been home. A good home for us.' He studied his son. 'You understand to live the way we have will be almost impossible elsewhere.'

'Even as brothers?'

Noah laughed. 'Questions would always be asked. And in Florence, well, Sam will no longer be that, will he?'

'So, it will be difficult for you both, then. I'm sorry, Papa.'

'Not as difficult as Sam being dead. I've faced that before and I've every intention of ensuring I don't do so again if it's at all within my power.'

Michael lowered the sail and used the oars to slow

the boat while Noah steered it towards its birth beside the Mirabel. Michael quickly jumped ashore to tie-off the lines before following his father up the gangway onto the ship's deck. 'Have you sailed into Lisbon before, Papa?'

'Many times, but not on our way out here. I didn't want to leave a trail. Not that it mattered in the end, did it?'

Surprised by a woman's voice behind them, they turned.

'I must see Hal. Is he here? She looked around expectantly.

Noah had seen this girl before. 'Remind me who you are, Lass?'

Michael moved to her, looking concerned. 'Are you all right, Marianne?'

Of course. Marianne Carlisle, the fort commander's girl. 'Hal's not with us today.'

She closed her eyes, swaying a little. Michael caught her arm to steady her. 'He sent me a note to say you're leaving soon. Please tell him I need to see him before he goes.' She stared hard at Michael's face. 'It's very important. You must tell him, Michael. I beg you.'

'Of course, I shall. May I see you back to the fort? You seem a little unwell.'

'I'm hot is all. But I should be grateful for your company. My servant is ... well. Thank you. You're most kind.'

Noah met his son's eyes. 'I'll fetch you a dip of water before you go, Lass.' When he had filled it, he gestured for Michael to cross the deck to take it from him. 'Christ's fucking wounds,' he whispered. 'Find out if she's with child. I bloody well knew it.' How could Hal not leave a bastard somewhere? Handing Michael the scoop, he bowed to Marianne and walked away.

Noah sat at the table in the cabin entering bills of lading into a ledger when Michael returned.

'Well, did all the barrels fit?'

He grinned. 'Of course they did, Lad. I never doubted it.' He put down his pen. 'What did she have to say for herself?' He waited somewhat impatiently to have his suspicions confirmed, trying to decide what should be done about it.

Michael sat down opposite him at the table. 'Not what you think. And it wasn't an easy thing to ask her, though I had the distinct impression when I raised it, she wished it were so.' He sighed. 'Her papa has found her a husband here on the island—'

'And she's not much taken with his choice?'

'Most decidedly not. This man is a planter twenty years her senior with several children and she will be wife number three, the other two having died in childbirth.'

'I see. Poor Lass. Though I fail to understand what Hal is expected to do about it.'

'Marry her himself, I believe. Take her away with us.'

'Christ.' Though if he had wished to marry the girl, he would have asked her once he knew they were leaving. That he had not told him all he needed to know. He also knew what Hal would do now. So, his dilemma was whether to tell him at all. He rubbed at his face. 'Well, she's an honourable lass that she chose not to say there was a child.'

'Perhaps she doesn't truly wish to marry him either. Yet it must seem her only way out, I imagine.'

'Marriage is a huge step. There must be another way, surely?' He sighed. 'Now, let's finish up here so we can get back.' He stood. 'And, Michael, perhaps don't mention this to Hal yet. Let me think about it for a while longer, yes?'

'You can't mean not to tell–'

'No. I mean to think on it.'

CHAPTER 49

Hal

Hal rode out from the stable yard not long after his father and brother set sail in the pinnace. He knew he was supposed to remain guarding Sam but after telling him why he needed to go, Sam had insisted he did so. First, though, he left instructions for men to watch the road and jetty, which did something to assuage his guilt.

He had sent a note to Marianne earlier, telling her he was leaving Jamaica. Yet the more he thought of it the more it pricked his conscience. He must tell her in person. How had he not understood that sooner? He urged his horse on up through the jungle towards the track into Port Royal. It seemed strange to think how soon he would be gone from this verdant place. Would he return to Rother-hithe? How alien it seemed now in his memory. Grey. The river brown, cold and fetid. He looked over his shoulder at the sparkling turquoise sea behind him. Breathed in air fragrant with greenery and damp earth. But what else could he do? He would be naïve not to realise that in all likelihood his father would return there too. Firstly, because he would wish to find the people behind the threat to Sam ... and God help them when he did. And, secondly, being with him in Florence would be impossible. Jesu, it would be hard for him. Hard for both of them.

Out on the open trail to the town the heat intensified, and he wiped his face on his shirt sleeve. This he would not miss. How could he explain that note to Marianne? Would she think him so indifferent to her he could not make the effort to see her? What was he thinking to send her such a thing? He guided his horse down the right-hand fork that would take him out to the garrison.

Riding in through the open gate, the sentries greeted him for he was not an infrequent visitor there, though Marianne's father would be surprised to learn of it. He stabled his mare to get her out of the sun and walked around the towering sandstone walls of the fort to the side where many ramshackle buildings made up all the kitchens and storerooms needed to feed the many militia men posted there, taking a moment to look out at the expanse of open sea, jewel-like in the relentless sunshine.

As he approached the entrance that would take him to the servants' staircase up to Marianne's rooms, a voice called out behind him. 'Hal? What are you doing here?'

He turned around and Marianne ran to him flinging her arms around his neck. She looked flushed, hot, and more than a little distressed. He quickly stepped out of her embrace. There seemed little point in attracting attention to them, even now when he was unlikely to see her again. He grasped her hand to lead her inside and up the stairs, not speaking until he closed her chamber door behind him. 'What's wrong? Where have you been?'

'I went to the Mirabel. Your Papa said you weren't coming today.'

'I wasn't. I shouldn't have. But that note. Well, it was inexcusable. Forgive me for it.'

She sat on the bed. 'I thought I'd never see you again.' Tears spilled.

He sat beside her wiping them away with his fingertips. 'No. Oh no, Marianne. I'd never do that to you.' And then, of course, his lips found hers. What could he do then but make love to her? When she lay naked beneath him, he moved away enough to see his hand moving slowly down the length of her, watching her smile. She was so familiar to him now; he felt another sharp stab of realisation that he would never lie like this with her ever again. 'Christ. You're so beautiful.'

She ran her hands down over his back, clutching him. 'So are you.' She gasped. 'Do it now Hal. I want you inside me now.'

He took his time until he heard her cries and felt

the abandon of her climax beneath him but when he began to pull out, she clung to him.

'Don't. Please don't. Just this once, I beg you.

He ignored her, moving up and finishing himself hard, groaning as his seed pulsed across her breasts. He rolled away then, sitting high against the pillows, and sweeping his loose hair away from his face, vexed with her. 'What's the matter with you? Why would you say such a thing?' Christ. It was hard enough without that. 'You want me to leave you with a child? Is that what you want? Holy God, Marianne, have you lost your mind?'

She moved up beside him and covered her face with her hands. 'Yes. I have. For that's exactly what I want.' Then she began to weep again.

It took him some time to get the full story out of her and afterwards he held her quietly for a while to let her gather herself. 'You won't marry this man. I swear to you. I won't allow it to happen.'

She looked up at him, her dark lashes glittering wet, her face tear streaked. 'Forgive me. I went to pieces. It shames me.'

'We all do sometimes.'

'Even you.' She raised her eyebrows. 'I find that hard to believe.'

'I do. I have. I promise you.' He shook his head. 'And it's not a pretty sight.' How could he not see himself weeping inconsolably in his father's arms? Snot flowing. He took a deep breath. 'I'll marry you, and you can sail with us on the Mirabel.'

She cupped his face, gently. 'But I don't wish to marry you, my sweet Hal. Any more than you wish to marry me, no?'

He tilted his head, not sure how he should feel about such a statement. 'But you want my child?'

'This wretched man wouldn't take me then, would he? Papa would have to send me back to my aunt in Dorset to avoid the scandal here.' Her eyes slid away. 'And there's someone there I love.'

He turned on his side to face her. 'You've never told me that. What would he make of another man's child do you think?'

'He wouldn't care a jot if it meant we could be together. Papa refused him for me. He's the son of one of our family's tenant farmers.' She shook her head, looking wistful. 'We've loved each other since we were fourteen.'

Hal was quiet again, thinking. 'Well, if this suitor of yours won't have you with another man's child in your belly–'

'I'd be damaged goods then, which wouldn't go down well in polite plantation society. Perhaps I might claim there is a child? That would work.'

'Yes, but what is it he expects from a wife?'

'Beyond she must be young enough to be his daughter?'

'Exactly. But why? Why doesn't he want a widow or an older woman, even though he has no need of more children? Marianne, he wants a virgin. And perhaps he now needs to be made aware you're not one.'

She seized his face and kissed him. 'Oh my God, Hal, that's it.' Her eyes danced. 'I can confess to my papa, full of contrition, concerned this man might think he intended to dupe him. And I won't have to lie to him, either.' She clutched her head. 'More scandal. He has to send me home now. He must.'

'And you're free to accuse me of the deed. I'll be far away by then and there'll be nothing he can do about me.'

She moved in tight against him. 'But it wasn't you, Hal. You must know that?'

He smiled. 'I do.'

'There's been no one else while you've been here, though.' She smiled. 'Which is more than can be said of you, I'm sure.'

Hal shrugged, grinning. What could he say? It was the truth. But no other in Jamaica. He lifted her hand and kissed it. 'Was it your lad in Dorset?'

'Kit. Of course. In all honesty, there's only ever been him and you.'

He moved in to kiss her. 'Well, then, I'm truly honoured my sweet.

They made love again before he left, both knowing it really was their last time.

CHAPTER 50
Noah

Sam was on the porch with Susannah when they arrived back. Michael barely acknowledged them before retreating to his chamber.

Sam raised his eyebrows in an eloquent, *'What now?'*

Hearing Paolo begin to wail, Susannah sighed looking down to see wet patches of milk spreading on the front of her gown. She stood. 'Jesu. This is a messy business. How had I forgotten?' The cries increased in volume. 'Fear not, your highness, your wish is ever my command.'

They watched her walk away. 'I know what you're thinking. And don't. Do you imagine any such notions ever occur to her?' Noah moved away to go inside their chamber. Sam followed. Noah sat on the bed to remove his boots.

'I know they don't. Yet it makes me a little sad not

to have shared such things with her. How can it not?' He sat beside him. 'Now, what's wrong with Michael?'

Noah told him. 'He's concerned I won't tell Hal about it.'

'And will you?'

Noah rubbed his face. 'Christ, I don't know. It's one of those dilemmas that seems not to have a right answer. Either I keep this from him and when he finds out, which he undoubtably will, he'll despise me for it. Or I tell him and watch him commit himself to something perhaps neither of them truly wants.'

'Yet you'd have felt quite differently had there been a child. That possibly neither of them truly wanted marriage would be of no consequence then, would it?'

'Of course it wouldn't. But it's entirely different.'

'It's still a marriage that neither may want. And, as we know, there are other ways.' He took a breath. 'So perhaps there is another way for the girl with this?' Sam stood. 'I promised Penny a walk on the beach while we still can.'

'Where's Hal, by the way?'

Sam shrugged 'Chamber, I imagine.'

Noah watched him leave. 'Well, Lad, if you can think of another solution this time maybe you'd care to tell me.' He moved out onto the porch and stood at the rail, watching Sam and his daughter move along the shore, hand in hand, foaming wavelets splashing over their bare feet. His heart ached for him. There was so much he must soon lose. And in that, he was not alone, of course. He moved away to the sofa to sit, closing his eyes, and allowing his thoughts to drift until sleep began to circle and close in.

The high piercing shriek sent him bolting upright, heart pounding. Penny. He Ran. Down the steps and onto the beach. Breathing hard and struggling to comprehend what he saw before him. Sam was lying on the sand with Penny kneeling beside him, sobbing and calling out his name. Somehow, he absorbed the running figure of a man, incongruous black coat flapping, as he made his escape. Sam had been attacked. He arrived beside him landing on his knees. 'It's all right. It's all right.' He was uncertain to which of them he spoke. Perhaps both, in truth.

Raphael landed on the sand beside him, and Penny launched herself into his arms, sobbing inconsolably. Noah took several deep breaths to gather his wits. Sam was bleeding freely from a shoulder wound and from a hasty inspection of the rest of his body, this seemed his only damage. 'You're all right, Lad. It's not deep, I don't think. He bent closer, carefully parting the edges of his shirt cut by the blade.

Sam clutched at Noah with his left hand. 'Fuck. It hurts like damnation.'

It was then he became aware of the stink. 'Fucking Christ. It's poisoned.' He scooped Sam up in his arms, ignoring his cries of pain, and dashed with him out into the sea. He tore his shirt away and held him close while he washed out the wound, watching the water around it turn red with blood as he vibrated with pain. 'This should get it out. Please God.' Sam groaned long and loud and then he swooned. Noah thought it probably for the best. Eventually he brought him out onto the beach, where Raphael and Penny stood watching, Raphael's arm tight around her. The little girl was deathly white.

'Is he dead? Is Sam dead?' Tears streamed down her face.

'No, sweetheart. He's fainted. What I had to do hurt him, I'm afraid.' He set off striding back towards the house and soon had Sam down onto their bed. He bent to sniff the wound again.

Raphael spoke from the doorway. 'The blade was poisoned? *Porcodio.*'

Noah heard Susannah soothing Penny out on the porch. Poor child. It must have been terrifying for her. He tapped Sam's face, trying to wake him. 'An old pirate trick. I've seen seawater used like that before onboard ship.'

'Did it work? Christ almighty. How would pirates have access to poison? What poison?'

'Sometimes it worked.' Pray to God this was one of them. 'And poison is more a description of the result. They use something far more readily available and just as effective. Human shit.'

Raphael crossed himself. '*Madre di Dio.* And you smelt it on him and knew what to do? I think Sam is a very lucky man.'

'I *have* been stabbed, Raphael,' Sam croaked. 'Not much luck in that.'

Noah sat beside him, smiling. 'Welcome back. And it could have been worse, Lad. A hell of a lot worse.'

Pearl arrived with a bowl of hot water and cloths for bandages. Michael beside her. He bent over Sam. 'It'll need packing to allow it to drain as it heals.' He turned to Pearl. 'Have you anything suitable to use?'

She nodded. 'Ma Gala has special moss and herbs. It heal good with em, you see.'

Noah frowned. 'I though her a midwife?'

'Oh, she much more. She a wise woman.' Pearl handed the water to Noah. 'I'll ride out to the village.'

'I'll come with you,' Michael said. 'I'd like to see which herbs she favours.'

'Perhaps I might have a spot of her opium syrup too, Pearl?' Sam called, plaintively.

After Sam was bandaged and dosed with herbal tea and opium, Noah sat with him holding his hand until he slipped into sleep. Outside he found Susannah, her sleeping infant in her arms, her head on Raphael's shoulder and his arm around her. Penny was on his lap, her head on his chest close to her mother. He spoke soft words of comfort to them in his own tongue. Noah's heart clenched seeing them all so close, wrapped in love. Thank God little Penny was safely back with them. Seeing them now reminded him that no matter all it had cost them, it had been more than worth it.

Raphael looked up when Noah stepped out. 'How is he now?'

'Sleeping.' He sat and closed his eyes for a few moments. 'I think we must plan to delay our departure by a week or so. Give him a bit of time to recover.' Christ, he hoped there would be no fever. They would keep dressing the wound with the old woman's herbs and dosing him with the tea Pearl set such store by. Sam had said it tasted like horse piss. How did he know? And he would pray, too. Not that he ever felt much listened to. 'Will you pray for him, Lad?' Perhaps Raphael's God would be more amenable. How could he forget Rifkind's last words? *He'll die. It's too late.* They would haunt him more than ever now.

'Of course.'

Susannah looked alarmed. 'You don't think he's in any danger?'

Noah shook his head as much to reassure himself as her. 'We've done everything we can. Pearl said the old woman thought seawater the right thing to clean the wound.' He sighed. 'But a word with God on it can't harm, can it?'

Susannah smiled, turning to Raphael. 'No. I'm a great believer in it when you do it, my love.'

Penny watched him. 'Did you pray for me, Papa.'

'All the time, *piccola*.'

'And God heard you, didn't he?'

Raphael smiled. 'He certainly did.'

CHAPTER 51

Hal

Once out on the track riding home, his mind drifted. His offer of marriage had been refused and he had to admit Marianne's words had rather shocked him. Had he expected her to be thrilled by his generous consent to marry her? Something she was quite aware he did not truly want. He shook his head, laughing at himself. And marriage was definitely not something he sought ... at all. Life was too good the way it was. The thought of Raphael and Susannah gave him pause, though. He had lived such a life and given it up for her. Yet he knew enough to be aware their marriage was a rarity that not many people were able to find. He promised himself it would be that or nothing for him.

He wondered whether his father would tell him of Marianne's visit to the ship? How would he feel if he did not? He surprised himself then with the realisation that he understood his decision, whatever it was, would come from his desire to do what was best for him. He had not intended to speak of it – he had abandoned Sam to make it, after all – but he would tell him now to take away the dilemma.

After emerging from the jungle shade, he narrowed his eyes against the white glare from the sea now the sun was lower in the sky. He saw the pinnace was already tied up at the jetty, so he must face his father earlier than expected. He felt certain Sam would not have told him of his desertion. When a stable boy come out onto the shore, he handed over his horse and crossed the sand to the back of the house.

The Rossi family were gathered with his father on the porch, one look at their faces froze the smile on his. His father appeared hollowed-out. 'Holy God. What's happened?' He sat beside him, hardly able to comprehend what he was being told. Penny buried her face against Raphael's chest while his father spoke. And he had left Sam. 'Papa, I wasn't here. I went to the fort to see Marianne, God forgive me.'

Noah touched his arm. 'It happened while I was out here ... sleeping. Don't blame yourself, Lad. If anyone's at fault, it's me.'

Raphael stroked Penny's head. 'You're not to blame. We were all here, Noah. No one is, apart for the wretch who attacked him.' Susannah chewed her lip, seeming unable to speak.

Hal hugged his father and stood. 'May I go in to him for a moment?'

'He's had opium. Nothing should wake him for a while.'

When Hal stepped inside the shuttered room, it was too dark to see for some moments after the bright sunlight. When his eyes adjusted, he looked down at Sam's naked form on the sheet, eyes closed, face slightly flushed, and strands of damp hair plastered to his forehead. He fought the urge to smooth it away. It was then he recognised the deep affection he now felt for him. Friendship between them had come almost immediately but he had not expected this. His father loved this man, knew his body as well as he knew his own. Strangely, that part felt a commonplace thing. Male or female, in truth, physical pleasuring was little different, surely? It was the love that lay outside his knowledge. How might it change the physical experience? He understood, too, the abyss of loss that must haunt such love. That omnipresent possibility of catastrophe. He took a long breath to gather himself before going outside again.

His father was alone now; his eyes closed. Hal sat beside him again, wishing there was something he could do to help him.

'How did he look?'

'A touch hot.' His father's eyes flew open. 'Peaceful, though.'

'Hot? Christ. Noah lurched to his feet. 'Wait here. We need to talk.'

'Of course, Papa.' He pulled off his jackboots and stockings and tossed them carelessly down onto the boards. Lord, the heat was oppressive today. He studied his father's face when he come out, quickly feeling reassured.

Noah smiled. 'No fever. Just a hot chamber, is all.'

'I hadn't realised how fond I've become of him.'

'And he's extremely fond of you.' He patted Hal's hand. 'Now what have you decided with Marianne. Whatever it is you'll have my support.'

'I know I shall.' He rolled his eyes. 'I told her I'd be prepared to marry her.' His father's slight gasp made him smile. 'She turned me down, Papa. Even after such a gallant proposal as that. Her heart is given elsewhere. And it was never about hearts anyway, which I'm sure will come as no surprise to you.'

'So, how was it resolved?' He had not kept the relief out of his voice.

'We decided her lack of maidenhead should be sufficient to send her home in disgrace to her sweetheart.'

Noah raised his eyebrows. 'Ah. I see. What would a marriage bed be without one?'

Raphael crossed the porch to join them. 'Infinitely preferable, in my opinion.

Hal laughed. 'Well, Marianne's lack can't be laid at my door but I'm glad it'll serve her so well. I'm sure it's not always so.'

'Or even often, perhaps?' Raphael changed the subject, turning to Noah. 'Susannah has asked Pearl to accompany us home as a nursemaid and she's agreed. She's good with Paolo and Penny's grown close to her.'

'I'm glad. There'd be nothing for her here after

we've gone bar men thinking employing her gives them rights to her bed. And she has no living family. Or none she knows of. She was a foundling, poor lass. Though what she'll make of London, Christ knows.' Noah stood. 'Now, I think I'll sit with him for a while.'

'My first impression of London? Dirty. Cold. Wet. And hideously crowded.'

Noah turned back with a chuckle. 'About sums it up.'

After he went inside, they sat in silence until Hal looked up. 'He will recover, won't he?'

Raphael crossed himself. 'Holy God, I hope so.'

'I can hardly bear to contemplate what would happen to Papa if he didn't.'

'He'd need you and Michael very much then, I think.'

'I'd never really thought about that side of love until today. It's always seemed a constraint best avoided when there are so many desirable women to choose from.' He shrugged watching Raphael smile. 'Is the fear of loss always there?' He frowned. 'Perhaps another reason to keep away from it.'

Raphael sighed. 'Yes. In the background but the important thing is not to dwell on it. And that's surprisingly easy just because it is so unthinkable. It's not just romantic love, either. It's all love. The moment you hold your child you're overwhelmed by love and by fear. You must know it too, with your papa? Your brother?' Hal nodded. 'But what I can say, Hal – and I've lived as you do now – is I thank God every day for the love I feel for my wife and hers for me. It changes everything.'

'How though? I can't see how making love can be better or even different just because you love a woman as well as desire her.'

'Oh, believe me it can. It is.'

Hal narrowed his eyes, sceptically. 'But how? You haven't explained.' He realised then that Raphael was under no obligation to explain anything to him, and he must have read it on his face.

He smiled. 'I don't mind trying to. It's simply a little hard to define it.' He took a breath and tilted his head. 'Everything is intensified. Physical pleasure. Everything. You feel a closeness, a sort of oneness with a woman after you make love, yes?'

'I suppose so, yes. Sometimes.'

'Well, when you love her that never goes away. It's a wonderful thing, believe me.'

'Forgive me, but I just can't see why that should matter.'

Raphael laughed. 'Well, I hope you will one day. I should be sad for you if you didn't. Though I was twenty-seven when I fell in love with Susannah. I'd never loved a woman before. So, you've plenty of time yet to meet the right one.'

Hal grinned. 'And I intend to make good use of it.'

CHAPTER 52
Noah

Noah woke with a start to find Sam's lips on his. They were hot. Too hot. He moved him away onto his back, his hand arriving quickly on his forehead checking for fever.

'I'm fine, Noah. I'm no warmer than you are. No warmer than we always are in here.' He moved Noah's hand strategically.

'Best not, Lad–'

Sam's hand moved onto him. 'Well, there's a part of you already disagreeing.'

Noah snorted. 'I don't claim my cock as a seat of judgment. You have an open wound. So not a good idea.'

'Oh, for Christ's sake, just kiss me.'

Afterwards, Noah gathered him in and in held him, gently. 'Better now?' Holy God. He felt almost overwhelmed by how much he loved him. That he suddenly seemed so insubstantial in his arms, terrified him.

'What do you think?' Sam said.

'What do I think? Well, I *think* it shouldn't have happened, Laddie.' When Sam made a disparaging sound, Noah smiled, knowing the look on his face that would accompany it, though it was too dark to see it.

Sam touched Noah's face. 'I noticed the extent of your reluctance. How could I not?'

Noah snorted. 'Well, I'm not a fucking saint. Never claimed to be.'

Sam laughed. 'No, I've noticed that, too. But I know you love me, which is vastly more important.' He sighed. 'Forgive me. I don't know why. I just had to–'

'It's what men do, Sam. Fight and fuck.'

'What? A brush with death brings some sort of atavistic desire to plant seed in fertile ground ... to leave something behind? He laughed. 'Not really appropriate in our situation, is it?'

'Tell that to a cock.'

Sam laughed again and closed his eyes.

'Sleep now, Lad. It's what you need to heal.'

The next time Noah awakened, he felt the heat radiating from Sam like a furnace burned within him. His heart beginning to pound as his hands reached his skin. Not that touching was necessary. He pushed Sam's drenched hair away from his face.

Sam groaned. 'This isn't good, is it?'

'Not especially, no. But we'll soon get you tended to. I'll fetch Pearl.'

'Oh God,' he croaked. 'Not more horse piss.'

When Noah found Pearl's chamber deserted, with her bed undisturbed, he knew where to find her. He didn't knock. They were asleep in each other's arms. He felt a lump in his throat at the sight of them. The sight of his son. 'Pearl. He has a fever. Sam is fevered. Will you come?'

Yet, as it turned out, it was Michael who seemed to know what to do, asking for a bowl of cold well-water to sponge his skin. 'The books would say to bleed him. Well, most of them. But I've read of this somewhere and there does seem some logic to it. After all, we warm ourselves with heat, don't we? Why not the other way around?'

So, Noah sponged him, sending a boy for fresh water when it warmed. 'Stay with me, Sam. Try and keep awake.' But he knew he was fighting a losing battle. When he fell into complete oblivion, finally, Noah was already expecting it. He turned to Michael who sat on a wooden bench beside the open casement where the sky was already taking on the first milky hue of dawn. 'He's insensible. What now? There must be something more to be done?'

Michael looked up, blinking, and shaking his head. 'Pearl's sent someone to fetch Ma Gala from the village,' he croaked, sleepily. 'She'll bring physic. Until then carry on trying to cool him, Papa.'

Noah found himself listening to each rasping breath, praying another would follow it; living moment to moment, oblivious to the daylight now filling the room or only aware of it because he could now see Sam's restless, sweating form – his hair soaked black – almost wishing he could not. Where was that damned woman?

Susannah spent time there, holding Sam's other hand, talking softly to him, only leaving to tend to her child when Raphael took her place. He spoke in Italian, talking of an olive grove near Sam's family estate outside Florence. A place Sam had never seen. He met Noah's gaze. 'He told me of it when I travelled with him to his trial. It's a special place to him. His mother described it so vividly.' Raphael looked down at Sam once more. 'You can show it to me, Sam, and I can show you my beautiful city. Your mamma's city.'

'Tell him about it, Lad. Tell him what he'll see.' When Raphael did as he asked, Noah found himself entranced by the churches and squares and ancient buildings honeyed by sunshine. By the river and its bridges. By its statues and fountains. He would see it all with him, too. He held tight to Sam's hand. *You won't leave me. I won't let you.* He blinked away tears, wondering how, in the name of God, he was back facing such a prospect, only this time he was so completely and utterly powerless.

When the old woman arrived at last, she clucked and hissed through her teeth, talking to Pearl in a patois Noah could make no sense of. Yet she seemed to know what she was doing, packing his angry wound, which now had red streaks coming from it out across his chest, with an evil smelling substance she produced from her canvas sack. She held the pot in her hand still and said something to Pearl.

She nodded. 'Roll him towards you. Some must go up arsehole.'

'What? You can't intend such–' Michael spoke from behind him. Noah had not even been aware he was still there.

'It's quite a common thing, Papa. As a way to give medicine.'

The old woman gestured, impatiently. Holy hell. Noah rolled him. The lad was insensible, it would matter nothing to him. She took a goodly dollop on her finger and proceeded. Noah looked up at Pearl. 'What does she say? Will he recover?'

'She say he will. Keep using balm. Give him herb-tea when he wake.'

The old woman spoke directly to him, then. 'Keep he cool for sweats. Wrap he for shiver.' She crossed herself. 'Pray, Chile.' And with that she was gone.

CHAPTER 53
Hal

Hal waited outside the chamber. Last time his papa had faced this awful thing, he had been at his side doing everything he could to help him save Sam's life. Now it seemed Michael had taken-on that task, and quite rightly. He sat up higher on the sofa when the old woman came out with Pearl beside her. There was nothing to read on either of their faces. Nothing to tell him how Sam was. Christ, he had looked bad the last time he checked on him. Michael came out then and lowered himself beside him. 'What's happening? How is he?'

Michael rubbed his face. A gesture he recognised as their father's. And his own too, now he thought of it. 'Ma Gala's dressed his wound again.' After telling his brother all of it, he laughed. 'Your face is the mirror of Papa's when she said she would–'

Hal held up his hands. 'I think I preferred your conversation when you planned to become a minister.'

Michael laughed again. 'Would you like me to list the medicines and treatments given–'

Hal stood 'No, I bloody wouldn't. Let's ride or swim ... or something. I need to get off this damn porch for a while.'

'Swim. We shouldn't be too far away if Papa needs us.' Hal nodded and ran down the steps onto the beach while Michael went to tell their father where to find them, should he need to. His brother sprinted to catch him up and they walked a little way further along the shore, stopping where they would be sure to see him if he came down to the water to hail them. Then, stripping off their clothes, they launched themselves into the sea, both grateful for the instant relief from the heat. They swam out strongly, racing for a short time without acknowledging it, until Michael pulled-up, laughing, and they both turned onto their backs to float.

Hal grinned. 'Well, Brother, good choice. You didn't stand a chance there.'

Michael grinned, too. 'No idea what you're talking about.'

Hal shook his head. *'Really?'* He loved the view from this far out with the whole bay visible between the headlands, lush green down to a strip of white to demarcate the border between land and sea. Something else he tried to imprint upon his mind, for whatever happened with Sam they would leave. From here it looked like paradise before the Fall. As though men had never walked upon it. No plantations. No slaves. No murderous fuckers with poisoned knives.

'Papa said you've seen Marianne but not what you've decide to do.'

So, Hal recounted it all again.

Michael looked pensive. 'I hope her father won't be too angry with her. Yet again life seems particularly unfair on women. I mean when I think of Papa's eagerness for me to lose my virginity.'

Hal laughed. 'No. It can't be much fun being a woman. But I always try to give virgins a wide berth.'

'So, you've never–'

'Came close once. I stopped when I realised it was her first time. It seemed too big a sacrifice to make just because I wanted a fuck. It deserved more than that.'

Michael raised his eyebrows. 'Admirable of you.'

Hal laughed. 'Not entirely. I educated her in other ways to please a man. I'm sure her future husband will be grateful, though.'

'Well then, I hope you reciprocated.'

'A gentleman always does, Michael.' How far his brother had come in the few short weeks he had been out here. Where was the eager boy who talked of little other than God? While he loved him fiercely, and always had, he thought he would like this one better. They swam out a little further before stopping to tread water. 'How are things with Pearl? You must be pleased she'll be living in London now.'

'I think she'll be spoilt for choice with admirers

there. And I'll soon be gone to Leiden. Though she does seem rather taken with red hair ... and medical books.'

'Or perhaps she's just rather taken with you, little brother.'

CHAPTER 54

Raphael

That night I sat with Noah and Sam in their chamber. Noah, lying on the bed beside him – holding him close when he was seized by shivering or moving away to sponge him cool when he thrashed as though burning up – had asked me to bring my rosary.

So, I told my decades and waited vigil, feeling I really should not be there with them. It seemed such a private thing. Yet what else could I do? If Sam had been of my faith a priest would be with him now, administering the last rites. I understood what comfort that brought to those who watched a life ebbing away. And how usual it was for the recipient to be insensible just as Sam was now. No. More often the comfort offered was for those left behind, knowing all sins were absolved at the last.

And how could I not recall that other night I had spent with Sam, though alone together that time,

458

when he would stand trial for his life the next day? I had got him drunk on strong ale, so he had ended-up insensible then, too. Though first he had wept in my arms. When Noah left the bed, I looked up from my beads, my fingers still moving mechanically along them, but realising my mind had long since moved away from God, I set them down.

'I'll dress it again.'

I nodded. Understanding Noah needed to do something. Anything to act. He opened the pot of unguent, its rank smell soon filling the room. 'We'll need more of this tomorrow, I think.'

I prayed it might be so. I stood and held the candle closer to Sam while Noah removed the bandages. 'It looks a little better.' I thought it appeared much as it had the last time Noah had changed the dressing. He placed his hand on Sam's forehead without comment. 'He seems more peaceful, at least.'

'That reeks like the devil's arse,' Sam croaked.

Noah appeared stunned and then grinning, tears spilled suddenly down his face. 'And you know this how?'

Sam tried to smile. 'Forgive me.'

Noah clutched his hand and kissed it. 'For what, Lad? For what?'

'For leaving you.' It was so clearly a struggle for him to speak. 'It will be soon now ... Oh, Christ I don't want to ...'

Incomprehension. Denial, until Noah's face crumbled. 'You can't. I won't allow it.'

I stood. My presence was an intrusion on them now–'

'Wait.' Sam's eyes were on me. 'You must hear it too.' His voice rasped, dry as sand.

Noah lifted his head and helped him drink a sip or two of water, tears still streaming down his face unheeded. 'What do you need to say, dear lad?'

He managed to lift his hand to touch Noah's face. 'That I love you. And I'm so grateful for it.' His eyes moved to me again. 'I must tell everything now. It can't die with me.'

'You saw the marriage certificate, didn't you?' In truth, we all knew he had but perhaps now we might learn the circumstances of it.

He pointed to the water cup and Noah helped him drink again. 'Palais de Louvre.' He found strength to speak from somewhere. 'Sleeping. The man wore a mask across his face. I thought he would hurt ... only saw his eyes. He looked old. Carried a lantern. There was a black leather box. Inside.' Sam panted a little.

'Rest now–'

He shook his head, feebly. 'Mustn't. Can't. It was inside. Charles Stuart. Lucy Walter. Looked his signature. 23 January 1749. Rotterdam. Don't know who he was ... or where.' He took a long shuddering breath, steeling himself to speak again. 'He said it would be fetched into the light in a time of extremis for only then would its purpose be truly served. He told me to remember.' Sam released his breath hard and rasping, as though letting go his last and then his eyes rolled up into his head, his lids open and slack.

Noah dropped to his knees beside the bed and began to gasp desperate sobs.

I felt numb, falling to my knees beside him, crossing myself and commending Sam's soul to God. *'Eternal rest grant unto him, O Lord, and let perpetual light shine upon him, through the mercy of God, rest in peace.'*

Epilogue

NOAH

Jamaica 1677.

The grey sky threatening imminent rain seemed almost a cliché considering their purpose in St Agnus's grave-yard that morning in the hills above Port Royal. Not a thunderstorm though, to bring some drama. Just ordinary mundane, shitty rain which could not hold-off until they were done. No surprise there. It felt like that sort of day.

This was their last task before they sailed for Lisbon that afternoon, seeing the white marble head-stone set in place, its inscription neatly carved and brightly gilded. Their little group grave of face around the grave. Raphael and Susannah. Michael and Hal. Pearl holding Paolo and keeping Penny well back. It was an upsetting thing for her to see. For how could it not be? She was his daughter, after all. Though it was not acknowledged on the stone.

Samuel Bartholomew
1652 – 1677
Most Beloved Brother and Friend

So, was it not cruel to put her through this? But they needed her distress. Susannah had agreed it, but Noah knew what it had cost her to do so. And Raphael too, even when he was unable to truly understand though had to conceal it from her, of course. She needed his unflinching support to get her through the thing, when it was plain the bleakness of it filled her with such melancholy.

With cargo and victuals loaded, the pinnace dropped the sea anchor so the crew could kedge the Mirabel away from the dock before being winched onboard for the crossing, they stood together at the rail as she finally sailed towards the harbour exit to leave this place for good, sheets already cracking loud and filling, straining for the open sea.

'How was it?'

'Unexpectedly emotional. What could have been, I suppose. How could I not think of it, Laddie?' Noah tried to smile. 'Have you ever met your Cardinale aunt?' he added, needing to change the subject, even though he already knew the answer.

Sam knew it, of course, and why he asked. He squeezed Noah's arm. 'I'd prefer not to think of it, either.' He gasped a quick breath. 'Aunt Serafina? No. No, she and my mother were twins. Sofia and Serafina. Very alike Mama always said. It will be odd to see what she would look like now, had she lived. I have many cousins to meet as well, I believe.'

How could Noah not think of the night they had thought him dead? The grief he had felt then still felt raw and terrifying, but he tried not to dwell on it, remembering instead his overwhelming joy and relief when Michael told him he still lived, though he was deeply unconscious. He had left the chamber to puke then. And weep like a child, his arms wrapped around himself while he rocked. It had taken Sam a week to come back to them, helpless as a new-born when he did. So, with the time it took for him to regain some strength, they had finally been ready to leave a month after originally planned.

Raphael and Susannah came to join them at the taffrail, Penny too, when the Mirabel made it into the open sea, for a last look at Hayes Bay.

Penny moved beside Sam, and he heaved her into his arms with a small groan. 'I didn't like seeing your name on that gravestone. It made me cry a bit, though I tried not to because I knew it wasn't truly you there.'

'I'm sorry it upset you, little one.' He glanced at Susannah.

She frowned. 'I know you thought it unnecessary for her to be there. But she would have been had it been real. Jesu. Wasn't that the whole object of putting it there, to look as though it was?'

Raphael put an arm around her waist, pulling her close. 'It's done, *cara*. Penny understands, don't you, *piccola*?'

She nodded against Sam chest. 'It's to keep Sam safe.'

Noah closed his eyes for a moment. To keep Sam safe. Please God it would if those who meant him harm believed they had been successful. That they maintained the fiction of Samuel Bartholomew, while Penny stood at his graveside should help convince them. Christ, they must believe it so. Then he could become Giacomo Cardinale and live safely, undiscovered by his enemies, in Florence.

Hal arrived and took Penny from him, glancing at Noah as he did. Good lad realised she was too heavy for Sam who was still far from fully recovered, but they had all shared a need to get away as soon as possible.

'I believe we have a ship to sail, Papa.'

Noah laughed to hear his own words, spoken so often to his son, now said to him. 'We have indeed, Lad. So, let's get to it.'

Hal placed Penny down onto the deck, knuckling his forehead with a grin, and walked away towards the foredeck.

Noah laughed, squeezing Sam's shoulder. 'Let's all look to Lisbon, now.'

Author's Note

The practice of indenturing servants remained consistent during the 17th and into the 18th centuries, with many transported under government auspices and others shipped by independent entrepreneurs. There were two categories of people involved, those sailing voluntarily and others going against their will. Volunteers were chiefly impoverished youths who hoped for a better life after the completion of a temporary contract. A supply which, as Raphael and the Bartholomews learn, dried up after reneging on such contracts became widespread.

Involuntary servants included convicts – often avoiding death sentences – individuals judged undesirable, such as prostitutes and vagrants, and those seen as dangerous such as religious, political, or military rebels. Many Royalist prisoners were conveniently transported by Cromwell during the interregnum. In addition to licensed contractors, 'spirits,' often illegally employed by apparently legitimate recruiting companies, were responsible for 'spiriting away' (kidnapping) people into servitude, many of whom were then 'barbadosed' or sent to the West Indies.

Producing sugar was especially demanding in terms of the amount of labour, capital and expertise required for success. Planting, weeding, and harvesting the cane and protecting it from rats and other pests was much more physically demanding work than producing cotton or tobacco crops.

The elite in Barbados chose a form of sugar production that yielded the greatest level of profit establishing large sugarcane plantations cultivated by slave labour. Many small family farms were bought up and amalgamated into these plantations. The Royal African Company and other slave traders were bringing increasing numbers of African men, women, and children to toil in the fields, mills, and houses. In the early 1640s there were probably 37,000 whites and 6,000 blacks; by 1684 there were about 20,000 whites and 46,000 blacks; and in 1834, when slavery was abolished, there were some 15,000 whites and 88,000 blacks.

In European markets, sugar was a scarce and therefore valuable commodity, and Barbadian sugar planters, particularly in the 17th century, reaped huge profits out of the early lead that the island established in sugar production. Increasing wealth brought consolidation of political power for a planter elite, and Barbadian society became a plantocracy, with white planters controlling the economy and government institutions.

From the time James Scott, Duke of Monmouth arrived at court in 1662 aged 13, there were rumours about the existence of a black leather box containing the marriage certificate between his parents Charles Stuart and Lucy Walter. At first Charles II was certainly ambivalent about legitimising his son, though always denying such a marriage had taken place. Many soon viewed Protestant Monmouth as a possible successor to Charles, and his political opportunities increased when the King's brother and acknowledged heir, James, Duke of York, converted to Roman Catholicism around 1668.

Though, as an illegitimate son, Monmouth was ineligible to succeed to the English or Scottish thrones unless he could prove the rumours that his parents had married secretly. Monmouth came to maintain that his parents were married and that he possessed evidence of it, though he never produced it. King Charles II, finally testified in writing to his Council that he had never been married to anyone except the Queen, Catherine of Braganza.

Historical background. The Stuart Restoration.

Following the English Civil War and the execution of Charles I in 1649, military rule under puritan Oliver Cromwell, lasted until 1659 when Richard Cromwell ceded power to parliament and Charles Stuart was invited to return. He ascended the throne in 1660 on a wave of support for the monarchy. His return represented a shift in the cultural and social landscape of England. London became the fashionable, social hub of the country and the playground of the nobility. Theatres were re-opened with women on the stage for the first time, public taverns and coffee houses flourished.

Charles II turned the previously staid English court at Whitehall into a hedonistic palace of pleasure, publicly acknowledging at least fourteen mistresses who were given enormous wealth, apartments at the palace, and political influence. Barbara Villiers, Countess of Castlemaine, Frances Stuart, Duchess of Richmond, and Louise de Kérouaille, Duchess of Portsmouth were amongst the most notable.

Charles also had countless liaisons with other women, including actresses and prostitutes.

With the mistresses came thirteen officially recognised illegitimate children. The King elevated them to the highest ranks of the nobility and provided them with apartments at the palace and estates in the countryside. They also received the most prestigious Offices of State and were granted pensions and annuities from the crown. That Queen Catherine had no children meant that Charles's brother James, Duke of York, remained heir to the throne.

The King had a wide variety of scientific interests, which led to the founding of The Royal Society and the Royal Observatory. And, in many ways, his style of rule laid the foundations of what is now recognised as the modern monarchical system.

Some time sequences have been adjusted for narrative purposes, and some linguistic choices are intentionally modern. Any historical errors or inconstancies are entirely mine as are liberties taken with Italian translation.

Dodie Bishop, Upottery, May 2022

About the Author

Dodie Bishop grew up in St Annes on Lancashire's Fylde Coast and in the New Forest in Hampshire, spending much of her life there before moving to Devon. Now living in the Blackdown Hills with her husband and overindulged cat, she has sons in London and Sydney. With a First-Class Honours degree in English Literature, she completed a Master's in Creative Writing and discovered her metier in historical fiction, so much so she now calls herself a time-traveller to the 17th century. She is a full-time writer, following an earlier career as a company director and an independent bookseller, so books are very close to her heart.

To learn more about Dodie Bishop and discover more Next Chapter authors, visit our website at www.nextchapter.pub.

Our Little Life
ISBN: 978-4-82414-409-6
Large Print

Published by
Next Chapter
2-5-6 SANNO
SANNO BRIDGE
143-0023 Ota-Ku, Tokyo
+818035793528

4th June 2022